FOXHEART

CLAIRE LEGRAND

FOXHEART

ILLUSTRATIONS BY
JAIME ZOLLARS

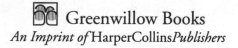 Greenwillow Books
An Imprint of HarperCollins*Publishers*

Foxheart
Copyright © 2016 by Claire Legrand

The text of this book is set in Adobe Garamond
Book design by Sylvie Le Floc'h

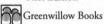

Library of Congress Cataloging-in-Publication Data is available.

ISBN 978-0-06-242773-1 (hardcover)

16 17 18 19 20 PC/RRDH 10 9 8 7 6 5 4 3 2 1
First Edition
Greenwillow Books

For my fellow Curators
Stefan, Kat, and Emma—
without whom Quicksilver would not exist

N
W — E
S

The Impassable
Mountains

The Shadow
Fields

Falstone

The Lady's Tree

The Nightwood

The Blackwood

King Kallin's
Castle

The Skullwood

Silverhair
Mountain

Belrike

The
Star
Lands
of
long ago

Mt. Korkaya

The Kivi Road

The Far North

The Black Castle

Ice Caves

Vorhaven

The Tarkalian Ruins

The Sea of Valkar

Valteya
The Winter Kingdom

Napurya

Lasunet

The River of the First Moon

Willow-on-the-River

The Viskan Hills

Koreva

The Cave of the Rompus

Bay of the Moons

The port city of Tavarik

Farrowtown

The River of the Second Moon

The Burren Bogs

The Sea of the Three Sisters

FOXHEART

.1.

PIGWITCH GIRL

For the first twelve years of her life, Girl had no name.

At least, she pretended that was the case. In fact, she knew very well that her parents had given her a name, but she didn't consider it to be anyone else's business.

When she was three years old, on a stormy night that haunted her memories, her parents left her on the doorstep of Saint Martta's Convent of the White Wolf. There was no note, no birth papers—only a small, drenched girl with a flat, upturned nose and a head of wild gray hair.

The gray hair in particular alarmed the Sisters of Saint

Martta's. It seemed to them too unusual for a young girl, and they had been taught all their lives to be suspicious of the unusual. But they told themselves that most of the witches had been killed, and that the Wolf King was even now hunting those who might remain, and forced smiles to their faces.

"What is your name, girl?" asked the sisters, again and again, that first terrible summer. But the sisters, clothed in their stiff black robes, their wrinkled skin painted white with powder, frightened Girl. She stared at them in silence and said not a word for two years, choosing instead to observe everyone around her with a frankness that made even stone-faced Mother Petra uncomfortable.

The sisters called Girl by no less than twenty-six different names, and she answered to none of them. Not Arja, not Brita. Not Inga, and certainly not Ruut.

"Perhaps one of these names will be more to your liking," suggested Sister Veronika, showing Girl the register, in which were kept the records of all the saints of the Star Lands.

"A most noble way to die, assisting His Grace the Wolf King," assured the sisters.

Girl's heart leaped with hope: had this, then, been her parents' fate? They hadn't abandoned her, no; they had gone north, to find the Wolf King and serve him! They had died heroically, and had been sainted for it. Surely their names were in the register; she would know the letters by sight.

Feeling cheered, Girl tried to read the register's pages and pages of tiny print, but soon found this task not only impossible but unforgivably boring. Her hope faded; none of the names she read meant anything to her. She remained stubbornly silent.

So the sisters, who, according to the Scrolls, were to distrust all disobedient children—for in disobedience lies the potential for great evil—spitefully began to call the child Girl.

"If you will not choose a name," Mother Petra told five year-old Girl from behind her enormous desk, "and if you will not answer to any we choose for you, then you will have no name at all."

And Girl was pleased, for it felt like she had fought some kind of battle, and emerged the victor.

The other girls at Saint Martta's, however, had no qualms about giving Girl a name.

Six-year-old Adele, with soft black curls and the clear voice of a bird, was the one to christen her.

"Oh, Pig!" Adele called out one morning, when Sister Helena had stepped out of the classroom. "Piggy!"

Girl did not at first realize she was being addressed. Then a wadded-up piece of paper hit the back of her head.

Girl whirled around to face Adele. "What'd you do that for?"

Adele pulled up the tip of her nose and flattened it. "Hey, Pig! Do you smell that? Something *stinks* in here. I think it's *you!*" She snorted enthusiastically.

"Pig! Pig! Pig!" the other girls began to chant, turning up their noses too.

Girl's skin crawled with anger.

That evening, she sneaked a mixture of herbs from the sisters' storage closet into Adele's stew. Girl hoped the concoction would leave Adele ill for the rest of her life—perhaps perpetually plagued with a burning stomachache, or unable to talk without violently sneezing. Instead it tinged Adele's skin blue, and boils popped up on her tongue. The sisters, tending to the sobbing Adele, were flummoxed. Who could have gotten past the locks and into the stores?

Mother Petra seemed to know; she made Girl scrub each stone in the courtyard with a bristle brush the size of a baby's finger. Girl obeyed, though for the thirty-six hours it took to complete her task, her mind was full not of penitent thoughts, but rather vengeful ones.

The following Tuesday, Mother Petra awoke to find that *someone* had stolen every piece of paper from her office and pasted them all across the convent's rooftop, covering the dark shingles in layers of fluttering white.

Instead of forcing Girl to retrieve the papers, Mother Petra told her, "When these papers have fallen free of their own accord and blown away out of sight—*every bit* of the paper, even the tiniest scraps—you may return to your room. Until then, you will sleep in the courtyard, with no blankets."

Girl obeyed, even in the blistering cold, even when the sky threw down sharp sheets of rain. Every evening she stood in the courtyard until Mother Petra went to bed. Then, once all the lights had been blown out, she crawled to the roof and slept beneath the bell tower, in a snug nook she had discovered while pasting the papers to the shingles. It was a better bed than her cot inside could ever be, for on clear nights, she fell asleep watching the stars.

One spring day when Girl was seven years old, a pack of boys from town peeked over the garden wall as the girls picked vegetables.

"What's wrong with your hair?" called out a boy, staring at Girl.

"It's gray, like an old woman's!" another boy cried.

"Are you sick? What's wrong with you?"

"How old are you, anyway? Hey! Are you listening to us? Are you deaf?"

"Maybe she's a witch!" suggested the first boy. They all fell silent, deliciously scandalized by the idea, and then they began to chant: "Witch! Witch! Witch!"

The other girls gasped. "Witch" was the most wicked word, a word that even the sisters whispered when reading stories from the Scrolls during lessons. Stories about how the Wolf King had begun hunting the witches of the Star Lands, earning the loyalty of all seven lords.

Girl's skin flushed as red as the tomatoes in her basket. It wasn't that she minded being called a witch. She knew she *should* mind, but as a general rule she found things the sisters deemed important—such as memorizing all one hundred and twenty Songs for the Black Castle—utterly uninteresting. And she found things the sisters deemed disagreeable or even dangerous—such as witches—*entirely* interesting.

No, it wasn't the witch "insult" that sent her blood boiling— it was the mere *existence* of this simpleminded pack of boys who felt it necessary to single her out and jeer at her, just because they were bored and because she looked different than the rest.

So Girl launched her tomatoes at them.

They screamed and fled, some of the younger ones crying, their faces splattered with juicy tomato pulp. Girl climbed the nearest tree, jumped from a sturdy branch to the top of the garden wall, and ran along the wall, chasing the boys down the road and flinging as many tomatoes at them as she could.

A yellow puppy with a torn ear flew out of the bushes on the side of the road and joined the chase. He galloped alongside the garden wall, barking like mad and kicking up dust, and every time one of Girl's tomatoes hit one of the boys, the puppy nipped at the boy's ankles. When Girl reached the end of the wall and could chase the boys no farther, she watched them run away and laughed.

The yellow pup sent one last bark after them before turning his panting, lopsided grin up at Girl.

Just then two dark figures in hooded robes hurried out from the chapel.

"Look, just *look* at what she has done," cried Adele, pointing up at Girl from the garden. "I know they shouldn't have been talking to us, that's against the rules, but did they deserve to have things *thrown* at them?"

Girl knew it would only make things worse, but nevertheless, she threw her last tomato right at Adele's lovely, astonished face.

As Sisters Gerta and Marketta dragged Girl to Mother Petra's office, she thought bitterly about how quickly the sisters appeared when she did something wrong, and how they were nowhere to be found when others wronged her.

"And who might you be, sweet child?" a charitable woman from town said when Girl was eight years old. Girl saw the woman's eyes flick to her nose and then to her hair, how the woman's mouth twitched, her eyes widening in genteel alarm.

By now, Girl was used to such looks, but that didn't mean she would let them go.

"I'm Pigwitch Girl," Girl said proudly, and then threw her arms around the woman's waist, snorting and squealing. When the sisters dragged her away, Girl called out, "Horrible to meet you! Please don't come back and visit!"

That earned Girl a week's worth of scouring the pans after supper, but she accepted the punishment—for no one had noticed her slip her hand into the woman's pocket and steal her tiny bag of coppers.

Someday, she thought, up to her elbows in soapy hot water, *I shall have enough coin to leave this place. I'll travel the world and steal what I need to get by, and I'll go north and find my parents, and if they're busy with the Wolf King, then I'll join them. I'll show them I can help. Hunting's not so very different from stealing.*

She knew stealing was forbidden. It said so in the Scrolls, and the Scrolls had been written by the great-great-great-grandparents of the seven lords of the Star Lands, back when the Hunt first began. But what did any of them know? All they cared about was keeping the Wolf King happy, so that he in turn would keep the witches away. Fancy lords in fancy castles didn't know what it was like to be a pigwitch girl. She was sure of that.

"Oh, Piggy?" Adele called out sweetly in the courtyard one Wednesday after morning prayers.

Girl, now ten years old, snorted inquisitively and rushed at Adele. Then she sniffed up and down Adele's clothes like a pig sniffing for slop.

"Sister Kata!" Adele burst into sobs. "Girl is being so cruel to me!"

"What is *wrong* with you?" Sister Kata hissed, hurrying Girl to her room.

"Well, I have a pig nose, for one," said Girl. "I have strange hair, for two. How do you know I'm *not* in fact some sort of witch, Sister? Perhaps I've come to eat you all!"

Girl was confined to her room for an entire month after that, with only thin gruel for meals. But every night after Mother Petra had gone to bed, Girl slipped between the window bars and retreated to her spot on the roof. She breathed in the clean air, free of incense and prayer oil, and watched the stars turn in the black spread of the sky.

It was during this month that the yellow dog started coming to see her. He was older now, long and lanky. At first he curled up in the flower bed beneath the bell tower and slept while Girl slept, and he was gone in the mornings. Then he began bringing food scraps—half-eaten chicken legs and savory meat pies and hot buttered rolls. He would hold them in his mouth and stare up at the bell tower until Girl finally climbed down to him.

"Did you steal this?" Girl asked him one night, holding up a tiny beef pie. It was soaked with drool and looked as though the dog had already torn off bits of it for himself.

The dog growled.

"I'm not angry if you did," Girl said. "In fact, I think if you did steal it, I would like you even more than I did before."

The dog tilted his head.

"Well," said Girl, "thank you. You're very clever, you know."

The dog curled up in the flower bed with a soft huff of annoyance. Girl scowled, stuffed the pie into her pocket, and returned to the rooftop.

A few nights later, Girl waited for the yellow dog with her heart in her throat. When he arrived, he held in his mouth a bag of powdered sugar cakes, and Girl took them with uncharacteristic shyness.

"Would you want to sleep up there, with me?" she asked, pointing to the bell tower. "You can see for miles. And the ground is cold right now, and up by the bell tower, the roof is warm because of the kitchen fires. What do you think?"

She held up a sack she had fashioned from her scratchy bedsheet. If she slung it around one shoulder, it was just big enough to hold the yellow dog close to her stomach while she climbed.

The dog eyed the sack dubiously.

Girl rolled her eyes. "Fine, then. It doesn't matter much to me if you freeze down here in the mud."

She turned to climb back up to the roof, her eyes stinging with tears that made her so angry she nearly lost her footing. Then, as she began to pull herself up, she felt something nudge her leg, and looked down only to get swiped with a slobbering tongue.

"You smell," she told the dog cheerfully, and helped him into her bag for the climb to the roof.

Later, as he lay sleeping beside her on the warm spot over the kitchen, Girl whispered to him, "I should like to call you Fox, for you are so very clever," and his ear twitched, and he smacked his lips and belched, and Girl took this to mean that was all right with him.

Pig. Witch. Girl. Pig. Witch. Girl.

On stormy days, when the world turned gloomy, something inside Girl cried out for her parents. She could only remember pieces of her past—a tired face, a soft touch, a hard voice. Her name, of course. The name she told no one.

On those days, the insults shouted at her landed like the blows of fists. After everyone had gone to bed, Girl would sneak out of her room and, instead of going to the bell tower, find Fox in his flower bed and retreat with him to the chapel, where she would gaze at the stained-glass windows for hours.

Girl did not possess the patience for prayers, and hymns were even more intolerable, but these windows, the painted icons, the intricately carved figurines of the doomed saints and the Wolf King protecting the Star Lands from evil—these things she loved. She did not understand them, but their beauty made the lost feeling inside her shrink and fade.

In the windows, the Wolf King chased witches, fanged and warty, with wild hair in unnatural colors—purple, green, blue. Girl tried to feel hatred for the witches; she knew from the Scrolls that she ought to. Perhaps if she did not look so unusual—and almost like a witch—the others would not despise her so much. Perhaps her parents would not have abandoned her and instead would have brought her along on their heroic travels.

But she could never bring herself to hate the witches. So they had strange hair. So did she. So they had irregular faces. Well, and so did she.

Perhaps witches were simply born funny looking and different. And no one understood them. And so they had been deemed evil. It did not seem particularly fair.

On those lonely nights in the chapel, Girl would hug Fox and stare at the Wolf King's golden crown until her eyes turned hot and the chapel became a sea of blurred color.

And this was Girl's life, from the day her parents abandoned her at the age of three until she was twelve years old: Punishments from Mother Petra. Memorizing the Scrolls when she felt agreeable, and stealing from the sisters or hiding on the rooftops when she didn't. Adele's soft black curls and cruel mouth. Pigwitch Girl! Pigwitch Girl! Pig. Witch. Girl.

Wondering about witches and magic, and about her parents too, and when they would return from the Hunt to find her. Wondering, wondering, with a lonely twist in her chest that she pushed down until it lodged deep in her belly like a stone.

This was Girl's life, until suddenly, violently, it wasn't.

.2.

THE WOLVES THAT WERE
NOT WOLVES AT ALL

Girl slipped between the window bars and dropped to the floor. When her bare feet touched the cold stone, her heart kicking inside her chest, she allowed herself a moment to catch her breath and let her eyes adjust to the darkness.

Then, spotting Adele's sleeping face, Girl grinned.

Pulling tricks on Adele, Girl suspected, would never lose its appeal, and the one she had planned for tonight was perhaps her best trick yet.

She hurried to the door and let Fox inside. He padded off into the darkness, the sack around his shoulders rustling.

Girl set to work.

First the patchwork cloak and gown, sewn together from scraps of cloth that Girl had stolen from Sister Veronika's mending bag over several long weeks. She slipped the gown and cloak over her own head, and then donned the hat, a lopsided, pointed affair made from the same materials. Then the false hooked nose—clay, baked on the hot roof at midday. She had already painted clusters of warts onto her hands using ointments stolen from the sisters' stores—would they *ever* manage to find a lock that could stump her?

Her hair, of course, required no alteration. It was strange and witchy on its own.

She adjusted her hat and looked around for Fox, excitement zipping through her body. If she was caught dressed like this, she would be confined to her room forever.

But she wouldn't be caught. She never was, these days.

And when she did get back to her bed without being caught, she would really have to sit down, look over her list, and decide on a proper thieving name for herself. If she was to be the best thief in all the Star Lands, she couldn't call herself Girl, and she certainly couldn't use her real name.

Perhaps the Rogue of Lalunet, or the Silent Shifter, or

Constance Craft, as a sly nod to Sister Veronika, who had tried to call Girl Constance for a six-month stretch when Girl was seven. Or perhaps—

Fox *whuffed* softly, and Girl shook herself. There would be time for choosing a name later.

She pocketed the coins on Adele's bedside table, which was the real point of this excursion.

"Ready?" Girl whispered.

Fox trotted back toward the door, the small cloth sack she had tied around his shoulders now slack and empty. He let out another small *whuff* of air.

Girl squinted in the dim light, saw the shiny black beetles scuttling across Adele's bedcovers where Fox had dumped them out—a trick that had taken *weeks* to teach him. She smiled and approached the bed, her shoulders hunched, her fingers bared like claws. She was ready to pounce, a wild cackle building in her throat—when Fox started growling at the door.

Girl froze.

"What?" she whispered.

The hair on Fox's back stood up in a bristly line. Girl heard the creak of the main gate downstairs as it opened and shut.

No one ever came to the convent at this hour.

Girl crept to the window, stood on her toes, and peered out. A cloaked figure swept through the courtyard, Mother Petra herself hurrying alongside it. Shapes Girl couldn't quite make out swirled above the cloaked figure's shoulders.

Shadows?

With another low growl, Fox darted into the hallway.

"Fox!"

Adele shifted in her sleep, smacked her lips. A beetle plopped to the floor.

Girl hesitated. She didn't want to miss Adele waking up to discover herself covered in beetles with a "witch" hovering over her—but Fox had never behaved like this before.

Girl hurried after him, down the hallway lined with the somber portraits of dead sisters, down the stairs, past the kitchen, and across the small stone yard to the classrooms.

Fox stood at the end of the hallway, a few paces away from Mother Petra's office. The door was ajar, letting out lamplight. Girl slipped behind the loose wall panel and crawled into her eavesdropping spot, Fox at her heels. After she'd pulled the panel shut behind them, she crouched and, through a small brass grate, peered into the office. She saw Mother Petra, her desk, and the cloaked figure.

"This is most unusual," Mother Petra was saying. "If Lord Aapo wishes to bring my students to see the capital, then I'm certain he would not send a *messenger*, if that is indeed who you are, to retrieve them in the middle of the night. Now, come. Tell me your full name." Mother Petra arranged pen and paper. "You can find a room in town, and I'll send a letter to Lord Aapo first thing in the morning, and we will get this sorted out. Until then, I'm afraid I will have to ask you to leave."

A low murmur of words then, but Girl could not quite hear. Fox started growling once more. Girl pressed a finger to her lips, and Fox obediently fell silent.

"I beg your pardon?" said Mother Petra, in a shocked voice.

"I said you are a fool, old woman. I tried to approach this as a human might have done, following human rules and courtesies. But you have exhausted my patience even more quickly than I had anticipated."

This new voice was strange, distorted. Girl could not quite fix her ears on it. Was there just the one person in the office speaking with Mother Petra, or were there many?

"Fool?" Mother Petra rose, tugging her dressing gown straight. "You are impudent, young man. That is no way to speak to Mother Petra of the Convent of the White Wolf!"

"Wolf?" A soft spill of unkind laughter. "Old woman, you know nothing of wolves."

Seven sharp, lean creatures slunk into Mother Petra's office from the hallway. Fox backed away from the grate, his tail between his legs. They were wolves. Seven wolves, each a different color: White, black, brown, gray, red, blue, and gold.

Understanding came to Girl slowly. *I know those colors,* she thought. *I have memorized them.*

Mother Petra fell to her knees. "It's you! I am so sorry. Forgive me, I didn't realize!" A wondering smile spread across her face. "I have dreamed of meeting you!"

"I doubt you have dreamed of this," came the reply—clear now, and cold.

The wolves lunged over the desk. Papers scattered; claws scraped wood. Girl could not look away. Mother Petra's screams rang in her ears.

The wolves . . . they were no longer wolves at all.

They were streaks of light, howling and hissing. Girl felt their heat through the grate as though she were crouched beside a crackling fire.

She caught flashes of animal shapes—a tail here, a snout there—but mostly she saw fire, and light, and the cloaked figure standing still as stone. They *had* been wolves, though, hadn't they? She had seen them with her own eyes. But now they were most certainly not.

Fox tugged at the hem of her cloak, whining.

Girl couldn't move. Her heart pounded, her stomach churned. The fiery wolves swarmed over Mother Petra, turning her papers to ash and scorching her great black desk.

And the cloaked figure, dark and terrible, stood watching.

Who was he? He couldn't be who Girl *thought* he was. That wouldn't make sense. The Scrolls, they said—

Fox nipped her leg, hard.

She turned, kicked out the wall panel, clambered to her feet, and ran, Fox right behind her. Heat and howls trailed after them. Down the hallway they raced, through the small yard, past the kitchen—out, out, *out*. They had to get out.

Out through the gate, down the lane, along the garden wall. Girl's bare feet pounded the rocky ground. The autumn wind bit her face and hands. Her witch's cloak caught on a briar, and in her terror, she thought it might be someone grabbing her. She cried out, turned, kicked blindly. Dislodged the cloak, reached for Fox. There was the rough scruff of his neck, his floppy ears. She ran and ran.

Behind her, she heard the screams of the other girls, of the sisters. Adele's scream—she recognized it, high and piercing—was loudest of all.

They were all waking up to find . . . what? What had *happened*? Was the Wolf King hurting them as he had hurt Mother Petra?

Girl did not stop running, stolen coins jangling in her pocket and her heart ablaze with fear.

.3.

GOLD AND SWORDS AND CAKES

After a day on the road, her stomach pinched with hunger and her feet raw from walking, Girl stopped to rest at a river. Countless stars, even more brilliant at night than they were during the day, spilled across the sky. In the light of the two moons—one near and pale violet, the other white, more distant—she saw a shabby, mud-colored town, its rooftops a tumble of mismatched shingles. A sign at the town's western bridge told her that this was Willow-on-the-River, where the sisters shopped for goods when their own small village's market ran low.

But she would not think about the sisters just yet, nor any

of the others back at the convent. First she must find food and a warm place to rest. Then she could sort out everything else.

"The Wolf King doesn't attack children and old women," Girl muttered to Fox, for the twentieth time that day. "He only attacks witches. And the witches are nearly gone."

She stopped at the town church, hesitated, then went inside. Though she was normally not one for prayer, as praying required her to sit still and recite someone else's words rather than her own, she lit a candle for everyone back at Saint Martta's. She even prayed to the Wolf King, as she had been taught, but then she thought of Mother Petra's screams and hesitated.

"I'm not sure he deserves my prayers," she whispered to Fox, who was keeping watch at the chapel door, "not until I know that wasn't him. Although I can't imagine that it *was* him. It couldn't have been. But I know what I saw." She paused. "Is that sacrilege?"

Fox whuffed in what sounded to Girl like enthusiastic agreement, his breath puffing in the chilled air.

So Girl clasped her hands and prayed instead to the ever-present stars above her, from which the Star Lands got their name. She prayed that the sisters and girls were unhurt, that they were not too terribly afraid, and that if they needed rescuing, she, Girl, would be the one to save them, and in reward they would give her gold and swords and all the cakes she could ever want.

Then she and Fox explored the town square, just outside the church. The closed market stalls stood in rows, heavy canvases pulled down over their fronts.

"I know. I'm hungry too, Fox," said Girl, rubbing her arms beneath her cloak to keep warm. Fox had offered Girl several quails and hares as they traveled, but Girl could not stomach raw meat and was afraid to build a fire in case the smoke gave away their position to any wolves prowling about. Since Girl did not eat the meat, neither did Fox, and Girl did not try to persuade him otherwise. They were partners, and it seemed to her that partners should eat together or starve together.

"I suppose I could wait until morning and buy something from the market like a respectable person would," said Girl, thumbing through the stolen coins in her pocket.

Fox cocked his head.

Girl grinned. "Or I could steal something, like a respectable *thief* would."

Fox wagged his tail.

"Come on, then!" Girl hurried through the dark streets,

assessing each house she passed. None of them would do—too many people inside, items that could easily be used as weapons against her lying out in plain view, foul cooking smells indicating whatever food she found would not be worth stealing.

Then, on a quiet, ramshackle street, Girl saw a humble house, crooked and narrow, squashed between two larger buildings. The arrangement of its door and windows gave it an expression rather like someone who had long ago resigned himself to a cramped and crowded fate. One of the second-floor windows was ajar.

"Wait here, Fox," whispered Girl. She started scaling the wall, using cracks between the stones to pull herself along. She looked back and saw Fox staring up at her, his torn ear sticking out crookedly as it always did.

She crawled through the open window into a dark room with an empty bed. She paused, crouching, listening for signs of danger and hearing none. Creeping out of the bedroom and down the stairs, she encountered nothing but bare walls and dust bunnies. Once she thought she heard someone moving about, but then realized it was only her own pounding heart. She opened the front door a crack and whispered to Fox, "I'm almost done. Stay right there."

Fox did not move from where he sat in the road, though he licked his chops and quivered with excitement.

Girl tiptoed, grinning, to the kitchen. *I knew no one was home,* she thought. *I sensed it right away when I saw this house. I really am the cleverest thief there ever was.*

But as Girl rummaged through the kitchen stores, it quickly became clear that she wasn't as clever as all that. The cupboards were bare. The pots and pans were cold and clean and neatly put away. There were no rolls, no pies, no potatoes. She even climbed atop a stool to check the highest shelves, but the only thing up there was a fuzzy layer of dust.

"What kind of kitchen is this?" Girl hissed, ready to smash every last maddeningly empty dish.

"It's not your kitchen, I know that much," said a voice behind her, and when Girl whirled around, she saw a shadowy figure standing in the kitchen doorway and the glint of a small, sharp blade.

.4.

A Name for a Thief

Girl fumbled for a weapon, and came up with only a spatula draped in cobwebs.

"Get back!" She whipped the spatula back and forth. "Don't touch me!"

"*You* get b-back!" The knife-wielding figure hurried away, tripping over a burlap sack.

It was only a boy. Girl thrust the spatula in front of her. The boy scrambled back, his knife clattering to the floor. Girl grabbed it and, knife and spatula in hand, advanced on him.

"Beware, boy!" she said. "My name is Quicksilver, and I'm

the best thief in all the Star Lands, and if you believe the tales, you're a bigger fool than you look, for they're not half so bloody as the *real* stories."

"Who? I've n-never heard of . . . *what* silver?"

Quicksilver. Girl's giddy heart danced.

Quicksilver was one of the dozens of potential thieving names on her list, but she had never given it much thought until now. She had, in all honesty, always been drawn to the alliterative. Constance Craft. The Silent Shifter. The Fleet Fox (in honor, of course, of Fox).

But now . . . now, she knew that no other name would do. The fact that she could make such a spectacular choice while her life was in danger reassured her of her own brilliance.

I am Quicksilver, she thought, and with each word, she stood up a bit taller. *My name is Quicksilver.*

"Quicksilver, you fool," she said to the boy, grinning, and with those words, she shed the name Girl like a sheath of dead skin. "Let me pass without any trouble, and I'll spare your life."

"Er . . . just wait a moment," said the boy, even as he continued backing away with his hands raised in surrender. All of a sudden, moonslight came in through the kitchen window, and Quicksilver saw a pale, freckled, lanky boy with hair the color of tallow. There were shadows beneath his eyes. He kept glancing up the stairs toward the second floor.

Quicksilver followed his gaze, her thoughts racing. Perhaps she hadn't surveyed the other rooms as thoroughly as she ought to have. "What's up there? What're you hiding, boy?"

"M-my name's Sly Boots," said the boy.

"That's a stupid name."

Sly Boots straightened. "Well, y-you have a stupid face."

"That won't matter much, will it, when I've robbed you blind and left you for dead?" Quicksilver jumped toward him with a growl. Sly Boots yelped and stumbled back against the wall, and Quicksilver ran up the stairs. She would make a quick search, grab whatever she could find, climb back out the window, and run away before the boy had even managed to regain his footing. Maybe he was hiding a stash of coins, or jewels, or—

At the door to the second bedroom, Quicksilver came to an abrupt stop.

A man and a woman lay sleeping in a bed, their skin pale and slick with sweat. The air in the room was stale and heavy. In the corner was a chair draped with a threadbare blanket, and on the table by the bed an empty bowl and spoon.

"Please . . . don't hurt them."

Quicksilver turned. "Who are they? What's wrong with them?"

"They're my parents," said Sly Boots, wringing his hands by the bedroom door. "And what do you mean, what's wrong with them?"

"I've seen sick people before at the—where I used to live."

"You haven't seen sickness like this before." Sly Boots inched past her warily, eyeing the knife. To remind him who had the upper hand, Quicksilver slapped his arm with the spatula.

"We were on a job in the hills," Sly Boots continued. As he spoke, he pressed his hands to his parents' foreheads, wiped their faces with a damp cloth, arranged their pillows. He scooped a dark, viscous liquid from a jar and spread it across their throats; their rattling breath quieted. Downstairs, he had been clumsy, faltering, but here, tending to his parents, Sly Boots moved almost . . . elegantly.

Quicksilver forgot herself for a moment and asked, in a hushed tone, "How do you know what to do for them?"

Sly Boots shrugged. "I've always been good at this sort of thing. I read whatever books my parents could steal for me. I used to watch Reko—he's the town apothecary—when he spoke to people in the market, and take notes and such. But he never liked me, seeing as how my parents are thieves, and then when I tried to steal from him a couple of weeks ago . . . well, I'm just lucky he didn't report me to the magistrate."

Quicksilver fixed on one word. "Thieves? Your parents are thieves?" She stepped back, assessing him in a new light. "Are you one, too?"

"Sort of. Well. No. Not really. See, they were on a job—my parents—but I went along even though I wasn't supposed to. And then I . . ." Sly Boots looked away, as if remembering who he was talking to. "I shouldn't be telling you these things."

Quicksilver shook herself too. This boy was a mark, not someone to have a conversation with. "No. Indeed it's rather careless of you. You don't know anything about me."

"You're a thief."

"The best there is. Better than your parents, I'll bet." Quicksilver approached the bed. She poked the man's foot with her spatula.

Sly Boots shoved her away. "Don't touch them!"

"Will I get sick if I do?"

"No. I'm not sick, am I?"

"*Are* you?"

Sly Boots sighed. *"No."*

"You look sick. You've got dark circles under your eyes."

"Are you going to leave now? I wish you would. As you can see, we don't have anything worth stealing." Sly Boots glanced at her. "How'd you get in without me hearing you? I wouldn't have found you if I hadn't come down for water."

Quicksilver shrugged. "A thief never reveals her secrets."

"That's what Mother always said." Sly Boots paused, staring at his mother's face, and then sat on the edge of the bed and put his head in his hands.

"Are you *crying*?"

Sly Boots, sniffling, didn't answer. Then he looked up at Quicksilver, his expression watery and hopeful. "Just how good a thief are you?"

Quicksilver narrowed her eyes. "The best there is. And I don't like repeating myself, so maybe you should pay better attention."

"Maybe . . . we can make a deal, then."

A *deal*. Quicksilver perked up. Could Sly Boots have coin stashed somewhere? Coin he could be persuaded to give up in exchange for her leaving quietly? "What kind of deal?"

"You can stay here, at my house—it's cold out, you'll lose your toes to frostbite soon—and in return, you help me steal.

We've no more money, and I've almost run out of medicine, and . . . well, you saw the kitchen." He paused, twisting his hands together. "You know, since you're . . . the best thief in all the Star Lands?" Sly Boots cleared his throat. "The legendary . . . Kicksliver?"

"Quicksilver," Quicksilver ground out.

"Right. Quicksilver."

"Why would you want some strange thief living in your house? Why would you trust me?"

Sly Boots's smile looked strange on his face, as though he weren't used to doing it. "I don't really have a choice. It's either trust you, or . . ." He fell silent, gazing at his sleeping parents.

"What happened to them? You have to tell me, before I agree to anything."

"We were on a job in the hills—"

"Which hills?" Quicksilver interrupted. "Be specific."

"The Viskan Hills." Sly Boots blinked. "You're really not from around here, are you? That's what we call them. *The* hills."

Quicksilver could have smacked herself. "You think I don't know that? You still need to refer to things by their proper names. It's the rules of storytelling."

"What rules?"

"*My* rules."

Sly Boots held up his hands. "All right, all right. Anyway, my parents were out on a job in the hills—the *Viskan* Hills— and they told me not to come because, well, I'm a terrible thief. Always knocking things over and making too much noise, and dropping things, and forgetting where to meet after, and . . . well, you get my meaning. But I followed them anyway, because I wanted to show them I'm better now than I used to be—which I am! I don't break things nearly as often now as I used to—"

"I don't need to hear your tragic life story," snapped Quicksilver.

"*Fine.* Well, they broke into this trader's carriage, and I followed them in, and they were mad when they saw me, I'll tell you that, but they couldn't do anything about it then. So we gathered up the loot, and my parents ran for it, but I tripped trying to climb out of the carriage and dropped everything, and there was this great crash—are you *laughing* at me?"

Quicksilver bit her tongue and attempted a sympathetic expression. "Just a frog in my throat, is all. How *awful* that must have been for you."

Sly Boots wiped his nose. "It was. My parents had to come back and help me, and the traders chased us into the forest.

We got turned around—it was dark, and they'd already gotten into scrapes with the magistrate twice before, so we couldn't get caught a third time, so we kept running, and . . . and then we found the witches."

"Witches."

"Yes, witches! They had—" Sly Boots glanced at Quicksilver's hair, which was sticking up every which way. "Well. I knew what they were."

Quicksilver ignored the gooseflesh prickling her skin and snorted. "You saw wrong. Almost all the witches are gone. The Wolf King—"

"Almost," said Sly Boots, his voice sharp. "And these were witches, I know it. My skin tingled around them, like a lightning storm was coming. And they hurt my parents. I don't know what they did to them, but something bad. I wager they would've hurt me too, if I hadn't fallen so far behind. I don't think they knew I was there." Sly Boots wiped his cheeks on his sleeve. "Those witches and their animals—strange animals, all lit up like fire, they were. If I ever meet another witch, I'll—I'll—"

"Oh, yes? You'll what? You'll fight them? Honestly. You couldn't even fight a girl with a spatula." Quicksilver rolled her eyes, but in fact she was thinking very hard about what

Sly Boots had said: *strange animals, lit up by fire.*

Like the wolves in Mother Petra's office?

"Insult me all you like," said Sly Boots, "but I know what I saw. It took me hours to drag my parents back home, and I got some funny looks, I'll tell you that, and now . . . I can't get them to wake up. They're better than they used to be. I got their fevers down, and they can still swallow, so I feed them broth, but it's getting harder to make them eat it, and—I don't know what to do. We've run out of everything, and if I don't keep giving them their medicine, they'll get feverish again and start crying out in their sleep, like someone's hurting them in their dreams."

Sly Boots's father shuddered, as if he had heard his son's words. His face contorted and then relaxed.

"You see?" Sly Boots reached for a fresh cloth. "It's already happening. You've got to help me, or else . . . or else I don't know what we'll do. Once our money ran out, I started trying to lift things from the market—just basic tonics for fever and the shakes—but I'm caught every time. I'm just hopeless at it." Sly Boots sat heavily on the bed. "It's my fault. If I'd just stayed home, like I was supposed to, if I hadn't tripped and fallen, if we hadn't run off into those woods . . ."

Sly Boots grabbed the empty bowl on the bedside table and flung it against the wall, shattering it.

Quicksilver's opinion of Sly Boots improved. Throwing and smashing things was much preferable to snotty crying.

"If they can't get better," said Sly Boots mournfully, "if they stay like this forever, it'll be my fault. They should never have had me. I should never have been born—"

"Oh, for the love of all the stars, would you please just stop talking?" Quicksilver smacked her spatula against the bed. "If you're going to whine about everything, I'll leave you right now, and I won't feel bad about it for a second."

Sly Boots looked up, his cheeks streaked with tears. "Does that mean you're staying? You'll help me?"

"I have some conditions. First, when I steal us food, you must cook me things that taste delicious."

Sly Boots nodded eagerly. "I'm an excellent cook."

"You'd better be. Second, you must not complain, ever, not even once, while we're out on a job. And if you're really as hopeless as you say, and I decide to send you home, you can't complain then, either—not one whining, sniveling word."

"I will only say cheerful, excited things."

"As long as they aren't *too* cheerful," said Quicksilver sternly.

"You can go too far in the opposite direction, you know."

"But how far is too—"

"And third . . ." Quicksilver took a deep breath. "You must help me find information about the man who attacked my convent. He had a pack of wolves with him, and—"

"Like the Wolf King?" Sly Boots's eyes grew wide.

No. It couldn't be the Wolf King. Because that meant . . . Quicksilver didn't know what that meant. "Would the Wolf King attack a convent full of little girls? That's a rather blasphemous thing to say."

But it might have been the Wolf King, a voice inside Quicksilver insisted. *And what then? What* then?

"Sorry," said Sly Boots sheepishly.

"These wolves weren't like real wolves. They glowed and changed, like—"

"Like the ones I saw," Sly Boots whispered. "Do you think it was a witch pretending to be the Wolf King? That'd be really clever. Pretending to be the Wolf King and getting into all these fancy places, maybe even a lord's castle, and then doing terrible things—"

"And my fourth condition," said Quicksilver, "is that you may never again interrupt me, or I'll make Fox rip out your throat."

Sly Boots frowned. "Who's Fox?"

Quicksilver gave a sharp whistle. From downstairs came the sound of the front door slamming open and something rapidly crashing up the stairs. Fox bounded into the bedroom and cornered Sly Boots with a growl.

Sly Boots threw himself back against the wall. "Is this yours?"

"Yes, and just so you know, I've trained him to kill on command." Quicksilver whistled once more for Fox, and he trotted over to her, his tongue lolling out of his mouth. She held out her hand to Sly Boots. "Do we have a deal?"

Sly Boots hesitated for only a moment before slapping Quicksilver's hand. "We have a deal."

.5.

THE RULES OF THIEVING

"The first rule of thieving," Quicksilver whispered the next morning, "is to always be aware of your body. That way you don't trip—say, over your own boots—and ruin a job." She cleared her throat. "If you know what I mean."

"Right. Be aware. Body. Got it."

Quicksilver watched witheringly as Sly Boots struggled to adjust the long striped scarf about his neck with one hand while clinging to the church rooftop with the other. "Was it really necessary for you to wear that?" she asked.

"Was it necessary to climb onto the roof? It's cold up here!"

"The second rule of thieving is to survey the area from as high a point as possible, so nothing takes you by surprise."

Sly Boots looked down at the ground and then quickly up, breathing fast. "We're going to fall and smash our heads open."

"We won't if you listen to me instead of panicking. I've done this loads of times, trust me. Now come on."

Quicksilver climbed farther up the shingled roof, her makeshift witch's cloak flapping in the wind. Sly Boots had loaned her a pair of his own boots; they were too big for her, brown and clunky, but she still scaled the roof with ease.

Sly Boots followed her much more slowly, muttering over and over, "Don't look down. Don't look down."

At the top of the roof, Quicksilver lay flat and hooked her elbows over the peak. From here, she could see the entire town square. She could see what the people of Willow-on-the-River put into their market baskets—bolts of cloth, wrapped parcels of fish, sacks of apples and potatoes, stoppered bottles of all sizes, bunches of garlic cloves, sprigs of rosemary, wool blankets tied with twine, charms made of beads and colored glass, and carved wooden figurines.

And, Quicksilver observed, some of the figurines were wolves—painted black, gray, red, blue, brown, gold, and white.

One wolf for each of the seven Star Lands. Seven wolves for the Wolf King.

Quicksilver pressed her cheek to the slanted roof, which was warm from the midmorning sun, and gazed north. Past the farmlands and rolling hills of her own kingdom, Lalunet, was the kingdom of Valteya. And past the cold mountains of Valteya was the even colder and more mountainous Far North. And there, somewhere, was the Black Castle, where the Wolf King lived. Many had traveled there, but none had returned. The Scrolls said the Wolf King was beautiful, and splendid, in that way that only kings can be. The sisters had explained that those explorers who braved the Far North in search of the Wolf King's castle never returned because they had found him, and been overcome with love for him, and agreed to stay and serve him in his great hunt.

Quicksilver had always believed this, as had every other child at the convent—and every other child in the Star Lands, she reckoned.

But now, looking north, where the barest shadowy hints of the Valteyan mountains reached toward the clouds, Quicksilver could think only of Mother Petra's terrified face.

She thought, as she had many times, about her parents—

no doubt traveling at the Wolf King's side, helping him hunt, offering him counsel. By serving the Wolf King, they were helping many, and by returning to Quicksilver, they would be helping only one small girl.

But if that horrible man at the convent *had* been the Wolf King, and he was somehow not what she had been taught—if he did indeed go about attacking orphans and old women—then such a person did not deserve her parents' help.

Her cheek pressed hard against the roof, Quicksilver whispered to the wind, "Come back. Leave him, and come back to me."

Below, in the square, a familiar bark alerted Quicksilver to Fox. He was circling a market stall from which floated the mouthwatering scent of cooking meat.

"Are we going to do this or not?" Sly Boots hissed beside her. He clutched the shingles, his feet slipping and sliding to find purchase.

Quicksilver blinked. "Of course we are. Stop moving around so much. You're distracting me."

"Are you crying?" Sly Boots scooted closer, his eyes wide. "What is it? Are we going to fall? Are we stuck? I knew it. We're stuck." He pushed himself up and opened his mouth to scream. "Help!"

Quicksilver tugged him back down. "The third rule of thieving is you never, *ever* ask for help from non-thieves. You die before giving yourself away."

"That's ridiculous! I don't want to die!"

"Look—I never need help, from anyone, so if you do as I say, you won't either, and then you won't have to worry about dying. Simple as that." Quicksilver took a deep breath and turned away from the north, even though it was hard to do, for thoughts of her parents lingered.

"Now, in that stall over there," she said, "is a woman selling some really excellent-smelling chicken—"

Sly Boots scrambled up to see, his scarf catching on the roof. "What about medicine for my parents? I see Reko's cart, right over there. They need a tonic for their fever."

"Food first. Medicine later." Quicksilver gritted her teeth. "You said Reko's on the lookout for you, so we'll work up to him. Now—"

Anastazia.

Quicksilver froze. "Did you hear that?"

Sly Boots looked around frantically. "Hear what? What is it? Did someone see us? Oh, stars, we're going to die. The magistrate will arrest us, and then we'll die."

"No, it was—"

Anastazia.

It was impossible. Quicksilver was hearing things. There was a voice on the wind, a woman's voice, and it was saying her name, and that was impossible.

Anastazia.

Not her thieving name. Not Pig. Not Witch. Not Girl.

Anastazia. Her *real* name, which only her parents knew.

Quicksilver's head buzzed with sudden fear and hope.

She crawled across the roof, ignoring Sly Boots's cries, and climbed up the church belfry until she reached one of the high arched windows. From there she gazed north again, and this time she saw a figure on the village's northernmost bridge. The figure wore a dark cloak, and even from this distance, she could see that the figure was gazing up at the belfry, right where Quicksilver stood.

.6.

THE STRANGER

"What is it?" asked Sly Boots, scooting his way across the roof toward the belfry. "Do you see something?"

"I . . . I don't know," replied Quicksilver. "I suppose it's just a traveler."

But Quicksilver knew, in her deepest heart, that this was no normal traveler. The sight of the stranger gave Quicksilver a chill, even with the sunlight shining down upon her. Something about the stranger seemed familiar—the way she moved, the shape of her hand holding the cloak at her throat.

Quicksilver climbed down from the belfry and perched

on a gargoyle shaped like a howling wolf. The stranger walked smoothly into town, cloak trailing through the mud, and when she reached the square, where the market bustled on, oblivious, the stranger found an unused stool and sat upon it.

And sat. And sat.

The stranger sat on this stool for such a long time that Quicksilver began to doubt her own memory. Had this person just arrived, or had she always been sitting there, on the south edge of the market, still and dark?

"Who is that?" whispered Sly Boots loudly, poking his head over the roof's peak. "Quicksilver?"

"Not now, Boots," said Quicksilver, climbing down the side of the church, using the stone wall's intricate carvings of wolves as handholds. Though Quicksilver could hear an increasingly unhappy Sly Boots calling after her, she ignored him. There was something much more important to puzzle out, now that she could see better:

Beside the stranger sat a dog with a small pack tied to his chest, and the dog looked remarkably like Fox.

He was older than Fox, his chin shaggy with white whiskers, his coat grayed. But she could not ignore the resemblance— there were his alert brown eyes. There was his torn left ear.

Quicksilver's Fox hurried over, even the slow-roasting chicken forgotten. He put himself in front of Quicksilver and growled at the stranger and her dog, his teeth bared.

"It's all right, Fox," whispered Quicksilver, although she could not be sure that it was.

A young boy in a tasseled linen shirt, passing by with a small bag of potatoes slung over his shoulder, glanced at the stranger, then glanced again, his eyebrows shooting up in surprise.

"Who are you?" the boy asked. He examined the stranger from head to toe and made a face. "You're ugly."

"And you are very unpleasant," said the stranger, in a voice warm and smooth as sleep. The stranger peeked out from her hood. Her strong, steady voice did not match her lined face, nor the chalky white skin flaking at the corners of her mouth.

"What of it?" demanded the boy.

The stranger shrugged. "Just an observation. Perhaps you'd be happier if you had something . . . pretty in your life?"

And with that, the stranger bent to scrape her knobby fingers across the ground. From the cracked cobblestones, she pulled a bouquet of purple and yellow flowers and presented it to the boy with a flourish.

The boy gasped, a grin spreading across his face. He ran

across the square, calling excitedly for his mother.

With a tired *whuff*, the old dog pulled a lumpy hat from beneath the stranger's cloak and laid it on the ground.

"Did you see that, Fox?" whispered Quicksilver. "She's good. She slipped those flowers out from her sleeve, I know she did. I've done something like that before myself. Remember when I dragged that garden snake out of my prayer robe and Sister Marketta fainted?"

Fox backed away from the stranger, whining uncertainly. He nudged Quicksilver's arm, but she did not budge.

Soon a crowd gathered around the stranger to watch her draw coins out of ears and frightened-looking rabbits out of coat pockets. She juggled ten apples at once, and threw her voice to make it sound as though she was speaking to the crowd from inside the church, and she turned water into milk using a special cup she withdrew from her cloak.

The villagers indulged her, tossing coins into her hat and exchanging smiles over the heads of their children. It was benevolent, innocent "magic," these tricks—sleight of hand, misdirection. Nothing to be concerned about. And did you see? She has perfectly respectable red hair, and it's graying with age, like a normal person's would. It's a wonder she's even still alive, by the looks of her face.

No, no witches here.

Quicksilver watched the stranger all morning, crouched in the shadows around the church. Sometime after the lunch hour, Sly Boots found her, his scarf half torn and his face dotted with scrapes.

"I got myself down, thank you very much." He slumped against the church wall, flinging an arm over his eyes. "I thought I was going to die. Perhaps I have died. Are we up in the stars now? Did you die too?"

"Sly Boots," whispered Quicksilver, "watch her dog for a while and tell me what you see. Not the stranger, don't watch her, or her tricks. Just watch the dog."

Sly Boots groaned and pulled himself upright. Then he sat up straighter.

"That dog," Sly Boots breathed. "It's stealing things. It's . . . it's moving so quickly . . . like—"

"Like the lit-up animals you saw with the witches in the woods?" Quicksilver interrupted. "Like the wolves at my convent."

As they watched, the old dog vanished in a soft flash of light. It then reappeared behind a man wearing a red cotton vest. The dog pulled a purse heavy with coins from his pocket and then disappeared again, with that same soft flash that could easily have been mistaken for a shift in the clouds, had you not been paying close enough attention.

The man in the red vest absently brushed his coat, as if scratching an itch, and applauded along with everyone else.

The old dog reappeared at the stranger's side, nudging the stolen purse beneath the ragged hem of her cloak.

Sly Boots grabbed Quicksilver's arm. "Do you think—?"

Quicksilver shook him off. "I can't be sure. But we've got to talk to her. Maybe she knows about the wolves, and your parents too."

"I'll kill her," said Sly Boots, in a voice so deadly it stole Quicksilver's attention. She placed a hand on each of his shoulders.

"You will do nothing of the sort," she said. "Are you stupid? If you kill her, we won't be able to ask her any questions. Plus, if she is a . . . well, you know. If she is, you probably wouldn't be able to kill her, and then you'd end up just like your parents, wouldn't you?"

The hard light faded from Sly Boots's eyes. His shoulders slumped, and he was the same mopey, clumsy boy she had met the day before. "I suppose you're right."

"Of course I am. Now—"

Anastazia.

Quicksilver spun around, searching for the voice on the wind and finding instead that the village square was empty, the market closed, and the world cold and dark with night.

"Wh-what?" Sly Boots threw himself back against the wall of the church, his eyes round as two moons. "What happened? What . . . where . . . ?"

"I believe the word you're searching for is *when,*" said a low, even voice. The stranger appeared before Quicksilver in a swirl of light. The light became dog-shaped, and then the old dog materialized beside her. When Fox, disoriented, swayed on his feet, the old dog appeared to *smile* at him.

It was not a particularly nice smile.

Quicksilver glared up at the stranger's shadowed face. "Who are you?"

"An interesting question, Anastazia—"

"My name's Quicksilver," said Quicksilver sharply. "I answer to no other name."

The stranger knelt and lowered her hood. Quicksilver could not help but flinch at her grotesquely marred face—her bulbous, scarred nose, her mottled skin. "An interesting question," she said again, ignoring Quicksilver. "But I don't think it's really the question you want to ask, is it?" Her eyes twinkled. "Odd and wonderful, how we land on the same name every time. Some things, I suppose, never change."

Sly Boots tugged on Quicksilver's coat. "Let's run. She's worked some kind of magic on us. Where are we? Have we gone mad? Oh, stars help us. . . ."

The stranger quirked an eyebrow. "The boy's not wrong. Who is he, by the way? I've never met him before. He's new."

"How do you know . . ." Quicksilver's voice shook and then gave out. She reached for Fox, and he bumped his cold nose against her palm.

"Yes, little thief? How do I know what?"

Quicksilver looked into the stranger's eyes and saw that they were violet as the near moon. Bright and sharp, they did not look as old as the rest of her, and there was something about those eyes—the shape of them, their mischievous light—that struck Quicksilver as familiar.

Something uneasy fluttered in her stomach. "How did you do this? How did you make it—"

"How did I make it night?" The stranger waved her hand carelessly at the stars. "Even I can't do that much. It was a simple spell that kept you and your breathless little friend immobile and hidden for a time, until I was ready to meet you." The stranger's eyes cut to Fox; the corner of her mouth twitched into something like a frown. "And your dog, of course."

"Teach me," Quicksilver blurted, though it was not what she had meant to ask: *Who are you? Why do you care about me and Sly Boots?*

How do you know my real name?

"Quicksilver," Sly Boots hissed, "what are you *doing*?"

The stranger smiled. "Why should I teach you anything at all?"

Quicksilver's words spilled out before she could stop them. "I'm the best thief in all the Star Lands."

"Then why should you need me?"

Quicksilver wished Sly Boots were not hovering quite so close, and that he would stop whispering, "What'll we do, what'll we *do*?" over and over.

"Because I want to *really* be the best thief," said Quicksilver, flushing, "and not just say I am. Because I want to find out what happened with those wolves."

Because, whispered her deepest heart, *I want to find my parents, and maybe magic will help me do it.*

She squared her jaw and tried to imitate the haughtiest of

Adele's expressions. "Because I'm not afraid of witches."

The stranger's smile was slow and horrid, revealing crooked black-and-yellow teeth. "Not yet, you aren't."

Sly Boots squeaked something unintelligible.

"Well?" Quicksilver insisted, though her throat was dry and Fox would not stop whimpering. "Will you do it?"

"I will, and this very night too," said the stranger, "if you can tell me this one thing." The stranger leaned close, and her breath smelled not of rot, but of snow—crisp and clean. "How do I know your real name, little thief? Tell me, in three guesses' time, and I'll teach you everything you want to know, and more."

Then she stood, returned to her stool, arranged her cloak about her in voluminous folds of night, and waited.

.7.

THREE GUESSES

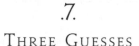

For what seemed to Quicksilver like the longest stretch of time she had ever endured, she stood watching the stranger, and the stranger sat staring back at her.

Sly Boots nudged her foot. "I don't understand what's happening."

"What a surprise," Quicksilver muttered.

"Well, pardon me for being more than a little confused when first, *oh*, there's a you-know-what and a dog performing tricks in the square, and then—*oh*! Suddenly it's hours later and it's night, and we're still here, but it doesn't feel like hours later to us, and then—*oh*! Some old ugly woman says she'll teach you magic. Right. I see. Because these are things that happen any old day!"

"Just let me think for a moment, will you? I don't understand it. No one knows my name. No one but me."

"And your parents," Sly Boots pointed out. "Right?"

Quicksilver crouched in front of Fox. "Fox, what do I do? What does it mean?"

Fox wagged his tail, his eyebrows bunching in an expression that seemed to say, "I'm not sure, but we'll figure it out together, and I love you."

Quicksilver smiled. Sometimes it seemed that, just by looking at his familiar face, she could determine exactly what he was thinking.

Exactly what he was thinking . . .

"I've got my first guess," Quicksilver announced.

The stranger crossed her arms. "That didn't take long. Are you sure you're ready to use one of your guesses?"

In fact, Quicksilver was not at all sure, but it seemed unwise to show a witch she was afraid.

"As long as *you're* ready to teach me magic," she shot back.

The stranger chuckled. "You always are an arrogant young thing."

What a strange thing to say, Quicksilver thought. If the stranger's laugh had been an animal, it would have been a snake, old and sly. Quicksilver's pounding heart seemed to fill every inch of her body.

"Let's just go home," urged Sly Boots. "Something isn't right here."

"My first guess," Quicksilver said, "is that you read my thoughts using magic, and that's how you found out my real name."

"Mind magic!" The stranger let out a sharp, rasping laugh that dissolved into a cough. "That's rich. And are *you* the kind of person to go around using mind magic without a care in the world? I hardly think so."

"But I've never used any magic at all!" said Quicksilver.

"Mind magic," the stranger muttered. "Mind magic indeed. I don't much feel like scrambling my skull like an egg on a skillet, do I? I don't much feel like losing my sense of up and down, and how to put one foot in front of the other, do I? No, indeed I do not. *Mind magic.*"

"All right. Fine." Quicksilver crossed her arms and began to pace. "So I got that one wrong."

"Ha! Mind magic!"

Sly Boots and Fox followed Quicksilver as she paced.

"Quicksilver, listen to me," said Sly Boots. "Let's get home, and we'll start again with our lessons tomorrow. Aha! We'll climb up onto the magistrate's house in the morning, how about that? Or the roof of the inn? Not quite so high as the church but much less steep, which I think you'll agree can only be an advantage—"

"Just let me *think*, won't you?"

"Two guesses left," the stranger called blithely from her stool, and Quicksilver's stomach clenched, for there it was again—that feeling of familiarity in the tone of the stranger's voice. That voice sounded like . . . someone. Someone at the convent, perhaps? But that couldn't be right. This stranger was obviously no one Quicksilver had met before—

"If she doesn't stop shouting, someone will hear!" Sly Boots whispered. He tugged on the ends of his scarf and groaned. "Oh, can't we just go home? My parents need to eat! What if they're in pain? What if their fever's returned?"

Parents.

Quicksilver stopped pacing, seized by sudden inspiration.

Come back, whispered the treacherous thought from earlier that day. A northern wind snaked through Willow-on-the-River, ruffling Quicksilver's hair. She drew her patchwork cloak tight around her body and felt, in that moment, that the world had never seemed larger.

"I have my second guess," she said.

"This is happening more quickly than usual," remarked the stranger, leaning forward to prop her chin on her hands. "You're a curious one, you are."

"Oh, and do you collect many little girls on your travels?" Sly Boots marched over to her with clenched fists. "What do you do with them? Do you eat them? Do you throw them into the sea?"

The stranger lifted an eyebrow; at her feet, her dog lifted his head and growled. "No, I only do that to boys who don't know when to shut their mouths."

Sly Boots shrank back behind Quicksilver. "She'll cut my throat, she will."

"You're my mother," Quicksilver tried to say, but fear clung to her voice, choking it, and though she tried not to hope—for what did hope ever do but leave you open to hurt?—she could not help it. A light, fluttery feeling bloomed inside her, and she could hardly look up at the stranger's eyes, uncertain of what she might find there—and what she might not.

"You're my mother," she said again, forcing her voice steady, "and that's how you know my name. Because you were the one who gave it to me."

The square fell silent, save for Fox's whimpers and the hiss of the wind. Even Sly Boots stopped wringing his hands. The stranger's face seemed caught between too many painful things, and in that moment, she looked not old, but young—a girl trapped in a crone's body.

Then the church bells rang midnight—twelve low, mournful strikes. The stranger rose to take Quicksilver's chin in her hand. Now Fox was the one to growl.

"You should forget about your parents," said the stranger. "They abandoned you. They're not worth thinking about. Don't waste one more moment on them. Doing so will only ever bring you pain."

Quicksilver's eyes filled with tears, but she refused to let them fall. "Oh? And how do you know that?"

"I know. Accept it, and let it be."

The stranger returned to her stool. The old dog leaned his head against her leg.

"One more guess, little thief," she said, her voice tired and thin. "Consider carefully."

Quicksilver glared at the stranger for a long moment, then

turned on her heel, marched over to the church, and climbed back up to the roof. Her clammy hands shook as they gripped the wall's intricate wood carvings.

"Quicksilver?" Sly Boots called. "Where are you going?"

But Quicksilver did not answer him. She settled herself atop one of the church's wolf gargoyles and stared out into the night, thinking.

She thought all night, neither tired nor afraid. Chilled wind blew softly past her, ruffling her hair. Sly Boots and Fox curled up near the church in the dirt, Sly Boots sleeping fretfully, Fox quiet and alert.

The stranger and her old dog sat alone in the square. Quicksilver watched them by the light of the moons. She hardly blinked. She moved not an inch. The stars slowly turned above her, a carpet of shining silver dust. The stranger's old dog belched and turned over, showing his belly. Below Quicksilver, Fox did the same a moment later.

And, at last, her body heavy but her mind afire, she knew. She *knew*.

As the first reaches of dawn crept into the sky, Quicksilver climbed down from her perch. The noise of the clock striking five roused Sly Boots. Fox *whuffed* a question.

"What happened?" Sly Boots mumbled, yawning. "I dreamed there was a witch—"

"I'm ready with my third guess," proclaimed Quicksilver, standing before the stranger. She felt warm and calm, and a little dizzy, as if the cold night had worn away her useless bits, and left only her truest self behind.

The stranger watched her keenly. "Well then?"

"You are me," said Quicksilver, "and that's how you know my name, for it is also yours."

.8.

WHITE, GRAY, BLACK, BROWN, GOLD, BLUE, RED

The stranger's mouth curled into a smile. "Very good. *Very* good. We don't always get it right. Sometimes we need hints. But not you, eh, little thief?"

Sly Boots's mouth fell open. "But that's impossible!"

"She wasn't using mind magic," said Quicksilver, not taking her eyes off her older self, "and she's not one of my parents. It's the only answer that makes sense."

"But it makes absolutely *no* sense!"

"Which is why you had to arrive at that solution on your own," the stranger—Anastazia—explained. "Otherwise your mind would not have accepted the impossible truth."

Quicksilver could believe that. Even now, though she had found her answer hours before and had spent the night coming to terms with it, her mind still felt unbalanced, as though the world had shifted beneath her feet, and she could not yet walk steadily upon it.

Fox crept closer to the old dog, touched noses with it, went very still, yelped, ran away, froze, crept close again.

Quicksilver would have bet her entire stash of coins that the old dog rolled his eyes.

"And that's . . . Fox?" she asked.

"Yes," said Anastazia. "Much older, of course."

"Of course!" Sly Boots laughed and dragged his fingers through his hair. "Why not? An older Fox. Naturally."

"Sly Boots, either accept what's happening or go home," Quicksilver snapped. Then, to Anastazia: "So now what? What does this mean? Why are you here?"

Anastazia opened her mouth to answer and then smiled instead. "It's rather difficult to explain. Perhaps I should show you instead. Fox?"

The older Fox stretched, shook himself, and pressed his snout into Anastazia's palm. Quicksilver's Fox trotted toward

Anastazia and then stopped, tilting his head. He looked back at Quicksilver and whined.

"This might get confusing," Quicksilver said, "to call them both Fox."

"Don't worry about that. It won't matter for—"

But Anastazia did not finish her sentence, for at that moment, the chill dawn air of Willow-on-the-River filled with howls.

Quicksilver's blood seemed to freeze in her body. She knew the sound of those howls.

Anastazia leaped to her feet. In a flash, the older Fox was no longer himself, but a dog of light, tinged scarlet and gold. He looked strong, lean, powerful.

"He's found me already," Anastazia whispered. Her breaths came faster, thinner—almost wheezing. "*Stars*, I thought I would have more time."

"Who?" Quicksilver asked, though she thought she knew.

"The Wolf King."

Sly Boots breathed a shaky sigh of relief. "The Wolf King! But that's good, isn't it? Well, maybe not for you, you horrible, lying witch lady, but—"

"It's not good for *anyone*, fool," Anastazia snarled. "Quicksilver! Grab my hand, and your Fox, and don't let go."

Quicksilver reached for Anastazia's outstretched hand, then hesitated and took a step back. "Why?"

"I'll take you somewhere safe. I promise. Hurry!"

Then a dark, cloaked figure burst into the square. He was surrounded by wolves—seven of them.

White, gray, black, brown, gold, blue, red, recited Quicksilver's frantic brain. *The pack of the blessed Wolf King.*

"Get behind me," Anastazia commanded. Quicksilver and Sly Boots hurried to obey.

"You've lost, old woman!" bellowed the Wolf King, in a voice that reminded Quicksilver of metal scraping against metal. Sly Boots, hiding behind Quicksilver, clapped his hands over his ears. Throughout the square, windows glowed yellow as candles were lit. The door of the inn opened with a creak.

"What's all this ruckus about?" called the gruff voice of the innkeeper.

The Wolf King flung out his arm, and two of his wolves broke away, running toward the innkeeper. As they ran, their bodies lengthened and brightened, and soon they were not flesh-and-blood wolves, but wolves of light and fire, and where their paws hit the ground, they left black, charred spots behind. They lunged at the innkeeper, latching on with their jaws. He screamed in terror. His screams did not last long.

The Wolf King thrust his arm toward Quicksilver. Three more wolves broke away and bounded straight toward her.

Anastazia turned, her eyes wild. "Quicksilver, grab my hand, *now*."

Still Quicksilver hesitated. As the sleepy villagers awoke and stepped outside to investigate, the wolves attacked, their howls discordant and shrill. Fires broke out where the wolves crashed through wooden market stalls. A wolf shimmering white tackled a woman and tore at her throat. The air filled with smoke and the sound of the villagers' screams.

"*Quicksilver!*" Anastazia cried, her voice cracking.

Quicksilver could stay here. She could run and hide from the Wolf King and try to help the villagers. She could help Sly Boots protect his parents; maybe she could find out what had happened to everyone at the convent.

Or she could grab Anastazia's hand and go with her . . . somewhere.

What if they went to a place that was even more dangerous?

What if they went nowhere at all?

She grabbed Sly Boots's hand and squeezed.

"Get Fox!" she screamed, and waited until she saw Sly Boots

scoop up Fox before turning to take Anastazia's hand.

The snarling wolves leaped, their fiery jaws open wide and blazing.

Quicksilver felt Anastazia pulling her close. "Don't let go!" Anastazia cried, and then she whispered, "Good-bye, old friend," and when Quicksilver raised her head, she saw the older Fox, glowing and magnificent, racing around them, faster and faster, spinning them up into a column of light that pulled and tugged, and made Quicksilver feel as though her limbs would snap off her body.

"Anastazia!" she cried, but her voice was swallowed away, and she could only hope that Sly Boots had a good grip on Fox, and that he hadn't let go of her hand, for she could no longer feel the squeeze of his fingers.

All she knew was the blinding ring of light around her, and an immense pressure upon her chest, as though she were being turned inside out. From amid the wolves' howls came the frustrated wail of a child—a boy. Was it Sly Boots? Where was he?

"Fox? *Fox!*" Quicksilver screamed for him, her throat raw from trying to breathe in this tight, hot place. She would not lose Fox, she would *not* lose him—

Then, without warning or ceremony, there was nothing but darkness, and a silence thick as an ending.

.9.

THE MONSTER'S DEN

The first thing Quicksilver heard was Anastazia's voice.

"Don't open your eyes," she instructed.

And then, of course, all Quicksilver wanted was to open them as wide as they would go.

A cool, rough hand pressed against her eyes. "I said *don't* open them. Not yet."

"Quicksilver?" That was Sly Boots, somewhere nearby. It seemed to Quicksilver that her ears were stuffed full of something heavy and scratchy, making it difficult to pick out sounds. "Where are we? I can't breathe!"

"Keep your eyes closed, Boots!"

"Don't worry," said Anastazia, "I won't let him do anything *too* stupid."

"*Fox!* Where is he?" Quicksilver cried, trying to pry Anastazia's fingers off her face. "Did he open his eyes? Is he blind? Is he hurt?"

"I'm more than all right, in fact—"

"He's fine," Anastazia said loudly. "Just keep your eyes closed while I see about getting us a room. Oh, where *is* that horrible inn?" Anastazia grasped Quicksilver's wrist and dragged her along. Quicksilver held tight to Sly Boots's hand and pulled him along with them.

The sun was hot on her skin. Sounds of a bustling market met her ears, but they weren't anything like the sounds of Willow-on-the-River's market. She heard hissing and croaking sounds, as if strange beasts were speaking to one another, and jiglike music played on discordant, reedy instruments. She smelled dough being fried and smoke that carried the scent of burning flowers. She heard the rattle of coins, the shouts of bartering, and a roaring sound that could have been a bear or a particularly ferocious man.

But none of these things were as interesting to Quicksilver as the question of who had said, "I'm more than all right, in fact."

The voice had been a man's voice, and before Anastazia had interrupted him, he had sounded both strange and dear to Quicksilver's ears, as if he had been someone she had always known but had never spoken to before.

She stayed quiet and considered this while Anastazia guided them up a set of steps and into a building. A door closed behind them, and the air was cooler. There was a bustle of chatter and dishes, the smell of food.

"Welcome to the Monster's Den," came a cheerful voice. "Would you like a room or simply lunch?" And then, much more bewildered, "Why are your children walking around with their eyes closed?"

"It's a surprise!" said Anastazia. "For their birthdays."

Quicksilver waited while Anastazia spoke to the bewildered someone, discussing prices and room sizes. Quicksilver put out a hand, feeling for Fox, but couldn't find him.

Anastazia turned Quicksilver around and sat her on a bench. "All right," she said, "you can open your eyes now. It should be safe. This little pinchbrain's giving me a hard time about our room. Just sit there and don't move."

When Quicksilver opened her eyes, she saw that they were

inside some sort of inn. Across the hallway was a high-raftered room where people ate and drank. The shades were pulled shut, but even so, the light streaming through the windows was near to blinding, making Quicksilver squint. Everything glowed—the windows, the glassware on every table, the aggrieved-looking man carrying stacks of plates. He had bright blue hair, done up in spikes, like a bird that had fluffed itself up to look larger.

Anastazia crouched in front of Quicksilver, inspecting her. Her violet eyes glowed like jewels, and her hair flamed red and silver—but a more vivid red and a more brilliant silver than Quicksilver had ever seen. "How do you feel? Is it too bright? Your eyes should adjust soon."

"Where are we?" Quicksilver cringed at how trembly her voice sounded. "Why does everything look so strange? And where's Fox?"

"Same place—Willow-on-the-River, in the kingdom of Lalunet, in the Star Lands—but a different time. Long ago, before the hunt began. And everything looks strange because, being before the hunt, the world is full of witches, and therefore full of magic. And Fox is right there."

Quicksilver turned. She would not have recognized the dog sitting before her, regal and poised, had it not been for the torn left ear and the big brown eyes. Whereas Fox had always had an air of perpetual hunger about him, this dog looked solid and healthy and altogether completely satisfied with himself, as if he had just enjoyed a gourmet feast.

"Fox?" Quicksilver whispered. "Is that you?"

"Of course it's me," answered Fox, raising an eyebrow. He grinned, showing off his sharp teeth. "Don't I look incredible?"

.10.

THE STAR LANDS OF LONG AGO

Behind Quicksilver, Sly Boots made a choked, squeaky sound. Quicksilver couldn't blame him.

It was a curious thing, seeing a human expression on the face of her dog, and hearing human speech from the snout of her dog, and realizing that her dog wasn't quite *there*, was no longer quite *solid*. He looked like a normal dog until he turned, and then a curl of light drifted off him, and his whole body was illuminated as if he were made of sunlight and fire. He looked as though he might soar into the stars and be rather at home there—and then he turned solid again, and licked his behind.

For the first time in her life, Quicksilver was left completely without speech.

Anastazia dropped a few coins into the innkeeper's outstretched hand. "Thank you very much! Always dependable, you are."

"But I've never seen you before!" said the innkeeper, just before the door slammed shut.

Anastazia ushered Quicksilver and Sly Boots down the hallway and up two flights of stairs. Through a window on the landing, Quicksilver looked out at a crowded market, though she could only open her eyes a crack against the blazing light. She saw that the hissing, croaking sounds belonged to a pack of furred lizards in a gilded cage, spitting fire at one another. And the roar she had heard did, in fact, belong to a particularly ferocious man, who was singing with great pathos about his lost love to a bemused crowd.

Quicksilver looked around for some familiar landmark that would confirm that this was indeed Willow-on-the-River, but everything looked utterly foreign. There was no church, the roads were larger and paved with clean stones . . . ah. There was the magistrate's house. And there was the river. And there, a giant willow tree sat, appropriately, on the river. The tree glowed a bright green, its slender boughs shimmering as if dusted with starlight. But there *were* no willows on the river—at least, not in the town they had left only moments before. Quicksilver had always wondered how the town got its name—and now she understood.

"I feel like I've gone mad," said Sly Boots, his nose pressed to the glass, squinting through the spaces between his fingers. "Do you think she's telling the truth? Oh, I'm going to be sick."

Sly Boots bent over and heaved onto the landing.

"Come, don't dawdle," said Anastazia, ushering them up the rest of the stairs. She coughed into her sleeve and wiped her mouth. "Your eyes need some time. Also, my feet are on fire, and I'd like a nice sit."

"I'd like an explanation." Quicksilver said sharply, once Anastazia had shown them into a quiet room with three beds and a cushioned couch by the window. "You've dragged us around quite enough."

"Have I now?"

Sly Boots stumbled into the nearest bed and lay there, moaning and rubbing his temples.

Quicksilver squared her shoulders. "Yes. I've reached my limit. Isn't that right, Fox?"

She said this automatically, having over the years gotten used to speaking with Fox as though he were a person and not simply a dog.

"Honestly, I'd rather not get into it." Fox sighed, settling on the couch to look down into the market. "There are much more interesting things to see here than you two arguing."

Quicksilver gaped at him. "I beg your pardon?"

"Did I misspeak? I said you're boring."

Often Quicksilver had amused herself by imagining what Fox's voice would sound like, had he been a human—but in none of those fancies had he ever sounded so . . . well, if not hateful, then certainly not *loving*.

She turned on Anastazia. "What have you done to him?" The shock of this new Fox left her with a dangerously upset feeling lodged in her throat. "This isn't my Fox. My Fox would never speak to me like that."

"You're right," Anastazia agreed. "This isn't your Fox. And yet you're wrong, because it *is* your Fox. He's the same, and he's different, and he's new, and he's who he was always meant to be. And so are you, my dear. See for yourself."

Anastazia pulled Quicksilver to stand in front of the mirror in the corner. Quicksilver saw her own reflection—and yet it wasn't her own reflection. Much was the same—her squashed, piggish nose, the shape of her mouth—but her hair was a bright, blazing red instead of gray, and her eyes were an even more brilliant violet than Anastazia's.

Sly Boots sat up, looking dazed. "I feel a little better now. What did you do to your hair?"

"It couldn't ever have happened in your time," Anastazia told Quicksilver, her eyes fixed hard on Quicksilver's face. Quicksilver, for her part, kept her expression blank, determined to give nothing away to this woman—nor to this Fox, sitting by the window as if nothing were amiss.

"Ever since the Wolf King began his hunt," Anastazia continued, "eliminating witches from the world one by one, magic likewise faded, for without witches, there can be no magic. Magic feeds on itself, you see. The more witches, the stronger the world's magic, the more you can see it in the forests and flowers, in the sky itself.

"In your time, so little magic is left that even someone whose blood is rich with magic will never be able to access it. Even blood as rich with magic as your own, Quicksilver." Anastazia paused and smiled wistfully. "As *our* own, I should say. But here, in this past . . . here, your blood sings. Magic is everywhere. Magic is at your fingertips. *In* them."

Sly Boots approached them slowly, his eyes wide. "Does she mean what I think she means?"

"You're saying I'm a . . . a—" Quicksilver swallowed hard.

"You're a witch, Quicksilver of Lalunet." Anastazia grinned. "Just like me."

.11.

ANASTAZIA AND THE WOLF KING

Anastazia had lunch sent up to their room—vegetable stew and hot, crusty bread and mint tea, plus a leg of mutton for Fox. They ate in silence, listening to the birds that perched outside the window. The birds' feathers glowed a rich, deep indigo tipped with glimmering gold, and they sang with eerily human voices. Past them, the stars shone like beacons in the midafternoon sky.

At last Anastazia turned to Quicksilver with a serious expression.

"Now that we've eaten," she said, "I suppose you'd like to know what's going on. I know I did, at this point."

Quicksilver folded her arms over her chest. "You might say that."

Anastazia took a deep breath and looked at the ceiling. "All right. This is always the hardest part. I know it will be difficult for you. I know because it was for me too. And for the Anastazia who taught me. And for the Anastazia before that, and before that, and before that."

"What is she talking about?" hissed Sly Boots, sitting with a pillow clutched protectively to his chest.

"I've brought you back to an earlier time in history," Anastazia said, ignoring him, "so that you might come into your witch bloodlines and learn how to work magic, so that you might help me find the bones of the First Ones' monsters and defeat the Wolf King, so that we might save our race from extinction."

"Nothing to worry yourself about too much," said Fox breezily, lounging on his cot. "A simple task, really."

Quicksilver wondered if she would ever stop feeling disturbed at this snotty, insufferable voice coming from her Fox's mouth. "Why me? Why couldn't other witches help you?"

"Witches don't help other witches," said Anastazia, staring darkly out the window. "Since our beginning, it's been our nature to quarrel, to try to best one another, even to steal other witches' magic, if we can. We know it's dangerous to do so—that the health of the world's magic depends on many witches having healthy magic, not witches constantly stealing and fighting. But that's how we are. That's how we've always been."

Quicksilver nodded. The one time she'd tried working with another thief had been recently, with Sly Boots—and look where that had gotten her.

"In this case, of course," continued Anastazia, "no one is helping me but me—albeit a younger *me*—which is perfectly acceptable. And any other witch who has ever tried to defeat the Wolf King has failed, while we have continued on, life after life after life. So"—Anastazia gave Quicksilver a hard, grim little smile—"I can only assume we're the only ones fit for the job. Why bother asking for help from anyone else? They'll only botch things."

All of a sudden, Quicksilver sat up straight. "Wait. Your Fox. Where is he?"

Anastazia's smile faded. There was a horrible silence, during which even Fox seemed to hold his breath.

"He's dead," Anastazia said at last. "He died to bring us here."

Fox whined, and Quicksilver's heart jumped to hear the

sound. She patted the bed, and Fox curled up beside her, pressing hard against her leg. Quicksilver smiled and had to fight the urge to scoop Fox up into her arms as she once would have done. Instead she stroked Fox's velvet ears, and he sighed his familiar, contented sigh.

Anastazia watched them with an unreadable look on her face.

"But . . . why did he die?" Sly Boots asked.

"Traveling through time is dangerous magic," said Anastazia. "It requires tremendous sacrifice—of the witch, and her monster. Which is why, as far as I know, I'm only one of two witches to ever have done it." She folded her hands in her lap, looking suddenly very small. "To willingly give up your monster, and therefore your magic, the very thing that makes you a witch . . . it's unthinkable. Witches would rather die than make that sacrifice. You'd have to be a fool to do it." She smiled tiredly. "So I suppose the rest of witchkind is truly lucky that I'm a big enough fool for all of us."

"Wait . . . what's a monster?" Quicksilver asked.

"Perhaps I should start at the beginning," Anastazia said, "instead of rambling on like the dotty old woman I've become. That's something to remember, Quicksilver: the older you get, the harder you must work to keep your thoughts in order."

"I won't be old for a very long time," Quicksilver pointed out.

"You'll soon find that a very long time isn't as long as you think," said Anastazia. "Now, listen to me and don't interrupt. I hate having to repeat myself."

Then Anastazia began to speak.

Once there were no witches in the world.

Then there were seven.

The first seven witches to walk the earth became known as the First Ones. They and their monsters were born out of the same ancient star, the same pool of magic—forever connected, forever sisters and brothers. Beloved by all, the First Ones were sought after for their magic, strength, and wisdom.

But soon they began to quarrel, each desperate to prove themselves the most powerful witch in the world. They went to war—a terrible war that lasted an entire dark age. And when the war ended, the First Ones had destroyed themselves.

Of course, throughout their long lifetimes, the First Ones had joined with many humans, and their children grew up as witches too—and their children's children, and so on. Long after the First Ones had gone, then, the world was still full of witches. But they

*carried the spirit of that long, dark war inside them, and lived full
of distrust for one another, more likely to quarrel than to join hands
in fellowship.*

*Now we witches say that when the First Ones disappeared, their
spirits went to rest in the stars, from where they watch over the seven
kingdoms we know as Lalunet, Falstone, Napurya, Belrike, Koreva,
Menettsk, and Valteya.*

*These seven kingdoms are called the Star Lands, and for a long
time, they enjoyed an era of peace.*

Anastazia bowed her head, letting her eyes fall closed. She
sat there for so long it seemed she'd fallen asleep. Quicksilver and
Fox glanced at each other.

"Er, well, that was a nice story," said Sly Boots, his eyes
peeking out over the pillow he still clutched to his chest. "But
that doesn't explain anything that's happened except for witchy
history nonsense that no one cares about."

"Everything I say is important," said Anastazia, her eyes
snapping open to glare at Sly Boots. "You'd do well to shut your
mouth and listen carefully."

Sly Boots obeyed, but with such a red-faced expression of
indignation that Quicksilver nearly burst out laughing.

But she didn't. She waited as Anastazia took a sip of her tea and then continued.

Once there was a boy born into an old witch family.

The boy's name was Ari, and the family's name was Tarkalia. They ruled the northern kingdom of Valteya, and their ranks were full of powerful witches.

Except for Ari.

He had little magical skill . . . so little that, when he turned thirteen years old, and still had not found his monster—which is to say, he had not yet come of magical age, as he should have   his family began to scorn him. And therefore the entire kingdom came to scorn him, and Ari's life turned lonely and cold.

One day the boy was wandering the mountains of Valteya, very near the Far North, and was greeted by seven voices. They told Ari that if he would act as their vessel in the Star Lands, give them a body in which to exist, they would find monsters for him. Not just one, but many. He would become a powerful witch, more powerful than his family, more powerful than anyone.

All he had to do was help them with this one simple task: he must act as their body in the Star Lands and help them find the bones of their monsters, for they had once been witches themselves, but were no longer. And once these bones were found, the seven witches could walk the earth again, as they had not done in many an age.

Having nothing to lose, and eager to seek revenge upon those who had ridiculed him, Ari agreed to this bargain at once. The spirits of these seven witches possessed his body, and Ari Tarkalia began working terrible deeds.

As had been promised, he soon found seven wolves—one for each of the Star Lands, one for each of the spirits now living inside him—and forced magic into them. The wolves became bound to Ari as his monsters, and since the wolves were forced into this bondage and did not come by it naturally, their magic was dangerous and sharp. The wolves hungered for violence, as did the witches who controlled them.

Using Ari as their eyes and his wolves as their teeth, the seven witches slaughtered his family, every last Tarkalia they could find, and then Ari was king of Valteya, though his throne was red with blood. But soon even Valteya was not enough. Ari left that kingdom, and the Star Lands, and appointed seven lords to rule the Star Lands in his name. They would be loyal to him, and him alone, and he would be the only king. Then Ari moved to the Far North and built a castle carved of stone so black it swallowed the starlight.

Finally Ari understood that the witches inside him were the spirits of the First Ones, who had nearly destroyed the Star Lands long ago, in that dark age of war. They were seeking the bones of their monsters, and once they found them, they would return to the world, powerful and terrible.

And so Ari Tarkalia became the Wolf King, and began the hunt, so that when the First Ones returned, there would be no other witches left to challenge them.

"So the Wolf King . . . is a boy?" managed Quicksilver, her voice hushed. She glared at Sly Boots, whose wide eyes peeked out over the edge of his pillow.

He reeled back from her. "What's that look for? What, because I'm a boy too? I can't help being a boy, you know!"

Fox lowered his head to the bed and put his front paws over his snout. "Someone make him stop shrieking, *please.*"

"Once, the Wolf King was a boy," said Anastazia. "But now he is something else. Something darker. I'm not sure there's anything left of the boy Ari inside the creature he has become."

"But what about us?" Quicksilver leaned forward. "You, and me? And our Foxes?" She waved her hand back and forth between them. "How are you me, and how am I you?"

Anastazia's irritated gaze softened—with fondness or sadness, Quicksilver couldn't tell.

"This last bit," said Anastazia with a tiny grin, "is my favorite part. I always like talking about myself, you know."

Quicksilver sat up a bit straighter. "I do too!"

"I know, little thief." Anastazia cleared her throat, folded her hands in her lap, and began the last part of her story.

Once there was a witch who didn't know she was a witch.

She lived in the kingdom of Lalunet. Magic had long faded from the world, thanks to the Wolf King. He had hunted the witches until hardly any remained, and those that did lived in hiding, praying to the stars that the Wolf King would never find them. The colors of the world faded, and the stars dimmed.

Worst of all, the Wolf King had sowed in the hearts of humans distrust and fear of witches. Humans came to revere him, the witch slayer, and erect churches in his name. He taught them false truths about witches, but no one still lived who knew the real truth and would speak it.

This witch—the witch of our story, who called herself Quicksilver—

♘ ♘ ♘

"Do you mean . . . you?" Sly Boots asked Anastazia. "Not *this* Quicksilver," he said, pointing at Quicksilver, "but you, Anastazia, when you were young?"

Quicksilver and Anastazia both glared at him.

"I'm talking about *us*," said Anastazia, pointing at herself and then at Quicksilver. "Not either of us sitting here right now, but the first version of *us* to travel back in time. Just let me tell my story, won't you? I've almost finished."

"Sorry," muttered Sly Boots. He glanced over at Quicksilver. "It's just a pretty good story, actually, you know? I'm getting overly excited."

Quicksilver threw him such a fierce look that he immediately fell silent.

The witch of our story, who called herself Quicksilver (though that wasn't her true name), didn't come into her magic until the age of twenty, which is much later than she would have, had the Star Lands still been full of witches and bright with magic, as they had once been.

When she was twenty, magic settled in her companion, an old dog named Fox, who then became her monster. There now existed a mighty bond between them, connecting their hearts.

Quicksilver didn't know much about magic—other than what she had learned at the convent when she was young—but she knew it was forbidden, and that the Wolf King hunted those who possessed it. Quicksilver lived nowhere and everywhere, stealing to survive. She was good at stealing, so though it was a lonely life, it was not a hard one.

Then one day Quicksilver was imprisoned in a town for thievery. Another prisoner there had been arrested for witchcraft and was gravely injured. His name was Filip, and he recognized Quicksilver for what she was. Together they escaped and fled into the wild.

Soon after, the Wolf King heard of their escape and gave chase. Every hour on the road made Filip and his tiny mouse monster weaker, but they managed to teach Quicksilver about magic—its shape, its taste, and most importantly, how to work with Fox to use it.

One cold night, with the Wolf King nearly upon them, Filip and his monster promised they could send Quicksilver and Fox somewhere safe, in thanks for helping them escape. Just as the Wolf King attacked, Filip and his monster made the ultimate sacrifice. Even though Filip knew it would kill his monster and leave Filip himself defenseless before the Wolf King, he sent Quicksilver and Fox back to an earlier time—a time when many witches still lived, and the Star Lands were bright with magic.

Quicksilver took her birth name, Anastazia, for she felt that she should leave behind the relics of her old life. Anastazia decided that if no other witches would challenge the Wolf King, she would. Once she had been the best thief in all the Star Lands. Now she would be the best witch—and nobody would get the better of her, not even a king.

When she realized the Wolf King was searching for the skeletons of the First Ones' monsters, she began searching for them, too, and found some of them, and lost some to the Wolf King when they battled, and stole some back from him, and fought him again, and lost, and won, and hid herself away, and this went on for long decades, while Anastazia crafted spells that extended her life far beyond that of any normal witch, and the Wolf King became desperate and dangerous.

Anastazia fought until she was a frail old woman—and then she found her younger self, the twelve-year-old orphan thief Quicksilver. Anastazia brought Quicksilver back in time, to an even earlier point than she herself had traveled, and taught her younger self how to use magic, and how to fight the Wolf King. And this happened again, and again—a cycle of war fought through the endless ring of time.

Anastazia and Quicksilver searched and stole and battled, for decades and centuries and lifetimes, over and over, and in none of

*these lives did they manage to defeat the Wolf King—though they
often came close.*

Each time—

"Did you come close to defeating him in *your* lifetime?"
Quicksilver interrupted. "You, yourself?"

"Yes, tell us about your battles," said Sly Boots, leaning
forward with shining eyes. "What was the worst one? And I
mean worst as in, a really *exciting* one, not one where the Wolf
King got the best of you and left you for dead, wounded and
defeated. . . ."

At the sight of Anastazia's furious expression, Sly Boots trailed
off and hid his face behind his pillow. "Sorry," he mumbled. "I
got carried away."

"Indeed," Anastazia snapped. "And yes, I came *quite* close
to defeating him during my own lifetime, thank you very much,
Quicksilver. This is the last time I'll tolerate such cheek from
either of you, remember that."

Then she cleared her throat, muttering to herself, "Ruining
the ending. Interrupting me. *Children.* Nasty little creatures,
truly."

☙ ☙ ☙

Each time, Anastazia hoped this fight would be the last, and each time, it was not.

Until, perhaps, now.

Silence fell. Sly Boots looked at Quicksilver, at Anastazia, then at Quicksilver again.

"Is that the ending?" he whispered. "She yelled at us because of two measly sentences?"

"So here we are, Quicksilver," said Anastazia, her body sagging against the pillows now that her story had concluded. "You and me—the next pair in this war, just as we have been many times over." She paused, drew a long breath, and fixed her tired violet eyes upon Quicksilver's matching bright ones.

"Are you ready to become the witch you were born to be?"

.12.

SOME SORT OF WITCHY THING

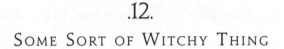

Quicksilver let Anastazia's question linger in the air while she turned it over in her head.

Was she ready to fight? Ready to become a witch? She could not imagine how to answer. So much had happened in the last few days—most of all in the last few hours—that she had hardly had time to catch her breath.

"Hang on a moment," Sly Boots spoke up, pounding his fist against the pillow. "The only thing we're going to do is return to our own time. I mean, is there really any question about this? My parents are there, our home is there. We can't just leave it behind." Silence met his words. He looked to Quicksilver, his face tense and earnest. "Quicksilver?"

She could not look at him. Now that he had said the words aloud, it was very easy to decide that she wanted to stay in this time after all. For what was there for her to return to? She had nothing and no one. The only creature in the world she cared about was sitting by the window—well, except for the girls and the sisters of her convent, but when had they ever cared about her? Although even they didn't deserve whatever the wolves had done to them.

"If we defeat the Wolf King," Fox murmured, as though he had heard the thoughts in her head, "then we'll change the future, and they'll be all right, won't they? They'll never be attacked, because the Wolf King will never have been alive to attack them."

Quicksilver considered his sharp, whiskered face. "I suppose you're right."

"I'm afraid there's no way to return just yet," Anastazia said. "Not only does such an act require much more powerful magic than we have access to at the moment, it also would require Fox to sacrifice—"

"Absolutely not," Quicksilver interrupted. "There will be no sacrifices here." She tilted up his face. "I promise I'll never make you do that, Fox. *Never.*"

Fox huffed indignantly. "I should think not."

"What do you expect me to do?" asked Sly Boots. "Leave my parents to die of fever or be killed by the Wolf King when he burns Willow-on-the-River to the ground?"

"Do keep in mind," said Anastazia evenly, "that if we succeed in our task, and therefore change the future, we could prevent your parents from ever getting cursed in the first place."

Sly Boots opened his mouth and shut it again, looking stumped.

"But in the meantime," Anastazia continued, "we cannot afford to concern ourselves with the fates of individuals. This is a war. We are fighting to save our kind."

"Witches aren't *my* kind," Sly Boots pointed out, his voice low. "They're the reason my parents are ill. And now they're the reason why I've been separated from them." The expression on his face reminded Quicksilver of how he had looked in his parents' bedroom, right before he had shattered the bowl against the wall.

Quicksilver rolled her eyes. "No one forced you to come thieving with me. You could have said, 'No thank you, I'd rather cry at home alone in my slippers,' and you wouldn't have been there when the Wolf King came, and Fox and I would have come back to the past by ourselves."

Flushing, Sly Boots said, "Well, I didn't ask you to break into my home and try to rob me, did I?"

"Hah! As if you'd anything worth stealing."

Sly Boots shot to his feet. "I would have had something worth stealing—lots of somethings—if I hadn't had to sell it all to get medicine for my parents, and *they* would have never taken ill were it not for you—you—"

Anastazia raised a cool eyebrow. "Yes? Go on. *Us* what?"

Quicksilver crossed her arms over her chest. "Yes, please. Do say whatever nasty word you were about to say."

Fox curled his tail around his body, his eyes twinkling. "Oh, this ought to be fun."

Sly Boots tossed the pillow onto the bed. "Never mind."

"Quite right." Anastazia sniffed. "Unless you would like to wander off into this world and fend for yourself against any rogue witch who might fancy making you her servant—and believe me, you have the air of a particularly useful servant—or some beast so savage not even your sleeping mind could have imagined it, then you will have to remain here, with us, and help us fight our fight."

Sly Boots glared at Anastazia, but his glare was sorely outmatched. He looked down at the bedcovers.

"I don't see any other way about it, Boots," said Quicksilver. "If we're stuck here, we're stuck here, but I don't like to remain stuck for long." Quicksilver rose to her feet. "If you'll teach me magic," she said to Anastazia, "I'll help you fight the Wolf King. Or find the what's-it things. The bones of the First Ones' monsters." She paused. "You already have some of them, right? You've managed to hang on to at least a couple of skeletons, maybe?"

Anastazia's face fell, her mouth thinning. "No. I had two of them, and then I lost them to the Wolf King before I found you. In every one of our lifetimes, we have found these skeletons hidden in different parts of the Star Lands, and they don't always stay in the same place for long. Before the First Ones died, they put a spell on their monsters so that their skeletons might never be found, and they did a fine job. They can cloak and glamour themselves to look different than what they are. They're here one instant, and three kingdoms away the next. You'll find one only to lose it a moment later if you don't grab it fast enough. That's what happened to me—for *ten years* I hid two of them, carrying them with me wherever I went. I was lucky. And then, only days before I found you, they vanished."

Anastazia took a deep, shuddering breath and then let out a rattling, wet cough. "I've brought you to a time in the past when the Wolf King hasn't yet found any of the skeletons—at least I don't *think* he has—but as for us . . . we'll have to start with nothing. No skeletons, no advantage . . ."

Quicksilver swallowed hard. "Well . . . once we *do* have the skeletons, we can destroy them, right?"

"We haven't yet designed a spell strong enough to do it, but we will," said Anastazia. "Each time we get closer. Meanwhile, we'll steal as many of them as we can and try to keep them out of the Wolf King's reach until that day comes."

Quicksilver was silent for a long moment. When she finally held out her hand, she tried to make herself seem more confident than she felt. "All right, then. It's a deal."

Anastazia, amused, slapped her palm. When their skin touched, a spark zipped between them.

"Agreed."

"And," said Quicksilver, turning to Sly Boots, "as soon as I figure out a way to return, I'll send you right back home, so you can be with your parents. I can't imagine it will take me long. If magic is anything like thieving, I ought to learn quickly."

"Hah!" snorted Anastazia.

"Don't worry, child," Fox said, stretching and yawning. "With me as your monster, you can't go wrong."

Quicksilver flushed. "Child? I'm *twelve*."

"Can't go wrong," Anastazia repeated, shaking her head. "Oh, stupid little fools. You've no idea what lies ahead."

Ignoring her, and Fox's smug face, Quicksilver thrust out her hand again. "Agreed, Boots?"

Sly Boots considered her. "You promise you'll do that for me? You'll send me home the moment you can? Even if . . . ?" He trailed off, glancing Fox's way.

"I won't do it if it hurts Fox, no," said Quicksilver. "But I'll find another way, I'm sure of it. I always find a way."

After a moment, Sly Boots gave a nervous smile, and they slapped hands. "Agreed."

Quicksilver wiped her palm on her coat. "You're always so nasty and sweaty. First thing I'm going to do is find some sort of . . . witchy thing . . . to fix that."

"It's called a spell," Anastazia hissed. "Witchy thing. Indeed."

"Well, how am I supposed to know what it's called?"

Fox stretched, sticking his rump into the air, and then sat up. "Shall we begin now? I'm still bored, you know. No offense, child," he continued, cutting off Quicksilver's indignant reply, "but when you're a monster, the rest of the world seems dull as pudding."

"I like pudding," Sly Boots offered.

"Of course you do," said Fox soothingly.

Anastazia, grumbling to herself, fluffed her pillows and blew out the candles. "First, we sleep. We'll begin in the morning—that is, if I decide not to run away and leave you noisy lot to your own devices."

With the candles out, the room soon fell silent. Fox padded over to the window couch and curled up in a ball with his nose tucked under his hind leg.

Quicksilver watched him for a long time, forcing her heavy eyes to stay open, for when he was like this—quiet and still—he was the Fox she had always known, and not the strange, sharp creature he had become.

.13.

A Bit Rough around the Edges

The next morning at dawn, while Anastazia settled their account with the proprietor, Quicksilver waited on the bench just outside the tavern's dining room, where other early risers were eating breakfast.

The woman serving coffee had luminous purple braids and wore a gray patterned dress with belled sleeves. (Her earrings, Quicksilver assessed, might have fetched twenty silvers back home.) A man and two children devoured a plate of eggs and ham (five coppers), their skin glowing like polished ebony lit up by fire.

And there, lounging at a table in the corner, was a bear of a man, reading a small book the size of his palm. He glowed brighter than anyone, his yellow-tipped green hair and the eighteen rings on his fingers all vivid as the sun.

On this man's shoulder perched a brilliant green bird with eyes like amber jewels. It watched Quicksilver without blinking.

"Is that a witch, do you think?" Quicksilver whispered.

Sly Boots, sitting beside her, mumbled something incoherent, leaned his head against her shoulder, snuggled into place, and resumed snoring.

"Ugh, wake up and stop drooling." Quicksilver shrugged him off, and his head hit the back of the bench. He smacked his lips and snored even louder.

"Yes, he's a witch," said Fox.

Quicksilver jumped to find him at her elbow. Anastazia had given her a pack that held two pouches stuffed full of food and supplies, and she hugged it to her chest, unable to meet Fox's eyes.

"I didn't hear you come over," she told Fox.

"I'm quite sly."

They sat quietly for a moment. Quicksilver used to tell Fox everything that was on her mind—her plans, her fears, how she sometimes imagined the north wind carried her mother's voice.

But now, she didn't know how to say anything to him, and she certainly didn't think she could trust him.

"Don't worry," Fox said blandly, "your secrets are safe with me."

Quicksilver scowled. "Can you hear everything I think?"

"Most things. Say, do you think I'd make a good bird?"

"What?"

"Just think about it. I'd be a good bird, wouldn't I? All gold and feathery? Long and sleek?" He paused, glanced sidelong at Quicksilver. "Maybe with white feathers in my tail?"

At his words, Quicksilver imagined such a bird. She imagined Fox's lanky dog body transforming into a smaller, feathered creature, soaring through the rafters overhead. . . .

"What in the name of the stars?" Sly Boots sat up, fully awake.

Quicksilver blinked. A bizarre creature half hopped, half flew across the dining room tables—gold feathered and gold furred. It had a wing on one side, and two pawed legs on the other. When it opened its mouth, its tiny beak was crammed full of canine fangs. It tried to fly and crashed into the breakfasting family's plate of hot rolls.

A hand grabbed Quicksilver's shoulder.

"Think of Fox," Anastazia instructed. "Think of him as you know him—a dog, and a dog alone."

An image of Fox flashed into Quicksilver's flustered mind. Something tugged on her heart, yanking her toward Fox, and she gasped. She needed to be near him, more than she had ever needed anything in her life. She ran to him, her pack swinging from her shoulders. With a flash of golden light, the bird-dog *thing* clambering across the tables became fully a dog, and slid right into the feet of the witch with the green bird on his shoulder.

Fox raised his head, woozy, and barked. Quicksilver fell to her knees beside him and scooped him into her arms.

Sly Boots hurried over. "Are you all right? What happened?"

Quicksilver did not know how to answer him. She felt as if she had stepped into an outlandish dream. All she knew was that she had needed to be near Fox, and now she was, and whatever had happened didn't matter much in the face of that. She buried her face between his ears and was relieved to discover that he still smelled of dog.

"Our apologies," Anastazia muttered to the witch with the green bird, not quite looking at him. "She just got her monster. A bit rough around the edges."

The witch man grimaced, avoiding Anastazia's gaze just as determinedly as she was avoiding his. "Not to worry. First few days are always tricky." Then he turned away, the air around him vibrating with animosity.

The witch's monster, in a soft thrum of emerald light, circled around Fox's head, squawking angrily, before popping back to the witch's shoulder with a second puff of light.

"Do it again, do it again!" shrieked the two children a few tables over.

"So sorry to burst into your morning like this," Anastazia called to the entire establishment.

The woman in the purple braids grinned. "I've seen much worse. Why, this one time, this witch from Belrike came in with her son, and—"

"What a wonderful story," said Anastazia, ushering Quicksilver and Sly Boots out of the inn and onto the street. Fox hopped along beside them, shaking out his paws. Quicksilver slammed her eyes shut as they stepped outside, but dared to open them again after a couple of moments, and found that the brightness of this long-ago world was no longer painful.

"Of all the careless, reckless things to do," Anastazia spat. "What were you thinking?"

Quicksilver frowned. "What do you mean, what was *I* thinking? Fox was the one who—"

"Fox can't do anything on his own. Without you directing him, he's simply raw magic. Shapeless and stupid."

"Excuse me," Fox interrupted, coughing out a tiny yellow feather, "but I am certainly *not*—"

"Stupid, yes. You looked ridiculous, flapping about like some newborn half-thing."

"But Fox was the one who started talking about being a bird," Quicksilver cried. "He told me to imagine it, and I did, and then I don't know what happened, but all I did was think, I promise!"

"*All* you did?" Sighing, Anastazia looked to the sky, stars glittering between streaks of dawn-lit clouds. "Quicksilver, magic is all *about* thinking. Your monster listens to your thoughts, reads them and interprets them, and does whatever they tell him to do."

Quicksilver whirled on Fox. "You *knew*. You told me to imagine it, and you knew what would happen when I did!"

"Not true," Fox protested silkily. "I thought you would actually think what you were supposed to think instead of botching it."

"How could I botch something when I didn't even know I was doing it?"

"It's not *my* fault you don't know these things. *She's* supposed to teach them to you."

"Dog, I will teach you things so beyond your current capacity that someday you'll look back on this morning and think yourself nothing but a dumb pup," said Anastazia. "And don't you use that tone with me. I mean it."

They walked in silence until Sly Boots burst into a fit of giggles, gasping and wiping his eyes. "I'm sorry, but I can't help it anymore. You looked ridiculous! A wing on one side, and . . . *paws* on the other! And a beak full of teeth!"

Sly Boots's laughter rang through the already crowded street. A fox glowing a fiery red bounded alongside a woman wearing a gauzy veil. A ruby flash, and he was a tiny red bird, flying overhead. Other flashes followed—monsters shifting into different animal forms, witches vanishing into columns of colored smoke—and the Willow-on-the-River market of long ago cheerfully bustled on.

It was a world of witches, a world where thoughts could turn dogs into birds.

Or *almost* birds.

Quicksilver laughed too, at the sheer outrageous wonder of it all. She clutched Sly Boots's arm, laughing so hard she almost fell over.

Fox sniffed, putting his nose in the air. A fluffy white feather fluttered on his rump like a flag, and Sly Boots and Quicksilver laughed at it all the way through town.

.14.

A MONSTER NAMED FOX

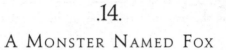

The first thing Quicksilver noticed about being a witch was that it would have been much easier without a monster getting in the way.

Or perhaps simply with a monster who wasn't so completely impossible.

Anastazia had taken them to a clearing some distance from town. It butted up against a pasture of cows, and thick clusters of trees shielded them from the road. Here, she said, they would practice the most basic of magical tasks—communication.

"Before you can try any actual spells," said Anastazia, "you must learn how to speak to each other—not as girl and dog, but as witch and monster. You'll read each other's thoughts, and know how to use your magic based on what you're thinking." Anastazia paused to rifle through a bag of mint-and-chocolate star-shaped candies she'd purchased in town.

"Do you have to practice here?" Sly Boots complained from his perch on the pasture fence, waving his hand about. "These cows stink."

"So do you, but you don't hear me griping about it," said Anastazia. "Now, Quicksilver. Let's try again. Fox, stop biting your rump and act civilized."

Fox gathered himself with dignity and bowed his head. "Of course, master."

Quicksilver snapped, "*I'm* the one you call master. *I'm* your witch."

"Are you quite sure? You don't seem to be a very good one, at any rate."

"*Fox,*" Anastazia scolded.

"All right, all right. Whenever you're ready. *Master.*"

Quicksilver rolled up her sleeves and stuck out her tongue at him.

"Now," said Anastazia, "try again."

Quicksilver closed her eyes and breathed in and out, steadying herself.

"Listen to each other," Anastazia continued. "The bond is there, connecting you—soul to soul. All you have to do, Quicksilver, is reach out and find the bond, follow it, and use it to show Fox whatever it is you want him to do. You must think your instructions in clear, easy-to-understand images. Remember . . . though he is now a monster, he's still a *dog*."

"And what is *that* supposed to mean?" huffed Fox.

Quicksilver allowed her breathing to carry her thoughts in and out of her mind, as though they floated atop a calm river.

Fox? she thought.

Nothing.

She tried again. *Fox? Hello?*

Still nothing, and yet she knew he was there, across the clearing. She could hear him scratching his ear.

Quicksilver focused on the rhythm of her heart. She followed it out, into the air, reaching, searching, until she sensed another heartbeat. At first she thought it was the echo of her own, but then she realized it was faster, and hotter, like Fox when he was panting.

Fox!

He sighed. *What?*

I've found you!

Well done, you.

Be serious, Fox.

Why? That's no fun.

I can feel you scratching your ear! No wonder you make those funny growling sounds when you do that. It does feel amazing.

"What's happening?" called Anastazia.

"I've found Fox," Quicksilver cried, her eyes still closed. "I'm talking to him!"

"Excellent. Now, try sending him an image, something simple. Picture it in your mind, and then send it toward him, like you might push an object across a table."

What shall I think of? Quicksilver wondered to Fox.

An image of Sly Boots sitting on the fence, picking his nose, flashed through Quicksilver's mind.

What was that? I didn't think that.

No, Fox said, *I did. Because that's what he's doing right now. Charming, isn't he?*

Quicksilver snorted. *What if we . . . ?* Then she pictured a scenario that made Fox stop scratching himself and perk up.

Oh, that's a superb idea, master.

Quicksilver beamed. *I thought you'd like it.*

But we'll have to surprise him.

Of course.

Otherwise it wouldn't have the same effect.

I quite agree. Then Quicksilver had another idea. *I've got it.*

She worked through the entire situation in her mind, step by step, which took a while to accomplish. She had never before realized how many thoughts go into one idea, and how they come jumbled and out of order, a messy tangle of sensations and colors. She forced herself to think slowly, imagining each step in their new scheme as if sketching it out with pen and paper.

"What are you two doing?" Anastazia asked. "You've been quiet an awfully long time."

"They're just standing there with their eyes closed," said Sly Boots. "It's starting to give me the creeps."

He gives me the creeps, thought Fox to Quicksilver. *All those freckles, that droopy smile . . .*

Quicksilver stifled her giggle. "We're trying something!"

"Trying *what*, exactly?" asked Anastazia. "You're only supposed to send him a single image."

"Oh, we're far beyond that," said Quicksilver. "Don't worry, we can handle it."

"Quicksilver—" warned Anastazia.

Go! Quicksilver thought to Fox, and opened her eyes.

In a soft burst of golden light, Fox disappeared and then reappeared as a sleek yellow bird—a proper bird this time, not half formed—hovering right in front of Sly Boots's face.

Fox squawked and flapped his wings.

Sly Boots screamed, teetered, circled his arms to regain his balance, and fell back into a clump of tall grass—just missing a questionable-looking pile of something buzzing with flies.

One of the cows gave a sorrowful moo.

"Quicksilver!"

Quicksilver flinched and turned sheepishly to face Anastazia. "Yes, O wise older self?"

Anastazia's cracked lips twisted into a not-quite smile. "Don't even try that face with me. I know that face. I *used* that face, and so have all of ourselves, for lifetimes and lifetimes. What did you do to poor Sly Boots?"

"I thought you didn't like Sly Boots."

"I don't, particularly."

"He just popped right up out of nowhere!" Sly Boots grabbed the fence rails and pulled himself to his feet. "How'd you do that? Did *you* tell him to do that?"

"It was only a bit of fun, Boots," said Quicksilver. "Besides, I had to make you stop picking your nose."

Sly Boots rubbed the back of his head, scowling. "You could have just asked me."

"But where's the fun in that?" said the yellow bird, perched atop a fence post.

Quicksilver thought of her friend in his true form, wanting him to be a dog once more—but nothing happened. Her mind met only a thick gray wall. "Fox, what are you doing? Change back!"

"I don't want to," Fox sniffed, turning up his yellow beak. "I quite like being a bird."

Quicksilver crossed her arms over her chest. "Anastazia, Fox won't do as I say!"

Anastazia looked up at the sky and closed her eyes. "May the stars send me patience. . . "

"All I can feel when I think instructions to him is this gray wall. He's keeping me away!"

Fox stuck out his pink bird tongue, fluffed up his golden feathers, and started preening.

"He's your *monster*," Anastazia explained to Quicksilver. "He can try to keep you away for a time, but ultimately he has to do as you say. Just breathe. Clear your mind of all thoughts except the one you need. Focus."

Though her cheeks were hot with temper, Quicksilver managed to slow her breathing and follow Anastazia's instructions. She pictured Fox—the dog Fox, sitting obediently before her like a well-trained pup, gazing up at her adoringly.

She cracked open one eye. There Fox sat, wholly doggish once more, looking grumpy.

"There," he muttered. "Back to normal, just as you wish. *Master.*"

Quicksilver plopped down onto the grass. "That was exhausting."

"It won't be, once you both get used to each other," said Anastazia. "Now, get up. Let's try again."

"I liked you better when I didn't know what you were thinking," grumbled Fox to Quicksilver.

"I liked *him* better when he couldn't talk," Sly Boots muttered, climbing back onto the fence. "Rotten mutt."

Quicksilver's temper flashed, and Fox obeyed her thoughts at once.

"What did you say?" Fox growled, appearing before Sly Boots as a snarling golden wolf.

Sly Boots nearly fell off the fence again. "N-nothing! Nothing, I swear!"

"No wolves." Anastazia marched over and pulled Fox away by the scruff of his neck. In her grip, his ears flattened and he tucked his tail between his legs. "The Wolf King's pack has become a bunch of bloodthirsty beasts, though they didn't ask for it. They represent death and pain for our kind. Remember that, Quicksilver."

Quicksilver mumbled an apology and told Fox to become himself again. He obeyed, albeit slowly. His reluctance made her mind feel like taffy, being slowly tugged this way and that.

Of course you know what all of this means, don't you? Fox thought to Quicksilver, as Anastazia started lecturing them about the improper use of magic.

A thrill jolted through Quicksilver's chest. She nodded to Anastazia, though she had no idea what the old woman was going on about. *That we could pull some really excellent jobs, with magic like this?*

Hmm. And that in a land full of witches, there are bound to be a lot of really excellent things worth stealing?

Quicksilver bit down hard on her tongue to keep from smiling. *And that, if you were, say, a mouse, you could squeeze into really small places?*

And that our friend Bootsie is most likely afraid of snakes? I think I'd look quite dashing as a snake, don't you?

Quicksilver's stifled laughter came out as a giant snort.

Anastazia turned, narrowing her eyes. "Were you listening to me?"

Sly Boots piped up from the fence. "You were talking about how magic must never be used to harm another person, unless that person is the Wolf King or one of his associates, or unless your life is in danger and you're forced to use magic to defend yourself—"

"Not *you*, boy. Quicksilver?"

"I . . . what Boots said?" Quicksilver shot Anastazia a hopeful smile.

Anastazia sighed. "Quicksilver, this is serious. You're a witch now. You can't act as though you've no responsibilities in the world. Your blood contains power that, when used improperly, could do a lot of damage. You must pay attention during these lessons. Otherwise you'll never be strong enough to face a unicorn, much less the Wolf King."

At the word "unicorn," the cows made alarmed noises and bumped into one another in their haste to hurry away.

But Quicksilver was already planning thieving jobs in her head, and imagining all the many ways she and Fox could trick their marks. How much magical, witchy loot they would bag, and how they would live in the mountains someday like kings, and never have to talk to anyone ever again.

We'll have to work hard, Quicksilver thought to Fox. *I'm not sure we could steal a piece of candy right now, much less riches and gold. That means you'll have to listen to me, do as I say.*

Fox's indignation was like a tiny black cloud in her mind. *As long as you actually pay attention to what you're doing,* he thought back, *we should be fine.*

Quicksilver stomped her foot and screamed in frustration. Fox stomped his paws and echoed her scream—only much sillier—and then rolled his eyes at her.

"Anastazia, he's being *incredibly* rude!" said Quicksilver, pointing at Fox. "Aren't you going to do something?"

But Anastazia only muttered, "I wasn't nearly this impossible when I was your age," and stalked away, popping candies into her mouth.

Quicksilver stared, her temper fading. The annoyed look on Anastazia's face was so familiar and so perfectly echoed how Quicksilver felt whenever *she* grew annoyed with something . . . it made her feel as though she'd stepped outside her body to float in the sky.

How bizarre it was, she thought, to look at this old, hunched woman and realize that, though her body would change over the years, her messy, grumpy soul would stay safe and unchanged inside her.

.15.

THE LITTLE HURTS

That night they slept on the ground near the cow pasture, on soft mounds of sun-warmed grass dotted with white flowers. Anastazia had fallen asleep with her bag of candies in hand. Her snores were wet and thunderous.

"Do I snore?" Quicksilver whispered to Fox, but he lay on his back beside her, his paws up in the air, twitchily asleep.

Quicksilver smiled at the sight, but a thorn of fear pricked her heart. She yearned for things between them to be as they once were—Fox and Quicksilver, Quicksilver and Fox. The best thief—and dog—in all the Star Lands.

"Things with Fox will get better," Sly Boots remarked, his voice hushed.

Quicksilver whipped her head around, ready to snap at him to leave her alone—but couldn't do it. Sly Boots lay on his back with his hands clasped behind his head, chewing on a long stalk of grass and staring up through the wind-whispering trees to the stars overhead.

He looked almost . . . tolerable.

"There's the Three Sisters," Sly Boots said, pointing to a cluster of stars. "See that bright one in the middle?"

Quicksilver blinked and looked away from him, settling her head back onto her pack. "Yes."

"That's the heart they share. And there—that's the White Bear, and that bright blue star is his eye. You follow that, and you'll go north, because that's where all the snow bears live, in the Far North." He sighed. "It's funny. I don't think I believed her, until now. Anastazia? I thought she'd spelled us into some odd witch land that only looked like home but wasn't *really* home. But seeing these stars, stars I've seen all my life . . . I don't think even witches could make stars look *that* real. And besides, if I squint really hard when I look at her, I can see you in her face."

Quicksilver harrumphed. "Her nose isn't the same. It's all swollen and crooked."

"I suppose she must have gotten hurt a lot, fighting the Wolf King."

The Wolf King. Yes, Anastazia had spent a lot of time fighting the Wolf King, or so she said, and now she wanted Quicksilver to do the same—though Quicksilver couldn't fathom how, or even *why*, she would do such a thing. So far the only witch Quicksilver cared about was herself—her*selves*—and she didn't see why they had to bother helping anyone else.

As long as she and Anastazia stayed away from the Wolf King, what did it matter what happened to the other witches? If they were stupid enough to get themselves hunted, then why did it fall to Quicksilver to help them?

No one had ever helped *her*.

She glared up at the sky. She hadn't thought of her parents once since arriving here, in this new time, but now that things were calm enough to think, her thoughts wandered to them. As she so often had when she was younger, she tried to remember their faces— perhaps her mother had gray hair too. Perhaps her father had a squashed nose. A crooked smile. A dimple or two.

She turned over on the hard ground, trying to shrink the

ache in her heart through sheer force of will. Out of everything she could do, she was best at that, maybe even better than she was at stealing—bearing down on the little hurts inside her to keep them from getting bigger and swallowing her whole.

"Are you nervous?" Sly Boots asked. His voice was soft, but it still startled Quicksilver.

"No," she said. She paused. "Nervous about what?"

"About fighting the Wolf King."

"Oh, him?" Quicksilver let out a breezy laugh. "To be honest, I haven't thought much about him."

"*I'd* be nervous."

"Well, that's you, isn't it? I'm not afraid of anything. You can't be afraid of anything, if you want to be a good thief."

"You're lucky," Sly Boots said with a sigh. "I'm afraid of everything. Always have been."

Quicksilver turned over to look at him. In the moonslight, Sly Boots seemed rather unlike himself—more freckled, but not so sad and hopeless, and with a serious, grown-up sort of look in his eyes that made Quicksilver feel as though she had never seen him before. She wished he would spit out that stupid piece of grass. Her head buzzed from working with Fox all afternoon, and the grass was distracting her. Every sound seemed magnified; her limbs ached.

"Sly Boots?"

"Hmm?"

"I'm sorry about your parents. You must feel awful." As soon as she spoke, Quicksilver flushed. Who was she to be sorry? *She* hadn't hurt his parents. *She* didn't have parents at all. She pounded the ground with her fist. "You know. For not being able to help them, and not being able to steal anything for them, and for mucking up that job in the first place."

"I do feel awful," said Sly Boots. "But thank you for being sorry. I don't usually have anyone to say they're sorry for me."

"Me, neither. I like being alone, though. When you're alone, people can't hurt you." Quicksilver dug her fingers into the dirt. She really needed to go to sleep and stop saying such things. Her pounding head was turning her into a babbling fool.

"I suppose that's true."

"I really will get you back to them, as soon as I know how."

"I know you will."

"It shouldn't take us long. Fox and I are already pretty good at this magic stuff."

Sly Boots smiled. "I noticed. So did the back of my head."

"Well, if you hadn't been picking your nose . . . and you know, Fox gave me the idea, at least part of it—"

"Really, it's fine."

Quicksilver fell silent. It seemed wise to do so. She couldn't seem to stop tripping over her own tongue. She stared up at the stars, her mouth in a hard line, until sleep had nearly taken her. Then an idea came to her. She shook Sly Boots's arm.

"I'm awake, you know," he said.

"I have an idea. Witches are alive in this time, right?"

"Yes . . ."

"So I reckon there are lots of witchy medicines and healing what-do-you-call-its all around the Star Lands. I'll find out which ones we need—I'll say, 'Oh, Anastazia, please teach me about witchy what-do-you-call-its,' and she'll say, 'Oh, of course, my brilliant and talented student,' and she'll tell me everything because she'll want to show off—and then Fox and I'll steal whatever we can find, and when we send you back to your parents, you'll absolutely be able to make them better!" Quicksilver grinned at him. "You get your medicine, and I get to steal things. It's the perfect plan."

Sly Boots stared at her. "You'd do that for me?"

"No, I'd do it for *me*, because stealing is fun. But it'd work out nicely for you too. Conveniently."

Sly Boots continued staring.

Quicksilver shoved him. "What? Stop it."

Before Quicksilver could stop him, Sly Boots drew Quicksilver into a tight hug and then let her go at once. "Good night, Quicksilver," he said, with a shy smile. "You're a good friend."

"I'm not your friend."

"Well, all right. I suppose we haven't known each other that long. But you will be. *We* will be, I think."

Then Sly Boots rolled over, and Quicksilver was left fuming until she fell hard into a dreamless sleep.

.16.

A COOPERATIVE WITCHLING

For the next day, and the day after that, Quicksilver and Fox spent their time learning how to be witch and monster, while Anastazia lounged on a rock in the sun, sometimes giving instructions and sometimes falling asleep in the middle of lunch.

"Again," barked Anastazia, after Quicksilver and Fox's fourth failed attempt at producing a successful glamour—a magical disguise that changed her face to look like someone else.

"But I'm tired," whined Fox, collapsing dramatically in the middle of the clearing that had become their home. The thick stretch of oak trees that hid them from the road rustled lazily in the warm breeze. "Can't we work on this later? Perhaps we could be on our way to find the bones and practice as we go?"

Quicksilver shot him a look. *I don't* want *to go yet!*

Ah, but I *do,* Fox replied. *Magic practiced in a safe, quiet clearing doesn't really count. We need to test ourselves!* He paused, cocking his head to look at her. *Are you frightened of leaving?*

All right, now you're just being mean. Of course I'm not frightened. I just like it here, that's all. But Quicksilver avoided Fox's keen gaze, hoping he couldn't sense the truth—that she was, in fact, the tiniest bit frightened of this unfamiliar, long-ago world.

And that she worried that hunting for bones would rather get in the way of thieving.

"Oh, yes, Fox, what a *grand* idea," said Anastazia, with an enormous roll of her eyes. "And what if we were to encounter the Wolf King on the road, with Quicksilver still getting worn out after only five minutes of work, and you only able to dependably shift into birdies and kitties and itty-bitty mouses?"

"Isn't it *mice*?" Quicksilver pointed out.

"I'll say it how I like, and so will you, once you're an old woman."

"So," said Quicksilver, putting her hands on her hips, "just because you're old, you can say whatever you like, even if it's wrong?"

"That's about the crux of it, yes."

"Well, that's the stupidest thing I've ever heard! I could never get away with saying wrong things, even when I was small!"

Anastazia sneered. "The sky is purple, unicorns are evil, and life isn't fair. These are the facts of it, my dear."

"Don't call me 'my dear,'" Quicksilver snapped. "I'm *you*. It's *strange*."

I'd consider backing off, master, Fox thought calmly to her. *She looks ready to burst.*

"She looks *ready* to collapse into a blob of wrinkles!" Quicksilver cried, so flustered that she forgot to keep her thoughts between herself and Fox.

Anastazia shot to her feet. "Look good and hard, girl, for this is your future. Now, *try again*, or so help me, I'll—"

But then Anastazia stopped. For of course she couldn't do anything at all these days, except for perhaps irritate someone to death. She no longer had a Fox, and therefore whatever magic remained in her blood lay cold and dormant.

Anastazia returned to her rock, arranging her cloak about her and avoiding Quicksilver's gaze. She looked out at the meadow full of grazing cows and said quietly, "If you'll try once more, please."

Quicksilver wished she wasn't so angry and could comfort Anastazia without losing something of her pride. To be without a Fox was not a fate she would wish on any version of herself, no matter how old and wrinkled and mean.

"Quicksilver!" cried Sly Boots, hurrying into the clearing, his arms full of goods from town. "Anastazia! Wonderful news—I've found help! A whole group of witches, traveling together. They were in town at the market, and I noticed them because of their monsters and hair, of course, and I told them about you, and how you're going to fight the Wolf King. They said they'd help us, so now we can do everything faster and go home sooner—"

Anastazia jumped up from the rock and slapped Sly Boots.

He dropped his parcels and held his cheek. "Are you mad?"

"Are *you* mad, boy? I don't want other witches here! We work alone. We can't trust anyone else! Our mission is dangerous, and the Wolf King has many spies. Anyone we meet might be listening with his ears, seeing with his eyes—"

Voices came from the nearby trees. "Hello?" someone called out. "Don't be afraid. We're friends, and we only want to speak with you."

Quicksilver saw the fear and anger on Anastazia's face and chose to do something about it. Urgency gave her mind a new focus. She sent an image to Fox: the four of them disappearing into a shell that, to others, would look exactly like the surrounding world.

Good idea, Fox thought, and in a flash of soft golden light, he dissolved and circled round them all like a curtain—except the curtain was invisible, and soon so were they.

"Move closer together," Fox murmured, from somewhere behind Quicksilver's left ear.

"What just happened?" Sly Boots whispered.

Quicksilver felt the touch of a rough hand on her own. "Excellent cloaking spell," came Anastazia's low voice. "Well done."

Quicksilver said nothing, though warmth blossomed inside her.

A group of people entered the clearing, led by a young man perhaps three years older than Sly Boots. His hair was white as the glowing far moon, as was the owl monster on his shoulder.

"Hello?" the young man called. "Is anyone there?"

When silence greeted him, the young man raised his hands. "I promise, we're not your enemies."

Anastazia snorted quietly. "But they would be, given the opportunity. I've seen it dozens of times. I've *done* it dozens of times. Witches can't be trusted."

"Does that mean I shouldn't trust you?" whispered Quicksilver.

"Only fools lie to themselves."

"Hush, both of you," Fox whispered.

"We too flee the Wolf King," said the young man. "We make for the western mountains."

"Hah!" Anastazia let out a single harsh laugh.

The young man's head whipped toward the sound. "Do you know, I think that might be the best cloaking spell I've ever seen? It's too bad you forgot to cloak your *sounds* as well. I might've given up and left in a moment."

Fox groaned. *Sorry, master. I tried my best.*

It's all right, Fox. We'll get better.

"I'm sorry, I couldn't help laughing," said Anastazia. "That anyone could *flee* the Wolf King, or be safe in the western mountains . . . it's too senseless an idea to be tolerated."

Quicksilver sighed irritably. "Show us, Fox."

Fox shimmered into existence at their feet. "All things considered, I was actually quite enjoying that," he said. "It felt like swimming."

"It felt like being *strangled*," Sly Boots hissed, patting himself as if to make sure nothing was missing.

The young man approached them with a smile. "Hello, sisters. My name is Olli—"

"Oh, save your *sisters* bit for the idiot you find next," Anastazia snarled. "We won't fall for it."

"Fall for what, exactly?"

Quicksilver stepped forward. "Who are you?" she demanded. "Speak clearly, or leave us be."

"Ah! A cooperative witchling! My name is Olli, and this is my coven." He gestured to include the witches standing behind him. Their monsters gleamed like jewels on their hats, on their shoulders, peeking out of their pockets.

"*Coven?*" Anastazia spat, but Quicksilver spoke over her.

"What's a coven?"

"Dear child, a coven is a group of witches who live and fight together," said Olli. "Surely you've heard the term?"

"Oh, yes, I've heard the term," Anastazia said. "I've heard of witches in covens turning on one another, falling prey to suspicion and jealousy, launching themselves and others into chaos, leaving many dead and wounded behind—including witches." Anastazia drew herself up, her lip curling. "Don't you understand what's happening, boy? What's beginning? The Wolf King won't stop until he kills us all, and we're doomed if we try to fight together.

Witches who try to live together only ever end up destroying themselves. It's our way. So make your covens, yes, go on and try it—and soon you'll have done the Wolf King's job for him."

Some of the witches in Olli's coven shifted restlessly, glancing at one another. Some moved away from the group to stand glowering in the shadows, their monsters pacing at their feet.

"But that's exactly why we have to try this grand experiment!" Olli put his hands on his hips. "If we stand and fight together, we will not be so easy to hunt."

"When a wolf pack hunts," Anastazia countered, "they corner a herd until it panics. Then they pick off the weakest. And these wolves will do this again, and again, and again, until we've been wiped clean from the world, because they never tire." She added, low, "I've seen it hundreds of times."

Olli's eyebrows shot up. "*Hundreds* of times?"

Quicksilver's heart jumped in fear. What would Olli do, if he figured out their secret?

Anastazia froze, and then recovered.

"Perhaps I was a little dramatic," she said smoothly, "but you understand my meaning. The only way to survive is to hide, and hide alone. If you want to fight him, go ahead. Just don't drag anyone else down with you."

"And is that the kind of life you would want for us?" Olli asked. "A lonely life in the shadows?" He turned to Quicksilver, his shock of white hair catching the sunlight. "What do you think, girl?"

Quicksilver bristled. "My name's Quicksilver. Don't call me 'girl.'"

"My apologies, Quicksilver. I meant no offense. What do you think of our little coven? Will you travel with us, even if only for a time? To try it out? We're stronger together. I truly believe that. And . . ." He glanced at Fox. "You've just started practicing, haven't you? He seems only days old."

The hair on Fox's neck stood up. "I'm six years old, thank you very much. That's *forty-two* in dog years."

"I only meant your monstrous age."

Fox sniffed and said nothing.

"Wouldn't it be nice to learn from not just one witch, but many?" Olli asked. "And from witches who still have their monsters with them?"

The clearing filled with silence, and Anastazia seemed to shrink where she stood. Fox trotted over to her, pressed himself against her leg, and licked her sleeve. Her gnarled hand shook as she petted his ears.

She misses him, Quicksilver and Fox thought to each other at the same time.

"I apologize, sister," Olli said quietly. "I don't mean to make light of your grief. The loss of a monster is a terrible thing."

"You know nothing about my grief," said Anastazia in a deadly voice. "So speak nothing of it."

Olli nodded, stood with his head bowed for a moment, and then said, "So, Quicksilver? What do you think?"

I think, Quicksilver thought to Fox, *that these witches' pockets look awfully full.*

I was thinking very much the same thing, answered Fox in a smug tone. *Must be quite taxing for them, to travel with those heavy packs.*

Perhaps we should relieve them of their burdens?

Master, I would be only too delighted to grant them such a courtesy.

Quicksilver swallowed her smile. "If we do travel with you—when we decide to leave, you'll allow us to do so with no trouble?"

Olli put his hand over his heart. "That's a promise, Quicksilver."

The sight of Olli smiling at her left Quicksilver feeling rather undone. She blushed and looked away.

Anastazia shoved her way between them.

"One moment, please," she said through gritted teeth. "I need to speak with my *student*."

Anastazia guided Quicksilver toward the fence at the meadow's edge. Then she bent down to meet Quicksilver's eyes, her joints popping. "What do you think you're doing?" she whispered. "You've never known witches as I have, we can't trust—"

"What we can't do," said Quicksilver, talking over her, "is practice in this field forever." *Even if we want to,* she added silently. *Even if we're afraid.*

Fox sent her a wave of encouragement through their heart link. *We've markets to rob and coin to steal, eh, master?*

Indeed we do, Fox. Quicksilver stood tall, forcing Anastazia to take a step back.

"You don't understand—" Anastazia began, shaking her head.

"I understand perfectly," said Quicksilver. "I'm the one with the magic now, so you can either come with us, or you can stay here."

Then, before Anastazia had the chance to reply, Quicksilver marched back over to where Olli stood waiting and held out her hand once more.

He grinned and lightly slapped her palm. "Welcome to the coven, Quicksilver."

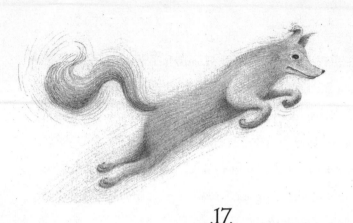

.17.

A THOUSAND BATTLES

For the next two days, Olli and his coven led Quicksilver, Fox, Anastazia, and Sly Boots through the meadows and woods west of Willow-on-the-River, staying clear of the road.

They were a large group—Olli's coven consisted of fifteen witches and their monsters—and they moved slowly, but no one seemed to mind the frequent stops to rest, talk, and eat. The sun was high but gentle, the wind soft; the cows grazing in field after field were placid and calm. The warm weather lulled everyone into a sense of peaceful contentment—everyone but Anastazia.

She refused to speak to any of them, instead choosing to

read a leather-bound journal she pulled from a large pocket inside her cloak and to communicate only through nasty faces or rude gestures.

At first Quicksilver enjoyed the respite from Anastazia's constant harping about magic, and how Quicksilver wasn't doing it right. She and Fox worked without the old witch, practicing glamours, cloaking, and shifting under the guidance of Olli and his friends Lukaas and Freja.

"Now, try it again, but this time, try to look like Freja," instructed Olli on their second afternoon of traveling together. They had stopped for the night, to pitch their patched tents and start cooking fires. The smell of smoking sausages filled the air. Olli took a bite of a crisp red apple. "And remember— concentrate on the details. The slightest inaccuracy can ruin the whole illusion."

Quicksilver closed her eyes and pictured Freja—a witch around twenty years of age who sported a purple birthstone on her neck and wore her vivid fire-orange hair short and spiky. She had fifty-three freckles on her cheeks, and her left eye was slightly smaller than her right one.

Change me, Quicksilver thought, keeping the image of Freja firmly in her mind and pushing the image toward Fox. Instantly she felt Fox receive the image, acknowledge it, and obey. He shifted into a shimmering gray swirl of fog, wrapped himself around her, and settled over her like a cool invisible cloak. And all of this happened in the time it took Olli to finish his apple and toss the core into the field for the cows.

Quicksilver grinned, her body tingling with happiness. Fox was beginning to understand what she wanted before she had even finished forming an image herself. They were getting better, and faster. Why, they'd be seamlessly thieving together in no time at all!

When Quicksilver opened her eyes, she looked down at her arms and saw Freja's arms instead, freckled and strong.

Olli applauded. Lukaas, his dark face framed with bouncing bright green curls, gave a sharp whistle and waved his faded patchwork cap like a flag. Freja admitted grudgingly, "Not bad."

"Not bad? It's a job well done, *very* well done!" Olli chuffed Quicksilver on the shoulder. "You're a natural at glamours, Quix."

Quicksilver grinned.

Fox made a gagging sound in her head. *Tell him to stop calling you that or I'll mutiny.*

But Quicksilver would do nothing of the sort. So what if Olli had given her a nickname? It was only practical. Her full name was something of a mouthful. And she *liked* having a nickname. It meant that she was important to Olli and his coven, and well liked.

Which meant they would never guess that she would rob them and abandon them, and the whole job would go off easy as stormberry pie.

Fox reappeared, panting. He rolled over and showed the world his belly. "Please, oh please, can we be finished now? I'm absolutely starving and can't possibly go on until I've had a sausage or twelve."

"Oh, you can do one more, can't you, Fox?" said Quicksilver, scratching his tummy. "I'd like to try making an Olli glamour next."

"But could you ever hope to truly capture my magnificent physique?" Olli posed in the sunlight, flexing his muscles. Lukaas threw an apple at him.

Quicksilver looked away, her cheeks burning, although she didn't understand why. Olli's smooth brown skin and bright smile were no concern of hers. He was a mark, not a friend.

But a pleasing-to-look-at mark, Fox thought mischievously. *Eh, master?*

FOXHEART

Shut it, Fox!

"Quicksilver!" called Anastazia, her voice crackling with impatience. "Come here at once."

Anastazia sat beneath a cluster of towering trees some distance away, thumbing through her journal. When Quicksilver stalked over to her, Anastazia didn't even look up.

"Have you finished playing games with your little friends?" Anastazia asked.

"We weren't playing games," said Quicksilver. "We were practicing magic. They're helping me, which is more than I can say about *some* people."

Sly Boots lay on the ground beside Anastazia, sniffing the air longingly. "I've been reading to you for hours, Anastazia. Can I go get lunch now, *please?*"

"Go get lunch for all eternity, if you wish," Anastazia snapped. "I've had enough of your whining."

Sly Boots sprang to his feet. "And I've had enough of your *everything*," he grumbled, storming off to the cooking fire.

Quicksilver smirked as she watched him leave. "What do you want, then?" she asked Anastazia.

"Your help." Anastazia patted the ground beside her. "Sit and look at this with me."

Reluctantly, Quicksilver joined Anastazia in the grass and looked at the map she'd unfolded from her journal. It was a map of the Star Lands, so covered with scribbled notes that Quicksilver could barely see the original lines marking the borders of the seven kingdoms.

"We'll have to head north soon," muttered Anastazia. "I can't believe I've let us linger for so long with these people. Must be losing hold of my senses at last." She pointed at a black star in the kingdom of Menettsk. "That's where I found the first skeleton when I was young—in the Burren Bogs of Menettsk. It's as good a place as any to start."

Quicksilver crossed her arms over her chest. "I'm not doing that."

Anastazia glared at Quicksilver, her eyes burning. "Have you forgotten why I brought you here, child? Oh, forgive me—*Quix?*"

Fox trotted over, his mouth full of food. "If there has ever been a more repulsive nickname, I can't imagine it," he snorted.

Fox, you're not helping.

Pardon me, O master Quix.

"You brought me here to fight the Wolf King," Quicksilver recited, "and to find the skeletons of the First Monsters, so that we can destroy them, because if the Wolf King finds them first, the First Ones will come back to life and kill everyone. And if we don't find the skeletons, we'll never be able to defeat the Wolf King, because the First Ones are working through him, and they're too powerful. But if we destroy them, then we can destroy the Wolf King, and everyone will be saved, and the witches will not be hunted away into memory and nothingness." Quicksilver glared back at Anastazia. "Have I got that all right?"

Anastazia chewed expressionlessly on her candy—a fresh bag of her beloved mint-and-chocolate stars that Olli had given her as a peace offering, to no avail. "You're remarkably flippant," she said, "considering how serious the situation is."

"And you're remarkably . . . annoying!" Quicksilver barely resisted the urge to knock the journal out of Anastazia's hands. "I don't know why you think I want to take part in any of this. Just because *you* did when you were my age doesn't mean *I* want to. I'm different from you. We may be the same person, but we're not the *same* person."

Anastazia lifted an eyebrow. "I've noticed as much."

Sly Boots stomped back and threw himself onto the ground with a half-eaten sausage in his hand. "Those monsters make my skin crawl. Animals aren't supposed to look so smart."

"I'd take offense at that remark," mumbled Fox, "if I weren't enjoying my lunch so terribly much."

"I think they're wonderful," said Quicksilver. "They're funny, and they like me."

"Are you talking about the monsters, or your precious *Olli*?" muttered Sly Boots.

Quicksilver bristled. "I mean *all* of them. They're certainly more pleasant to talk to than either of you."

"The Wolf King is pleasant too, if you catch him on a good day," grumbled Anastazia. "But if you're not careful, before you know it he's talked you into a trance and slit your throat, and you're left wondering what happened as you lie dying in the dirt."

"Such a cheerful person you are," said Sly Boots. "I can see where Quixxy here gets her temper."

"Listen, *Boots*—" Quicksilver rolled up her sleeves.

Then Anastazia began coughing—a terrible dry, hacking cough that made Quicksilver's throat hurt just to hear it.

Quicksilver and Sly Boots watched in horrified silence as Anastazia's body spasmed. Black flecks flew out of her mouth, dotting her lips in slimy clumps.

"What do we do?" Sly Boots whispered, his face pale.

Quicksilver did not know how to answer him. She sat frozen

in shock until Anastazia's breathing turned steady again.

"Anastazia?" Fox asked, his whiskers full of crumbs. He curled up beside her, put his snout in her lap. "What is it?"

"Everything all right over there?" called Olli from the cooking fire.

"Splendid," Sly Boots answered. "Just leave us be for once in your life."

"As if we've been traveling with them for our entire lives," spat Quicksilver.

"Well, that's certainly what it feels like!"

"We don't . . . have much time," said Anastazia, her breath rattling like teeth in a cup. "I won't . . . be here forever."

Quicksilver shifted uncomfortably. "What do you mean?"

"It's what happens when . . . you spend your life . . . fighting a mad king." Anastazia closed her eyes. "This old body's full of holes and curses like you wouldn't believe. Should've died long ago, but he won't beat me that easily."

Quicksilver settled quietly beside her. "The Wolf King?"

Anastazia nodded and handed Quicksilver her journal. "Boots has been reading to me, helping me remember. Now it's your turn. Someday this will be yours, after all."

"What is it, exactly?" Quicksilver turned page after page. The paper was old and stained, filled with maps, charts, drawings, and notes—all written in variations of the same scribbled handwriting. Sly Boots read over her shoulder.

"It's us, isn't it?" asked Quicksilver. "It's all the yous and mes. We kept notes."

"Yes," whispered Anastazia, absently stroking Fox's head. He remained perfectly still, his eyes closed in happiness. "Everything we've discovered, in all our lives—all the important clues and locations. All our battles. All the spells we've designed to extend our lives past their natural boundaries. It's all there."

"Not much of it makes sense," Sly Boots observed, crumbs flying onto Quicksilver's arm. "At least not to me. At one point I got lost and just started reading nonsense to her—blah-blee-bloo, hoo-diddy-day—and she nodded as though I was quoting poetry."

"Some of it's a bit . . ." Anastazia murmured, and then fell silent.

Fox lifted his head, and Quicksilver's heart went cold with fear.

"Anastazia?" Quicksilver shook her older self. "Anastazia, wake up!"

Anastazia's eyes fluttered open. "Sorry, sorry. I'm just a bit tired, that's all."

Quicksilver shared a glance with Sly Boots, who looked as uneasy as she felt.

"As I was saying, some of these notes are rather patchy," said Anastazia. "Sometimes I wrote in code when I was in the more dangerous parts of the Star Lands. Sometimes . . . well, the longer you live, the more your mind fades. Not even magic can prevent that. But I'll help you through it. As much as I can remember, anyway."

Quicksilver frowned. She held the journal right side up, and then upside down. "What are these? I can't make them out."

"The skeletons," said Anastazia, glancing blearily at the journal. "A starling, and a snowy hare. A hawk, a cat, a mouse. An owl. An ermine."

"Those were the First Monsters?" Quicksilver peered at the scratchy illustrations.

"Those are the skeletons we *must find*." Anastazia placed her hand on Quicksilver's, her palm cracked and callused. "Quicksilver. I know this is difficult. I've tried to give you time to adjust. But I must insist that we be on our way, and soon. These skeletons will not be easy to find." Anastazia squeezed Quicksilver's hand, letting out a shuddering breath. Her shoulders slumped. "To have to start over," she whispered, "when I spent so many years collecting them . . ."

"We'll find them," Quicksilver said briskly, snapping the journal shut.

Will we? Fox's surprise swept through Quicksilver. *I thought we were going to forget about all that Wolf King nonsense, and rob the Star Lands blind.*

Well, she doesn't have to know that, Quicksilver replied. *Not yet. We'll keep her happy for now.*

"Shouldn't be a problem for us, should it, Fox?" Quicksilver went on, looking pointedly at Fox. "Remember breaking into Sister Veronika's office to steal the love letters from her secret beau?"

Fox shuddered. "Please don't remind me of those. I wanted to scrape my brain clean with a knife."

"You actually *read* them?"

"I said, don't remind me!"

"Quicksilver, this isn't like our games at the convent." Anastazia's eyes drifted shut. The harsh sunlight made her look as creaky and brittle as the ancient trees around them. "This is real, and we can't . . . let him win. We can't let him hunt us all until there's nothing . . . left. No one else will stop him. But we can. We *have.* A thousand battles, all part of one long war, and we could be the ones . . . to finish it."

Anastazia began to snore, her head nodding to the side. With Sly Boots's help, Quicksilver settled her in the soft grass, balled up her cloak, and tucked it beneath her head like a pillow.

"Tomorrow?" Anastazia murmured sleepily, cracking open one eye.

"We'll leave tomorrow," Quicksilver reassured her, tucking the journal back into her cloak.

Once Anastazia was asleep, Quicksilver and Sly Boots sat in a silence that seemed ill fitting with the cheery summer day.

"What will you tell them?" Sly Boots said at last, gesturing to Olli and the others, who were playing games around the fire. Some of the witches sat apart, sullen and sharp faced, watching Olli and his friends suspiciously. But Olli did not seem deterred; he grabbed the hands of an older, stone-faced witch named Bernt and swung the man around for a dance. Bernt's bright fuchsia-colored badger monster growled in warning, fluffing up its fur, and Bernt himself glowered down at Olli like he was ready to give him a hard thump on the head, but Olli merrily ignored both of them.

The fool, Quicksilver thought. *Can't he see they don't like him? Witches aren't meant to live in covens. It's unnatural. You can't trust anyone.*

You sound just like her, Fox said, picking twigs from Anastazia's mess of red and silver hair. With barely a thought, Quicksilver shifted Fox into a small, speckle-breasted wren, so he might have an easier time of it. He flitted happily around Anastazia's head.

Well, and so what if I do? Quicksilver settled back and sat frowning at the world. *I am* her. Suddenly the past two peaceful days with the coven seemed small and silly in comparison to everything Anastazia had endured. *She's fought the Wolf King her whole life. What have* they *ever done but play stupid games and make fools out of themselves?*

As if to illustrate her point, Olli cartwheeled out into the grass and stood on his head. Bernt stalked back to rejoin the sour-faced witches clustered in the shade of the trees, none of whom looked impressed.

"Hello?" Sly Boots waved his hand in front of Quicksilver's face. "Did you hear what I said? What will you tell them?"

"Nothing," Quicksilver said. "Our business is none of theirs."

We'll steal everything we can, Quicksilver thought to Fox, *and then we'll leave, tonight.*

.18.

LIKE A PIECE OF NIGHT

That evening, Quicksilver pretended to sleep while Olli and his coven set up camp at the base of a wooded ridge. Tomorrow they would arrive in Farrowtown, a village on the border between the kingdoms of Lalunet and Belrike. There Olli hoped to convince more witches to join the coven.

"And how will you do that?" Quicksilver had asked, after a grueling practice of cloaking Fox, and then shifting him into ever smaller animals—a cat, a black rat, a moth—so that he might creep into tight spaces unseen. The difficult maneuvers left them both cranky and with nasty headaches.

Olli had shrugged. "I'll tell them the truth—that it's safer to travel in a group. That being suspicious of other witches is a tired tradition that will end up being our ruin. And," he had concluded with a grin, "that we throw marvelously fun dinner parties. As you now know. Here," he had said, tossing her an apple. "Eat something. It'll help the headache."

Quicksilver had taken a huge bite of the apple, and then given a piece to Fox, who made a sound like a purr. Then he became a cat and griped at Quicksilver for shifting him.

It had been a long day.

Now, they were all asleep. Quicksilver waited until she heard everyone's breathing level off and steady snores begin.

It's time, she told Fox.

"It's time," she whispered to Sly Boots.

While Sly Boots gently awoke Anastazia, Quicksilver crept past the sleeping coven and their monsters, her body and her footsteps both cloaked by Fox. She nudged purses loose from packs and coppers loose from pockets. At times it felt as though she were guiding Fox; at other times, it felt as if he was leading her down a path only he could see. He pushed, she pulled, and then the opposite.

Soon, the pouches in Quicksilver's pack were full. She

hurried back to Sly Boots, her hands full of coins, and filled his pockets. Then they fled the camp.

"You were so fast!" Sly Boots whispered gleefully, helping Anastazia through the dark cow field. "How much did you get? My pockets feel like they're full of bricks! Oh, think of the medicine this will buy!"

"I didn't stop to count." Quicksilver adjusted the now-heavy pack on her back. "Stop talking!"

Anastazia glanced sidelong at Quicksilver, her expression decidedly stern.

"What?" Quicksilver whispered. "You didn't like them. What does it matter if I steal from them? This will help us as we search for the you-know-whats! We can pay people to give us information! We can buy food!"

"I only wish you'd told me the plan," said Anastazia. "I woke up and had no clue what was going on."

"Well, that's what happens when you sleep for twelve hours and belch at us when we try to wake you." Quicksilver paused. "Fox?"

Fox, in his dog form, had stopped and turned back to face camp, his ears pricked and his tail standing out straight.

"Something's wrong," he said quietly.

"What do you mean? Are they following us?"

"No—"

I hear something happening, he thought to Quicksilver, *but I don't understand what it is.*

"Wait here," said Quicksilver.

"Why aren't we leaving?" Sly Boots whispered after her. "What's going on?"

"Quicksilver!" hissed Anastazia.

Quicksilver and Fox slipped back through the tall grass, keeping low to the ground. Sounds floated to them through the woods—screams, and a low, rumbling roar. When they reached the ridge that overlooked the camp and peeked through the undergrowth, Quicksilver could hardly believe what she was seeing.

A great hulking figure as tall as a three-story house lumbered through the camp, scooping up the witches—and their monsters—as though they were nothing but toys. The creature was dark, like a piece of night cut away from the sky. Its arms were as thick as boulders, its legs twice as large as that. On its tiny pin of a head glowed two round white eyes.

Caught unawares and still half asleep, the coven did not stand a chance. Two witches ran away into the darkness with their monsters, as fast as they could, not even bothering to help the others fight. Quicksilver watched in awe as Olli sent his owl monster soaring at the creature like an arrow from a bow. The owl became a bolt of lightning, vital and sizzling. When it hit the boulder creature, the creature stumbled and roared in pain—but the owl flew crookedly back to Olli's shoulder with a hurt wing. The creature couldn't repel magic, then. But it would certainly take more magic than that to fell it.

With a high peal of laughter, the creature scooped up Olli and his monster, crammed them into a tremendous sack with the rest of the coven, flung the sack over its shoulder, and lumbered off into the woods.

.19.

THE ROMPUS

Quicksilver and Fox dashed back through the field, found Anastazia and Sly Boots exactly where they had left them, and proceeded to shout over each other about what they had seen.

Anastazia listened calmly and then said, "Well, good riddance, if you ask me. Shall we continue on?"

"But do you know what that *thing* was?" Quicksilver insisted.

"Could have been any number of *things*, but based on the information you've given me, I can't very well say. Now, shall we—"

"But we have to go find them!" Quicksilver interrupted.

Anastazia's eyebrows flew up. "Oh, yes? And why do we *have* to do that?"

"We were going to leave them anyway," Sly Boots pointed out. "And, ah, to be honest, I don't much fancy the idea of chasing after some giant, bloodthirsty creature."

"I wanted to leave them, yes," said Quicksilver, "but I didn't want them to *die*. There's a difference."

"We left my parents," said Sly Boots sullenly. "You didn't seem to have a problem with that."

"Boots, we're getting back to your parents as soon as we can," said Quicksilver impatiently. "But not until we do this first, and by the way, it's not like either of you can stop me. I defeated you with a spatula," she said, pointing to Sly Boots. "And you're a witch without a monster," she added, pointing to Anastazia. "So if I wanted to, I could bind you both up with Fox rope and float you in front of me all the way to wherever we're going, and you couldn't do a thing about it."

Sly Boots looked ill. "Please don't do that. I don't want to be squeezed up tight against *her*."

Anastazia studied Quicksilver with an unreadable expression. Then she said, with great dignity, "Very well. Lead the way, Quix."

"Wait just a moment." Sly Boots's eyes narrowed. "Is this about that nitbrain Olli?"

"Oh, shut it, Sly Boots!" snapped Quicksilver.

Sly Boots, quite wisely, fell silent.

The creature's tracks were easy to find and follow—at first.

Tremendous blunt-toed indentations marked a path of flattened trees and undergrowth that led them into deeper and deeper woods. But soon the tracks became smaller—narrow and clawed—and then they disappeared altogether.

"Fox?" Quicksilver whispered. "Do you smell anything?"

Fox rummaged about in the trampled grass and then pointed with his front paw.

"That way," he said, "but careful . . . I smell bones."

"Bones?" Anastazia perked up.

"*Fresh* bones, if you know what I mean."

"I smell something too," said Sly Boots, wrinkling his nose. "Something awful."

Quicksilver thought of Olli and the others, smashed into bloody bits, and felt that evening's supper turn in her stomach. But she led them on through the tangled woods until they found the source of the increasingly rancid scent—a cave, dug into a rocky hillside. A tiny brook nearby gurgled and glimmered.

The tall round mouth of the cave, easily big enough to accommodate the creature they had seen, gaped at them like someone caught in the middle of a yawn.

"Well, that settles that," Sly Boots said, a slight hysterical edge to his voice. "I'm not going in there. You'll have to bind me up with Fox or knock me over the head, or . . . or—Quicksilver, please don't make me go in there!"

Anastazia sat on a large rock, flipping through her journal. "I'm inclined to agree with him, for once. While I myself have never seen a creature like the one you described, I've just found a note written by one of our previous selves, and if I'm reading this correctly . . ." Anastazia held the journal to her nose, squinting. "Blast it all, why couldn't she have written this even somewhat legibly? Anyhow, it's either a . . . Pompous, or a Bumpits, or a . . . rompus?"

"Rompus!" called a voice from the cave, and before any of them could react, a fat black snake slithered out to coil at Quicksilver's feet. It looked up at her expectantly, with eyes white as stars.

Sly Boots squeaked in dismay.

"Er . . . hello there," Quicksilver hedged. "Who are you?"

"Hurry, hurry, add them to the rest," muttered the snake, and as it spoke, it grew, and fattened, and its voice boomed like drums. Soon it was all hard edges and boulder-rough hide. Starry white eyes blinked on a tiny head.

"It's you," whispered Quicksilver.

"Rompus," agreed the creature, and scooped them up into its meaty hands.

When Quicksilver groggily opened her eyes some time later, she was met with the rather unexpected sight of a lace-covered table set for tea, complete with heaping plates of cakes, cookies, and tiny frosted pies.

The Rompus loomed above her, with those same glowing white eyes—but it was no longer a boulder creature, nor a snake. It was a dragon with gleaming purple scales and a set of black horns. It watched her unblinkingly, its narrow, scaly chin propped up in its claws.

When it saw that Quicksilver was awake, it clapped joyful, thunderous claps. The cave around them quaked, raining dust from a ceiling of shadow and stone. Quicksilver could only see the outside world through the cave mouth some distance away. A staggering array of portraits hung from fire pokers jammed into the walls. Each portrait displayed a person in a stiff collar and fine hat.

"I painted them meself," the Rompus announced. "Would you like one?"

Upon examining the paintings more closely, Quicksilver noticed, with great alarm, that the painted figures were . . . *skeletons*.

"All the ones I've ate," the Rompus explained, pointing. "That one was me first. That one laughed all the way down me throat. That one tasted like dung."

Fox? thought Quicksilver.

Right here, master, answered Fox, tickling her neck. *Fox the invisible mouse, at your service and not at all terrified out of his wits.*

And Sly Boots? Quicksilver's throat dried up with fear. *Anastazia?*

I'm not quite sure.

Quicksilver pretended awe at the arrangement of ghastly paintings. "These must have taken you quite a long time. I've not the skill for painting, but your talent is plain to see."

The Rompus grinned—an unnervingly toothy sight. "That's what I tell meself every day. Oh, it's been so long since I had a visitor, and I do like the look of you. You're as ugly as me." The Rompus circled the tea table. "How many sugars in your tea, Pig Face? Twenty? Thirty?"

Despite the perilous situation, Quicksilver felt her temper

rise. "I'm afraid you've gotten my name wrong, my talented friend. It's Quicksilver."

The Rompus paused, a tiny flower-patterned teakettle pinched between its massive claws. "I like Pig Face," he declared.

Quicksilver clenched her fists beneath the table, but before she could do anything rash, Fox pressed his tiny, warm mouse nose against her neck again.

"You know," she said, calmer now, "you're right. That *is* a better name. And I'll have fifty sugars, please."

The Rompus laughed, the gust of hot air blasting Quicksilver's hair back from her face. "Fifty sugars! Pig Face is a brave little thing." The Rompus filled a pink porcelain cup with a mountain of misshapen sugar lumps. "Stole these from lunch number four hundred and one. Sugar merchant. You'd think he'd taste sweet, wouldn't you, but he was more of a . . . what do you call it? A savory flavor. Rather tangy."

Slightly sickened, Quicksilver glanced up at the painting where lunch number four hundred and one smiled through a broken jaw.

"Who would have thought?" she asked faintly. "So, tell me . . . Mister . . . Rompus. Why have you brought me here?"

"For breakfast!"

Quicksilver felt sick. "You mean—"

"It'll be a good one today," the Rompus said, clacking his teeth as if already chewing away. "Nice and fresh."

Quicksilver followed the Rompus's ravenous gaze to a nest of shadows against the wall. There she saw, to her horror, Olli and his coven, and their monsters, *and* Anastazia and Sly Boots, trapped in a gently spinning net made of glowing white rope. The net hung over an enormous roaring fire. An elaborate system of lines and pulleys held the net in place, and as Quicksilver watched, the pulleys began to turn—lowering the net, inch by slow inch, closer to the fire.

.20.

On the Toasty Side of Things

Quicksilver watched the net creep toward the fire, a scream of horror lodged in her throat.

Breakfast. They were going to be *breakfast*.

She felt like she was stuck in thick, syrupy mud. She couldn't move; she could hardly *think*.

Are they . . . ? Quicksilver thought frantically to Fox.

Not yet, he answered. *I can feel their monsters. They're a bit on the toasty side of things, but they're still alive. It appears to be a rather slow-cooking fire.*

Quicksilver peered closer at the clump of spinning witches

and saw Sly Boots come into view, his face frozen in an expression of terror that perfectly matched the whimper piping from his lips.

Anastazia, squished beside him, glared at Quicksilver. The look on her face clearly said, "Do something. *Now.*" Then they spun out of view, and Quicksilver saw Olli, Lukaas, Freja, Bernt, and their monsters, all trapped and immobile. Thirteen witches and thirteen monsters.

Why can't they move? Quicksilver wondered. *They look frozen.*

Fox was quiet. Quicksilver felt him stretch her magic out into the room like a tendril, seeking and tasting.

The net's been spelled by a witch, Fox concluded, the instant before Quicksilver did. *He must have stolen it from . . . well, from one of his meals, I suppose.*

Quicksilver's stomach turned. *Can we undo it?*

The magic's keeping them bound up tight, said Fox. *But we should be able to help from the outside, if we can distract this brute for long enough, that is.*

Quicksilver thought fast, her mind racing through horrible scenario after horrible scenario. She searched the room for something—*anything*—she could use as a weapon against the

Rompus, who was happily arranging cookies on a plate.

Then she saw it—a gleam of something shiny at the mouth of a tunnel in the far wall.

"What's that?" she asked, pointing.

The Rompus turned to look. His mottled reptilian face brightened.

"That's me collection," he said. Then he jumped to his feet and began hopping around in excitement, knocking over the entire tea setting and causing the whole cave to shake. "Do you want a tour, Pig Face?"

The net holding the coven lurched closer to the fire. Hidden in Quicksilver's collar, Fox let out a squeak of alarm.

"Yes, *yes*, but you have to calm down," she said anxiously. "You don't want our breakfast to cook too fast, do you? Slow roasted, that's the proper way."

The Rompus clapped a hand over his mouth. "You're so right, you are," he said, his voice muffled.

Quicksilver gestured toward the tunnel with a tense smile. "Well then? You promised me a tour."

"Of course, yes! Let's go!"

"*Quietly.*"

"Yes," whispered the Rompus, tiptoeing across the vast portrait gallery toward the tunnel. "Like mices. Which I thought we could have for dessert. Mices crunch nicely."

Quicksilver let out a weak laugh. "I was just going to say."

Where is he taking us? Fox dug his tiny paws into her neck as the Rompus led them into the dark, winding tunnel.

No idea. But maybe we can find something back here to distract him—oh, my.

The tunnel opened into a series of rooms connected like a honeycomb, each one stuffed to the brim with what looked like every object in existence: polished tables and ornate chairs had been set and arranged as if for a feast fit for hundreds. Gems the size of Quicksilver's head sparkled atop high glass pedestals. Shelves that disappeared into the darkness overhead were crammed full of books bound in shimmering fabric, porcelain turtle figurines, jars of gold coins, dolls with immaculately brushed curls, feathered caps, jewel-encrusted goblets.

"Well?" The Rompus grinned toothily down at Quicksilver. "What do you think of me treasures?"

I think, thought Quicksilver, *that if we had five minutes to ourselves in this place, we could steal enough loot to buy a kingdom.*

She clutched her hands to her heart. "Oh, it's marvelous! Truly exceptional!"

The Rompus puffed up his chest, his nostrils spewing smoke. "Stole it all meself, every last piece."

And where's the challenge of thieving, Fox sniffed, *when you can just terrify your marks into giving you whatever you want?*

"Did you *really* steal it all?" asked Quicksilver, ignoring Fox. "How *clever* of you!"

"These are me teakettles," said the Rompus proudly, trotting along on his massive paws. "I've got two hundred and nineteen so far."

He paused at an oak table, every inch of it covered in gleaming teakettles, and leaned over to inspect one of them that was painted with fluffy yellow ducks. He opened his great jaws to puff out hot air, then buffed away a spot with the end of his tail, leaving the kettle flawless once more.

TEAKETTLES read a piece of paper nailed to the table, the handwriting large and crooked. TABLE ONE.

"Is that one your favorite?" asked Quicksilver, looking around for something she could grab—a sword, or a club. Even a kitchen knife.

"Of course!" said the Rompus, smiling fondly at the

kettle. "Nothing fluffier in this world than tiny wee ducks."

"What about tiny wee sheep? They're rather poofy all over, don't you agree?"

The Rompus frowned. "Now there's a thought."

Do you feel that? asked Fox, suddenly alert.

Feel what? But then Quicksilver felt it too: something, somewhere in these rooms, was big. Powerful.

It pressed against her spine like the feeling of someone watching from the shadows.

I'll go have a look, said Fox.

Quicksilver felt him scamper down her sleeve and away. The feeling of missing him lodged in her heart like a blade.

Hurry, Fox.

I won't leave you, he promised.

"On we go," rumbled the Rompus, ducking into the next room. "To your left, you'll see me collection of birdcages—"

The Rompus led Quicksilver through the birdcages, then the dressmakers' mannequins, then the dozens of baskets stuffed with distressed-looking puppets.

On the far wall hung a huge rack of swords, some longer than Quicksilver was tall—some just the right size for a girl like her.

Fox? she thought. *I see swords. Where are you?*

He didn't answer.

Fox? Fox!

I'm here, he said at last, his voice quivering with excitement. *Master. He's got monster skeletons. I suppose he's collected them over the years. They're making a racket—they sound like a whole mess of people talking over one another—but I can pick out individual voices if I concentrate hard enough. Weasels and chipmunks, otters and even a wolverine or two. And one of them is . . . master, I could swear that one of them is a snowy hare. It's quiet, it's trying to hide, but I'm fairly sure I'm right. Can you feel it?*

Quicksilver concentrated on Fox, thinking along the magical connection that bound them together, and felt a sharp chill creep up her arms. A snowy hare—could it be? The page from Anastazia's journal flashed before her eyes.

You mean, she said, *it's one of the . . . ?*

One of the First Monsters, yes, maybe. We have to at least look and see. And if it is . . .

Then it could disappear at any moment, like Anastazia told us. Quicksilver fought not to grin. *Think of the coin we could get for it—*

We wouldn't even need any of this other rubbish, Fox agreed.

Then he paused. *Or we could use it to fight the Wolf King.*

Yes, of course. But Quicksilver promptly dismissed the thought. All she could imagine was how good it would feel to have that skeleton in her possession—a rare find, and she would steal it right out from under this fool creature's nose.

We'll be rich, Fox, she thought dreamily, *but we'll have to move fast—*

"Pig Face! You're not listening!" The Rompus suddenly appeared in front of her, spewing smoke into her face. He held a smiling puppet in his claws. The Rompus's teeth gleamed, each fang the size of Quicksilver's foot.

Quicksilver yelped and jumped back, and in her fear she imagined the most comforting thing she could—Fox as a dog.

There was a crash from somewhere beyond them, in one of the Rompus's many rooms.

Oh, dear, said Fox. *So much for that vase.*

The Rompus whirled, dropping the puppet and knocking four chairs to the ground.

"What was that?" he squeaked, his voice startlingly high. "Pig Face? What was it? Did you see?" He hid his face and peeked out from between his gleaming claws. "Go look, won't you?"

Inspiration shot through Quicksilver. *Fox. He's afraid. He's a complete baby!*

Pardon me?

Hurry, distract him. Act like a monster while I find the skeleton.

Fox's outrage raised the hair on Quicksilver's neck. *I am a monster, thanks very much.*

No, I mean like a real *monster.*

As opposed to the fake *monster that I currently am?*

I mean like a ghost, or a demon, or something really scary!

"Rompus," whispered Quicksilver, placing a hand on his spiked tail, "is your cave by chance haunted?"

"HAUNTED?" wailed the Rompus.

"That sounded like a ghost to me." Quicksilver put a hand to her ear. "Listen." *Fox. Now!*

And how am I to know what a ghost, or a demon, or whatever is supposed to sound like?

Improvise!

Fox groaned in disgust. *Fine.* Then, after a pause, Quicksilver heard a flat, utterly indignant voice call from somewhere in the distance:

"Oooooo. Look at me. I'm a ghost."

Fox. Really? You can't be serious—

"I heard it, I did!" The Rompus ducked behind Quicksilver, and his tail coiled tightly around her. "What is it, Pig Face, can you see it?"

"Let go of me at once," she said, "or I'll leave you to fend it off on your own."

The Rompus squeaked in dismay and released her.

Again, Fox!

This is ridiculous—

Now!

A pause, and then two giant crashes sounded from the back of the room, followed by a bloodcurdling scream.

The Rompus screamed too, and dropped to the floor. "What was that?"

I'm impressed, Fox, thought Quicksilver.

Fox grumbled something under his breath and then darted to another part of the room before letting out an otherworldly howl. Quicksilver closed her eyes and focused on following Fox with her mind. The bond that connected their hearts led her rushing through the caves right along with him— knocking over vases and dinner plates, crashing through an assortment of ladles hanging from the ceiling. She felt his irritation every time he howled or screamed; he dove into a barrel and knocked it over, and the metallic scent of spilled coins filled her nose.

Quicksilver grabbed a teakettle shaped like a fat speckled owl. "Rompus, this ghost sounds like quite a nasty one. We'll have to fight."

He peered up at her, his scaly lips trembling. "Fight?"

"Grab a weapon. You go that way, I'll go this way. We won't let that ghost ruin your collection!"

The Rompus grabbed a dressmaker's mannequin wearing a floaty pink dress and gazed at Quicksilver with watery eyes. "You'd help me fight?"

She forced a smile. "What are friends for? Now run!"

Fox, still invisible, ran across a row of pianos shoved against a wall. The discordant notes plinked out an eerie song, and the Rompus tore off after the noise.

"This way, Pig Face!" he bellowed.

Quicksilver ran in the other direction. *Fox, can you tell where the bones are?*

A little busy at the moment, Fox panted. *This fellow's faster than he looks.*

Just stay invisible and you'll be fine.

But even as Quicksilver said that, she felt the Rompus's paw swipe right by Fox, barely missing him and smashing into one of the pianos instead.

"My song maker!" wailed the Rompus.

Behind you, Fox gasped, *and hurry.*

Quicksilver felt it now too—a gigantic mess of old monster bones. They crackled in the distance like a warm fire in a cold house.

She dashed through another room, and then another.

To your left—can you feel them? They're down that hallway.

I think so. Are you all right?

A roar and a crash sounded—followed by an eerie wail from Fox and a shriek of terror from the Rompus.

Oh, just lovely, answered Fox. *He's whacking at everything he can find with that stupid mannequin. As if that could hurt a ghost.*

I'll hurry!

No need. I could do this for years—wait, stop! There they are!

Quicksilver froze at the entrance to the largest room yet.

Where? Which way?

Right in front of you. It's big.

Quicksilver looked up—and up, and up. For the only thing right in front of her was an enormous chest of drawers. It took up the entire wall, as tall as a house, and had as many drawers as there were stars in the sky—all of them tiny and unmarked, with little brass knobs. There was only one label, nailed to the ground in front of the chest:

TO BE SORTED, it read, in the Rompus's handwriting. EVENTUALLY.

"You have *got* to be joking," Quicksilver muttered to the empty room.

She felt Fox darting beneath the Rompus's paw. The creature's clawed fist hit a mirror, sending glass flying everywhere. *Why?* said Fox, panting. *Have you encountered some trouble?*

It's a chest of drawers, none of them labeled.

So open them and find the right skeleton, then!

"I've almost got him, Pig Face!" roared the Rompus, his booming voice echoing through the caves.

But there have to be a thousand drawers!

Well, just start looking!

Quicksilver flung open every drawer she could reach. All of them were stuffed full—buttons and socks, wooden whistles and tiny silver bells. One drawer held playing cards that had been enchanted to sing winter carols. Quicksilver slammed the drawer shut on them, though their cheery voices didn't stop singing.

It's higher up, came Fox's gasping voice. *Concentrate!*

I'm trying! Quicksilver closed her eyes, tried to find the skeleton's pull once more, but her mind was too scattered to focus, and all the bones collected in this chest were too loud for her to pick them apart. *This is too hard—*

Fox wailed a ghostly wail. *Does this fellow* never *get tired?*

The crashing noises were getting closer, Fox leading the Rompus on a wild chase through room after room.

"Bad ghost!" roared the Rompus. "You're making a mess!"

Quicksilver wiped her sweaty hands on her skirt and climbed the drawers, using the tiny knobs to pull herself up. She followed Fox's directions—*To the left! No, the* other *left! No, wait, it's much higher than that! Climb higher!*—and opened drawer after drawer. A buzzing warmth tingled just past her fingers, always out of reach. Just when she thought she had gotten close to its source, there was a jolt, a *whoosh* like something flying past her, and then the feeling of something very small but very powerful jumping to another drawer, and then another—on the other side of the chest, in the top row of drawers, in the bottom row.

Fox, I think it's running away from me!

Anastazia did say the skeletons liked to do that—

She flung open drawer after drawer, chasing the skeleton through the chest—there! A drawer rattled and hissed. There, to the right! Another drawer flew open and slammed shut.

But each drawer she opened revealed yet more of the Rompus's treasure: Pocket watches and hairbrushes, silver coins and bags of marbles, matchbooks and silk gloves—and bones. Monster bones—brightly colored, whispering to one another, laughing quietly at Quicksilver's distress. But none of them were *the* monster. None of them felt quite right.

She felt ready to scream in frustration—until one of the drawers she touched stung her hand.

She yanked her arm back with a cry. *Something bit me!*

That's it, that's it! That's the one! Fox's relief and excitement flooded through her.

She pulled open the stinging drawer and peeked inside. . . .

Bones. Tiny, delicate ones, glowing light brown like a sandy beach blazing bright at midday. The power emanating from them made her feel as though she was turning headfirst into a gusting hot wind.

Quicksilver's heart pounded as she stared at them. All the other noise in the world faded away. She heard a faint voice—no words, just gibberish. Were the bones *speaking?*

Grab them! yelled Fox.

Quicksilver scooped up every last bone and shoved them

into her pockets, clinging to the drawers with one clammy hand. Last of all, she reached for the skull—only a couple of inches long, with those wicked-looking hare's teeth at the end.

Master, look out!

She turned, skull in hand, just in time to see the Rompus crash into the room, the broken mannequin dangling from his claws.

He stared at her—first in confusion, and then, his face darkening, in rage.

"You're stealing from me?" he growled, black smoke puffing from his nostrils. One of his hind feet pawed the ground. He raised himself to his full height, his horns brushing against the ceiling.

Jump, master! yelled Fox.

She squeezed her eyes shut and thought of Fox, held her breath, and jumped—and right before she hit the hard ground, Fox darted below her, invisible, and cushioned her fall. She landed in softness—warm fur and itchy whiskers and a cold nose kissing her face.

I've got you, said Fox. *You're all right.*

The Rompus gaped. "How did you do that?"

"It was the ghost," said Quicksilver, jumping to her feet. "He works for me!"

As she spoke, she shifted Fox into an enormous, lion-sized spider, ghostly and gray. He lurched at the Rompus with a rattling roar, and the Rompus's eyes rolled back into his head.

He's fainting! yelped Fox, as Quicksilver shifted him into a dog once more. *Run!*

Quicksilver raced from the room just as the Rompus crashed to the floor. She and Fox darted back through the caves, the bones of the First Monster hot and sizzling in her pockets. The skull sent out little waves of magic that nipped at her skin like teeth.

They reached the portrait gallery, where sunlight poured in through the mouth of the cave—and froze.

The net holding Anastazia, Sly Boots, and the witches had nearly reached the flames.

We forgot about them, whispered Fox, and a heavy, hot shame settled between them. *How could we have forgotten about them? What if we hadn't been in time?*

Quicksilver shoved down the awful guilt tightening her throat and ran toward the fire. *Doesn't matter now. We're here, aren't we?*

"Fox, can you bite through that net?" she shouted out loud.

"I can try," said Fox.

Fly, instructed Quicksilver, shifting him into a golden

eagle. He alighted on the net and started slicing through it with his shining beak. Meanwhile, Quicksilver ran back and forth between the fire and the Rompus's table, dousing the flames with water and tea. When that wasn't enough, she kicked up dirt from the cave floor.

A despairing howl rang out through the cavern: *"PIG FACE!"*

Olli and his monster dropped to the floor. Before he could say anything, Quicksilver shouted, "Go! Run! I'll hold him off!"

Olli didn't question her. As Fox cut the net, the others jumped free, and Olli hurried them out of the cave, his owl monster leading the way.

The Rompus burst into the room, flinging treasure at Quicksilver. She dodged fistfuls of coins, soaring dolls in lacy white gowns. A goblet hit her hard on the top of the head, and she swayed. Fox swooped in to cloak her.

Hold on, master, Fox whispered, warm all around her. *Don't fade on me, or we're both dead.*

Quicksilver gritted her teeth against a wave of dizziness, grabbed her pack from where the Rompus had tossed it beside the tea table, and ran. She wove in and out of the Rompus's legs as he chased them through the room, grabbing at the air in search of them.

"But you was my friend!" he cried, dripping ropes of snot and tears.

Everyone's safe, came Fox's steady voice, *and you've got the bones. Keep running. You're almost there.*

Quicksilver did not stop running until she was out in the woods, huddling beneath a felled tree with Fox wrapped tightly around her. The Rompus's wails of grief rang through the night.

It's biting me, Quicksilver informed Fox as the snowy hare skeleton squirmed and hissed in her pockets, *and I think I'm about to faint.*

Then, without further warning, she did.

.21.

THE THIEF DAGVENDR AND HIS MANY NEARLY PERILOUS ENCOUNTERS WITH DEATH

Quicksilver awoke to the sound of cheers.

"You're awake!" cried Olli, smacking a kiss onto her cheek. "She's awake, everyone!"

Quicksilver blinked and looked around. She was surrounded by the smiling coven. They seemed to be in the tavern of an inn. She sat on a cushioned high-backed chair that had been draped with an only slightly stained tablecloth, and on her head, she wore a crown made out of butcher paper. Anastazia and Sly Boots sat at a table to the side. Anastazia looked amused; Sly Boots looked incensed.

Quicksilver blushed and stifled an assortment of garbled words.

"Quix, we don't know how to thank you," gushed Lukaas, his bright green lizard monster curled happily about his neck. "You saved us!"

"I . . . I did?"

"So modest, you are. Without you and Fox outwitting that beast, we'd never have escaped!" Lukaas raised his arms and conducted Freja and Olli in an enthusiastic, if more than slightly out of tune, rendition of "The Jolly Old Queen of Greenhart," substituting Quicksilver's name for Queen Lemvala's.

Quicksilver squeezed her way through the singing, dancing witches to Anastazia. By the time she reached her, Quicksilver's cheeks were wet from sloshed drinks and sloppy kisses. Irritably, she wiped her face on Anastazia's robe.

"Where are we?"

"Farrowtown," said Anastazia. "Olli's monster, Pulka, found you and Fox, and we brought you here straightaway. Six of the others left after escaping the cave, which is right smart of them, if you ask me. Seven stayed—including Lukaas and Freja. I'm not entirely convinced Olli hasn't bewitched them into following him around like puppies. No offense, Fox. The inn's called the

Laughing Farmer." Anastazia toyed with the speckled meat on her plate. "Their supper menu leaves something to be desired."

Quicksilver's head felt heavy. She didn't even protest when Sly Boots started fussing over her many cuts and bruises, treating them with an ointment he'd scraped together somewhere. The paper crown kept sliding down to her nose, and she knocked it off in a fit of frustration, abruptly ending Sly Boots's nursing.

"Fox and I found one of the skeletons," she said.

"The snowy hare," mumbled Fox as a mouse, tucked beneath Quicksilver's collar. "At least, we think it's one of them."

Anastazia's face lit up. "All of it? Please tell me you have the whole skeleton."

"Every last bone." Quicksilver made a nest out of her paper crown and gently settled a snoring Fox onto it. Then she fished the hare skull out of her pockets. When Anastazia touched it, a set of ghostly white teeth chomped down on her fingers. She yanked her hand away with a hiss. The teeth disappeared, cackling to themselves.

"That's one of them, all right," grumbled Anastazia, though she couldn't hide her relieved smile. "Good work, Quicksilver."

"It really doesn't like you," Quicksilver observed.

"We're both nasty pieces of work."

"Why don't we just hide the bones in different places while we look for the other skeletons?" Fox mumbled from his nest. "They'd be much harder to find that way, much safer than keeping them all in one bag."

"I only wish we could do such a thing," said Anastazia. "But do you remember how I told you that the First Ones and their monsters were all born of the same pool of magic, the same ancient star? The bones of each skeleton *want* to be together. You can separate a skeleton for a time, but its bones will always find their way back to one another." She scowled at the skull in Quicksilver's hand. "The little fiends. Put it away before it makes any trouble."

Quicksilver rearranged the contents of her pack, filling one of its pouches with all their food and coin, and carefully transferring the snowy hare skeleton into the other pouch. As she handled the bones, she felt as though something very small and very angry was biting her. By the time she tied the pouches shut, her fingers were red and throbbing.

"What if the bones disappear while I'm carrying them?" asked Quicksilver, dunking her fingers into a cup of water.

"Hey, that's my cup!" said Sly Boots.

Anastazia nodded grimly. "They could disappear—or maybe

you'll get lucky. Remember, those two I lost just before I found you, I'd had in my possession for ten years. Others I only managed to hold on to for a matter of days. It's all a matter of luck. The First Monsters were vain creatures, and so are their remains. All you can do to try to keep these skeletons near is pamper them. I've found them to be particularly fond of singing."

"I hate singing."

"I'll sing!" said Sly Boots. "I'm good at it. My mother always said so. There's this one song about the thief Dagvendr. My father used to sing it to me when I was little, and it goes like this." Sly Boots cleared his throat. *"Oh, the wise old thiever Dagvendr, he had a wicked plan, he—"*

"Not just now, Boots," groaned Quicksilver, as Olli, Freja, and Lukaas launched into the twelfth verse of "Queen Greenhart." "I've had quite enough singing for one day."

Sly Boots flung himself out of his creaky chair, scowling. "Fine. Just see if I sing for you next time you ask me."

"There is absolutely no danger of that happening."

Sly Boots's scowl deepened, and he stomped off to another table to sulk.

Anastazia snatched a plate of hot buttered rolls from the serving boy and tossed one to Quicksilver. "Something wrong?"

Quicksilver tore off a chunk of bread with her teeth. "I almost didn't save them," she mumbled at last. "Or you and Sly Boots, either."

"Oh?"

"I wanted to get the bones. I was focusing on that, and I . . ." She paused. "I forgot about all of you, stuck in that net."

Anastazia nodded. "You were thinking like a witch. Those bones are more important than any of us. Well done."

"But they think I'm a hero!" she said through a mouthful of bread. "I'm not the heroic type. I would've let them get roasted, if I'd had to."

If I had left them, maybe Fox and I could have gone off on our own, sold this stupid skeleton for a lifetime's worth of coin. Quicksilver hunkered down in her seat, miserable and angry—at herself, or maybe at the world. She couldn't decide.

"They don't need to know that," said Anastazia, shrugging. "Could have, would have. That's none of their business."

"But . . ." Quicksilver swallowed and stared hard at the floor. "I would have left *you*. I mean . . . myself. I don't know what I mean."

"And you should have, if it had come down to that," said Anastazia briskly. "My life doesn't matter much, these days. I've done my part, and now this is your fight. I'm only your shadow now, and I'll help you for as long as I can manage it."

My fight, Quicksilver thought. *But what if I don't want it? What if I just want to be a thief?*

Anastazia squeezed Quicksilver's hand and went upstairs to bed, and Quicksilver was left alone with her thoughts, Fox the mouse sleeping on the table, and Sly Boots bumbling through a conversation with a pretty serving girl in blue braids. Olli's coven sang Quicksilver's praises long into the night, until the innkeeper came down in her robe and nightcap and told them they'd better make the singing stop, or she'd deny them hotcakes in the morning.

.22.

A Tiny Bit Heartless

Though she was rash, and impatient, and a tiny bit heartless, Quicksilver was not one to forget things, nor one to break promises (unless, of course, a promise was made in the course of thievery), and so she did not forget the promise she had made to Sly Boots.

After everyone had gone to sleep that night in Farrowtown, Quicksilver crept to Sly Boots's bed, Fox at her heels in dog form. Quicksilver placed her hand over Sly Boots's mouth and shook him.

"It's just me," she hissed. "Get your shoes on. We're going out."

"Out?" Sly Boots hopped around in his socks, pulling on his boots. "Where?"

"I told you we would steal medicine for your parents, and I meant it."

Quicksilver led Sly Boots down the twisting stairs. The inn's front door creaked awfully, but when Quicksilver thought to Fox, *Whisper us,* Fox transformed himself into a wispy cloud that glowed faintly and bore the snout of a dog. In this form, Fox wrapped himself around the door and muffled the noise.

Outside, the air was still and warm. They wandered the streets of Farrowtown, keeping to the shadows while Quicksilver searched for a promising target.

"I thought you'd forgotten about that," said Sly Boots, watching his feet. "About my parents, I mean."

"I don't forget things," Quicksilver replied.

"But Olli, and the coven . . . I don't know, I thought maybe you cared more about them than anything else back home. We could have just left them to the Rompus, but you went after them. You risked your *life* for them in that cave."

Quicksilver bit down on the truth—that she had nearly been too late to save any of them, including Sly Boots—and then said calmly, "I'm a thief, not a murderer."

"But . . . you left my parents to come to the past, and dragged me along with you."

"I had to make a fast decision. Coming back to the past with Anastazia saved our lives."

Sly Boots considered her carefully. "So you don't fancy Olli?"

"*Fancy?* Great stars, Boots. What does that have to do with anything? I've got no time for fancying people. I've got magic to learn and skeletons to find. Now are you going to help me rob this place, or aren't you?"

Sly Boots looked up at the narrow, crooked house in front of which Quicksilver had stopped. A wooden sign hanging above the stoop read THE CURIOSITY SHOP: APOTHECARY, ANCIENT RELICS, AND ANTIQUE APPRAISAL.

"The place looks ready to fall over," he said.

"Well, then, we'd better move quickly, hadn't we?" *Fox,* Quicksilver thought to Fox, who sat patiently beside her in dog form, *find us a way in.*

I thought you'd never ask. Fox transformed into his yellow mouse self. He squeezed under the front door, and then Quicksilver felt him climb up to the latch and unlock it. Quicksilver cracked open the door to slip inside, and then suddenly she and Sly Boots were wrapped in the warm, furry cloak of invisible Fox, Quicksilver's nose mashed against Sly Boots's chest.

"Fox," she said through gritted teeth, "*if* you don't mind."

"My apologies, master," murmured Fox, adjusting his cloak so that Quicksilver could wiggle loose. She and Sly Boots crept through the shop's candlelit foyer, which was crowded with bulging crates and marble statues and dark tables weighed down by tall stacks of books.

"Remember," whispered Quicksilver, "*I'm* the witch here. You're only the—"

"*Only?*"

"Fine. You're the monster. But when you do things without asking me first—"

"Chaos ensues, the order of magic is upset, and you yell at me." Fox huffed, annoyed. "It's just I *knew* you were about to ask me to cloak you and Sly Boots, so I did it. It's called taking initiative, master. What if I'd waited for your instruction back in the Rompus's cave? We'd have been stomped flat."

"Life-and-death situations are one thing," said Quicksilver, "but when it comes to normal life situations, I'll thank you to wait until I say so—*ow!*"

Quicksilver rubbed her arm. The skeleton of the snowy hare, though tucked away in her pack, had apparently decided to announce its presence. A set of grinning, ghostly rabbit teeth hovered by Quicksilver's elbow and then faded away.

"What was that for, you horrible thing?" demanded Quicksilver.

"I don't think it likes that you two were fighting," said Sly Boots.

"Of all the stupid things you've ever said, Sly Boots, that might be the most—"

The ghostly set of teeth reappeared and chomped down on Quicksilver's thumb.

Be nice to it, Fox thought to her. *Isn't that what Anastazia said? It likes to be cared for.*

Quicksilver forced a sweet smile and crooned to her pack, "What a nice skeleton you are. So polite and kindly. Of *course* we should not have been fighting. Of *course* we are all friends here, and love one another."

A happy sigh drifted from the pouch holding the skeleton.

"I think it's working," Sly Boots whispered.

Quicksilver showed him her thumb, from which the set of teeth still dangled. "Is it, now?"

"Didn't Anastazia say you should sing to it?"

Quicksilver closed her eyes in an attempt to find patience.

"Oh, yes," added Fox in a suspiciously cheerful tone. "I do believe Anastazia said that exact thing."

"Who's there?" called a voice. Still concealed within Fox's cloak, Quicksilver and Sly Boots turned to see a tiny, spectacled woman with short purple hair peeking down the stairs just ahead of them.

Sly Boots nudged Quicksilver. "We never shut the door!"

It was true—the front door stood ajar behind them. Quicksilver crept back toward it, pulling Sly Boots with her, and quietly kicked the door closed. Then they stood in silence while Fox's cloak swirled slowly around them.

The woman squinted about the hallway and inspected the door's handle. Quicksilver, Fox, and Sly Boots flattened themselves against the wall between a suit of armor and a tall blue cactus crowned with white flowers.

Finally the woman shook her head and retreated back up the stairs. "The children's books are at it again," she muttered to herself.

"Well?" Sly Boots asked, once she was gone. "Shall I sing to it, or do you prefer walking around with skeleton teeth hanging off your thumb?"

And so, as Fox ushered them invisibly through the house— which was undoubtedly spelled in some way, for it was much larger on the inside than it appeared to be from the outside—Sly Boots sang all twenty-two stanzas of "The Thief Dagvendr and His Many

Nearly Perilous Encounters with Death." Soon Quicksilver's pack was as quiet and warm as a basket of baby bunnies.

"Fox, let me out," said Quicksilver.

"Whatever for?" Sly Boots asked.

"I just want to try something," Quicksilver explained. "Take the pack, Boots, and keep singing to the bones. Fox, help him get up to the roof. I'll meet you there."

"But the medicine—"

"I can steal it much easier on my own."

Master? Fox questioned. Quicksilver felt a soft paw on her arm.

Go on. Trust me?

You know I do, said Fox, and licked her cheek.

Licking cheeks isn't very dignified for a monster, is it, Fox?

We must always respect our heritage. Mine is about licking things and chasing sticks.

Once they had gone, Quicksilver felt a weight lift off her shoulders. No pack, no Sly Boots, no Fox. No magic. She was alone and free and light as a leaf.

She moved silently through the apothecary stores, darting up and down ladders, climbing dusty shelves lined with mortar and pestles, squeezing between stacks of heavy burlap sacks that smelled of herbs. A box of empty vials nearly toppled as she brushed by them. She passed closed doors; from behind them came the sounds of people snoring, but Quicksilver moved so quietly that no one came out to stop her. And with no Fox to hide her, she felt rather thrillingly exposed, as she had when sneaking through the convent, magic-less and solid as any human.

By the time she'd navigated her way up through the house's five floors, through the cramped, cluttered attic, and out onto the roof, Quicksilver felt ready to crow with joy.

"There you are!" Sly Boots whispered, hurrying through the roof's forest of chimneys with the pack full of bones in his arms. "It's about time! Why'd you leave us like that? Do you know how creepy it is, sitting in the dark and singing to a skeleton?"

I did it, Fox, Quicksilver thought to Fox, who was foraging through the rooftop garden. *I stole things all on my own. Even without you, I'm still a good thief.*

Of course you are. Fox trotted over to her with a fat carrot in his mouth. *You always were. But may I remind you, master, it would have all happened much more efficiently, had I been with you.*

"Here, Boots, make sure I've got everything." Quicksilver emptied her pockets to show them the medicines she had stolen—jars of ground crumwort, stoppered bottles of essence of moxbane, tied packets of dried weatherwurst.

Sly Boots stared at it all with wide eyes. "But how did you know what to steal? I didn't tell you, but it's all here! This is exactly what I need!"

"The fourth rule of thieving is to always notice everything around you," Quicksilver explained, with not a little puff to her chest. "You never know when it might come in useful. Your parents' bedroom back home was full of these things—empty bottles and such, of course, but . . ."

Sly Boots gazed up at Quicksilver, and Quicksilver uncomfortably observed how the stars reflected in his eyes. It was not an altogether terrible sight.

"Stop staring," she said shortly. "It makes you look funny."

"You're the best thief in all the Star Lands, Quicksilver," he declared.

The words were exactly what she wanted to hear. Feeling generous, she patted his shoulder. "I know. Now, let's get back before you have to start singing again. I'm not sure my thumb could survive that twice in one night."

"I'll help you carry these," Sly Boots asked, reaching for the medicine.

Quicksilver slapped his hands away. "No. They stay with me."

His eyes narrowed. "And why is that?"

"So I know you won't leave me."

Sly Boots blinked, looking rather baffled. Fox stopped munching his carrot and lifted one furry eyebrow.

Quicksilver blushed furiously. She hadn't meant to say that, but now, of course, it was too late, and she was left standing there looking like the biggest fool there ever was.

Sly Boots laughed. "Why would I leave you?" he asked. "Without you and Anastazia, I can't get back home."

"Right. You're absolutely right."

"So . . ."

"So just stop talking to me, how about that?" Quicksilver shoved the medicines into her pack, in the pouch that held their food and coin, making sure to avoid Sly Boots's steady gaze.

Making sure not to think about the convent girls, and the sisters, and her parents, and all the other pieces of her life that she'd already lost.

Thinking about such things made her pause, and think too much, and hurt. Not to mention say things that she shouldn't. And if she were to become a truly great witch thief, she would need to keep her heart hard.

For witches, Anastazia had said—and thieves, Quicksilver knew from her own experience—were better off alone.

.23.

Too Late for Warnings

The next day, the group left Farrowtown and followed the Kivi Road west into the kingdom of Belrike. After some weeks of traveling, Olli explained, they would arrive at the impassable western mountains, and though reportedly everyone who had attempted to cross the mountains had died doing so, they seemed to by all accounts last longer and, in general, have a better time of things if they started out on this particular footpath at the base of Mount Korkaya.

"That's the most disturbing explanation about why to go somewhere that I've ever heard," Quicksilver told Olli. "When people start out here, they live a *little* longer than other people—but still end up dying anyway! Hooray!"

Fox and Sly Boots laughed, but Olli seemed neither amused nor offended. He simply kept his eyes on the road and, in a much more serious tone than he typically used, said, "I don't know where else to lead my people, Quix. The Wolf King hunts the witches of the Star Lands, so it makes sense that we should go elsewhere, even if the way is impossible. Otherwise we should stay here and die. Is that what you'd prefer?"

Quicksilver had nothing to say to that, and, frowning, fell back to walk alongside Anastazia.

"My people," Anastazia muttered, loudly enough for Olli to hear. "Pah! Some people they are, most of them running scared when things get hard. One little Rompus, one little roast over a fire, and away they go! Do you think, *Quix*, they'll stand by him deep in the mountains, in the brutal claws of winter? Or what about when the Wolf King tracks them down? Will they help their beloved leader fight, or will they run away in a panic and leave him for dead?"

Olli's shoulders tensed, and his mouth became a hard line. He hurried to catch up with Freja and Lukaas. Pulka, perched on his shoulder, glared back at Quicksilver and Anastazia with sharp purple eyes.

"Why do you have to be so mean to him?" Quicksilver

demanded. "He's not doing anything wrong."

"I'm trying to do him a bit of good, make him see how foolish he is before it's too late," said Anastazia. "We'll leave them, tomorrow, just like we'd planned to before this whole Rompus ruckus began. When we're with them, we're harder to hide, slower to move."

Quicksilver kicked a pebble out of her path, startling Fox, who had been tracking a quail.

"Well, I think that's a grand idea," said Sly Boots loftily. "We could have been a lot farther along without them, you know, if they hadn't distracted us. Maybe you could have even tried some time-traveling magic by now—"

"Oh, shut it about time travel, Sly Boots," Quicksilver snapped. "You're just jealous because Olli's funny, and kind, and brave, and you're just a—a nobody! You're not a witch, and you're not a thief. You're just a boy."

Fox looked up from his sniffing. *That was harsh.*

Quicksilver glared at the ground, her cheeks flaming. *It's the truth!*

I think you're still worried about losing him. Master, I mean this with all due respect, but . . . not everyone is going to be like your parents.

Fox, that is one thing we will never—never—talk about. Do you understand me? My parents are not your concern.

Silence, and then Fox thought quietly, *As you wish, master.*

Steeling herself, Quicksilver lifted her gaze back to Sly Boots. It was remarkable, how his face had changed, how it hardened and closed like a door slamming shut on a bright room, leaving everything else in darkness.

"I'm a nobody, eh?" he said quietly, and then stormed ahead down the road before Quicksilver had a chance to say anything more.

"Well done," Anastazia murmured, squeezing Quicksilver's shoulder. "We don't need him. We don't need anybody. If we play this right, we can leave him behind, too. He'll only slow us down, just like the others."

Quicksilver nodded but said nothing. She hadn't meant to shout at Sly Boots like that. Only last night they had enjoyed stolen sugar cakes on the roof of the Laughing Farmer, their pockets bulging with goods from the apothecary, before finally crawling back into bed at dawn.

And now . . .

We're not actually going to leave him behind, are we? Fox asked quietly.

Perhaps it would be best if we did, Quicksilver responded. *I'm afraid I'm a splendid thief but a terrible friend.*

Well, so is he. Always going on and on about his parents, as though you aren't in fact doing your best to learn magic and help him—

"What was that?" Anastazia asked

Quicksilver realized she must have said something aloud. "I said, I'm no good at being someone's friend."

Anastazia laughed. "Well, thank the stars for that! What do friends ever do but get in the way? The only people a witch can trust are herself and her monster."

Did you feel that? Fox asked, pausing at Quicksilver's side.

Feel what? Quicksilver glanced around. They had stopped beneath a towering tree with a white trunk and leaves as blue as lightning.

Someone's here. The fur on Fox's back stood up.

But Quicksilver saw nothing out of the ordinary.

We're not alone, Fox insisted, and at that moment, darkness flitted across Quicksilver. Looking up, she saw a strange shadow darting through the leaves overhead. There were two, and they moved like birds might, wheeling about through the branches before perching on one to leer down at her. They were both human shaped, but only somewhat. Their bodies swirled like trails of smoke, and their shifting faces wore horrible, hungry grins.

"Anastazia." Quicksilver tugged on her older self's sleeve—but then the howls began.

It was too late for warnings.

The Wolf King had arrived.

.24.

A STORM OF FUR AND FANGS

The wolves came first, surging onto the Kivi Road in a storm of fur and fangs. White, black, red, gold, brown, gray, and blue—the Wolf King's pack of monsters.

The brown wolf lunged for Olli, its fangs gleaming. Olli shouted to Pulka, and Pulka soared around Olli, her white wings forming a shield of light. The brown wolf smashed into her and collapsed, whimpering.

The red wolf, blazing like fire, rammed Lukaas in the stomach and sent him crashing to the ground. Lukaas's belly was scorched black. His bright green lizard monster leaped onto the red wolf's back, shifted into a fiery green wildcat, and sank her teeth into the wolf's neck. The wolf, pinning Lukaas to the road, grabbed the wildcat's tail with its teeth and flung her to the side. Lukaas screamed.

A teenaged boy wearing a fur-trimmed cloak clasped with a silver wolf pin sauntered out of the forest, laughing. The two shadows from the tree now hovered over his shoulders like a pair of malevolent crows.

"Boots!" Quicksilver cried.

Sly Boots, standing frozen with shock, whirled around in the chaos, but Anastazia grabbed Quicksilver's arm and hurried her away down the road. Fox ran alongside them, whining frantically.

"Where are you taking me?" Quicksilver pulled against Anastazia's grip. "Where's Boots?"

"We can't worry about him," Anastazia snapped. "We have to hide, keep that skeleton safe. Now run!"

But Quicksilver was the witch. *She* was the one with the monster. She would not be dragged away.

"Quicksilver!" came a faint cry—Sly Boots's voice, cracking with fear.

Anger flared up inside Quicksilver. *Fox, free me.*

Right away, master, and with a muttered apology, Fox shifted into a mouse and plummeted down Anastazia's shirt.

Anastazia twitched and squirmed, batting at her clothes. Fox sank his tiny mouse teeth into her shoulder. She yelped and let go of Quicksilver.

Quicksilver turned and ran back toward the fight. *Fox, I need you!*

Fox jumped out of Anastazia's cloak, shifted back into a dog, and tore after her. Anastazia screamed at them to stop, but they kept running. They were witch and monster, girl and dog, and they were not afraid.

Quicksilver spotted Sly Boots scrambling through the undergrowth, hurried toward him, and yanked on his collar. He yelped and hid his face.

"It's just me!" she hissed. "Are you all right?"

Sly Boots turned, his cheeks smeared with bright pink pollen from the tiny flowers scattering the forest floor. "I-I'm . . . yes. I'm fine, I think."

"Go with Anastazia and hide," she said, pointing back down the road.

"Quicksilver, get back here!" shouted Anastazia, hurrying toward them as fast as her frail body allowed.

"But—" said Sly Boots.

"Go!"

Quicksilver shoved Sly Boots at Anastazia and then turned and raced toward the coven. She did not pause to strategize or think. Her blood roared and her heart pounded, and she understood what she must do like she understood how to put one foot in front of the other.

She pointed at the nearest wolf, the gold one, and said to Fox, *Do not spare him.*

Fox raced for the golden wolf, which had pinned Freja and her snake monster to the ground and now stood over them, licking its chops. The faster Fox ran, the more he glowed, until he was a furious ball of light, surging toward the wolf.

The wolf's head snapped up right before Fox slammed into him. They toppled, wrestling down the road, snarling and snapping their jaws. Freja and her monster struggled to their feet and fled.

To me, dear Fox! Quicksilver pictured him in her arms instead of locked in combat with the much bigger wolf. A pain in her heart tugged, the cord between her and Fox snapped back to her, and then Fox was there beside her, panting and disheveled.

But there was no time to waste.

Again! Quicksilver pointed to the black wolf, who was dragging an unconscious, bleeding Bernt toward the Wolf King. Fox shifted into a hawk and let out a piercing cry. He flew at the black wolf and pecked at its eyes.

The coven's seven remaining witches shifted their monsters into wildcats and boars and bears. Colored streaks of energy zipped back and forth between them like bolts of lightning. Each time Quicksilver saw another witch in trouble, she sent Fox flying over to help, and when she felt teeth pierce him or claws scrape him, she shoved her own pain away, thought him back to her, and held him close.

I'm here, she told him.

I'm all right, he answered.

But the wolves were too powerful, and they did not tire. The Wolf King watched from a distance, leaning against a tree by the road, directing his pack with lazy flicks of his fingers. He appeared to be talking to the two shadows perched on his shoulders.

Who are they? What's he saying to them? Is he . . . laughing?

Fox did not answer.

Quicksilver whirled in time to see him slammed to the ground by the gigantic golden wolf.

"To me!" Quicksilver cried, her voice breaking, and the pang of magic that pulled Fox out of danger and into her arms was so enormous it knocked her flat.

"Fox, Fox," she whispered, snuggling him to her chest. "Are you hurt?"

I'll be fine, master, he thought to her, weary. *We monsters are resilient creatures, didn't you know?*

A tingle down Quicksilver's spine alerted her to the Wolf King, who was watching her from across the road with eyes cold and hard as knives. He was no longer smiling.

The bones in Quicksilver's pack shifted and hissed words she did not understand.

As one, the seven wolves froze and turned to her.

The two shadows on the Wolf King's shoulders rose into the trees, stretching tall and thin. Then they swooped down toward Quicksilver, twin waves of howling darkness big enough to drown her.

She realized, with a sort of slow falling feeling, that this was the end.

I'm sorry, master. I tried.

It's all right, Fox. Maybe the others will escape, at least. Quicksilver drew a deep breath. *Shall we give it one more try?*

I don't intend to die lying in the dirt like some dog, Fox agreed. *I mean . . . well, you know what I mean.*

Quicksilver got to her feet and gathered up everything she had inside her—every fear and every hope, every dream and every nightmare. Her thoughts turned to fire in her mind, and then her heart, and then her fingertips, until she was nothing but the calm, hot certainty that her death would be one that people would tell stories about for the rest of time.

When she flung out her arms, she sent Fox flying toward the oncoming darkness in a glorious arc of light.

He cut right through the twin shadows, and the growling wolves, and settled over the wide-eyed Wolf King like a shroud.

Then Fox disappeared.

And the Wolf King shuddered.

And Quicksilver felt the cord connecting her to Fox snap tight in her mind, and she saw . . . *everything*.

The images came in sharp flashes—colors and shapes, sounds and textures. She saw a castle in snow-covered mountains, a village being burned by a young boy with night-black hair. A blood-spattered family cowering before a pack of wolves. The same night-haired boy chasing a deer through the forest—calling after it, asking it to stay with him.

A canvas of swirling stars. Seven figures with eyes as deep as the seas, wearing robes of blinding white. They looked down upon the Star Lands as though studying a map in a book. They clawed inside the night-haired boy's mind and made him scream, turned his eyes to stone.

A starling, and a snowy hare. A hawk, a cat, a mouse. An owl. An ermine.

The First Ones, the part of Quicksilver's mind that was still her own whispered. *And their monsters.*

A scream began, somewhere deep and muffled, and rose higher and higher until it pierced Quicksilver from gut to skull, and threw her back onto the hard ground.

She lay there, dizzy and gasping, feeling as though she had been pounded in the stomach by marble fists.

Across from her sprawled the Wolf King, looking just as disoriented as she felt. Light leaked out of his ears and nose and mouth, and then the light gathered in a quivering puddle at his feet, and then it became a dog—Fox, limping over to Quicksilver.

Quicksilver buried her face in his coat. *Fox, what did you do?*

Only what you instructed, master. Fox's legs buckled beneath him. *I gave it one more try.*

The Wolf King shook his head and staggered to his feet.

His wolves hurried to him, their tails between their legs, yipping and whining. When the Wolf King's eyes cleared, he spotted Quicksilver in the dirt, and in that moment he seemed not a fearsome king but merely a boy. He backed away, his face waxen, his dark hair plastered to his skin.

It almost looked like he was *afraid* of Quicksilver.

The two shadows wrapped themselves around the Wolf King like scarves, hissing indecipherable words. The Wolf King called to his wolves, "To me," in the voice Quicksilver remembered from the convent—a choir of voices, and buried within them, the clear voice of a boy. The wolves circled around him, faster and faster, becoming a swirl of indistinguishable colors. Then they disappeared altogether, and took the Wolf King and his two shadows with them.

In the booming silence that followed, Quicksilver could hardly breathe, her mind working furiously.

"What happened?" Olli rasped. He sat nearby, cradling Pulka in his arms. One of her wings looked broken, but her owl eyes were sharp and clear.

"I saw his thoughts," said Quicksilver slowly, which sounded ludicrous, even though she knew it was the truth. "Fox went into his mind, and through him, I saw . . . I saw the Wolf King when

he was little. His family. I saw the First Ones. I saw . . . I saw
their monsters. . . ."

Olli stared at her. "But *how?*"

"Anastazia!" Quicksilver jumped to her feet. Despite her
shaky legs and pounding head, she was smiling. Fox wasn't dead,
and neither was she, and *look* what they had done! "You won't
believe it—I know where they are! The skeletons! It makes no
sense, but—"

Then Quicksilver lost her voice, for there was Sly Boots,
kneeling on the ground with a hopeless expression on his face,
and beside him, completely still, lay Anastazia.

.25.
MIND MAGIC

Quicksilver ran to them, her throat choked with fear.

"She's not dead," said Sly Boots, rubbing his forehead with a grimace, "but she's bad off."

"Anastazia?" Quicksilver took the old woman's face in her hands, wiping away specks of mud. Dry skin flaked away at Quicksilver's touch. "What happened? Are you all right?"

"She broke the link," said Olli, limping over to them. Pulka crawled up to Olli's shoulder and gingerly tested her wing. "I saw her run over like . . . well, like a much younger witch, if you don't mind me saying so. She shoved you to the ground, and it must have severed the connection between you and the Wolf King. It threw her back from you, though, hard. Magic flew off everywhere, like shattered glass. I barely missed getting hit myself."

"What did you see?" Anastazia's eyes fluttered open. "Quicksilver . . ."

"Don't speak," said Quicksilver, settling Anatazia's head in her lap. What a strange thing it was, she thought, to hold yourself in your own arms. "Just listen." She glared up at Olli. "Do you mind?"

Olli inclined his head and hurried to help the others. Quicksilver saw Freja cradling a broken arm, her monster snake hanging forlornly about her neck. Quicksilver grabbed Sly Boots's hand to keep him there beside her.

"Stay, Boots. Please?"

Sly Boots blinked, and then Quicksilver had to blink, too, because it had looked, for an instant, as though his eyes had changed color, as though something fundamental about his face had shifted. But then he smiled and sat next to her, and he listened closely as she told Anastazia everything—the images she had seen while connected to the Wolf King, and how frightening they had been. How she hadn't *meant* to perform mind magic, but how it had just sort of happened, because she had been prepared to die and had thrown everything she had at him, and how she had seen the First Ones, it must have been them, and their monsters too, and—

"I think I know where to go next," Quicksilver said. "Well, at least I have an idea." She frowned, working through the chaos of the last few minutes. The images she had seen while connected to the Wolf King's mind still stormed within her, and she shuddered to look at them. *That burned village, those people, covered in blood. The night-haired boy, doing such horrible things . . .*

Fox placed a reassuring paw on her leg. Quicksilver found her courage and continued. "I suppose it does make sense," she said. "The First Ones are using the Wolf King's body, so when I was connected to the Wolf King, I was also connected to them. Right? So of course I saw them, and pieces of their thoughts and memories, and their monsters, just like I did the Wolf King's. And . . ." She trailed off. *Fox? I don't know how to explain.*

"We feel pulled by the skeletons of the First One's monsters," said Fox. "We did before, in the Rompus's cave, but that was just the feeling of big magic nearby. It was confusing, jumbled. This is more than that. More focused. Before it was like . . ."

"Like hearing a shout in a crowd," said Quicksilver, "but not recognizing the voice."

"Yes! And now we know the voice. We know the monster it belongs to. And it's much easier to hear." Fox fixed his warm brown eyes on Quicksilver. "We need to go to the Belrike–Falstone border. Beyond that, I'm not sure yet. But that's where the nearest skeleton is, I'm sure of it."

Quicksilver looked hopefully at Sly Boots. "That makes sense, doesn't it?"

Sly Boots appeared to be navigating an impossible maze. He blinked several times and then rubbed his eyes. "I . . . think so? You both talk very fast. It's making my head hurt something awful. Perhaps if you start over—"

"That's right." Anastazia wheezed. "You're . . . right. Quicksilver. My good girl." Two tears slid from Anastazia's clouded eyes. She kissed Quicksilver's hand. "You frightened me, running off like that. Please, you must be careful."

"I promise you I will." Quicksilver leaned down, her shimmering red hair forming a curtain around them. "I didn't mean to, Anastazia, I swear I didn't. I was just so angry and afraid, and . . ." She paused, grinning. "It was fairly excellent, what I did, wasn't it?"

A hint of a smile tugged at the corner of Anastazia's mouth. "You still . . . have the skeleton?"

Quicksilver nodded, patting her pack. "Will you be all right?"

The hint of a smile became a full-fledged one. "I've had worse, believe me."

"Then we'll go north?"

Anastazia clasped her hand around Quicksilver's and squeezed, and Quicksilver was relieved to feel some of Anastazia's old strength return.

"North we will go," Anastazia agreed.

While Sly Boots helped Anastazia to her feet, Quicksilver hurried to Olli, who was helping Lukaas construct a splint for Freja's arm. Lukaas's face had been slashed by claws; remarkably, he still had both of his eyes, but blood streaked his skin. Three other witches lay unmoving beneath the trees. Bernt and his badger monster, their fuschia hair and fur spotted with blood, moved between the fallen witches, tugging their cloaks up over their faces.

Quicksilver hardened herself against the sight—only four witches left of the coven's original fifteen. She could spare no feeling for them, or she would sit right there and cry, and she couldn't do that. She needed to *move*.

"We have to leave you," she said to Olli, once they had stepped away from the others. "I'm sorry, but it's for the best. Our group is too big to travel safely, and where we're going . . ."

To be honest, she thought to Fox, *we don't know where we're going, exactly. Yet.*

They're better off without us, Fox reminded her. *If we're right, and we start finding these skeletons, the Wolf King will be after us, not them. They'll make it to the mountains safely.*

A tiredness overcame Quicksilver as she thought of chasing and being chased, perhaps for the rest of her life. *I wish I had never seen those memories. Now that I have . . . I can't do nothing anymore, can I, Fox? I can't keep living like you and me and thieving are the only things that matter. The Wolf King is dangerous. He's evil, he's . . .* She trailed off, shivering.

It's still your choice, master. No one here can make you do anything you don't want to. We could sell that skeleton and use the coin to live out our lives in peace.

And when the Wolf King finds us, when everyone else is dead?

Fox had no answer to that.

It would be easier to take the skeleton and run, to abandon Anastazia's fight—but that, Quicksilver thought, might not be the sort of life worth living. She wished, for an instant, that she weren't so terribly clever, and could go through life without having to consider such things.

You're not clever as all that, Fox teased.

Quicksilver let out one small laugh, her eyes nearly spilling over with exhausted tears. "Olli, take your coven and hurry west. Don't worry about us, and don't look back."

Olli's gaze moved from Quicksilver to Anastazia to Fox and back to Quicksilver. "What's this all about, Quix? How did he know to find us here?" He paused, ducked his head to look her straight in the eye. "What are you and the old woman up to?"

You don't have to tell him anything, Fox warned.

But the weight of what had happened pushed hard on her shoulders—what she had done, how fragile Anastazia now looked, how the Wolf King's blood-soaked memories sat heavy within her like festering heaps of rot. She turned away from the others and opened the pouch in her pack that held the skeleton.

Olli frowned at it. "Bones?"

But Pulka, still cradled in his arms, let out an alarmed squawk. "Is that . . . ?" The owl fluffed her feathers in distress. "Child, what have you done?"

Olli's eyes widened—as Pulka's thoughts came to him, no doubt. "You mean, that's really the skeleton of—"

"Yes," said Quicksilver, and then she explained everything to him—their mission, collecting the bones, Anastazia's many lives. Traveling through time, again and again. How Anastazia had found them in Willow-on-the-River, back home. The longer she spoke, the more easily she could breathe, as if by getting out the words, telling her story, she was also letting out some of her fear.

When she had finished, she waited, weary and sore, her head aching, her throat dry. The mind magic had indeed left her mind feeling scrambled like an egg on a skillet, just as Anastazia had said it would, that first night in Willow-on-the-River.

Olli ruffled a hand through his hair and looked away.

"I don't think we need to tell you how important it is that this information stays secret." Fox growled, baring his teeth.

"Oh, your secret is safe," Olli replied, "and even if I did want to tell anyone, no one would believe me. Quix." He knelt, took Quicksilver's hands in his. "You don't have to do this. You can come with us."

Quicksilver laughed faintly. "Over a mountain we'll die crossing?"

"I believe that, together, we stand a good chance of surviving even those mountains. I *must* believe it. The Star Lands are lost. Witches have tried to fight the Wolf King before, and they've failed. He may have gotten scared off this time—and I don't blame him, considering what you did—but he won't scare so easy next time. You know that, don't you?"

"I have to try," she said, but even to her own ears, she didn't sound convinced. "I saw . . . Olli, when I was in his head, I saw terrible things. I didn't realize . . . I didn't *know*—"

Olli nodded. "Yes, the Wolf King has done terrible things, and he'll do many more. But it isn't your responsibility to stop him. You're just a girl, Quix. You're not a hero. None of us are. Heroes are for tales and bedtime stories." He touched her cheek softly. "I know the old woman—er . . . the older *you*, I suppose—has this grand plan, and it's admirable, truly. Powerful she may have been—and you certainly are. I'll give you that much. I've never seen mind magic done like that before, especially not by such a young witch. But you've never succeeded, in all of your lives. Isn't that right? What makes you think you'll succeed this time?"

The bones in Quicksilver's pack shifted and grumbled. A sensation of thorns prickled against her back.

They'll need some attention soon, Fox suggested. *And perhaps a song. Unfortunately.*

Quicksilver took hold of her fear with a long, steady breath, and welcomed it into her heart. "I am not the sort of witch who runs away from evil," she said to Olli in a firm, clear voice. "I am the sort of witch who hunts it down."

Olli's face fell. "Quix—"

"I've made up my mind. So let us leave peacefully. You've seen what I can do. Don't test me."

Then Quicksilver held out her hand, refusing to meet Olli's eyes. After a moment, he slapped hands with her, and she endured a hug from him, and heard him say quietly, "You're a brave witch, Quicksilver, and we won't forget you." She ignored the sudden tears in her eyes, and how frightened and tired she felt. She muttered good-bye to Freja and Lukaas, who surely noticed her flaming cheeks and bright eyes, but did not comment on them.

"Only four left," Sly Boots observed as he, Quicksilver, Fox, and Anastazia turned off the road and into the forest. "Do you think they've really got a chance, like Olli hopes?"

"That isn't our concern, boy," said Anastazia, with a sputtering cough. "They were fools before we met them, and they'll be fools yet again."

Quicksilver did not want to think about Olli and his now-tiny coven any longer. Each step she took away from them was difficult enough, even though she knew she was doing the right thing.

Wasn't she?

"Here, Boots," she said harshly, tossing her pack at him. "Sing it a song or recite poetry or something. The Wolf King got it into a nasty temper."

While Sly Boots sang, Quicksilver kept her eyes on the bright blue star she could see through the treetops—the eye of Valkar, the White Bear, which pointed the way north.

.26.

RATS, MOST ASSUREDLY

In the kingdom of Belrike—which sat to the south and west of Quicksilver's home of Lalunet—there lived a king named Kallin.

His castle was squashed and gray, perched precariously on the side of Silverhair Mountain. Five tiny villages dotted the foothills below the castle, linked by several slender bridges, for the mountainside glittered with a web of tiny rivers. King Kallin had a queen and five beloved daughters—the youngest of which, Tatjana, would soon turn thirteen.

On the very day that Quicksilver, Fox, Anastazia, and Sly Boots entered his kingdom by way of the forest known in those parts as the Skullwood, King Kallin was preparing to hold a grand party in celebration of his daughter's accomplishment—that is, having survived thirteen years without being eaten alive by the numerous skeletal remains housed in the catacombs beneath their castle.

The king and his wife, Voina, sat in the royal dinghy as it glided across the still black lake at the bottom of Silverhair Mountain.

"My dear," said Queen Voina to her husband, and not for the first time, "don't you think you're worrying yourself into a fit over nothing? Must we really do this *again*?"

King Kallin rubbed his bald head and scanned the water for any signs of disturbance.

"In two days the castle will be crawling with well-wishers," said the king. "Do *you* want to risk their lives unnecessarily?"

Queen Voina raised one bored eyebrow. "Well, I wouldn't mind terribly much if your cousins disappeared under mysterious circumstances. Now *there's* a good use for the royal witches' talents. Never mind spells and traps and—"

A fish jumped out of the water and plopped back in. King Kallin yelped and drew his cloak tightly about his body. "What was that?"

"A fish, my darling husband. No haunted skeletons chasing us tonight." Queen Voina smiled slyly. "Not yet, anyway."

"Don't even joke about that!" snapped the king. Then he drew himself up and attempted to look regal as the boat approached the castle's three massive sewer pipes, which drained into the lake. The king's guards lifted a man out of the boat's bow, untied his hands and legs, and shoved him into the nearest pipe.

The man picked up his shoe to inspect the bottom and wrinkled his nose. "So all I have to do is get up through the catacombs and into the castle proper, without dying . . . and you'll let me go free? You'll pardon me?"

"Of course, young man," said King Kallin, with a magnanimous flourish. "Consider it penance for your crimes. The way is hard. Long and dank. Lots of sewage and the like. Rats, most assuredly." The king twiddled his fingers, recoiling as the water nudged the boat closer to the pipe. "Good luck!" he called out to the prisoner, and then hissed to his guards, "Back off, back off! Return to shore, for the love of all the stars in the skies!"

Queen Voina rolled her eyes and splashed water at her husband. The king screamed and flung himself at one of his guards, who patted him on the shoulder and settled him back into his seat.

As the boat glided back to the royal docks, the king kept his head tilted toward the pipe, listening. Only when he heard the prisoner's screams, the roar of fire, and the clatter of bones did he relax, for that meant the test was successful, and that the traps throughout the catacombs were in working order.

King Kallin shuddered to think of the generations upon generations of kings and queens buried beneath his home. Catacombs were a nasty tradition, but no matter how hard he tried to convince his court, no one would allow him to change the law and simply dump the bodies of dead royals into the sea. Everyone told him skeletons were merely bones, and could not come back to life, and that it was disrespectful to simply discard bodies like old handkerchiefs. No one believed the story about Old Throop, the legendary witch who had, as revenge against Queen Varaline the Fourth, cursed the catacombs' contents to come alive unpredictably and without warning—but King Kallin believed it. Years ago he had commanded one of his own royal witches to set a series of magical traps in the catacombs, so that when the cursed skeletons did come alive, they would never make it up into his castle.

But even the best spells required regular testing. And no one made for better test fodder than the criminals filling the royal jails.

So, in remarkably good spirits at the sound of this latest prisoner's dying cries, King Kallin kissed his wife and suggested they all sing a rowing song to pass the time.

.27.

DOES IT SMELL LIKE SKELETON?

"I can't believe we spent the rest of our money on *this*." Quicksilver held up the hem of her gown as if it were a piece of dung rather than a fine length of satin. Her pack, hidden on a belt under her huge ruffled skirts, was much lighter now, with so much of their coin gone. "Fox and I should have just stolen what we needed."

"An unnecessary risk," Anastazia muttered. "Better to keep our heads down when we can—"

"Yes, I know, I know. Just let me complain without explaining why I'm wrong, won't you?"

"Well, I think we all look fantastic," said Sly Boots, marching alongside them. "Besides, how else would we get inside? Sneak past the entire royal guard in our filthy everyday clothes?"

Quicksilver glared at him. He looked far too content dressed in that vest and silk shirt. The cap on his head reminded her of the well-dressed people from town who had visited the convent from time to time and pretended to care about orphans.

"Stop waving at everyone," she grumbled at Sly Boots. "We're not here to make friends."

"We're at a party." He jabbed her in the side, a little too sharply. "We should act like it."

"Oh, and you've been to many a party, then? You were a regular partygoer, back home?"

Sly Boots ignored her, waving at a pretty girl with glowing spring-green hair down to her feet, who wore a billowing satin dress adorned with plum-colored ribbons. The girl waved back and then hid behind her hands to whisper to her friends. Sly Boots puffed out his chest like some featherbrained bird, and Quicksilver wondered, with a hot flash of fury, how she could ever have stood the sight of him.

"Are you certain the bones are here?" muttered Anastazia, glaring at the crowd from within the folds of an excessively ruffled collar. "I feel like the most ridiculous twit in this getup."

"Why, Anastazia, you've never looked better!" crowed Sly Boots, bowing gallantly to her.

Quicksilver and Anastazia exchanged a look.

Can we accidentally lose him in the crowds and leave him here? Fox grumbled from Quicksilver's hair. He hid behind her ear as the tiniest mouse he could make himself, and the slight softness of him against her scalp made her enormous, flouncy dress almost bearable.

Almost.

"I'm sure it's here," said Quicksilver under her breath. "Fox feels it, and so do I. It's somewhere in this castle."

"Like an itch you can't scratch because it's just out of reach," said Fox.

"I think this one is the cat." Quicksilver concentrated on the Wolf King's memories, swimming chaotically through her mind. *You're close,* they seemed to purr. *Here. Almost.* "Don't you think? It feels like a cat."

"Of course, it *would* be a cat that would drag us into such a place," said Fox. "Miserable, wretched creatures."

"Somewhere in this castle," murmured Anastazia drily. "That shouldn't be a problem."

They stepped through the castle doors, which had been thrown open to receive visitors, and into a grand receiving hall decorated with garlands of luminescent flowers and banners embroidered with the young princess's likeness. Hundreds of candles lined the room, and an orchestra of fiddles, trumpets, and tambourines performed a merry jig from a stage in the corner—in front of which Princess Tatjana twirled from dance partner to dance partner, her golden curls flying.

The hall itself was thrice as tall as the church tower back in Willow-on-the-River, and twice the length of the Convent of the White Wolf. From where Quicksilver stood gaping near the doors, she saw a dozen staircases, fifteen curtained balconies, dozens and dozens of amber-glass windows.

"Stop staring," muttered Sly Boots through a fixed smile. "You might as well run through the hall screaming, 'Hello, I don't belong here!'"

Quicksilver bit down on her angry retort. He was right, after all. "Fox?"

"Working on it." Fox peeked out of Quicksilver's hair, his mousy whiskers tickling her neck as his nose twitched "Yes. Yes, I think . . . there. Head for that corridor, on the far left. The air smells more exciting there."

"Does it smell like skeleton?"

"It smells like *something*."

Quicksilver blew out an exasperated breath, but nevertheless made her way across the tremendous room, pausing only to sample the punch.

This way, Fox thought to Quicksilver, tugging on the magic that bound their hearts, guiding her to the left through the crowded room.

By the time they reached the corridor, Quicksilver felt ready to punch the next person who got in her way.

"Is this what all parties are like?" she asked Anastazia. "So many people, all of them hot and sweaty. It's unbearable."

"Haven't been to a party in quite some time, myself," muttered Anastazia, staring up at the ceiling with her mouth hanging open.

Quicksilver followed her gaze but saw nothing there.

Fox, Quicksilver thought, *is Anastazia quite well?*

Right as she thought this, Fox was thinking to her, *What's that fool boy doing?*

Quicksilver turned and immediately saw what he was talking about: Sly Boots leaned on a tall table near one of the hall's towering windows. He flashed a surprisingly charming smile at two witches nearby—one with yellow curls and a bright green frog monster sitting in her pocket, the other with orange spiky hair and a bluebird monster perched on her elaborately coiffed hair, from which dangled a wild assortment of baubles. The girls laughed at something Sly Boots said and swished over to him. Sly Boots beamed, and something about his smile made him seem . . . taller. Happier. More *together*, from his freckles down to his overlarge feet.

In other words, he looked nothing like himself at all.

For a moment, Quicksilver stood in shock. A strange sort of pain hooked deep into her gut.

Something wrong? thought Fox, looking at her curiously.

"Nothing," Quicksilver bit out. "Just a stupid boy in a stupid vest who apparently can't be bothered to stay with his friends at a party."

Fox thought delicately, *And here I thought you found Sly Boots more of a burden than a friend.*

Quicksilver spun around and snapped to Fox, *Hide us*, and when Fox's cloak settled around her and Anastazia, Quicksilver did not look back. She grabbed Anastazia's wrist and led her down the corridor, leaving Sly Boots and his jabbering girls behind.

She did not stop until they had gone down that corridor, and then ten others, and then through a door behind a tapestry, and then down three flights of stairs that spiraled deeper and deeper into the palace—all while following Fox's whispered instructions as the call of the skeleton pulled them farther on. Whenever they encountered a locked door, Fox wiggled through whatever cracks he could find and let them through. The farther they went, the more clearly Quicksilver could hear the skeleton's movements and memories, all tangled up in her mind—its purrs, its tiny hisses, the clack of its thin claws against the floor.

Definitely the cat, muttered Fox.

At last, at the end of a quiet, shadowy corridor, they pushed open a heavy stone door and emerged into a dark series of caverns. Passages snaked off into the shadows, marked by engraved stones. Quicksilver marched onward and then, at a sharp cry of alarm from Fox, stopped.

Before her, the stone dropped into a wide, dark chasm. A gust of cold wind raced up the sheer walls and blasted her in the face.

Shaking, Quicksilver found a small rock on the ground and threw it as hard as she could. The rock clacked against stone, and then stone again, and then silently disappeared into blackness.

"What's happening?" Anastazia murmured, peering over the chasm's edge. "Where are we?"

Quicksilver pulled her back to safety. "Listen to me carefully: You're going to follow me and do exactly as I say until we find this skeleton and get out of here. No wandering off, no leaning over the edges of chasms, and no asking questions. We have to move quickly. Do you understand?"

Anastazia nodded eagerly.

What's wrong with her? Fox inquired.

I don't know, but we can't worry about that right now. Quicksilver edged closer to the drop. There was a set of narrow steps carved into the chasm wall. *How far down do you think this goes?*

I'd rather not think about it, master, but I do know the skeleton is down there.

"Right, then." Her skin tingling with nerves, Quicksilver started down the steps, Fox in front of her and Anastazia following behind.

"Stairs!" Anastazia clapped her hands gleefully. "Hooray!"

They crept down the stairs, deeper and deeper into the darkness. It was too quiet for Quicksilver's liking—the air thick and still, Fox's yellow glow the one lonely light. The longer they walked, the more the snowy hare skeleton, tucked safely away in the pack beneath Quicksilver's skirts, squirmed and fussed. Quicksilver hoped that was a good sign—that it meant they were getting closer to the next skeleton.

Your guess is as good as mine, Fox thought to her. *Or maybe it's just fussing for the sake of fussing.*

Maybe. Only when they at last reached the bottom of the winding stairs did Quicksilver feel like she could breathe safely once more.

"Now what?" Even her whisper seemed booming in this quiet. The world above them was total darkness, whatever ceiling there was too high to see.

We're closer. Follow me. Fox led them farther into the caverns, down a twisting series of passages with low stone ceilings, until they finally emerged into a vast chamber lit with torches.

It was littered with thousands and thousands of bones.

.28.

LET'S LEAVE THE CREEPY CAVE

"These are not the bones of animals, Fox," said Quicksilver calmly, though calm was not at all what she felt.

"Indeed they're not." Fox sniffed a human skull, nudged it with his snout. "Some have been here a long time. Others . . . not so long."

Quicksilver felt suddenly very aware of her own skeleton. Such a fragile thing it was, kept in place by a sack of skin. She swallowed. "Well, how are we supposed to—?"

She whirled, at the same moment Fox did. They had both felt the same tug—and it felt somehow . . . mischievous.

Here. Almost.

Quicksilver's pack shuddered and jerked; the hare skeleton cried out shrilly.

Anastazia plopped down in the midst of the bones as though preparing to have a picnic. When she caught Quicksilver and Fox staring at her, she smiled and waved.

Quicksilver gritted her teeth. "Leave her for the moment. I think we're close."

She took a step, and then stopped—for there, right before her feet, appeared a skeleton. Smaller than the others, more delicate, and glowing a bright blue.

Quicksilver crouched, peering at the skull's huge eye sockets, elegant jaw, and sharp fangs. A cat. *The* cat, one of the First Monsters. The power drifting off it, reverberating up through her own bones, was unmistakable—hot and thrumming.

And though it was no longer alive, Quicksilver could have sworn it had just *winked* at them.

She exchanged a glance with Fox as she bent to retrieve the skeleton. "That . . . was easy."

But just as her fingers brushed the skeleton, it vanished. The bones in her pack slammed themselves against her with a hiss.

Quicksilver jumped back. "Where did it go? I *had* it!"

There. Fox pointed with his snout at a spot a few paces away, where the cat skeleton reappeared, twinkling with satisfaction. They ran for it, but the piles of bones on the cavern floor came midway up Quicksilver's calves, slowing her down. The sharp bits of broken bones scraped her legs, snagged her skirts. She kicked them in frustration. Fox darted ahead with a soft flash of light, swooped down—

But the skeleton disappeared once more.

Quicksilver growled. "What is it *doing?*"

"Anastazia said they might be spelled to move around from place to place, to avoid being discovered," Fox reminded her.

"Well, how are we supposed to—?" But then the skeleton reappeared only a few paces away. "Fox!" she cried, flinging him after it.

They chased the cat around the chamber, Quicksilver hissing every foul word she could think of under her breath. Every time they got close, the skeleton disappeared and then reappeared somewhere else. Quicksilver coughed, her throat full of dust. She was ready to sit down, right there in all those bones, and scream—when the cat skeleton appeared at her feet.

She froze, breathing hard. *Fox. Careful, now.*

Fox, now in his mouse form, inched his way closer.

Quicksilver crouched as slowly as she could. They reached for the skeleton at the same moment, and this time, when Quicksilver put her hand on the skull, it stayed put.

Hurry, master!

She gathered up the skeleton, though touching it felt like digging through a snarl of briars, and put it in the pouch with its snowy hare brother. Once she had drawn the strings of her pack shut with both skeletons safely inside, she sat back on her heels and sighed, her hands throbbing from the sting of the cat skeleton's magic.

From inside her pack came the sound of a purr. A sense of relief washed over her, and she wondered if it was not only her own, but if the hare and cat skeletons were relieved too, glad to be together once more.

They and their monsters were born out of the same pool of magic, the same ancient star—forever connected, forever sisters and brothers.

"We did it," Fox said quietly. "That's two. Now we only need five more."

And still, to Quicksilver's mind, it felt too easy. What had convinced the skeleton to stop taunting them? Would it soon disappear again?

I suppose there's no knowing, Fox said. *Whatever we do, can we get out of here first? I don't much like the smell of this place.*

"Where in the name of the stars are we?" asked Anastazia from behind them.

Quicksilver turned to find Anastazia sitting where they had left her, looking confused but clear-eyed, herself once more.

Quicksilver sighed. "Anastazia? You're all right?"

"I'm fine, I—" Anastazia fiddled with her ruffled collar. "Quicksilver, I fear . . . I may not be entirely well. When I interfered with the Wolf King, and broke your connection with him . . . do you remember how Olli said that magic flew everywhere, like shattered glass? I fear some of that shattered magic might have hit me, and . . . well, after all, it takes a great patchwork of spells to keep me going in the first place after all these years, and . . ."

Then Anastazia's face turned soft and blank. She gazed up at Quicksilver. "Are we to play a game? I do so love games."

Quicksilver had to look away. If Anastazia were indeed ill from breaking the mind magic connection, then there might not be a way to heal her. And if they couldn't . . . the idea of finding the First Monsters' skeletons without her made Quicksilver want to curl up in a ball right then and there.

Thankfully, these morose thoughts lasted for only a few seconds.

"Why, yes," Quicksilver said, dusting herself off, "we are indeed going to play a game. It's called Let's Leave the Creepy Cave and Go Back to the Party."

"And then Leave the Party as Quickly as Possible, and Never Attend Another One?" Fox suggested hopefully.

Quicksilver grinned. "Sounds like the best game I can imagine—"

A noise from behind her made her pause. A rattling, sliding sort of noise.

"Friends!" cried Anastazia, waving over Quicksilver's shoulder. "Hello! Come and play with us!"

A feeling of dread crept over Quicksilver, and when she turned to see who Anastazia was talking to, she saw a hundred human skeletons rising from the sea of bones around her.

.29.
A Sea of Bones

The skeletons wore jewels around their necks and crowns on their heads. Some carried scepters, which they used to stab the stone floor and drag themselves forward. Wisps of hair clung to their chins; their ragged cloaks stank of sewage.

In Quicksilver's pack, the snowy hare and the cat shrieked and whined. Under her skirts, the pack strained toward the exit, urging her to move.

Quicksilver grabbed Anastazia's arm, pulled her to her feet, and ran. The skeletons followed—some running, others crawling. Their breath wheezed and rattled. Their bony feet slapped against the stone floor.

Anastazia's giggles died abruptly. "Have I gone completely mad, or are there skeletons coming at us?"

Quicksilver tugged Anastazia on, back up the twisting stone passages—but now they were slippery, nearly impassable, coated with gunk and slime. Something had changed. A force pushed at Quicksilver like an invisible hand against her chest, trying to slow her progress. Every few steps, her feet went out from under her, and Fox swooped over in a glowing, dog-shaped cloud to cushion her fall.

"Don't worry about me!" Quicksilver cried, crawling up the passage on her hands and knees. "Worry about *them*!" She flung her arm behind her and thought to Fox, *Break some bones.*

Fox flew back toward the skeletons, an enormous, growling dog with huge, hulking shoulders. He zipped between them and kicked bones from their frames. A femur crumbled at the lash of his tail; a cluster of phalanges scattered across the ground like a handful of dice.

Quicksilver emerged into the main cavern, panting hard. Dragging Anastazia had left her arm feeling sore and burning. Anastazia was slick with sweat, her skin tinged a pale yellow-green.

"Quicksilver," gasped Anastazia as the sounds of Fox battling the skeletons rang through the cavern, "if you have to leave me—"

"I won't, so don't bother asking."

"I'm not asking, I'm ordering."

"You're not a sister, and you're not my mother."

Anastazia drew herself up, her violet eyes flashing. "I'm your elder—"

A yelp sounded from behind them. Quicksilver's heart seized. *To me!* she cried, and Fox appeared in her arms as a tiny, trembling pup.

There are so many of them, he panted. *I'm sorry, master. I need a moment.*

"We don't have a moment, Fox," Quicksilver replied grimly. "Just hold on to me."

He obeyed, pressing his face into her chest and digging his claws into her shirt. Quicksilver ran for the stairs that snaked up the side of the sheer black chasm, Anastazia right on her heels. But as they ran, the ground beneath them began to shake. Quicksilver fell hard and hit her head. Her vision tilted and swam.

The wave of skeletons broke and became chaos. Some of

them fell into the chasm; others dangled from the edge, swinging over the endless dark. Others crawled across the quaking ground toward Quicksilver, Fox, and Anastazia, pushing past one another with blank-eyed hunger.

A bony hand grabbed Quicksilver's foot; she kicked wildly. A set of cracked teeth bit down on her leg, and she screamed.

With a furious bark, Fox tried to shift into his dog self and defend her. Quicksilver felt the urge in his heart, ferocious and blazing. But she held him tight, clamping down on his magic.

No, Fox! Save your strength!

Anastazia kicked away two skeletons and grabbed Quicksilver, pulling her to her feet. They started up the stairs again, but when Anastazia's foot touched the first step, the entire staircase erupted into flame.

She cried out and stumbled back. Quicksilver sent Fox to her, and he wrapped himself around her, dousing the flames on her boot.

"Are you all right?" Quicksilver shouted above the roar of the flames and the rumbling rock.

"Fine," yelled Anastazia, a shaky hand at her throat. "My boot, however, is ruined."

"Fox, can you get us to the top, past the fire?"

Fox looked up at her forlornly, panting so hard his entire body trembled. "Putting out the fire took the last of me, master. I need more time to recover. We're still fairly new at this, you know."

The skeletons were almost upon them, a sea of bones and broken jaws and reaching hands. Quicksilver yanked out her pack from under her skirts and drew out the cat skull. It glowed a bright blue, scorching hot against her palm, but she held fast.

"Quicksilver, don't be a fool—" Anastazia protested.

"Do you want this?" Quicksilver called out. She held the skull up high, and the skeletons froze, their empty eye sockets trained on it. "Pretty, isn't it? Don't you want it back?"

The skull growled softly, like an annoyed cat, but Quicksilver ignored it. The mob of skeletons watched the skull as she swung it back and forth above her head. As one, the skeletons reached for the cat skull, howling, *"Mine, mine, mine!"*

"Anastazia, when I say run, follow me and run as fast as you can," said Quicksilver.

Anastazia gasped. "Oh! Is this a new game?"

Fox, do you think you have enough strength to at least catch this thing before it falls to the bottom?

I can manage that much, Fox answered. *Only that much.*

It would have to do.

"If you want it," Quicksilver shouted coyly to the skeletons, "then you'll have to catch it!"

Then she flung the skull over the side of the chasm.

In one huge, scrambling wave, the skeletons jumped for the skull, clawing, reaching, reaching . . . and diving off the cliff into blackness.

Fox, go! Quicksilver thought to him, but he was already away, soaring after the falling skull as a faint yellow bird.

Quicksilver tied the skeletons' pouch shut, threw her pack over her shoulders, and ran in the opposite direction, away from the chasm and the fire. She pulled Anastazia after her and sent as much love and strength as she could to Fox.

I'm here, Fox, I'm here. I'm not leaving you. Come back to me. I'm here.

He did not answer, but she felt him—still there, wings still beating. Careening, flying through blackness, reaching, reaching . . .

Some skeletons had not fallen for the trick. They chased after Quicksilver, crawling lightning fast, like giant bony spiders. They grabbed her and threw her to the ground. She kicked them and sprang back up, bleeding where she'd fallen. Anastazia was half running, half crawling, trying to kick off the torso of a skeleton that clung to her skirt and wouldn't let go.

A soft flash of light, and Fox reappeared—an even smaller puppy in her arms, quivering and helpless. His front paws held the cat skull, which seemed to be in a fit of temper—hissing and yowling as any angry cat might.

"You did it, Fox!" She kept her voice strong as she ran, even though the sight of him frightened her.

"*We* did it, master," he whispered. "But where are we going?"

"No idea. I hadn't thought ahead that far."

"I think our path is clear," said Anastazia, jogging unsteadily beside her.

Quicksilver followed her gaze to where the stone floor ended. Past the drop rushed a river of black water. From somewhere not too far away came the roar of a waterfall.

"You don't mean it," said Fox.

"We have to." She paused, set Fox down beside her. "Hold on to that skull, Fox, whatever you do, and stay close. Anastazia, can you swim?"

"Like a fish!" she called cheerfully.

Quicksilver allowed herself one pang of worry at Anastazia's gleefully oblivious expression. Then she grabbed Anastazia's hand, pinched her own nose shut with the other, and jumped, Fox at her heels.

Falling into the water was like breaking through a sheet of putrid ice. She surfaced, gasping, spitting out sludge. Anastazia, coughing, still clung to her right hand.

"Fox!" Quicksilver cried. Water rushed at her face in waves. Spluttering, looking up, she saw skeletons jumping into the water after them. The current was swift. Cold fingers brushed against her feet, grabbed on, pulled her under.

She inhaled water, kicked, clawed, lost sight of Fox, spun around, opened her eyes, saw a skeleton looming close through the murk, and punched it right in the face. It fell away, and Quicksilver swam back to the surface, gasping and coughing.

Fox found her, jumped onto her neck, and clung there as they struggled through the water. Quicksilver grabbed Anastazia's hand again and kicked until her legs and lungs burned.

"Look, up ahead!" Fox pointed his nose at the round opening of a pipe in front of them, through which they could see a spread of stars and a spray of water.

"Hold on!" Quicksilver cried, just before the river sucked them through the pipe and then spat them out into a quiet black lake. They plunged under the surface, and the cool, clear water swallowed all sound away.

Quicksilver saw Fox's faint glow in the darkness—and the blue glow of the cat skull still clasped between his paws—and followed him up, kicking as hard as she could.

Fox! I can't breathe!

Keep swimming, master, came Fox's steady voice. *We're almost there.*

When they at last reached land and dragged themselves up onto the shore, Quicksilver's body was weak as a newborn. She coughed up lake water and whispered Anastazia's name.

"Here," replied her older self, faintly. Trembling, they collapsed into the mud, still holding hands. Fox the pup circled around them, licking warmth back into their skin while the cat skull watched calmly.

"Did they follow us?" Quicksilver squinted back at the lake, lit by the twin moons. The water seemed undisturbed, but she could just see a mob of bony hands reaching out of the sewer pipe, grabbing greedily at the air.

"I'm not sure they can," Fox mused. "Whoever spelled that cave did a fine job of it."

"Almost *too* fine a job of it," Quicksilver muttered, shivering.

She longed fiercely for a hot bath. She wouldn't be able to shake the memory of those cold, bony fingers grabbing her legs any time soon.

A low sound from Fox caught her attention. His ears drooping, he held up Quicksilver's sodden pack from where she had dropped it in the mud.

The pouch containing the bones was safely closed, its contents intact—but the other pouch was empty, its strings hanging loose.

Quicksilver swayed, dizzy with despair.

Their food, what little remained of their money—and, most horribly, the stolen medicines for Sly Boots's parents—had all been lost to the catacombs.

.30.

A STAR-BRIGHT THREE SECONDS

"What are you looking at?" Quicksilver snapped at every scandalized expression tossed their way. "Don't you have anything better to do? Careful, or I'll wipe myself clean on your fancy dress!"

She stomped through the courtyards of King Kallin's castle, which glowed in the moonlight—incandescent lilies, manicured walking paths lined with glowing blue and green moss, gauzy banners tied between shimmering white trees hung with tiny silver bells.

Getting past the soldiers guarding the castle grounds had been easy, with Quicksilver and Fox working together to distract them and slip back into the party. They hadn't even needed to use magic. But that did nothing to cheer her up. She was cold, she was tired, and she was not looking forward to telling Sly Boots the news.

By the time they found him, chatting gaily away in a circle of laughing young people—witch and human alike—the mud coating Quicksilver and Anastazia had hardened into a shell of grime.

His eyes widened when he saw her. He jumped to his feet and hurried to her, leaving his new friends looking curious and confused.

"Quicksilver, what happened? Are you all right?" And then, before Quicksilver had a chance to berate him as she so longed to do—for talking to these beautiful people with normal noses, for leaving them to face those horrible skeletons all alone—Sly Boots yanked Quicksilver into an enormous, crushing hug.

Immediately Quicksilver's eyes filled with unexpected tears. She allowed herself three seconds to stand there and be held, which was not a thing she had enjoyed much in her life. Then, just before she was ready to shove him away . . . he did it for her.

He stepped back, pushing her away slightly, and wrinkled his nose. "You smell terrible."

Quicksilver stared at him, fuming. "Well, so would you, if you'd bothered to come with us!"

"I'm sorry," he said, scratching his temple. There was a red mark on his skin; he must have been scratching that spot over and over. "I got . . . I was busy. I didn't realize . . . so you're not hurt, then?"

Quicksilver brushed off her sleeves, as if that would do any good at all. "No, I'm not, but—"

"And Anastazia, you're all right?"

"As all right as all right can be," Anastazia murmured absently, picking a clump of mud off her shoe and tossing it in her mouth.

A gawking lady nearby, her hair pulled into bunches of aquamarine netting, fainted dead away at the sight.

"Er . . . what's wrong with Anastazia?" asked Sly Boots.

"Nothing," said Quicksilver. "Well, something, but I don't know what. Listen—"

"Did you find the skeleton?"

"Oh, we found skeletons, all right," remarked Fox.

Sly Boots straightened. A smile tugged at his mouth. "*Multiple* skeletons?"

"The bad kind, unfortunately. Aren't you sad to have missed out on all the fun?"

"Listen," Quicksilver snapped, so fiercely that even Fox

looked startled. Flushing, she opened her pack so Sly Boots could see what was missing. "I'm sorry," she told him, "but everything's gone. Our food, our money. The medicine for your parents. I thought you should know."

Sly Boots's expression froze, and then fell, and then turned flat and hard. A strange light flickered through his eyes, and was gone.

"I didn't mean to lose it all," said Quicksilver. "We went into the catacombs, and at first everything was fine, but then all the dead people came to life. We tried to get out, but everything was spelled to keep them in. The skeletons, I mean. There were steps that exploded into fire, everything was shaking—"

A shriek pierced the air. The crowd turned to see King Kallin, who had just come around the corner surrounded by his advisers. He stared in abject horror at Quicksilver.

"You there!" He pointed a trembling finger at Quicksilver. "Did you say . . . did you say something about skeletons?" He took one unsteady step toward her. "So it's true, then? They're . . . *alive?*"

Queen Voina stalked forward. "Oh, help us all, I'll never get him to sleep now. Mud girl! Come here at once! Tatjana, is this a friend of yours?"

A giggling Princess Tatjana came forward with a group of her ladies-in-waiting, all of them clothed in shimmering gowns of pearl and peach and cornflower blue. The princess squinted and then recoiled. "I've never seen that girl before in my life. If it *is* a girl, that is. I can't quite tell!"

The ladies-in-waiting burst into peals of laughter. Quicksilver stood seething, her muddy hands clenched into fists.

Fox sighed. *I guess the party's over, then?*

Hide us, Quicksilver thought to him, and an instant later, Fox cloaked them in a vaporous veil, and they ran.

Behind them, the crowd shouted in dismay, and King Kallin dissolved into hysterics. Quicksilver glanced at Sly Boots's hard, quiet face and wished, for a terrible, aching moment, that they could go back to that star-bright three seconds in which the only thing she knew was how it felt to be hugged by a friend.

Quicksilver plopped herself down on a log and flipped furiously through Anastazia's journal.

The spot they had found to make camp for the night was a good three miles from King Kallin's castle, in a copse of trees that stood between downy hills. From their camp, the castle and the lines of lights stretching across the surrounding bridges looked like child's toys.

Sly Boots immediately set to work tending to Anastazia's and

Quicksilver's wounds as best he could, but his movements were rough and hurried. He soaked a ripped section of Quicksilver's skirt in the creek nearby and used it to clean the rawest patches of skin. Each time the cloth scraped too hard, Quicksilver gritted her teeth but said nothing. Sly Boots ground up moxbane flowers with a rock and sprinkled the pieces of petals onto the cuts on Quicksilver's right arm, then ripped the sash from his vest and used that as a makeshift bandage. He tied it far too tightly, and Quicksilver yanked her arm away.

"Thanks very much, but I'm fine," she ground out.

His eyes narrowed; he said nothing.

Quicksilver looked away, back to the journal in her hands. "I don't know how I'm supposed to understand any of this. Her handwriting looks like some chipmunk popped out of a tree and decided to give it a go."

"Give that here." Sly Boots snatched the journal out of her hands so roughly that a page sliced her palm.

Quicksilver watched him, a sudden coldness gripping her insides. "What's wrong with you?"

"What's wrong with me? What's wrong with *her*?"

Anastazia lay in the grass, pulling radiant chartreuse flowers off a low-hanging branch. "I am," she said dreamily with each plucked petal, "I am not. I am. I am not." She paused, considering, and stared at Quicksilver. "Are *you*?"

Quicksilver ignored her. "If you're angry, you should just say it."

"Oh, are you telling me what to do again?" asked Sly Boots. "What a surprise."

"I'm telling you to stop being a dung head and talk straightforward-like!"

Sly Boots threw the journal into the weeds. "Fine. I'll talk *straightforward-like*. How could you lose that medicine, Quicksilver? *How?*"

Quicksilver retrieved the journal and shook flowers loose from its pages. Clumps of pollen left glowing pink smears behind. "I told you, it was an accident! And don't you dare throw around Anastazia's journal like it's some piece of trash. Don't you know what this is?"

"It's a book full of a silly old woman's mad ramblings."

Anastazia nodded to herself. "Well, that's rather the truth."

"Now, Anastazia, listen to my voice," said Fox reasonably, dusting flowers from her hair. "You're fine, aren't you? You've just had a hard few days, but you'll be good as new after some more rest, eh?"

"She's not a silly old woman," Quicksilver shouted.

Sly Boots started pacing, his hands in fists. "You used to call her that yourself!"

"Sometimes I say things I don't mean!"

"Like how you promised you would learn time-traveling magic and get my parents medicine and get me back home as soon as you could? Like when you said *that*? Did you not mean *that* either?"

"Look, I'm doing the best I can. You know we have to find the skeletons first. It's important, Boots. You saw what happened with the Wolf King. You saw how dangerous he is!"

"Ah! *Ah*. So you're saying your witch friends are more important than me and my parents?"

"I'm saying that if I can stop the Wolf King—and I can, I know I can—then I must. And I have to concentrate on that before anything else! Think about it, Boots—there are thousands of witches in trouble, compared to your two parents. Besides, I don't know why you're so upset. We'll just go get some more medicine! I've stolen before, and I'll steal again."

"But before we do that, we need to move on," said Fox. "If we go back into town, someone might recognize us as the—if you'll pardon me—mud-covered mad people from the party. There could be questions."

"We'll find another apothecary down the road, Boots," Quicksilver said. "I promise. I've always promised to help you. That hasn't changed."

Sly Boots laughed harshly. "So you say. It's good to know what you think is important and what isn't. Bones first, everything else second. You've made that very clear. I like how your precious skeletons made it through the catacombs safe and sound. But you couldn't take a second to make sure my parents' medicine was safe too?"

"We were running for our lives! I told you, I'm trying my best!"

"Well, that's obviously not good enough."

Quicksilver stepped back as if she'd been slapped. "*You* were the one who went wandering off into that party like a besotted fool, leaving *us* to fight an army of skeletons by ourselves!"

Sly Boots, looking taller and more solid than he ever had before, marched up to Quicksilver. The shadows moving across his face drew strange shapes, and his eyes sparked like fire. "Well, maybe I wanted to spend time with some nice, normal people for once! People who are kind and pretty and actually *like* me. Is that so horrible?"

Quicksilver stopped in her tracks, her arms going stiff at her sides.

Fox turned slowly, growling.

Sly Boots paled. The strange light in his eyes faded, and he seemed himself again—long arms and long legs and soft, candle-colored hair. A boy dressed up in fancy clothes that didn't fit quite right.

"Quicksilver," he said softly, "I didn't mean that."

"Yes, you did. You meant every word. I told you to speak your mind, and you did, and I thank you for that. Now I know how you really feel, and there's no more confusion." Quicksilver returned to the log, opened the journal, and sat facing away from them all. "Now, if you don't mind, I'd like to keep looking for a way to help my friend."

Quicksilver heard Sly Boots take a few steps toward her and stop. She waited, breathing carefully, as he moved about the clearing, and when she turned around at last, she found that he was gone.

Oh, Fox, Quicksilver thought, hating the sound of her own pitiful voice.

Fox said nothing and instead lay on her feet, for her thin dancing boots were wet and worn through, and her toes were icy cold. She read the journal until she could no longer see the words, hoping she might find a spell that could cut away the hurting pieces of her heart, and replace them with pieces made out of stone.

Sly Boots returned in the quiet night hours when the moons were bright as coins, but Quicksilver could not be bothered with him.

"I've found something," she whispered to Anastazia, settling beside her in a patch of clover that shifted in color from pale peach to deep violet at her touch. "Sit up, won't you?"

Anastazia, her hands folded across her stomach, did not move from where she lay in the clover. Her tattered ball gown seemed more ridiculous and ill fitting now than ever. Quicksilver removed Anastazia's cloak from her pack. It had folded down, most marvelously, into a square the size of her fingernail, which was a spell Anastazia had promised to teach her someday—if, that is, she could still *remember* it. Quicksilver unfolded the cloak and arranged it over Anastazia's body, tucking it close about her.

Anastazia raised a questioning eyebrow.

"That dress simply isn't your color," Quicksilver said.

"I see."

"As I was saying, I think I've found something in here." Quicksilver held up the journal. "Look at this—"

"I've failed you."

Quicksilver frowned. "What do you mean?"

"I thought this would be it. That *this* would be the time we would beat him. You and me, after all the other yous and mes. And yet . . . I can feel it happening, Quicksilver. I can feel my mind slipping away from me like books piled too high on a shelf. Teetering, swaying, falling . . ."

Anastazia closed her eyes, her mouth twisting. "I should never have let us tag along with that . . . that *boy* and his delusional followers."

"Olli?"

"Yes, *Olli*." Anastazia batted her eyelashes.

Quicksilver heard Sly Boots shift in the grass behind them and wished he would go stomp off and sulk some more. The night was too quiet; she did not want him to hear.

"If we had gone our own way, we might have been able to avoid the . . ." Anastazia's mouth pursed.

"The Wolf King?" Quicksilver suggested.

"It was too soon for you to meet him! You know hardly anything at all. I haven't had time to teach you."

"You've taught me quite a lot."

"Pah! Not nearly enough. We will need so much more to defeat him."

Quicksilver bristled. "I *did* use mind magic, you know. That's not impressive?"

"You didn't know what you were doing! It was an accident, Quicksilver, and if you were to try it again, it might hurt you, or worse. You could have died, all because I didn't prepare you properly. And if you die, then I'm all alone. And even if I manage to survive long enough to find another you, in the future, I've no Fox to send you back in time. . . ." Anastazia rubbed her temples. In the moonlight, her skin was pure white, her wrinkles canyons carved into clay. "I'll fail you. I'll fail all of us."

"Nonsense. *You* are *me*, and *I* don't fail at anything. I'm the best thief in all the Star Lands, don't you remember?" The words felt strange on Quicksilver's tongue. She used to utter them with pride, and now they felt pale and small in the face of everything else. "And someday I'll be the best witch. I mean, we've already got two skeletons, haven't we? What's five more? That's nothing for you and me, is it, Fox?"

"Easy as finding sticks in a forest," said Fox promptly.

"See there?"

Anastazia smiled up at Quicksilver. She pressed Quicksilver's hand between her own. "I remember that young heart, how it felt to know my own strength, no matter what anyone said."

Anastazia cupped Quicksilver's cheek. "I didn't think I would like meeting you, you know. I thought you would be endlessly frustrating. I remember myself, after all. But now . . ."

The soft, gooey look in Anastazia's eyes made Quicksilver squirm. "Yes, I'm sure we're all very much in love with ourselves. Now, look at this."

Quicksilver held open the journal to a page that included a list of scratched-out words and sketches of symbols—half-moons, ocean waves, a crossroads.

"Runes?" Anastazia asked, puzzled. "You're not that advanced yet, my dear."

"No. *This*." Quicksilver pointed to two words circled some fifty-odd times with black ink: COLLECTIVE MAGIC.

Anastazia's face became a web of hard lines. "That's nothing," she said, and she tore the page out of the journal before Quicksilver could stop her. "A foolish idea from one of our past selves, who was obviously too naive to know better. Never trust a witch. Didn't I tell you? We can only trust ourselves." She ripped the page into scraps and then turned away, hugging herself. "Don't make me," she said, in a soft, girlish voice. "I don't want to go there."

Quicksilver settled down in the clover beside Anastazia, wrapping her arms about her and squeezing tight.

She would not forget this idea of collective magic, no matter what Anastazia said about it. She had read the page so many times that she knew the words written on it by heart:

ONE CAN BE STRONG.

A FEW CAN BE STRONGER.

MANY WILL BE MIGHTY.

.31.

Backward and Upside Down

Quicksilver was well and truly sick of trees.

I like them, said Fox, trotting to the nearest one and lifting his leg to prove his point.

Quicksilver rolled her eyes. *Is it still steady?*

Is what still steady?

Is what still—? Fox. Are you trying *to irritate me? The skeleton we're tracking. That. Is that still steady?*

Yes, and getting stronger.

And you still think it's the mouse?

I know you can feel it, too. Why are you asking me this again?

It's just that—

It's a mouse. I know it, you know it.

Yes, but—

All tiny and whiskery and perpetually frantic.

Quicksilver snapped off a sprig of moss and tossed it to the ground. *Mice aren't the only tiny, whiskery animals in the world. Maybe we've got this all wrong—*

Fox, nosing through the undergrowth for sticks, snorted indignantly. *We sorted through the Wolf King's stolen memories, didn't we?*

Yes—

We stayed up all night listening to them and working it out together, didn't we? We agreed they smelled and felt and sounded like a mouse?

Yes, Fox, but—

Then stop doubting us. Fox trotted ahead, proudly holding a new stick. *Have some faith.*

In what? Quicksilver glared ahead at Sly Boots, who was walking much faster than the rest of them, his shoulders hunched and tense. He dragged his own stick across the moss-covered tree trunks, leaving behind a ragged, angry path in the bark. *The Wolf King's evil. Magic is good, after all, and so are witches . . . mostly.*

Anastazia's going nutty on us. The sisters and the girls and Sly Boots's parents back home might die if we don't save them. Not to mention all the witches might die. We might die. Sly Boots is mad at us. And my parents—

She shook her head and kicked a thick, curling root, which did nothing but hurt her big toe. *Everything's backward and upside down. What am I supposed to have faith in?*

In me. Fox dropped his stick and licked her palm. *And in yourself. Mostly in me.* He stretched, grinning a cocky dog's grin.

Quicksilver rolled her eyes and marched on.

Days ago, they had left King Kallin's Skullwood far behind, and then entered a darker forest called the Blackwood, and then an even darker one called the Nightwood, and now they were near the border of Falstone, where there was nothing but forests for long, lonely miles. And not even pleasant forests full of soft green paths and picturesque clearings. No, these forests were dense and tangled, the trees thick and towering, the clammy air as still as deep sleep.

There wasn't even a proper path. They had to climb over colossal fallen trees and pick their way through bramble patches. Fat green beetles with shimmering orange wings plopped out of the trees with alarming frequency. Round, summer-gold eyes

glowed from the shadows. The quiet air trapped every smell—
the musk of animal fur, the sour turn of damp rot, the heady
sweetness of the tiny moss flowers. When Quicksilver passed a
clump of them, with Fox at her side and the skeletons in her
pack, the flowers sighed happily, their dim glow turning brilliant.

"Tasty, don't you think?" said Anastazia, poking her head
through a sheet of hanging moss to smile at Quicksilver. It
looked like Anastazia suddenly had a head of flowery green hair
instead of her normal hair, and her lips shone bright pink with
pollen, but Quicksilver couldn't find the will to laugh.

"I wouldn't eat the flowers, Anastazia," said Quicksilver.
"Might spoil your appetite."

Anastazia nodded gravely. "Indeed. Good thinking. I'll try
the moss instead." And then, promptly, she did, and belched.

Quicksilver guided Anastazia away from the trees and
continued north, trying to ignore the hard knots of worry in her
stomach. Anastazia spoke less every day—or at least, what she
did say hardly made sense. And things with Sly Boots felt sticky
and cracked. She glanced at him, saw the back of his pale head
for an instant, and then blazed so hot with anger that she had
to look away.

He had not apologized for what he'd said, and Quicksilver

was not going to bring it up. As far as she was concerned, he did not yet—and would perhaps not ever deserve her forgiveness. Maybe it was better this way, the two of them walking in angry silence forever.

But there were no villages out here, not even a lonely woodsman's cottage. Quicksilver could not imagine that they would stumble upon any apothecaries or curiosity shops in such a forest. So, that night, when she and Sly Boots and Anastazia sat silently on a wide, flat stump, sharing yet another handful of wild berries, Quicksilver's anger turned to a sick, twisting guilt.

She should have been more careful, that night in the catacombs. She had been so concerned with keeping the skeletons safe that she hadn't even thought to check the other pouch. How long would it take them to find medicine like that again? And what if Quicksilver never even got the chance to learn time-traveling magic from Anastazia because her older self was now too dotty to teach her?

And what if Sly Boots's parents died, alone and ill in the future, and it was all because of her?

Parents, she thought, should stay far away from her. They just ended up lost.

As soon as she thought that, Fox growled. *You know that*

what happened to his parents is no fault of yours. You are doing the best you can, and you were right, what you said the other night: when you look at things straight on, a thousand witches are more important than two humans. You are thinking of the greater good.

The greater good? Really, Fox? Witches who don't trust me, and who I'm not supposed to trust either? Why bother saving people who want nothing to do with one another?

Because it's the right thing to do. Fox bounded after a butterfly whose long wings changed color with every flutter—from emerald green to dazzling turquoise to mustard yellow.

Quicksilver watched him, envious. Fox was the only one who seemed happy about anything anymore. She curled up in a patch of soft, shimmering blue-and-indigo grass while Anastazia sang a gibberish song at the base of a thick, knotted tree. Her blistered feet throbbed in her ruined dancing shoes.

I'm glad you're happy, Fox, she thought as exhaustion crept up on her. I'm glad somebody is.

Fox abandoned the butterfly to snuggle against her chest, and did not complain when she squeezed him too tightly.

Everything will be better soon, master. We're all just tired and sick of eating forest food. Anastazia will be herself again once we find a town and get some sugar cakes and sunlight. You'll see. Don't worry.

Quicksilver peeked through the hair that had fallen over her eyes to watch Sly Boots sleeping restlessly near a stand of crooked trees. The distant light of the half-moons illuminated his tense face.

Would everything be all right? She could not say. She had found nothing useful in the journal to help Anastazia—at least, nothing legible. All she could keep thinking about were those three lines:

ONE CAN BE STRONG.

A FEW CAN BE STRONGER.

MANY WILL BE MIGHTY.

Each time she recited these words, they made her angrier.

Only *many* can be might? Pah!

I am mighty, she told herself. *Me. Alone. I do not need Sly Boots. I do not need Anastazia. I need no one but myself.*

And me, Fox mumbled sleepily.

Quicksilver kissed his snout and recited the words over and over until she fell asleep:

I am mighty.

I need no one.

.32.

THE LADY IN WHITE

Quicksilver awoke to a pale dawn and the sound of a woman singing.

She sat straight up and listened. Except for Anastazia, she was alone. Fox was gone. Sly Boots was gone.

"What is that?" she whispered.

Hush. Fox was creeping away through the trees, his body tense. *I think we're close.*

To the skeleton?

Close to . . . something.

Quicksilver settled Anastazia on a fallen tree and shoved the journal into her hands. "On one of these pages," she said, "I've written a tiny secret message for you. It's very hard to find, but you must sit here quietly and look for it until I get back. Do you understand?"

Anastazia immediately bent over the journal, her eyes darting back and forth across the pages.

Quicksilver threw on her pack and followed Fox, tearing through vines sticky with sap and brambles lined with vicious bloodred thorns. Across a brook, down a muddy slope, through a tangle of the shimmery hanging moss—and finally, breathlessly, out into open air.

She blinked in the sudden light. She stood at the edge of a vast clearing surrounded by black trees that twisted into a layered canopy overhead. At the far side of the clearing stood a tree as fat as a castle tower, its roots spilling across the grass like a mass of dark snakes.

It seemed to Quicksilver in that moment that everything in the Star Lands radiated from this tree, and was held up by its branches. Vines with leaves as large as houses hung from the tree in glossy curtains. The billowing mounds of grass at its roots were deep green in the shade and a vivid pink where the sunlight hit.

Sitting on one of the great tree's roots, in a pool of green forest light, was a pale Lady all in white. A filmy white dress clung to her slender frame. Her hair fell down her back in cascades of pearl and moonslight and cloud. She sat unmoving, one hand up as if in greeting.

Quicksilver cried out and ran toward the Lady, her eyes hot with sudden tears. She had to touch her, tell her how much she loved her, tell her how long she had been waiting, desperate, to meet her—but Fox bit her tattered hem and tugged hard.

Wait, he whined. *Something isn't right here.*

Quicksilver struggled to break free. "Let me go! I must see her!"

The Lady's mouth curved into a gentle smile, and though her lips did not move, Quicksilver knew it was her voice singing, filling the clearing with silver bell tones. She could not understand the words, but they nonetheless overwhelmed her with longing, making it nearly impossible to breathe.

Then she saw Sly Boots emerging from between two of the tree's massive roots, crawling toward the Lady. His face was open and soft, his smile unfamiliar because it had been so long since he had looked anything but angry.

He reached for the Lady's hand, and she leaned closer, her flowing hair brushing against him.

"Let go of me, Fox!" Quicksilver screamed, kicking and clawing. She thought him into the shape of the butterfly he had been chasing the previous day and ran for it, clambering over the tree roots toward the Lady. Sly Boots couldn't be allowed to touch the Lady before she did, he just *couldn't*—

A sudden, sharp pain stabbed Quicksilver in the back. She cried out and tripped, fell between the roots, and caught a handhold in the bark at the last second. The snowy hare and cat skeletons, hissing and yowling, nipped up and down her spine through the pack.

"Oh, be quiet!" she spat at them. Then she gritted her teeth and pulled herself back up onto the root—just in time to see Fox bounding across the roots toward Sly Boots and the Lady, barking madly. The fur of his ruff stood up in angry bristles.

Now, so close, her head cleared, Quicksilver understood the Lady's song:

"The Lady in White guards the gate
Starved for love and full of hate.
Come closer, kiss our loyal ward.
Put down your bow, put down your sword.

The Lady in White was once our foe,
Hair like silk and lips like snow.
But now her heart is bound to bough.
Only you can save her now."

Quicksilver! Fox cried. *Don't listen to her. She's not what she*
appears to be!

Slowly Quicksilver made her way across the giant tree's roots
toward the Lady. Sly Boots had snuggled into the Lady's embrace,
and she held him on her lap, stroking his hair. Her own long
hair wrapped about his body in wispy tendrils. As Quicksilver
approached, the Lady's cheeks hollowed and her eyes darkened. A
patch of scarlet bloomed on her chest, and the silky coils of her hair
became fat and scaly—a wriggling mass of white, eyeless snakes.

"The Lady in White was once our foe . . .
Only you can save her now."

"I *will* save you," Sly Boots mumbled dreamily, kissing the
Lady's gnarled, blistered hand. "Don't worry, my darling."

The Lady looked at Quicksilver. Her cracked, bloody lips
twitched with a small smile.

Lightning-fast fear shot through Quicksilver. She raced toward them, leaping from root to root. She plunged her hands into the Lady's writhing hair and yanked hard on the snakes holding Sly Boots close to the Lady's bleeding chest. But the fat, icy-cold coils slipped from Quicksilver's fingers. A snake slithered around her arm and sunk its fangs into the crook of her elbow. Red flashed before her eyes; a hot pain flew up her arm. She stumbled away, dizzy and seeing stars.

We'll come back for him. Fox's warm weight pressed against her, keeping her upright. *I can feel the mouse skeleton, can't you? It's close! We have to find it before it's too late!*

Quicksilver concentrated, her mind fuzzy. Yes, she felt the tug of the skeleton, somewhere very near. The other monster skeletons were shrieking and clawing the inside of her pack; she feared they would soon tear it apart.

But she could not leave Sly Boots. She was furious at him, he had been terrible to her, and by all rights she should leave him there to rot in the Lady's arms. Everything inside her screamed at her to run—except for her traitorous heart, which kept her rooted to the spot.

She wished, for a hopeless, frustrated moment, that she had never met any of these people, that she had run away from

Anastazia the moment she saw her. No Anastazia, no Boots, no Olli or coven or Wolf King. Just her and Fox, forever, and no guilt or obligations or *feelings* to weigh her down.

"Boots!" she cried, tugging on his arm. "Boots, come with me! Come *on*, you stupid boy!"

The snakes wound around Sly Boots from head to toe, wrapping him into a cocoon of slithering white. His freckled face was turning blue. His breaths wheezed.

Her head spinning, Quicksilver collapsed at the Lady's feet, trying desperately to free Sly Boots's legs. Snakes struck at her, biting her hands. Starbursts of pain danced beneath her skin. The enormous tree root beneath her suddenly seemed like a fantastic place to lie down for a nap. She watched, dazed, as snakes struck Fox's paws and snout.

"Boots, get up," she said, fighting for breath. "*Please* get up! I'm sorry, all right? I'm sorry." She squeezed her eyes shut, pounding weakly on the snakes wrapped around his ankles. "I don't want to leave you."

"Do you seek the bones?" said a high, rasping voice.

Quicksilver blinked up at the Lady, who glowed in the green forest light.

"What bones?" she asked carefully.

The Lady grinned, her smile rotten and black. "I see right through you. I see what you seek."

"Then why ask me?"

"A mouse," the Lady murmured. "First a hare, then a cat." She licked her lips. "Now a mouse. I see right through you. You think you're the first?"

The skeletons in Quicksilver's pack shrieked, jerking toward the Lady. Fox, panting, crawled to Quicksilver's side.

Master, I don't like this—

Quicksilver ignored him, forced her bloody, tingling hands into fists. "Are you going to help me or kill me?" she asked the Lady. "Or just sit here asking pointless questions?"

The Lady inclined her head. "Perhaps the mouse came to me and asked to stay awhile. Perhaps I agreed, for I was lonely. Perhaps."

Quicksilver rose unsteadily to her feet. "Where is it?"

"Do you love him?"

"Do I—" Quicksilver followed the Lady's black gaze. "Who, *Boots?* Absolutely not!"

May not be the right answer, master, Fox suggested.

"Er . . . yes. Yes." Quicksilver patted Sly Boots's leg. "I love him *ever* so much. We are . . . betrothed. Secretly. He is . . . a runaway prince, and I am a mere kitchen girl—"

Fox winced. *A little too far.*

"Yes, all right, fine. I love him," snapped Quicksilver.

"I can see that," murmured the Lady. "I knew when I first saw you." The snakes slithered aside so the Lady could kiss Sly Boots's forehead. "I also loved, once. Long ago. Perhaps I could love again."

Fox whined, his ears flat. *What in the name of all the stars—*

Quicksilver tried not to panic at the sight of Sly Boots's blue face and closed eyes. "Do you . . . want Sly Boots?"

The Lady laughed. Her breath smelled like layers of damp leaves rotting on a forest floor. "I want to go with you. With him."

Quicksilver shifted nervously. "I'm not sure that's—"

Suddenly, a dozen long, fat snakes shot out from the Lady and coiled around Quicksilver and Fox.

Fox!

"Find my heart," whispered the Lady. "Free it. Take it with you, and give it to the boy, so he may guard it for the rest of his life. And you shall have your love, and your bones."

Then the Lady released them, and they fell between the tree's roots into blackness.

.33.

BOUND TO BOUGH

Fox hovered above her, a tiny golden wren, flitting back and forth.

"Good, you're awake," he said. "On your feet. We need to find a way out of here."

Woozy, Quicksilver sat up. Her arms and hands still stung from snakebites, but Sly Boots depended on her. She couldn't sit and cry about it. She shook her head to right her tilting vision.

"Are you all right?" she asked Fox.

"As all right as you are. Don't worry about me."

"Where are we?"

"Under the Lady's tree."

Quicksilver looked up at the web of twisting black roots overhead. Long strands of silver moss hung from them. Through spaces between the roots, she could just see the green world above.

But here, below, was a world of darkness and shadows. The tree's tremendous roots formed knotted walls and arched passageways—a web of long and narrow tree caves. Water trickled past her in shimmering streams. Phosphorescent slugs and bats clung to the underside of the roots. Gigantic sunset-colored flowers bloomed in thick clusters, their petals gaping open like mouths and lined with tiny quivering lights.

"Well . . . this is new," said Quicksilver, hugging herself. The air sat thick and damp against her skin.

Do you hear that, master? It's that song again.

Quicksilver listened. The song about the Lady in White was much clearer than it had been above. Quicksilver felt tears return to her eyes and impatiently swiped them away.

Shall we follow it, Fox?

It seems like a terrible idea, but I can't think of a better one at the moment.

Find my heart. That's what the Lady said. Then she'll give us the bones—and Boots.

Do you think she was telling the truth?

Even if she was lying, we have to try. I'm not leaving Boots, and if I don't get that skeleton, these *two will tear me to pieces.*

Fox put his front paw on her leg. *I'll wear it and give you a rest.*

Are you sure? You're hurt, too.

Fox licked her hand. *Let me help.*

Quicksilver arranged the hissing pack on Fox's back, tying the straps around his belly. Snakebites, raw and red, dotted his coat. A hot lump formed in her throat.

Fox—

And don't you think it hurts me to see you bleeding, too? Fox bumped her arm with his cold nose. *Let's get through this and back to our friends. We'll heal later.*

Quicksilver planted a kiss between his ears.

"Settle down back there," Fox called to the skeletons. "How about we all sing for a while?"

Fox started singing the Lady's song, too. The sound of his chipper voice made everything seem a bit less sinister as they set out past knots of mossy roots and columns of stone, following the song. They learned quickly to avoid the sunset-colored flowers, each of which unfurled a second set of petals at their approach—these lined with tiny black teeth.

"But this goes on forever!" Quicksilver cried, after pushing her way through a stubborn cluster of thick vines the width of her arm. The world below the tree seemed to stretch in every direction, as far as they could see.

Fox stopped singing. *Wait a moment. What is that?*

Quicksilver turned and saw, in a glade lit with a wash of green sunlight, a creature she had never seen before. But she knew at once what it was. The Scrolls said they had lived in the Star Lands long before humans or witches, and that brief mention had been enough to captivate all of the girls at the convent, even Quicksilver.

"A unicorn," she breathed.

The Lady had been lovely, but the unicorn was so glorious the sight of it made Quicksilver's dizziness fade. Its eyes were large and dark, its tail a banner of ethereal cloud. The thin, spiraled horn on its forehead gave off soft silver light.

There was another—no, *three* of them. They circled a tiny white tree, its net of delicate branches like fine lace. A dim beam of sunlight shone down through the tangled roots overhead, turning the tree and the unicorns a luminous white.

Quicksilver felt she ought not to stare at the unicorns but couldn't help herself. They tossed their heads and let out soft whuffs like sleepy laughter. She felt their hoofbeats on the mossy ground like the pulse of her own heart.

Boom.

Boom.

Boom.

But that wasn't *her* heart.

Quicksilver's head shot up. *Fox, the Lady's heart. It's in that white tree! The* heart *is the thing that's singing! Listen!*

Fox pointed at the tree, sniffing. *Do you think we can just . . . ask them to let us pass?*

Quicksilver approached the unicorns, keeping her gaze lowered. She had never been the bashful sort, and yet she could not stand up straight before these creatures. The weight of their beauty sat heavy upon her. She felt low and small, easily squashed.

"Pardon me," she mumbled, "but could we . . . that is, my friend and I . . . could we please, if it isn't too much trouble . . . pass by you?"

The unicorns froze and turned to stare at her. Their horns glinted in the sunlight.

Quicksilver's mouth went dry.

Say something nice! Fox suggested.

"You are . . ." Quicksilver swallowed. "You are more beautiful than . . . than sunsets, than dreams, than . . . *anything.* Thank you."

Thank you? Fox stamped his paw. *For* what? *They haven't let us by yet!*

Quicksilver stepped forward hesitantly. "It will only take a few moments, I promise you. Then we'll leave you in peace."

One of the unicorns flicked its tail abruptly.

Quicksilver took another step. Two.

As one, the unicorns bolted toward her—and once out of the sunlight, they . . . *changed.*

Their bright white coats darkened to coats of shadow black and rot brown and bruise green. Their elegant bones turned sharp and jutting, their muscles bulging and monstrous. Clumps of moss and weeds for manes, ropy black vines for tails. They let out horrible, shrieking cries that revealed long, gleaming fangs.

They lowered their heads and charged at Quicksilver, three gleaming obsidian horns aimed at her heart.

She swerved, ducked, and rolled, narrowly avoiding their stomping black hooves.

To me! Quicksilver thought, and with Fox at her side, they ran for the tree.

But the three unicorns were not alone. Others tore out of

the shadows, screaming like wildcats. Still others crawled out of the roots, like the tree itself was creating them, spitting out one after another after another.

Quicksilver whirled around, trying to count all of them. They were a swarm, and their horns shone like black swords.

Spare them not, she thought to Fox, flinging him toward the unicorns like an arrow from a bow. A bolt of pure, blazing gold energy, he zipped between them, leaving charred streaks on their coats. One, wounded, stumbled into the sunlight and collapsed, pure white once more save for the vicious wound on its heaving side.

Quicksilver paused, her heart seized by a sudden fierce pity. "So beautiful," she whispered, stepping toward it.

No, master! Go!

At Fox's voice, Quicksilver turned and ran. At the white tree, she skidded to a halt and placed her hand against the trunk. Its bark pulsed, warm and smooth to the touch—like skin. She leaned closer, put her ear against it.

Boom.

Boom.

Boom.

The heart was in the tree—but how to get it?

Behind her, a unicorn snarled and Fox let out a whimpering cry.

Fox?

I'm fine!

Quicksilver hurried around the tree, looking for a way into the smooth, hard bark—and then she saw it. A tiny knothole surrounded by scarred red wood, too small for even a squirrel to get through.

Fox, to me!

He flew to her, a streak of fiery golden light, and became a dog once more. She ripped the pack from his back.

Can you fit inside?

We'll see, won't we?

Fox shifted into his tiny mouse form, squeezed through the knothole, and disappeared.

Quicksilver turned to face the unicorns. Twelve of them— no, *twenty*—circled the tree.

Think, Quicksilver, she thought not to Fox, but to herself. *Pretend you're back at the convent. Sister Marketta found the beehive you left in the dining hall. She's sent everyone after you, and you have to get to the roof before they lock you up for good.*

She pictured Anastazia, alone in the woods—confused and

possibly, by now, afraid. She thought of Sly Boots, still and blue in the Lady's clutches.

She clenched her fists.

I am mighty.

I need no one.

I've got it! came Fox's jubilant cry from inside the tree. *It's . . . wait, that can't be right.*

Quicksilver thought him to her—*To me!*—and he appeared in her palms, quivering. He had wrapped himself around a crimson jewel that hung from a heavy gold chain with a long, wicked clasp. His yellow fur was soaked red with blood.

"But now her heart is bound to bough," sang the jewel, in a forlorn woman's voice. *"Only you can save her now."*

Quicksilver held Fox close, nearly gagging on the scent of blood. *Dear Fox. Just hold on to me. I can handle this.*

She ran—dodging the unicorns, sliding under their slashing hooves and horns, crying out when their fangs grazed her but not stopping, never stopping, never, *never.* The sunset flowers' forked tongues lashed about her ankles; the unicorns' cries pierced her aching skull.

Anastazia. Sly Boots.

Anastazia. Sly Boots.

Run. Run. Run.

Then she saw, dangling just ahead, a single white snake. Though it had no eyes, she knew it was looking at her.

"May I?" she shouted.

The snake seemed to nod, once. Quicksilver grabbed it with her free hand, which was slippery with the jewel's blood. The snake coiled about her and drew her up, and when the unicorns nipped at her feet, Quicksilver almost lost her grip—but then she was above the roots, and there was the Lady.

Quicksilver fell to her knees. Breathless, she offered up the jewel—except now it was not a jewel, but a pulsing, fleshy heart.

The Lady snatched it, and Quicksilver fell back. She gently shifted Fox into a dog and cradled him against her chest.

Fox?

Here. He hid his face in her hair. *I'm here.*

The Lady pulled aside her dress to reveal a gaping maw in her chest, surrounded by bloody puncture marks. With a faint, fluttering laugh, she shoved her heart back into place.

The singing stopped. The Lady closed her eyes and breathed deep. She sighed, and tears rolled down her cheeks before disappearing in tiny ashen puffs. When she opened her eyes, they were empty sockets. One by one, the snakes shriveled up into tufts of brittle hair.

Sly Boots slid out of the Lady's lap, and Quicksilver caught him before he could stumble and fall between the roots. As she watched, the Lady's body jerked left, then right. Her chest collapsed, her back snapped. With one last shuddering breath, she whispered, "Give my heart to your love, witch girl."

Then the Lady was gone. All she left behind were a tattered white dress, a red jewel on a chain—and a set of impossibly tiny bones that glowed gray like a storm-lit sky. Quicksilver watched in astonishment as the snakebites on her arms and hands disappeared. She checked Fox, and found his bites had vanished, too.

The skeletons in Quicksilver's pack gave twin cries of excitement.

Sly Boots shook his head and blinked awake. "What happened?" He saw the Lady's abandoned dress and recoiled. "Where'd she go? Where are we?"

The roots beneath them creaked and quaked. An angry, distant cry sounded from the world below.

Fox nudged her. *We should go!*

Quicksilver scooped up the glowing mouse bones and poured them carefully into the proper pouch in her pack.

Then she shoved the heart jewel at Sly Boots. She could not look at him; she *would not* look at him. It was unbearable to see him standing there, alive and healthy, when only moments ago he had been cold and blue on the Lady's lap.

"That's for you to keep, by the way," she snapped. "The Lady said. I think she liked you, though I can't imagine why. Don't let anything happen to it, or I'll pound your face in. Now come on, before the unicorns eat us."

Sly Boots stared at her, slipping the heart jewel's chain around his neck. *"Unicorns?"*

But Quicksilver had already turned away to climb down the mountain of roots. Tears stung her eyes, and she did not understand them.

He is not *my love, Fox. That Lady didn't know anything. Witches and thieves do not love. Not boys. Not older selves. Not even monsters, Fox. Not anyone.*

I know. I expect you're just tired, to feel this way.

"That's right, I'm tired," muttered Quicksilver, and she ignored Sly Boots completely as the unicorns' furious screams chased them back into the friendlier part of the forest.

.34.

FLAMES FOR EYES

Anastazia was furious and pacing.

"Where have you been?" she yelled. She stalked across the little clearing where they'd made camp the night before and crushed Quicksilver into a ferocious hug. Then she pulled away, saw the dried blood on Quicksilver's hands, and scowled. She inspected Sly Boots, who still had a dazed look about him, and her scowl became more terrible. She resumed pacing.

"I found myself sitting here with my journal. . . ." Anastazia gestured, the journal's pages flapping. "Completely alone, no note, no *anything*. Hours pass by. Day turns to night. And then, *finally*, you show up—with *blood* all over you?" Anastazia put her hands on her hips. "What do you have to say for yourself, Quicksilver?"

Quicksilver was so relieved to see Anastazia back to normal, clear-eyed and clearheaded, that she simply grinned and held up her pack.

"We found the third skeleton," she announced.

Anastazia stared at the battered bag. "You did?"

"Yes, and it's a mouse," said Fox proudly, bumping his nose against Quicksilver's leg. "Just as we thought."

A slow, crooked grin spread across Anastazia's face. "How? Where?"

"Well," said Quicksilver with a sigh. "It's . . . complicated."

Then she told Anastazia everything. About the Lady, and the unicorns, and the tiny white tree. As she spoke, she kept glancing over at Sly Boots, wondering if he would add to the story—but he didn't. He toyed with the long, sharp clasp of the Lady's heart jewel and gazed out into the forest.

She waited for him to thank her for saving him. She waited for him to tell her that he had heard what the Lady had said, and wasn't it funny, the idea that he could be Quicksilver's love? They would make faces and joke about it, and perhaps then they would slap hands and forget about the last several days.

But this did not happen.

So Quicksilver ignored him.

"You entered unicorn country," Anastazia said, "and you survived. I'm sorry, child."

"Sorry? Why?"

Anastazia shook her head, staring at the ground. When she looked up, her eyes were bright, her smile wobbly. "I'm so proud of you. Even though I'm a shabby, broken old woman, and you're having to take care of me . . . even so, you're still doing marvelously. Better than I ever did when I was a young Quicksilver, having to put up with my shabby old Anastazia."

Quicksilver grabbed Anastazia's outstretched hand, feeling a rush of tiredness that left her shaky and weak. Maybe, with Anastazia looking and talking so well, Quicksilver could lie down and let someone else do things for a change. She only wanted to rest for a while, clean the blood from her hands, let Fox worry about the monster skeletons chattering away in her pack. . . .

Sly Boots cleared his throat. "So, what will we do next?"

Quicksilver watched Sly Boots worry the Lady's jewel between his fingers. "We'll rest," she replied. "It's night, I've just fought a whole pack of bloodthirsty unicorns, and I'm tired."

"In the morning, you and Fox should sort through more of the Wolf King's memories," said Anastazia. "The more quickly we move, the better. The more skeletons we gather, the easier it will be to find the rest. The seven of them want to be together, you know. The First Ones were made out of the same ancient star, so the pieces of them are drawn to one another—"

"Yes, yes, yes." Quicksilver yawned. "We know all of that."

"I would like it," said Sly Boots evenly, "if we found a town where you could steal some more medicine for me."

Fox, who had curled up in a pile of moss, lifted his head. "Oh, indeed? That's what you would like, is it?"

Sly Boots, staring impassively at Quicksilver, ignored Fox. She tried to match her tone to the strange coolness of his face.

"We'll find a place eventually, Boots," she said. "And then of course we'll stop. Until then, what do you want me to do? Make a town out of thin air?"

Sly Boots's expression did not change, but it felt to Quicksilver that something dark had been drawn over his eyes.

Anastazia flung her journal onto the forest floor. "I'm hungry! I don't want to walk anymore, and you can't make me."

Quicksilver's heart flipped and fell.

Sly Boots smiled, a cold, slight thing that hardly moved his face. "No matter what you do next, I suggest you leave the old woman behind. She's a problem, and she's only getting worse. When she fades, she'll drag you down with her."

Fox jumped to his feet and growled.

Anger lashed against Quicksilver's ribs, swift and searing. How could he say such a thing? How could he hold himself so carelessly, and smile as though this was all some sort of pathetic joke?

"Or perhaps I should have left *you* behind!" she cried. "In the Rompus's lair, or at that princess's ridiculous birthday party, or back there"—she flung her arm behind them—"half dead in the Lady's arms!"

"Don't be a fool." Sly Boots sighed, clearly bored. "You wouldn't have done that."

Quicksilver thought of watching the stars with Sly Boots, and eating stolen cakes with him on the roof of the curiosity shop, and she felt such disgust at her past self that she could hardly see straight. "I should have! I'd be better off without you!"

"How dare you treat me this way, when all of this is your fault?" Sly Boots snapped. "You forced me to come here. You took me away from my home." Even though he hadn't moved, he seemed to suddenly loom closer. The strange light returned to his eyes. "You, witch, are made of poison, and so is your entire kind."

Fox darted between them, his lips curled back to reveal his teeth.

"I found it!" Anastazia cried, digging in the dirt. "The secret message you left for me!" She squinted at the ground. "Is it something about meat pie?"

Quicksilver thrust up her chin and marched toward Sly Boots. She would not let him see how thoroughly he was frightening her.

"If you hate me so much," she said, "then why don't you leave and go fend for yourself? Go on! I'd like to see you try it."

Sly Boots glared at her for a long moment. "I don't think so, witch. You owe me a debt, and I'm not leaving until you pay it."

Then he settled himself on the ground at the base of a hunched tree marked with bulbous growths, folded his hands in his lap, and stared at her.

Quicksilver lay down in the grass and scooted close to Anastazia, hiding her face in her older self's cloak. She did not trust herself to say anything more; her exhaustion was too complete, her throat tight and aching. Even with Fox standing guard, and Anastazia absently stroking her palm, it took Quicksilver a long time to fall asleep, and her dreams were full of boys with flames where their eyes should have been.

ⓔ ⓔ ⓔ

The next morning, Quicksilver awoke to find that Sly Boots had already gathered breakfast.

"Wake up, fellow travelers!" Sly Boots nudged Quicksilver's foot with his own. Morning sun peeked through the trees overhead, casting his face in shadow. "It's time to eat!"

"Pie?" mumbled Anastazia hopefully.

"Even better—figs! Roots! Blackberries!"

Anastazia rolled over. "More forest food," she grumbled.

Quicksilver sat up, instantly suspicious. "Why are you so happy this morning?"

"I thought about everything a lot while you slept. Couldn't sleep a wink! I kept thinking and thinking. The forest is so quiet at night. Lots of room for thoughts." As he spoke, Sly Boots paced through the surrounding trees, his gaze flitting around wildly.

Something's odd about him this morning, Quicksilver. Fox scratched his ear. *He sat there all night, not moving, hardly even blinking.*

Quicksilver munched on a handful of berries. *I don't care, as long as he stays like this. He almost looks like his old self again.*

Hmm. Fox ignored his own berries and put his snout on his paws, watching Sly Boots carefully.

After breakfast, Sly Boots urged them to their feet. "Come on, there's more where that came from!" He gazed north, his hands on his hips. "I figure we should stock up, gather as much as we can carry. That way we don't have to stop again for a long time! Searching for a market could take us far out of our way. We have to keep pressing on, right? Find all those bones?"

Quicksilver slipped on her pack, clucking her tongue at the fussing skeletons. "Well, yes, but we haven't figured out where to go yet—"

"Come on, slowpokes!" Sly Boots cried, hurrying off into the trees.

"Wait! Boots!" Quicksilver jumped to her feet. "Fox, go after him! He'll get lost!"

I say we let him wander around until he falls off a cliff.

Fox—

Fine, fine. Fox bounded away into the forest after Sly Boots.

Anastazia spat out a half-chewed date. "I hate this sort of pie. It tastes nothing like it should."

Quicksilver tugged Anastazia to her feet, an anxious feeling spiraling in her chest. She squinted into the trees, looking for Fox's yellow tail among the moss and shadows.

Suddenly, everything felt wrong. Too quiet, too still.

Something's wrong, Quicksilver.

What is it, Fox?

I'm not sure—

Quicksilver shoved Anastazia forward. "Come on, hurry—"

"Stop *bullying* me!" Anastazia shook her free, scowling.

Quicksilver grabbed hold of her again, pulling her on. "We don't have time to dawdle. Come on, pick up your feet!" She helped Anastazia climb over a fallen tree and called into the forest, "Fox? Boots? Where did you go?"

Sly Boots shouted back, but his voice was so faint she couldn't make out the words.

Then the dull, buzzing worry of Fox's thoughts became a sharp stab of fear. He jumped out of the undergrowth to slide in front of her.

Wait, Quicksilver, no—!

But it was too late. Quicksilver had already emerged into a small clearing, where the air was fresh and cool—and the Wolf King stood smiling, his hands behind his back. Two long, twisting shadows hovered over his shoulders like curls of smoke.

Beside the Wolf King was the white wolf. It had pinned Sly Boots to the ground, and it flashed Quicksilver a shining canine grin.

.35.

THE TRUE DANGER

"Give the skeletons to me, witch," said the Wolf King, seven deep and booming voices growling all at once, "and perhaps I'll let him go."

Time moved slowly. Quicksilver noticed everything in excruciating detail—the Wolf King's fine dark cloak, his high collar of chain and leather, his black hair, his gathered red sleeves tied with tasseled cords. The shadows beneath his eyes, and how they made him look not tired, but older and formidable.

The other six wolves emerged from the trees, surrounding them. Quicksilver's skin tingled with icy waves of fear.

Quicksilver, Fox thought urgently, *I can get us out of here. Let's go, now, while we still can.*

"I'm sorry, Quicksilver," Sly Boots choked out. "He told me he would get me home, he said he could heal my parents—"

With a savage growl, the white wolf snapped its jaws, only a hair away from Sly Boots's scrunched-up face.

Anastazia's hand tightened around Quicksilver's arm. "Stars help us . . ."

"Ah!" The Wolf King's haughty smile widened. "The old woman is herself again—but not for long, I'd wager. My curses have been eating her alive for years, but now she looks worse than ever." His cruel gaze flicked to Quicksilver. "You're obviously taking *wonderful* care of her."

The bile rose in Quicksilver's throat at the sound of his laughter. It was high, careless, like a child's.

"Run, Quicksilver, and don't look back," Anastazia commanded.

The skeletons in Quicksilver's pack shrieked. They slammed into Quicksilver's shoulders, straining toward the Wolf King.

Beside her, Fox shimmered into a growling dog double his normal size. *Say the word, Quicksilver, and I'll get you out of here.*

Anastazia gripped her shoulder, pushing her back toward the forest. "Go, child, *go!*"

But Sly Boots's eyes were wide with terror, and they held Quicksilver in place. She could think of nothing else but her fear for him, how close the white wolf's fangs were to his throat.

She tore off her thrashing pack and flung it at the Wolf King.

Anastazia and Fox cried, "No!"

"Now let him go!" Quicksilver demanded, immediately understanding how foolish she had been, how rash. She clenched her fists.

The Wolf King laughed. "Oh, yes? Or what? You didn't think that through very well, did you?" He picked up the pack, and the two shadows hovering over his shoulders swooped down and circled around him. They appeared almost human shaped now, long and stretched out. They caressed the pack with thin, smoky fingers.

Suddenly the Wolf King's stolen memories lit up like the sun in Quicksilver's mind, and she and Fox understood what they were seeing at the same horrible moment:

Those two shadows were First Ones—not returned fully to their human forms, not yet. But someday, when all seven monster skeletons had been reunited, they would be.

*Those shadows were with him when he attacked the coven,
Quicksilver.*

Quicksilver felt sick. *He already had two of the monster
skeletons that day. And now, thanks to me . . .*

He has five.

The shadows already looked more solid, more alive. Dark
eyes and sharp cheekbones unfurled across their faces. Their
smiling mouths filled with teeth. They cradled the pack of
monsters between them like a newborn.

"Brothers," one crooned.

"Sister," cooed the other.

The pack seemed to shudder, and so did the Wolf King. His
body jerked and shook, and his mouth opened wide, too wide,
his jaw cracking. Three new shadows, wispy and pale, unfurled
from the Wolf King's mouth. Five shadows, pale and dark, now
swirled around the Wolf King. They screeched and jeered, their
cries thunderous.

Five skeletons. Fox growled, his body shaking with anger.
And five First Ones.

The clearing turned still and cold. Quicksilver could
hardly breathe for her fear.

"What have you done?" rasped Anastazia. She shook Quicksilver. "What have you *done?*"

"Oh, give it up, old woman," the Wolf King drawled, his face pale and slightly green, his chest heaving. What did it feel like, Quicksilver wondered, to have long-dead spirits crawl out of your mouth?

"You've lost," said the Wolf King. "It was only a matter of time." Then he snapped his fingers, and the white wolf released Sly Boots.

And Sly Boots scurried to the Wolf King on his hands and knees, and knelt, his head bowed.

The Wolf King smiled at him. "Thank you, boy. Your loyalty will be rewarded."

"You traitor," Anastazia spat. "You weak, unforgivable boy!"

Anastazia lunged, throwing herself toward the Wolf King with nothing but her two frail hands as weapons.

The Wolf King flicked his wrist. The white wolf flew toward Anastazia, an arc of blazing flame, and slammed her into the ground. It raked its claws across her chest, sending up sprays of blood.

Quicksilver screamed. *Fox, can you get us out of here?*

At once! Fox bolted toward Anastazia, a streak of gold, and

Quicksilver raced alongside him, pumping her legs as fast as she could. She threw herself over Anastazia's bloodied body like a shield and held on tight. As Fox wrapped around them in a swirl of light, Quicksilver glanced one last time at Sly Boots, hoping, hoping . . .

But his smile was an echo of the Wolf King's, smug and sleek. Whatever had happened to him, he was now surely lost.

And so were they.

All this time, Anastazia had been warning Quicksilver about the danger of trusting other witches, and the true danger had been right in front of them.

The wolves attacked, raging and fiery. Quicksilver shut her eyes against them. She meant to concentrate on her connection with Fox, and help him disappear them away to safety—but all she could focus on was the heavy, sinking feeling of betrayal. Sly Boots had *betrayed* them. They had lost the skeletons. Now the Wolf King had five. Anastazia was hurt. Everything—all of it—had been for nothing.

The best thief in all the Star Lands? Pah.

I am the most complete fool in all the Star Lands, Quicksilver thought. Her limbs turned to stone. Her heart became a block of ice. She couldn't move, and she didn't want to. It was nice, feeling so heavy and cold. She pictured herself sinking to the bottom of a black, icy lake. She would lie there, frozen and alone, for all eternity, staring up through the frigid water at the cruel world above. She would be safe there. It would be quiet and still, beneath the water, where no one could ever hurt her. . . .

Master! Fox cried. *Stop! Something's wrong!*

Of course it was. Everything was wrong. *She* was wrong.

They passed through a cold veil—not cold like winter, but cold like nothingness. On the other side of the veil, a harsh wind was blowing. Fox released them, and Quicksilver fell onto gray, rocky ground.

"Well," said Fox, "now you've done it."

When Quicksilver looked up, she saw a sky, a forest, and distant mountains—and all of them were made of shadows.

.36.

THE SHADOW FIELDS

"What is this place?" Quicksilver whispered. The thick gray haze surrounding them swallowed her voice, leaving her wondering if she had said the words at all, or if she *was* at all.

She sent an experimental thought to Fox, and he immediately obeyed, shifting with a weak pulse of yellow light into his mouse form.

How could you do that? He climbed up to her collar, his tiny nose twitching furiously. *You gave the skeletons to the Wolf King, and for what? In exchange for that traitor's life? And it didn't even work!*

So she *was* still alive, and so was he. She looked around,

scanning the gray world for Anastazia—but she was nowhere to be found.

I'm sorry, Fox. She needed to look for Anastazia, but she was so *tired.* She rubbed her eyes. They felt full of grit, like she'd been asleep for a long time. *I wasn't thinking.*

That's right, you weren't thinking. And you did . . . something while I was trying to get us out of there. I don't know what it was, but I felt how sad you were, and how angry, and scared, and all of a sudden I couldn't think straight, I couldn't focus, and now . . . Fox climbed up through her hair to perch on top of her head. *Where have you brought us, master? If you've killed us, I swear to the stars, I will—*

Quicksilver plucked him from her head and brought him right in front of her nose. "What? You'll do what?"

Fox narrowed his beady mouse eyes and said nothing.

"That's right. You won't do anything, because you're only the monster, and *I'm* the witch, and you do as I say!"

"*Only* the monster?"

"Yes, *only!*" The louder Quicksilver shouted, the harder it felt to breathe, as though invisible fingers had wrapped around her throat, choking her. Her eyes filled with tears—from exhaustion, from the effort of talking, from the heaviness crushing her chest.

Sly Boots. How *could* he have done this to them?

"We should never have let that boy tag along with us in the first place," grumbled Fox. "Just because you thought he was nice to look at—"

"Oh. *Oh.* Is that what I thought?" Quicksilver barely resisted the impulse to shake him. "I let him tag along because I felt sorry for him!"

Fox scoffed. "You wanted to show off." He cleared his throat and assumed a high-pitched voice. "'Oh, I'm Quicksilver! I'm a big bad thief! Watch me steal things, pathetic little boy! You're so adorable it makes me stupid and careless! You're so dreamy it makes me give away really important magical skeletons for no good reason at all!'"

"Even if he were as handsome as a prince—even if I *cared* about handsomeness and princes—I'd still hate him right now, I'd hate him more than anything—"

Quicksilver stopped, gasping for air. She dropped to her knees, and Fox took his dog form.

Quicksilver? he thought, in his normal voice. *What is it?*

It's so hard to breathe. Don't you feel it? Quicksilver placed her hand on her chest. Her heartbeat was a stampede. *It's like trying to get out from under something heavy.*

"The Shadow Fields," Anastazia said faintly. "They . . . are not for the living. Oh, child. Why? Why have you . . . brought us here?"

Fox dashed through the mist to Anastazia, who lay nearby, half-hidden in a shifting pool of blackness. Quicksilver followed, slowly, part of her hoping that if she turned now, and ran away, what she saw before her would disappear. . . .

Anastazia's chest rose and fell rapidly. Bright red ribbons of blood on her arms, neck, and chest marked where the white wolf had attacked her.

"I'm sorry, Anastazia," Quicksilver whispered, holding her hand. "We're sorry for fighting, we didn't forget about you, we were just—"

Anastazia shook her head. "The Shadow Fields . . . they do that. They sit heavy . . . upon the souls . . . of the living."

The blackness in which Anastazia lay gathered and pulled apart and gathered again around her body. Dark, shivering tendrils caressed her face and snaked around her wrists.

Quicksilver slapped them away. "Get away from her! What are these things?"

"The Shadow Fields . . ." Anastazia's eyes fluttered shut.

Fox hurried around Anastazia, pawing at the tendrils, trying to yank them away.

"Anastazia?" Quicksilver shook her. "Don't fall asleep, all

right? Let's get up and go on. We'll find the nearest town and ask someone to help us."

When Anastazia opened her eyes again, they were dim and cloudy. "The Shadow Fields," she said, her voice a thin thread of sound, "are where . . . the shadows of witches and monsters go . . . after they . . ."

The smoky tendrils returned, greater in number this time, and no matter how much Quicksilver slapped and kicked at them, they kept growing, and swarming, until it was difficult to see Anastazia at all.

"Anastazia!" Quicksilver clawed at the cloud of blackness enveloping her older self, watching as her dull red hair faded to white, and the blood on her skin caked and turned gray. "Stop it! Leave her alone!"

"It's all right, child," whispered Anastazia, touching Quicksilver's arm. "You will be fine. Just think of . . ."

Quicksilver stared in horror. Anastazia's arm was dull as a gray sky, and just as vaporous. When she touched it, her fingers slipped right through.

"Anastazia? What's happening?"

But there was no longer anyone there to answer her—only slowly shifting darkness. Quicksilver clawed through it, searching for something warm and solid to grab on to. Perhaps they were in some sort of bog, and Anastazia had slipped beneath soggy ground. Quicksilver would find her, and drag her out. They would laugh about this later, telling stories to everyone they met about that silly moment when Quicksilver thought Anastazia had died and left her all alone to navigate a strange, sunless world.

"Oh, yes! I had nearly forgotten about that. Wasn't it the funniest thing?" Anastazia would say. "You were so frightened, my child." And then she would kiss Quicksilver on the cheek, and Quicksilver would pretend she hated being kissed, but in fact she would not at all, and then they would move on to the next town without a care in the world, for of course by that time, they would have destroyed the Wolf King, and the Star Lands would be safe and beautiful, and they would roam the kingdoms forever as the greatest pair of witches to ever live. . . .

For a long time, Quicksilver simply sat there and stared at where Anastazia had once been. Her shabby cloak and gown lay in the dirt, the old leather journal atop them.

Fox nudged her arm with his snout. "Quicksilver . . ."

"I don't understand. Where did she go?"

"I think it's best if we—"

Quicksilver whirled to face him. "Where did she *go*, Fox?"

Fox gazed up at her with sad brown eyes. "She's gone, Quicksilver. I'm sorry."

"I don't believe you."

"Believe me or not, I'm afraid it's the truth."

Turning on her heel, Quicksilver stormed away from him. She ignored the bizarre country around her—the clusters of thorny black flowers that bobbed in the unfriendly wind. The shadows that flitted from one dark tree to the next, watching her progress. The black mountains on the gray horizon.

Fox, Anastazia's cloak and journal between his teeth, trotted to catch up. "Where are you going?"

"I'm going to find her, Fox. Those—those shadow things, they obviously took her somewhere, and I'm going to find them, and when I do, I'll tear them apart so fast they won't even get the chance to beg me for mercy."

"A rather violent sentiment," Fox said dryly. "Will you use your fangs or your claws, when you do all this tearing?"

"Fox, this isn't funny!"

"No, it isn't." Fox cut in front of her and dropped the journal and cloak at her feet. "Put on this cloak, and put the journal in your pocket. You're shivering."

"I am not," protested Quicksilver, though now that Fox had said it, she realized her skin was covered in goose bumps. The wind here had teeth. Tiny shapes that reminded Quicksilver of snowflakes—though they were black and gray instead of white—gathered around her feet in drifts. Her shoes were soaked through.

"Please, master." Fox nudged the cloak toward her. "You won't do anyone any good if you freeze to death."

"I'm not cold," Quicksilver said, more quietly now. She picked up the cloak.

"I know," said Fox soothingly.

Quicksilver settled the cloak about her shoulders, fastened the clasp, and slipped the journal inside one of the cloak's many pockets. The fabric was heavy, lined with sheared wool, and though it had been ripped and mended many times over, it still warmed her. It smelled like Anastazia—like the chocolate-and-mint candies Olli had bought for her, and like her clean, cracked skin.

"I'm not cold," she whispered, sitting down, wrapping her arms about her legs, becoming a tiny ball of girl on the ground.

Fox scooted beneath the cloak to curl against her chest and tuck his face beneath her neck. As Quicksilver cried into his fur, he said nothing more aloud, and instead sent her the same thought, over and over, *I'm here, I'm here, I'm here.*

.37.

WORTHLESS, USELESS

Quicksilver did not sleep. She existed in a fuzzy state between sleep and waking.

It was gray there, as gray as the world around them, and quiet, and warm, and smelled of wool and Anastazia and Fox. She kept very still in this cocoon. Even flexing her feet or shifting her body sent pain flooding from her heart to her fingers and toes, and reminded her of where she was, and what had happened.

But when she lay still and quiet, all of that faded. *Everything* faded. She stared blankly at the grayness around her. Shapes shifted and gathered to watch her, peeking out from behind the dark trees before flitting away. Shapes moved through the sky like birds, and crawled along the gritty, rocky ground like rats, and still Quicksilver lay there, unmoving.

Who cared if a bunch of shadowy shapes were looking at her? If they wanted to eat her, they might as well do it. She was worthless, useless. She had failed Anastazia, and Fox, and Sly Boots, and all the witches. She had no parents, and she was alone.

You didn't fail Sly Boots, Quicksilver. He made his own choice. You cannot blame yourself for his betrayal. And your parents—

"Don't," she whispered.

She wasn't so sure Fox was right about Sly Boots not being her fault. He hadn't been himself recently—the look in his eyes and the way he talked, so sharp and strange. Where had his fear gone, his nervousness and clumsiness? Slowly all of that had disappeared, and he had become an angry, coldly smiling boy who had led them right into the Wolf King's trap.

It was like cruelty had slowly sunk inside him, changing him. Did that have something to do with the mind magic? Had some of it snapped off and hit him, like it had Anastazia? Made him vulnerable to the Wolf King just as it had turned Anastazia's mind mushy and confused?

Had Quicksilver ruined everything in that one frantic moment?

Of course she had. It was her destiny, to ruin things.

Maybe, she thought, gazing at the flat, gray sky, *if I fill up with stones, I really* will *never be able to get up. How nice that would be.*

Fox lifted his head, growling.

Maybe, Quicksilver thought, *if I fill up with stones, there will be no more room for anything else, and I won't be able to remember Anastazia anymore.*

A sob escaped her. She was not used to crying, and the more she tried to stop, the more she felt like her chest would squeeze itself into a hard, unbreakable knot. People died all the time; this she knew. But how did the people they left behind ever go on? How did anyone bear this feeling?

If you don't stop thinking like this, I'll bite you, just see if I don't, Fox thought angrily. *We don't have time to grieve, Quicksilver.*

A sharp pain pricked Quicksilver's side.

"Ow!" She rubbed her hip and glared at Fox. "What'd you do that for? Just leave me *be,* Fox."

"I didn't do anything, what do you—*ouch!*"

Fox darted from the cloak, licking his backside. Something

shadowy hung from his stomach—something shadowy in the shape of a squirrel.

Quicksilver smacked it away—but her hand went right through it, sending a jolt of coldness up her arm.

The squirrel jumped to the ground and hurried off into the trees.

"What was that?" Fox sniffed the air. "It *bit* me, but I don't smell anything. How does something not have a smell?"

Something slipped into Quicksilver's sleeve, skittered up her arm, and came to rest at her neck. She shrieked, clawing at her clothes. A tiny weasel plopped to the ground before hurrying away. Like the squirrel, the weasel was made entirely of shadow.

"I don't understand—" said Quicksilver, but then another pinch on her leg, on her back, on her thumb, alerted her to more shadow creatures. They scurried out from beneath shadow rocks and dropped down from shadow trees—voles and rats and hares, birds and beetles, lynxes and foxes. A shadow deer bounded out from the nearby shadow forest; a shadow hawk wheeled down from the sky.

They swarmed Quicksilver and Fox, nuzzling, biting, clawing, licking. They screeched and chittered and howled and yowled, but each sound was muffled, as if coming from a very far distance. Every time Quicksilver touched one of the creatures, plucking and shoving it away, her fingers met nothing but cold vapor. It was like trying to move pieces of the wind.

And yet they responded to her touch, hurrying off when she struck them, only to scuttle back an instant later, like they couldn't help themselves. An owl landed on Quicksilver's shoulder, shoving a shadow wren out of its way. A shadow bear lumbered out of the forest and scooped Fox into its arms, letting out a low roar of despair.

"Fox, what's happening?" Quicksilver cried, slapping away the shadow creatures swarming upon her. "What are they?"

Fox squeezed out of the bear's embrace and hurried back to her. A flock of shadow birds landed on him and pecked through his fur as if searching for bugs.

Quicksilver tried to stand and run, but there were simply too many of them now. She could hardly breathe; she could barely open her eyes. The coldness of the creatures weighed her down, flattened her. She reached for Fox but could not find him.

"Get away from them, you beasts!" roared a voice. "They're not for you!"

Instantly the shadow creatures disappeared. Quicksilver sat up, gasping. Fox slammed into her chest, and she threw her arms around him. He panted against her cheek, and she had never smelled anything sweeter than his familiar, musty dog breath.

A dark hand pulled Quicksilver to her feet. A numb feeling shot through her arm, and she looked up to see a figure made of shadows—not an animal, but a woman.

Her face was featureless, and yet it somehow carried the gentle impression of a smile. Beside her sat a whiskered, familiar-looking shadow dog.

Fox gasped, and Quicksilver staggered back. It could not be.

"Don't be afraid, child," said the woman. "It's only me. Or, I should say, it's only *you*."

Quicksilver recognized that voice now, and recognized the shape of this woman—the wild hair, the hunched back, the long shadowy cloak. The whiskered dog at her feet.

It was, impossibly, Anastazia—and the older Fox.

.38.

THE BRAVEST ME

"Who are you?" Quicksilver demanded. "What sort of trick is this?"

"No tricks." Anastazia held out her hands as if to prove it and then turned them over to examine them. "My, I look so strange now, don't I? But I suppose it's not really *me* anymore." Then she stroked the old Fox's ears with one shadowy hand. He leaned into her with a little sigh.

"I've missed you terribly, master," he said.

Anastazia leaned down and kissed him between his ears. "And I you, old friend."

Quicksilver's Fox backed away. *Quicksilver?*

For what felt like the hundredth time in a short span of days, Quicksilver felt herself near tears. Even though she knew it was childish, she stamped her foot in frustration. "I don't understand any of this."

Anastazia approached with her arms outstretched. "I know. I can see how it would be very confusing, from your perspective—"

Quicksilver flinched, and Anastazia lowered her arms.

"Please don't be afraid," she said. "Let me try to explain."

"I'm not afraid," insisted Quicksilver.

"You're Anastazia's shadow," said Fox, facing his older self with a keen look on his face. "And this is your Fox's shadow."

The woman nodded. "Right on both counts."

"But that's impossible," said Quicksilver.

"Not so. This is where the shadows of witches and monsters go after they die—the Shadow Fields, a land just beyond the world of the living."

Fox touched noses with the older Fox and then sneezed, sending tiny curls of shadow flying.

Quicksilver stared at the ground, her arms folded tightly across her middle. "And what if I don't believe you?"

"You do believe me," said Anastazia crisply. "You just don't want to. Those creatures attacking you . . . please don't think too unkindly of them. They are the shadows of monsters who have died, and they simply want a living witch to belong to again. The urge to survive is a powerful thing, as you well know."

Quicksilver glared up at her. If this shadow woman was trying to befriend her, she would have a difficult time of it. Quicksilver was a girl of ice and stone. She lived in a gray cocoon, where everything was soft and safe, and she had no heart left to give anyone, least of all an echo of a person she had once known, a person she had once—

Quicksilver swallowed hard against the tight ache in her throat.

Anastazia sighed, her form shifting. "There are still so many things about the witch world that you don't know. Things I was supposed to teach you, and never got the chance to." She lowered her head. "I'm sorry for that, child. I never wanted to leave you so soon."

Not ever in her entire life had Quicksilver felt more alone than she did at that moment. The loneliness built up inside her like a cresting wave, ready to break.

"And just how many things will I have to teach myself?" she snapped. "How will I defeat the Wolf King on my own?"

Anastazia knelt, grayness and blackness softly swirling about her like a cloud of dust. "Quicksilver—"

"Wait, I know the answer—I *can't* defeat him on my own!" She turned away, threw her hands into the air. "I haven't even learned how to use Fox to cast spells beyond shifting and glamours, or how to guide Fox to read runes, and I certainly have no idea how to teach myself time-traveling magic, or how to extend my life when the time comes so I can grow old and grumpy like you, and find my younger self. . . ."

She fell silent. The thoughts running through her head were too terrible and hopeless to say out loud.

Anastazia said gently, "I know you're afraid—"

"I'm not," Quicksilver said again, but a cold finger lifted her chin so she was forced to meet Anastazia's eyeless face.

"You are, and that's all right. It's good to be afraid, for when we are forced to feel that fear—the shape and taste of it, how it sits in our hearts—and must continue living even so, we discover how brave we truly are. And Quicksilver, my darling girl, you are the bravest me I've ever known."

Quicksilver's eyes spilled over. She didn't even try to brush away her tears this time. "Can't someone else do it?"

"Do what?"

"Find the First Monsters' skeletons. Defeat the Wolf King. Someone older, someone who knows more than I do."

Quicksilver thought of Sly Boots, of his parents rotting away back at home. She thought of the Wolf King, and how five shadows now hovered around him instead of only two. She hung her head and whispered, "I can't do anything right. The only thing I've ever been good at is stealing things, and playing tricks, and that's . . . silly."

The shadow of Anastazia was quiet for a long time. Then she said, "Someone else *could* defeat the Wolf King, perhaps. No one has, in all the lifetimes I've experienced. No one's even tried. You know this. We talked about it before."

"But maybe you're wrong!" Quicksilver cried. "Maybe the reason why no one's tried is because we've been doing it for them. Maybe because of us they've been able to run away and hide like a bunch of stinking cowards—"

"Maybe," said Anastazia firmly. "We can travel through time, but we can't understand it. Who knows what may or may not happen sometime in the future, if we do or don't do a particular thing? There are a thousand possibilities, a thousand different futures. But we can't worry about that, Quicksilver. We can only worry about now, about what *we* can do. About what we *should* do. Because we are not people to sit idly by and let others determine our fates, are we?"

Quicksilver bit down on her tongue and stared at the ground.

Anastazia cupped Quicksilver's face in her hands. A chill ran through Quicksilver, head to knees to feet.

"*Are* we?" Anastazia urged.

"No," Quicksilver said, low. "We're not."

"*We* determine the fate of our world. Say it."

"We determine the fate of our world," Quicksilver mumbled.

"That's not good enough."

"We determine the fate of our world," Quicksilver repeated, a little more loudly.

"Louder!" Anastazia bellowed, stretching to her full height.

"We determine the fate of our world!" Quicksilver shouted, her face streaked with tears and her fists clenched at her sides. Even though it made her body shudder with cold, she moved into Anastazia's embrace and buried her face in arms that were not really there. A frigid sensation brushed against her scalp—Anastazia's fingers, stroking softly. Fox leaned against Quicksilver's leg and whined. The older Fox pressed his cold, shadowy nose against Quicksilver's other leg, with a comforting *whuff*.

"Sometimes," Anastazia said, "it isn't about being the most powerful person or the person who has the most knowledge. It isn't about being the oldest person, or the strongest person, or the person who makes all the right decisions. Sometimes it's about being the person who decides to stand up and fight."

Anastazia took a step back and wiped Quicksilver's cheeks. The gesture was completely ineffective and did nothing but make Quicksilver's teeth chatter, but she leaned into the touch anyway.

"And that's me?" she whispered.

"I have never been one to let something scare me away from what's important," Anastazia answered. "And neither have you. I love you, Quicksilver. I believe in your strength. My greatest hope is that someday you will learn to do the same."

Never in Quicksilver's life had anyone said those words to her. She had heard about love, and seen it in the way some of the sisters at the convent had treated the other girls—but she had long ago decided such things were simply not meant for her, and so there was no reason to fret about it. Fretting would only distract her from becoming the best thief in the Star Lands.

But now the words had been said, and her hungry heart grabbed hold of them. She felt a warm thrill at the realization that she, Quicksilver, parentless and squash nosed—could receive love . . . and that she could, possibly, give it in return?

I love you. She formed the words in her mind first, and then on her tongue. They felt uncomfortable there, clumsy and too big for her. But she was not one to run away from things that frightened her.

"I love you," she told Anastazia, in a mumbled rush. A rush of warmth flooded through her, somehow leaving her feeling both lighter and more frightened. "I love you. I really do."

At the same time, both Foxes barked and wagged their tails—and then looked at each other suspiciously.

"I know how hard that was for you," Anastazia told Quicksilver, the sound of a smile buried in her strange, muffled voice. "And so I thank you. Shadows, I think, do not get many such gifts."

Quicksilver tried and failed to tighten her fingers around Anastazia's drifting black cloak. "Do you have to stay here? You could come with me, you know. I wouldn't mind having two shadows. We could spook people, play tricks on them!"

Anastazia laughed softly. "Your world is no longer my world. I'm afraid I will have to stay here. But . . ." She looked at the older Fox, and a ripple of excitement seemed to pass between them.

"I've found something for you that might make leaving easier," said the older Fox, his tail wagging even harder now. "Wait here. I promise we'll be back." Then he and Anastazia drifted off into the darkness.

Quicksilver waited, trying to hide her disappointment, hoping the new holes in her heart did not show on her face.

She thought her Fox into his mouse form and held him close, stroking his silken ears.

Fox?

Yes, Quicksilver?

I . . .

She stopped. She had thought she could say the words twice, but . . .

Fox nuzzled her palm. *It's all right. I know.*

When Anastazia and the older Fox reappeared, their dark forms peeling away from a nearby tree, Anastazia's hands were behind her back. "We shadows have two tricks that make existence bearable," she said. "One is that we can travel great distances across our realm in a very short time. Shadows, you see, are all made of the same stuff, no matter what they are shadows *of.* And the second is that we are drawn, inexorably, to things that find their way into the Fields from the world of the living— whether they come here by accident or because they're looking for a place to hide. For things from the living world create their own light, and shadows have none of our own left to enjoy."

And with that, Anastazia held out her hands, in which rested a tiny handful of slender bones, glowing faintly, warmly red—the skeleton of a starling.

.39.

SHARP EDGES AND BRIGHT SKIES

As Quicksilver gazed at the bones, she felt a pulse of recognition deep in her chest. The memories they had stolen from the Wolf King came back to her in dim echoes of light and sound:

A blood-splattered young boy.

The same young boy chasing a deer through a forest.

A figure in hooded white robes, a brilliant red starling perched on its shoulder.

"It's one of them," she whispered. "One of the First Monsters!"

A tiny ray of light worked its way through her stormy thoughts. She reached out for the bones. At her touch, they rattled and hissed.

A ghostly beak manifested out of thin air and pecked her hand.

Quicksilver grinned.

"So," said Anastazia's shadow, "you have one skeleton now, instead of none, and can return to your world with something good in your pocket."

"How did it get here?"

The older Fox stretched and yawned. "It probably thought it would be safe in the Shadow Fields, that no one would ever find it. Perhaps it comes and goes, and we were lucky enough to be here at the right time."

Anastazia put a cool hand beneath Quicksilver's chin. "However it came to be here, I hope, child, that you'll never find yourself here again."

Quicksilver opened her cloak to reveal its inner pockets, and Anastazia carefully poured the bones into the largest one.

"You'll want to get a proper pack for those soon," she suggested.

Trying not to think of what had happened to her *last* pack, Quicksilver nodded. "Of course."

"And don't forget to keep them interested and happy, or they'll disappear on you."

"Oh, don't worry about that," said Quicksilver's Fox. "I'm quite the bone nanny at this point."

The older Fox made a delicate scoffing sound. *"Bone nanny?"* Quicksilver's Fox haughtily turned up his nose.

"Does this mean we have to leave you now?" asked Quicksilver.

"You don't *have* to do anything of the sort," Anastazia said, "unless you'd prefer to stay here and waste away, with no food or water, while a horde of shadow monsters slowly pick away at what's left of your light."

At the mention of water, Quicksilver realized how parched her throat was, how difficult it was to swallow. She tried not to think about leaving Anastazia forever and stood as straight and tall as she could.

"How do we leave, then?" she asked.

"Well, I could send you out right where you came in," the shadow of Anastazia replied. "Or I could send you out somewhere more advantageous. Somewhere, perhaps, closer to another skeleton."

"The Wolf King has five," said Fox, "and we have one. There should just be one left."

"And do you know where it might be hidden?" asked the older Fox.

Quicksilver shook her head. "We haven't tried to find it yet. Fox? Shall we?"

Quicksilver sat on the ground, settling Fox on her lap. It was easier, she had found, to sort through the Wolf King's memories with Fox in his true form.

For how long they sat there, speaking to each other along the connection between their hearts, Quicksilver was not certain. Without sunlight to mark the passage of time, it could have been minutes or hours. When she finally opened her eyes, she felt like she had been swimming for miles. She heard the ghostly echo of tiny clawed paws against stone, felt the soft press of pure white fur.

"The last skeleton is the ermine," she said, her voice faint with exhaustion. She remembered looking up at the White Bear and its blue eye, how Sly Boots had drawn the bear's shape across the stars for her. "We must go north to find it, to Valteya."

"The winter kingdom," murmured the older Fox.

"You must be careful there, child," said Anastazia. "They say that land has been haunted, ever since Ari Tarkalia murdered his family, and I don't disagree. Winter can sow malice into even the kindest hearts. And Valteya borders the Far North—"

"And the Far North is where the Wolf King's castle is, yes, I know," Quicksilver snapped, to cover her nervousness. "Can you tell us where to go or not?"

Anastazia seemed pleased. "You are starting to sound more like yourself."

"Someone's got to be the grump, now that you're not around to do it."

"Am I doomed to be the only pleasant person left on this trip?" asked Fox.

Quicksilver scratched behind his ears. "It's a great burden, but I appreciate your sacrifice, Fox."

"Hold on to each other," Anastazia instructed, wrapping them in her arms, "and try not to move too much. Walking by shadow is the quickest way north, but it might feel a bit . . . jarring."

Quicksilver obeyed, grabbing Fox just before Anastazia and the older Fox yanked them into a cloud of darkness. Quicksilver caught glimpses of shapes as they moved—trees and black rivers, hills and shadow creatures. They hopped from patch of darkness to patch of darkness. Each time they burst into light and then back into shadow, a heavy, cold feeling sucked at Quicksilver's skin, like she was being squeezed into a too-small space.

When they at last stopped moving, they were still in the Shadow Fields, but no longer in a forest. Two black snow-capped peaks towered ahead of them, one on each side of a twisting mountain pass that climbed gently upward until it disappeared. Black snow fell from the sky in gusting flurries.

Anastazia's shadow lowered Quicksilver and Fox to the ground. "Sorry about the rough passage but you must understand you're not *meant* to shadow walk. For us it feels like nothing, like gliding through air."

Quicksilver held her spinning, aching head. "It wasn't too bad."

Fox swayed in place, his legs splayed like a newborn colt's. "Speak for yourself."

The older Fox snorted, but not unkindly. "Amateur," he said, and then licked the young Fox's cheek.

Anastazia knelt between Quicksilver and Fox, and pointed at the range of mountains to the north. "To leave the Fields, you must think about things shadows do not have—hope, and light, and joy. You must imagine yourself weightless, flying out of the heaviness of the Fields and into the brighter world beyond."

Quicksilver clutched the cold nothingness of Anastazia's arm. "I don't want either of you to live here like that."

"We don't have a choice." Anastazia's voice held a gentle smile. "We are the shadows of a witch and a monster who no longer live, so we are bound to this place. But you are not. And besides, we'll have each other, Fox and I."

Quicksilver took a deep breath and closed her eyes. "Will it hurt me, to leave?"

"It always hurts a little, to leave the darkness, for in shadows lies a certain safety."

A soft, gray cocoon of shadows. Quicksilver imagined herself staying in such a place for the rest of her life, not feeling anything, not seeing or even moving. The thought of that place—where no one could hurt her, where she would be safe from her own mistakes—had brought her here in the first place.

To leave, then, she must think of something else . . . of feeling everything, even the things that hurt. She must think of sharp edges and bright skies, warmth and summer and living a life even with thorns of grief in your chest—the grief of never knowing one's parents, of making terrible mistakes that hurt others, of losing, forever, the people you love.

She had bones in her pocket and Fox at her side. Somewhere out there lay one last skeleton, and somehow they would find it. What came after that, she could not say, but no matter what, Anastazia had loved her, and Quicksilver had loved her back, and she would carry that feeling inside her, forever.

Quicksilver's arms and legs tingled with a floating warmth, like she was swaying on the blissful edge of sleep. The cold heaviness in her chest felt lighter; the hot, hard lump in her throat melted away.

She weighed nothing at all. If she pushed off the ground, she would drift up into the air and fly.

So she did.

She kept her eyes closed, kicked her legs and pushed her arms through something that felt like thick black water. The harder she kicked, the higher she rose. The water warmed and lightened. Beyond her closed eyelids shone a brighter and brighter sun. Heat soaked through her skin right down to her bones.

"Travel safely," called the older Fox, "and swiftly!"

"Good-bye," whispered Anastazia. She sounded so far away that Quicksilver felt a jolt of shock and turned to find her—but the Shadow Fields were no longer there. Instead, Quicksilver saw the slope of a snowy mountain passage, and tall, shivering stands of green fir trees, and a vast spread of forest, far below her, stretching to the southern horizon. The setting sun painted the snow-capped mountains in vivid shades of pink, violet, and orange, bright as fire. The north wind stung her nose. She could breathe again, her mind clear of shadows.

And she was alone.

Fox? She whipped around, searching for him.

Coming. Don't worry. After a long moment, he tunneled out of the shadow of a nearby fir tree, like gold fur being squeezed out of a tube, and pranced through the snow to her side.

"Where were you? What were you doing?"

Fox shook himself from snout to tail. "Nothing important. She wanted to talk to me for a moment, told me to watch out for you and make sure you take care of yourself."

She rubbed his silky ears, then stepped back to look more closely at him. "Fox, what is it?"

"Hmm?" He was avoiding her gaze.

"You look frightened."

"Nonsense." He thrust his snout into the snow and ate a large chunk of it. "I'll just miss her, is all." He turned to face north, his nose dusted with white—and still, he wouldn't look at her. "Well?"

"Well," Quicksilver agreed, and together they started climbing—though Quicksilver kept glancing Fox's way, trying to determine what had shaken him so badly. But every time she searched his thoughts for the answer, she ran into a dead end, as if someone had planted a door where a hallway had once been.

She realized, with a slight twist of unease, that maybe Fox was lying . . . that maybe Anastazia had told him something he didn't want her to know.

.40.

THE WINTER KINGDOM

At the top of the mountain passage sat a small village winding between rocky outcroppings. Snow covered the sagging rooftops and drifted along fences that surrounded empty animal pens. Most windows were dark, but a few, in the largest building at the center of the village, glowed warm and yellow.

Quicksilver headed that way, holding her hood tight around her face. From the nearby trees, a crow cawed three times. A crooked sign marked the village as Vorhaven.

"What a dismal place," Fox remarked.

Hush. Quicksilver thought him into his mouse form and

slipped him into an empty pocket in her cloak. *Sorry, but we're too far north for you to be out in the open. Anyone could be spying for the Wolf King. I'm going to pretend to be a normal girl. You stay out of sight.*

You could have just asked, Fox grumbled.

The building with the lit-up windows included an inn, a tavern, and a small store that sold ice picks, snowshoes, packs of dried meat, and fur-lined cloaks and boots that looked splendidly warm—but the shopkeeper, though he appeared to be reading a book, kept glaring around as though he suspected catastrophe at any moment. Quicksilver wouldn't risk lowering her hood, or using Fox to steal any supplies, not until she knew the village was safe for witches. But she did stroll by a table in the corner and swipe two hot rolls from a snoring man's plate.

As Quicksilver ate at another table in the opposite corner of the room, sneaking bites to Fox while the fire thawed her toes, the door opened to admit a gust of icy wind and a group of snow-dusted travelers. They tromped in, stamping their boots, and ordered supper from a serving boy who eyed the now wet and snowy floor with despair. After he had hurried back to the kitchen, one of the travelers lowered his hood, revealing a familiar shock of white hair.

Quicksilver rushed over to throw her arms about him before she could think better of it. Something about the sight of a friend, when she hadn't thought she would ever see one again, left her feeling wild and careless, like she could climb to the rooftops and yell out her happiness for all of Valteya to hear.

Olli knew her at once and burst out laughing. "Quix? What are you doing here?"

"What are *you* doing here?" She stepped back, grinning. "I thought you were going to—"

Olli clapped a hand over her mouth. "Not so loud. You don't know who's listening, this far north."

Quicksilver glanced around. The room was largely empty save for the snoring man and the shopkeeper. "Listening to what?"

Pulka peeked out from Olli's coat to glare at Quicksilver. "You stink of bones," she declared, with a stern owlish gaze.

Olli leaned closer. "Did you find them, then?"

"Well . . . something like that." Quicksilver took a deep breath and settled on a bench beside Olli. Across the table sat Lukaas, still bearing raw red scars from the fight with the Wolf King, and Freja, her freckled face grim. Grumpy Bernt, one of the four surviving members of Olli's original coven, glared at Quicksilver from beneath bushy, fuchsia-colored eyebrows speckled with silver.

Not too happy to see us again, is he? Fox observed.

Can you blame him? The last time we were around, the Wolf King attacked.

The rest of Olli's coven—six witches Quicksilver didn't recognize—sat at nearby tables, hovering over hot drinks. Every now and then, a flicker of bright color darted out from a sleeve or hood to grab a bite of food.

Quicksilver took a deep breath and told Olli, Lukaas, and Freja everything—about the catacombs, the Lady in White, the Shadow Fields. When she came to Sly Boots's betrayal, Olli's expression darkened, and Freja pounded her fist against the table, startling the serving boy so badly he dropped a tray of drinks.

"That rotten scum," Freja growled. Her bright orange snake monster, peeking out of her sleeve, hissed in agreement. "I knew he wasn't one of us, but I never thought he'd do *that*."

Lukaas placed his hand over hers. "It sounds like he wasn't quite himself."

"Doesn't matter," she said. "Even if the Wolf King got his hooks in me, I wouldn't betray any of you."

"And now you're on your way to find the last skeleton," said Olli thoughtfully. "All by yourself?"

Quicksilver lifted her chin, ready to snap out something defensive—but then an idea came to her. The words from Anastazia's journal whispered through her mind.

Tucked inside her cloak, Fox perked up. *Now that's an interesting thought.*

"Or you could come with me," said Quicksilver, without meeting Olli's eyes. She clutched her mug of hot cider, breathing in the steaming warmth. "All of you could. We could . . ." She swallowed hard. She couldn't imagine how they would react to this. "We could use our magic, together. We'd find it faster that way, I'll wager."

Collective magic.

Many will be mighty.

Lukaas snorted. "You're joking, Quix."

"Come on, now," said Freja. "I'm not in the mood for such ridiculous talk."

Olli, however, sat up straighter. "Collective magic."

"You know what that is?" asked Quicksilver.

"It's a wild idea," he said, leaning closer with sparkling eyes. "Only a few witches throughout history have ever dared talk about it aloud, and they've always been run off or killed for it. Forming a coven is one thing, and risky enough. But the idea of sharing magic with other witches is—"

"Absurd!" Freja burst out. Across the room, the shopkeeper grumbled and flipped a page in his book with a snap.

"It's just not done," Olli conceded, with a wry smile. "But I've always wanted to try."

Quicksilver gripped the table's edge and sent Fox a wave of hope. "So will you do it, then? Will you come with us?"

Olli glanced around at the others. "Freja and Lukaas will come, but beyond that—"

Freja snorted and crossed her arms. "Oh, will we, then?"

Olli gave her a pointed look. Lukaas's green lizard monster poked its head out of Lukaas's sleeve and flicked its tongue with the air of someone preparing to give a good scolding.

Freja slumped, rolling her eyes. "All right, all right, of course we will."

Olli smiled at her. "But the others . . . I don't know. Out of our original coven, only Bernt is left. And our new brothers and sisters . . . I can't be sure."

"Who are they?" asked Quicksilver, looking around.

"There's a witch settlement not far from here. Very unusual, but they've had to band together for survival since they're so close to the Wolf King's castle. But they keep getting in fights and setting off all kinds of magical mayhem. Scaring off livestock, setting buildings on fire. And that means the humans in the nearby villages—including this one—have to pick up the pieces."

Olli shook his head and dragged a hand across his face. "And the more trouble they make, the more attention they draw to themselves—which means they're easier for the Wolf King to sniff out. When we heard about it, I knew we had to find them, convince them to come west with us and leave this place. For their sakes, and for the humans' as well."

"And will they go with you?" Quicksilver asked.

Olli sighed. Though he was only a few years older than she was, Quicksilver thought he looked, in that moment, as old as Anastazia.

"Some of them have already agreed to come with us, but others . . . they refuse to leave. And so this is where they'll be when the Wolf King arrives, alone and fighting among themselves." Olli clenched his fists.

"And we've heard the Wolf King's on his way," Lukaas whispered. "Coming home for the summer, maybe."

"Or looking for the same skeleton I'm looking for," said Quicksilver.

I wonder why he hasn't already found it? Fox thought to her. *Shouldn't he be moving more quickly than we are? He's more powerful, he's got the First Ones helping him, and he probably didn't get stuck in the Shadow Fields, either.*

But Fox—maybe Anastazia brought us faster than he can travel. I bet the Wolf King can't travel by shadow, like we did.

Maybe. Fox sounded worried.

"You do know where to find it, then?" asked Olli. "The last skeleton?"

Quicksilver tried to appear more confident than she felt. "Mostly I know where to go. But Fox will still have to track it down." She hesitated, and then clasped Olli's hand.

Witches, she knew, were not supposed to trust each other—but then, she was no ordinary witch.

"Please, come with me," she said. "We're strong on our own, yes. But think how much stronger we could be together. And think how angry the Wolf King will be when he gets here and can't find his bones."

After only a slight hesitation, Olli grinned and placed his other hand over Quicksilver's. "I'm in. Freja? Lukaas?"

Lukaas added his hand to theirs. "Why not? You haven't steered us wrong before, Olli."

"Sure he has, plenty of times." Freja glared at all of them. "But if I refuse, neither of you will let me have another moment of peace for as long as I live, will you?"

"No," Olli and Lukaas answered in unison.

Freja sighed and looked to the ceiling. Her monster snake wound around her neck, nuzzling her.

"Fine." Freja slapped her hand down, too. "Let's go be a bunch of fools, together."

"I'll ask the others," said Olli, nearly bounding across the room in his excitement.

Freja leaned forward and fixed Quicksilver with a hard glare. "You'd better know what you're doing, Quix."

Quicksilver smiled. "Oh, Freja. Haven't you noticed? I always know what I'm doing."

I hope you're right, Fox thought to her.

I hope I am, too.

.41.

ODD, BUT MARVELOUS

Collective magic, Quicksilver decided, felt like being bound to other witches by a net stretched far too tight. And if you did not move with care, the net would snap apart, and everything it held would *whoosh* away to the edges of the world.

Quicksilver, Olli, Lukaas, Freja, and the three other witches who had agreed to accompany them—Lumi, Aleksi, and grumpy, frowning Bernt—and all seven of their monsters—moved cautiously up into the mountains, as though making their way across thin ice.

Quicksilver kept her head low against the wind and watched

her feet trudge through the snow. Olli, Lukaas, and Freja had scraped together enough coin to replace her long-ruined party clothes with a new pair of sealskin boots trimmed with fur, a proper set of wool trousers, and a long wool tunic. With gloves, a scarf, and a fleece-lined hat with ear flaps, in addition to Anastazia's cloak, Quicksilver felt warm and bulky.

"Still steady?" Olli called to her over the howling wind.

Quicksilver paused to scan the net of their collective magic. The others had agreed to funnel their magic through her and Fox, so that the two of them could lead the way and guide the group. It had taken them the whole night to figure out how to do such a thing, huddled in one cozy, shabby room at the inn, and before they had figured out the right balance, Quicksilver had glimpsed more of the others' thoughts than she would have cared to see—how completely Bernt doubted her. How Olli secretly loved Freja (which, Quicksilver was glad to realize, made her feel nothing but happiness). How quiet, stoic Lumi was so quiet and stoic because so much of her broken heart remained south in the kingdom of Napurya, with her sisters.

How frightened they all were that the Wolf King would arrive before they could find the last skeleton.

Now, as they climbed the mountain in the early hours of

dawn, Quicksilver could hear six other witches and six other monsters whispering through her mind—not too loudly, just loud enough to remember they were there, all of them different colors and shapes and sounds. The net of magic tugged and stretched and bunched between them, each invisible thread tethered to Quicksilver and Fox.

Quicksilver was constantly aware of the other witches and reached out to them with her mind to ensure they were all right, to tell them where to turn next, or if she saw a dangerous drop ahead, and when they needed to rest, even if stubborn old Bernt insisted they didn't.

Quicksilver spotted Fox ahead of her in the snow, in the form of a polar fox with fluffy yellow fur. Olli had bought him his own pack, which he proudly wore strapped to his back, the starling bones from the Shadow Fields contained safely within.

Fox? Are we still on the right path?

As near as I can tell, yes. The skeleton should be up there, in those caves.

Quicksilver followed his gaze to a series of dark spots lining the mountainside to their right. She closed her eyes and pictured each of her fellow witches, and his or her monster. She listened to their hearts' rhythms.

Olli.

Freja.

Lukaas.

Aleksi.

Lumi.

Bernt.

When she felt she had a good hold on each, she used their magic to delve even deeper into her own mind. It was like lifting a heavy stone with not just one set of hands, but seven.

Inside her, the Wolf King's memories shifted and flashed like a storm—dark, angry clouds here, blue-white flashes of lightning there. Fox helped her navigate the tumultuous memory, flickering ahead of her like a beacon.

"Quix?" Olli called.

Quicksilver opened her eyes. The others stood around her, tensely waiting, their snow-crusted furs covering everything but their eyes.

"Up there!" She pointed to the ice caves and felt the other witches' dismay in a rush of thoughts and feelings.

No, no, no.

On foot? With no magic?

It's so high.

We'll fall.

We'll freeze to death.

I'm so tired.

Quix will keep us safe.

This last was Olli, and Quicksilver sent him thanks in a warm wave of feeling that flushed her cheeks.

We can't use magic to climb the mountain, she told the group, trying to keep her voice steady and firm. *The link of our collective magic is fragile. We've never done this before, and we're not practiced at it. If someone grows careless, lets their thoughts wander, the link could break . . . and we'd all fall to our deaths.*

Dread rushed through them, swift and black.

Fox cleared his throat. *That was cheerful.*

"We climb!" Olli shouted over the wind. "Stay close, go slow and steady!"

Olli turned to Quicksilver, gave her a nod. She glimpsed his hopeful eyes shining between layers of fur and felt a bit more hopeful herself.

They made their way up the slippery cliffs on foot, keeping as close to the mountain face—and as far from the sheer drop—as possible. Even with her new clothes, Quicksilver's entire body was stiff with cold, and every breath burned. The path was narrow and packed hard with ice. When they turned a corner and the north wind hit them full in the face, Quicksilver began to shudder and shake—until tall, solid Aleksi placed a hand on her shoulder.

Steady, he thought to her, in a low, smooth voice. *You're doing a fine job, Quicksilver of the Far-Off Time.*

Her mind was too tired to send him complete sentences. Instead she wearily pushed a feeling of gratitude and comfort toward him. It was the softest, warmest image she could muster up—herself and Fox, warm and safe on the roof of the convent kitchen, snuggling up for sleep.

Immediately, tall Aleksi stood even taller, straightening like something had repaired itself inside him. And the feeling crept down the line to the others, warm and warmer and warming.

So they kept marching on.

And marching on.

And marching on still farther, up the mountain and through the snow and into the blistering, burning cold until all that was left of Quicksilver's warm Fox feeling was a faint tingle in each of their chests.

Cold.

Keep going.

Left foot, right foot.

Cold, scared, too high.

I won't give up, never, never.

Move, keep moving, don't stop.

Left foot, right foot, left—ahhhh!

A bolt of fear shot through them all, zipping hot and desperate from person to person.

Lukaas! Fox cried. *Freja!*

Quicksilver whirled just in time to see Lukaas slip over the cliff, dragging Freja down with him.

Freja let out a fierce roar and caught hold of the ice. They hung there, Freja clinging to the cliff's edge, Lukaas clinging to Freja's waist. Their monsters—the shivering green lizard, the snow-crusted orange snake—held on to their witches, too shocked to move.

Make a chain! Quicksilver hurried through the snow to them, the others right behind her. They threw themselves onto the ice, flat on their bellies. Olli grabbed Freja's arms, and Quicksilver grabbed Olli's ankles, and Bernt grabbed Quicksilver's ankles, and so on. Pulka shot into the air in a frenzy of white feathers, screeching.

The net of collective magic wavered. They were seven spiders sharing a single fragile web, and two threads had broken, drifting in the wind.

Many will be mighty, Quicksilver shouted in her mind,

clinging to Olli's ankles while Fox bit down hard on her cloak and dug his paws into the snow.

Olli glanced back at her, his eyes wide. "What?"

Quicksilver hadn't meant to say that. The words had come instinctively, desperate and stubborn, from somewhere deep inside her.

Many will be mighty, Quicksilver thought again, louder and more firm, and then once more: *Many will be mighty!*

The more she said the words, the stronger she felt, and when she pushed that feeling along to the others, she felt them grow stronger too. Fear faded, confusion cleared. Together—seven minds, working as one—they sent their monsters swooping over the cliff, shifting them into a great multicolored eagle, yellow like Fox and white like Pulka, orange like Freja's snake and green like Lukaas's lizard.

The eagle grabbed Freja and Lukaas with its talons, soared back over the mountain path, and deposited them safely into the snow. Then the huge bird wavered and dissolved, and became seven monsters once more.

Olli tugged the scarf off his mouth and beamed at Quicksilver. "How did you do that, Quix? Is that a spell the old woman taught you?"

"Not a spell," Quicksilver replied, trying to think of an answer that Anastazia would approve of. "Sometimes words are more powerful than magic, for they can remind us how strong we truly are."

Shaking his head, Olli tucked his scarf back into place. "You're a marvelous witch, Quix, do you know that? Odd, but marvelous."

"You're one to talk, Ol," Lukaas shot back, still dusting the snow off his clothes.

Olli's boisterous laughter rang out as they started back up the path. "Bernt? Lumi? Aleksi? How about a song? Like when we were creeping across that frozen lake?"

The three witches chuckled and began singing, Bernt's old, raspy voice loudest of all:

"Once upon the southern seas
As blue and still as glass
I crashed upon a mint-green isle
And saw a golden lass.

She wore a crown upon her head
And diamonds in her smile

And though her eyes were black and cold

I thought I'd stay awhile."

Olli, Freja, and Lukaas joined in, their voices almost lost to the howling wind. Quicksilver stomped happily up the path behind them.

We did that, Fox. Can you believe it? We helped them. We saved them.

No, Quicksilver. Fox nudged her gloved hand. *That was all you.*

A thought came to Quicksilver then—a tiny, quiet thought that she kept tucked deeply away so that maybe not even Fox could hear it. She thought that maybe, if her parents could see her now, leading this group of witches up a treacherous mountain near the Far North, they would be proud.

But then a second thought came unbidden, right on its heels: even if they could see her, she wouldn't care. She was not theirs; she was Fox's and Anastazia's, and maybe even Olli's. She did not need parents to feel strong; she was strong on her own. She was doing impossible things, and she was proud of herself, and perhaps that was all that really counted, in the end—feeling content in her own skin. Feeling the power of her own will.

I've been saying that all along, Fox could not resist chiming in. She let him enjoy his smug moment, and by the time they reached the mouth of the first cave, she hardly noticed the cold at all.

"In here!" Fox called, shifting out of his polar fox form and back into a dog. Then he dashed into the cave before anyone had the chance to speak. "I feel it very clearly up here! Shouldn't be much longer!"

Fox and the other monsters sped ahead, their colorful glows creating eerie shadows on the sloping stone walls. They pushed deeper and deeper into the mountain, down rocky passages slick with ice and through mazes of stones covered with luminous blue lichens.

After crawling through a narrow tunnel so tight that Aleksi kept hitting his head on the ceiling, even while on his hands and knees, they emerged into a tremendous cavern, bigger than anything they had seen thus far. The ceiling high above them pulsed with a million tiny glowworms, creating the illusion of a starry night sky. The worms bathed the entire space in a warm pink-and-blue glow. Shimmering water creatures darted from here to there beneath the surface of a frozen lake.

A sharp, dense forest of rocks thrust up through the frozen lake.

There, Fox thought. *The skeleton's somewhere in there, in all those rocks. The ermine.*

As his thoughts echoed to the others, Quicksilver felt their rising excitement like warming rays of the sun.

Olli squeezed Quicksilver's shoulder and smiled down at her. "Well done, Quix. You and Fox should be the ones to retrieve it. This was your plan, after all."

Quicksilver turned to face the rocks, trying not to betray how pleased she felt. They had done this—she and Fox. Olli and his brave little coven had helped, certainly; with their magic boosting Quicksilver's own, Fox had been able to follow the skeleton's call much more easily than if they had been alone.

But they *would* have found it, eventually, no matter what— because, together, Quicksilver and Fox were an unbeatable team. She put a hand on Fox's head and stroked the soft spot behind his left ear.

Ready, Fox?

He wagged his tail. *Always, for you.*

Quicksilver shut her eyes, determined to take her time and get this right. She imagined Fox gliding effortlessly across the ice, speeding through the forest of rocks, and thought to him, *Away with you.*

She felt a slight, swift tug in her chest, opened her eyes, and saw him zip into the rocks—a comet trailing yellow light—and disappear.

Silence. Waiting. Olli sat cross-legged on a low, flat stone, clasped his hands against his mouth, and stared hard into the rock forest. Freja paced, her monster coiled nervously on her head; Lumi stood, her eyes closed, her arms crossed over her chest.

Finally Fox barked, the jubilant sound echoing through the cave.

Quicksilver's heart leaped into her throat. *Is it there?*

Yes! Every last piece! Just give me one moment. It's a right nasty little thing. Sharp teeth.

Then there was silence, thick with anticipation. Quicksilver felt Fox pick up each bone with his teeth and delicately drop them into his pack. The Wolf King's memories of the ermine monster drifted easily through Quicksilver's mind, and Fox's, too—an ermine's soft white fur and clever eyes, lean body and scrappy sharp claws.

At last Fox said, *Finished! I'm ready.*

Quicksilver smiled. *Come back to me.* And then Fox was safely back on the shore of the frozen lake, the bones tucked away in his pack, and the entire coven was cheering. Fox sat, accepting their pats and ear scratches, looking so entirely satisfied with himself that Quicksilver had to roll her eyes.

Am I the best monster in all the Star Lands, he asked, *or am I not?*

But Quicksilver did not have the chance to answer. For just then, in a brilliant flash of blinding light, the white wolf appeared beside her, and with a ferocious growl, knocked her flat to the ground.

.42.

NOTHING BUT A THIEF

$\rightsquigarrow$

Quicksilver lay sprawled on the ground, gasping, a sharp pain blooming on the back of her head.

The white wolf's mammoth paw pressed on her throat, cutting off her air. She clawed at the paw, tearing out tufts of fur. The wolf pressed down harder. She gagged, choking. The wolf snarled, a nasty grin curling across its long, sharp snout. Its hot, stinking breath burned her cheek.

She couldn't sense the rest of the coven—where they were, what they were thinking, what they planned to do. Their collective magic had snapped and broken. The only thing she could feel besides the paw on her throat was Fox—and he was furious.

Get off her! He tore across the cave to the white wolf and rammed into its side. The wolf staggered but didn't move. Fox leaped onto the wolf's back, bit into his shoulders, and tore at his fur with furious paws. A spray of hot blood hit Quicksilver's cheek. The white wolf roared, released Quicksilver, then slammed Fox to the ground and hit him in the stomach with one massive white paw. Fox yelped, skidded across the icy lake, and slid headfirst into one of the giant rocks.

Quicksilver screamed. *Fox!*

She scrambled away from the wolf and shot to her feet. Six streaks of burning light flew past her, whipping her hair around her face. Six lights—blue, gray, black, brown, gold, red. The lights whirled around Olli, Freja, Lukaas, Aleksi, Lumi, and Bernt like blinding bright cyclones. When the air stilled, six wolves stood in a semicircle between Quicksilver and the exit. Each held a monster in its jaws.

The other witches, wide-eyed and trembling, writhed at the wolves' feet. Olli reached for Pulka, gasping. The owl flapped frantically, trapped in the blue wolf's jaws. When Olli crawled toward her, the wolf gave her a violent shake.

The world tilted around Quicksilver, too slow and too fast both at once. Fear choked her voice, her mind, her whole body.

. . . Fox?

I'm not hurt, came his faint reply. He stood up and shook himself. *Well, not irreparably so. Rotten fellow's got a mean punch.*

Can we connect with the others? Our collective magic—

Not like this, not with their monsters trapped. They're in too much pain—

We have *to try! Help me!*

With Fox guiding her, Quicksilver reached out to the others, trying to re-create the magical net that had helped them up the mountain. She held out her power like an open hand and shouted at them, *Grab on! Make the net! Many will be mighty!*

But nothing happened. Their magic buzzed, dull and dim, at the tips of her fingers.

A throng of voices rang out from behind her—seven voices, booming and full of rage. And one eighth, tiny voice—a boy's voice—trapped within them.

"Give me the skeletons," roared the voices, "and there's no reason for further violence. At least for now."

Quicksilver turned to see the Wolf King walking across the ice, his hands clasped behind his back. She nearly gasped when she saw how much he had *changed*. His face was so gaunt she could almost see the skull beneath his skin. The shadows under his red-rimmed eyes had grown so immense that his entire face was drawn in shades of gray. His eyes leaked tears, though Quicksilver could not imagine what he had to cry about.

Five shadows, more solid and human shaped than the last time she had seen them, floated over the Wolf King's head.

The First Ones, Quicksilver thought to Fox.

No matter what happens, we can't let him get the last two skeletons.

I agree. Quicksilver forced herself to stand tall. *No matter what happens.*

"I don't know what you're talking about," she said.

A slow, mocking smile spread across the Wolf King's face. "Of course you do. I know who you are. I know who you've *been*. I—" He screamed, clutching his head, and fell hard to his knees.

One of the First Ones snapped its dark head around and hissed—and out from behind an icy boulder hurried Sly Boots, in a fine coat trimmed with shining fur.

He offered the Wolf King a sip from a leather drinking pouch and wiped his forehead with a cloth. He glanced at Quicksilver and then away, his eyes wide and watery.

Rage swept through Quicksilver in hot, crashing waves. She ran at Sly Boots, screaming, "You evil, you traitor—"

Pulka squawked, bringing Quicksilver to a halt. She whirled. Olli fought to raise himself to his hands and knees. He reached for Pulka, cried out her name. The blue wolf flung the owl to the ground and pinned her there. Its claws dug into her white chest, drawing blood. Olli sank back to the ground, moaning in agony.

The Wolf King rose unsteadily to his feet, his arm around Sly Boots's shoulders. "I wouldn't do . . . anything rash, witch," he said, his voice faint and low. "Unless you want to . . . hear your friends screaming in agony . . . see them split open right in front of you."

Quicksilver glared at Sly Boots, her stomach turning at the sounds of the other witches—all of them crying for their monsters, all the trapped monsters screeching and whimpering.

"So this is what you do now, is it, Boots?" said Quicksilver. "You play nurse to a bloodthirsty murderer?"

Sly Boots said nothing, just stared at Quicksilver. He widened his eyes and glanced pointedly at the First Ones, then at the Wolf King, then at the First Ones again as they circled over the group like storm clouds.

Quicksilver ignored him. Whatever he was trying to tell her, it was just another lie.

She held her cloak open so the Wolf King could see her pockets. "All right," she said, "if you want the bones so badly . . ."

Behind her, Olli let out a strangled cry. "No!"

Fox? Quicksilver thought, her heart pounding. When she did this, what would happen to them?

Ready, Quicksilver.

". . . then you can have them." Quicksilver reached into her cloak pocket.

The wolves leaned toward her, the trapped monsters held tight between their teeth and under their paws.

The First Ones drifted lower, like birds of prey circling a kill.

The Wolf King watched her with bleary eyes, looking tired enough to fall over.

Slowly Quicksilver withdrew her hand from her pocket . . . and held out an empty palm for everyone to see.

The wolves howled in rage. The First Ones shot up toward the ceiling, five angry columns of black. The cavern shook; worms fell from the ceiling, pink and blue and wriggling.

The Wolf King once again cried out and collapsed, holding his head.

And through the chaos, Quicksilver watched with grim satisfaction as Fox ran out of the cavern to safety, the starling and ermine skeletons secure in his pack.

I'll come back for you, Quicksilver. The warmth of Fox's love flooded through her, making her less afraid.

I know you will—

Agony ripped through her, and she screamed and fell. Her leg was on fire. The white wolf, his teeth piercing her calf, dragged her across the cave floor to the Wolf King.

Quicksilver? Quicksilver!

She couldn't think a word to Fox. She clawed at the ground, trying to pull herself away, but the wolf held fast.

The Wolf King stood looking down at her, his face shining and sickly with sweat. The First Ones roiled at his ears, whispering.

Sly Boots hovered behind the Wolf King, staring fearfully at Quicksilver.

"You're nothing but a thief," the Wolf King said coldly.

Quicksilver gasped, tried to breathe. The wolf's teeth sent white-hot streaks of pain shooting up her whole body. Tears rolled down her cheeks, but she flashed him a hard grin anyway. "That's right. The best in the Star Lands."

A small smile crossed the Wolf King's face, and for a startling moment, Quicksilver thought it might have carried a sort of sadness in it. "We shall see if that's still the case when you're screaming for me to stop hurting you."

"Leave her alone, you beast!" Olli bit out, his voice thick with Pulka's injuries. "She's just a child!"

"So was I, once," said the Wolf King calmly, and with a flick of his wrist, he sent the white wolf, now a bright arrow of light, straight for Quicksilver's heart.

.43.

FOR YOU, QUICKSILVER

At first, when the arrow pierced her skin, Quicksilver did not react. She refused to let the Wolf King have the satisfaction of watching her squirm.

But then the arrow burrowed into her chest and spun, digging deep and deeper. Lightning bolts of pain slammed through her body, hot and crackling. A scream tore its way out of her throat, and another and another—and then, just when she thought she could bear no more, everything stopped.

She opened her eyes, lungs heaving, and saw the white wolf standing beside her.

The Wolf King lowered himself to one knee and stroked her cheek. "That can't have felt good. I won't do it again, if you give them to me."

Quicksilver gazed up at him, her vision swirling and dim. She heard Olli and the coven, still trapped behind her. Freja called her name; Bernt, his voice deep and rasping, told her not to be afraid. Lukaas begged the Wolf King to stop.

Quicksilver? Fox's thoughts hurried to her through the haze of hurt. *Are you all right? Talk to me.*

She curled her gloved fingers against an icy rock and squeezed her eyes shut. *I'm fine. Remember . . . he can't have the bones, Fox. No matter what.*

The Wolf King shrugged and stood. "As you wish."

"Sir—" said Sly Boots, reaching for his arm, but the white wolf had already transformed, and the arrow once again pierced Quicksilver's chest. Pain surged through her in searing waves. Screams shredded her throat.

I'm here, Quicksilver. Just listen to my voice and ignore all the rest.

Quicksilver imagined burying her face in Fox's fur and breathing in his warm dog smell—but stopped herself from imagining it too vividly. She would not—*would not*—bring him back to her. She would die before she allowed the Wolf King to win this game.

We decide the fate of our world, Fox. Remember?

Again and again the pain came and went, and each time it returned, Quicksilver heard, as if they belonged to someone else, her desperate screams echo through the cave. Her mind began to leave her, her thoughts scattering like terrified prey. She called for Olli, for Anastazia. She called to everyone she could think of, and to no one.

She forgot to be angry, and asked Sly Boots to help her. She forgot to be proud, and begged the Wolf King to stop.

But she would not call for Fox.

Quicksilver, don't be afraid. Fox's voice brushed against her like a soft blanket. She felt his fear, how he paced somewhere in the caves, shaking with anxiety. *Let me come back. I can help you!*

No, was the only thought Quicksilver could form. *No, no, no . . .*

My darling friend, I can't listen to you any longer. My duty is to help you, not to abandon you.

No, Fox. Stay away!

Quicksilver, I cannot bear it—

The pain lifted once again, and the Wolf King nudged her

with his foot. "Are you still alive, girl? Give me the bones, and maybe I'll stop."

Quicksilver tried to tell him that he might as well kill her now and get it over with, for no matter how much he hurt her, she would never give up the bones again—but she couldn't speak. She lay facedown on the cold cave floor, and when she opened her mouth, she inhaled icy grit and coughed, which sent her body shuddering once more.

The Wolf King sighed. "Maybe she'll be more cooperative if we try the others."

When the Wolf King turned the white wolf on Olli, Quicksilver tried not to listen to his screams. *Fox?*

I'm here, my girl. I'm not going anywhere.

What'll we do? I don't want to help him, but . . . She drew in a shaky breath, flattening her palms against the ground. *Fox, I don't want to die.*

And I won't let you die.

"Here, drink some of this," whispered a voice.

Quicksilver cracked open her eyes and saw a sharp clasp, a gold chain—and a dark red jewel, glinting in the eerie light. The Lady's heart jewel.

"Boots?"

Sly Boots helped her sit up and held the Wolf King's drinking pouch to her lips. The feeling of his hand curling around the back of her neck should have disgusted her, but Quicksilver, her throat raw and her lips cracked, could only feel thankful for the water.

"Listen carefully," Sly Boots muttered beneath the sounds of—now—Freja's screams. "The Wolf King doesn't want to fight anymore."

Fox's surprise was vicious. *Careful. We can't trust him.*

"Are you mad?" Quicksilver rasped. "Get away from me."

But Sly Boots didn't budge. "The Wolf King— his name was Ari once. Remember Anastazia's story?"

"How dare you talk about her!"

"*Listen.* Ari wanted to help the First Ones back when they came to him. He truly did. Everyone made fun of him—his family, the kingdom. It wasn't right, but I understand why he did it. But when he saw what the First Ones really wanted, how bloodthirsty they were, he knew he'd made a mistake. They made him do terrible things, things he wanted no part of. They used him to kill his own family."

"That's why you don't cooperate with evil spirits," Quicksilver hissed. Lumi, stoic Lumi who missed her sisters, began to scream. Quicksilver tried to stand and winced.

"He was just a child, Quicksilver, just like us, and the First Ones have been using him as a tool. They tricked him. They're driving him mad, all of them living in his head like they are. It makes it hard for him to concentrate, hard for him to think. His mind's in pieces. He needs a rest, but he's been chasing after you so hard that he hasn't had the chance. And every time he fails, they punish him. If the other two First Ones come back, they won't need Ari anymore. They'll kill him."

"And he's killed many, so I say that's fair."

"But it's more complicated than that!"

Quicksilver flinched as Bernt began screaming. Would he die? He was old and graying; the climb up the mountain had exhausted him, and yet he had never once complained.

"I'm sorry for what I did," said Sly Boots. "I was stupid, and I was angry at you, and I wanted to go home to my parents. And ever since you did that mind magic . . . I started hearing his voice. The Wolf King's voice. He talked to me, said . . ." Sly Boots's face darkened. He tucked the Lady's heart jewel back under his shirt and shook his head. "It doesn't matter what he said. What matters is that I listened, and I shouldn't have. I'm sorry. I truly am. You may never forgive me, but—"

"Get away from her," snapped the Wolf King. He kicked Sly

Boots in the ribs. "See to the others, make sure they don't die. Yet. They could be useful."

Sly Boots limped away and offered water to Olli. Olli, blood dripping down his face, kicked the drinking pouch out of Sly Boots's hands. The blue wolf holding Pulka gave her another shake. Bloodied white feathers went flying, but she didn't screech. She fixed her bright eyes on Quicksilver, as if waiting for something.

Waiting for . . . what?

For you, Quicksilver.

Quicksilver's aching body went still. *What do you mean, Fox?*

I mean, they climbed a mountain for you. They walked toward death for you. When you're ready, they'll fight for you.

"Well?" The Wolf King crouched before Quicksilver. "Are you ready to help me, or not?"

The First Ones spun above her, a black cloud spitting insults: "Nothing but a thief. A puny, miserable, pathetic thief."

Quicksilver ignored them, gazing past the Wolf King to focus on the coven—Olli, Freja, Lukaas. Aleksi, Lumi, Bernt— and their six bloodied and beaten monsters, trapped by six impossibly strong wolves—

All of them, waiting for her.

Many will be mighty.

The Wolf King grabbed her arm. "I could break your wrist," he mused thoughtfully.

I'm sorry. The voice was small and clear. A boy's voice.

Startled, Quicksilver glanced up at the Wolf King to see his eyes wide and clear. A tendril of mind magic stretched between them—nothing like what had happened before. A faint thread, just enough to hear these few, pleading words: *Please. Help me.*

Quicksilver stared at him. Could Sly Boots have been telling the truth?

But then the wolves began growling, and the Wolf King looked up, toward the entrance to the cavern. Whatever Quicksilver had seen on his face disappeared. In its place curled a triumphant grin.

Quicksilver turned, too—and saw Fox approaching, the pack holding the starling and ermine skeletons in his jaws.

.44.
TWO HEARTS

"Fox!" Quicksilver cried in shock. "What are you doing?"

Fox stood proud, not looking at her. *I'm sorry, master. I couldn't stand to let him hurt you again. I love you too much for that.*

Love! This is more important than love, Fox!

You're wrong. Nothing is more important than love.

The Wolf King glared at him. "Give me the bones, dog."

"Once I ensure my master is unhurt," said Fox, "I'll give them to you, and gladly. But one wrong move, and I'll disappear and take them with me."

"And leave your master to a painful death?"

Fox did not flinch. "Even so."

The Wolf King smirked. "How touching." The First Ones, drifting above him, also smirked. Their dark, smoky expressions perfectly mirrored the Wolf King's own. "While you inspect your beloved master, I know you won't mind if I return to my work?"

And with that, the Wolf King turned and set his white wolf upon Freja. She writhed on the icy ground, and her screams rent apart the air. Olli called for her, his voice cracking.

Fox, how could you have done this? I told you to leave!

We still have these skeletons. All is not lost.

No matter how fast we run, he'll catch up and steal them back from us!

And then, because everything was going wrong, and they might not survive whatever was about to happen—she kissed Fox's velvet ears, buried her face in the soft patch of fur between them. With him at her side, her heart beat true once more. *Fox, Fox, you stupid dog. I'll never send you away again, ever.*

Quite right, you won't.

Do you have a plan?

Fox snorted. *Of course. We run. Now, while the First Ones are distracted.*

Quicksilver's heart shattered, even as she knew it was the only way. *What about the others?*

They'll fight for you, give us time. You know they will.

And if he catches up with us?

He won't. Not you and me. But we must hurry.

Quicksilver hesitated. She watched Olli strain toward poor Freja, unable to reach her. The rest of the coven lay crumpled on the ground, gasping and shuddering.

The white wolf's crackling arrow, half buried in Freja's chest, twisted and turned.

The other six wolves watched, their eyes bright with hunger.

The shadows of the First Ones hovered over Freja, cackling and jeering at her screams.

Quicksilver saw Bernt look toward her. Their gazes locked. He gave her one slight, small nod.

She flattened her palms against the ground and braced herself to push off and run, every muscle coiling and ready—

But then the Wolf King let out a sharp cry. His body jerked to the right, convulsed and went rigid, then collapsed in a crumpled heap. Sly Boots hurried to him, wiping the sweat from his brow.

Quicksilver's heart sank. She wanted to run, she knew she *should* run, but—

But we can't leave Boots and Ari, Fox.

The traitor and the witch hunter? You're joking.

In a flash, Quicksilver showed him everything Sly Boots had said. *I think he spoke to me. Ari. Not the Wolf King, but Ari the boy. He didn't want to hurt me.*

Fox sighed. *Wonderful. This makes things more complicated.*

A great, misshapen shadow fell over them. Quicksilver looked up.

"Give us the skeletons, witch," commanded the First Ones, swirling overhead. Their bodies flickered, almost solid, and then shifted back to curling smokiness. They were so close Quicksilver could see the sheer folds of their shadowy robes, the jewels floating around their necks. One moment they had long black teeth; the next instant, their teeth dissolved to mere puffs of black smoke. *"NOW!"*

The seven wolves slunk toward Quicksilver, licking their chops, their ravenous eyes trained on her.

They had abandoned the coven and their monsters lying on the cave floor—all of them seemingly dead. Sly Boots huddled by the monsters, tending to the shuddering Wolf King.

Then Olli cracked open an eye and winked at Quicksilver.

Freja, pale and bloody, clenched her fist. Her snake raised its head.

Lukaas, Aleksi, Bernt, Lumi—they all tensed, waiting. Their monsters, feigning death, twitched on the floor.

The First Ones reached toward Quicksilver, their dark hands shifting from smoke to fleshy fingers and back again.

Quicksilver looked to Olli. He nodded, once. *Go,* his determined expression seemed to say, *and good luck.*

Then he jumped to his feet and cried, "To Quicksilver!"

As one, the bruised and bloodied coven rushed at the wolves, flinging their monsters ahead of them like arrows. Pulka led the way, a churning ball of white streaked with red. Light shot out from each monster, connecting them in a furious web of power. The monsters grew in size—stronger, faster, brighter, hotter. Behind them, their witches raised their bloodied arms in unison and directed their monsters into battle.

Collective magic.

The wolves turned, ears flat, fangs bared, and pounced. Wolves and monsters collided in an explosion of light that sent sparks ricocheting through the cave. The crash shook the rocks protruding from the frozen lake; the ice itself cracked and splintered.

The First Ones shrank back from the noise and dove into the fight, weaving in and out of the fighting monsters, witches, and wolves.

Hurry! Fox nipped Quicksilver's hand. *Now's our chance!*

Quicksilver limped to Sly Boots, gritting her teeth against the pain of her bitten leg.

"Get up!" cried Sly Boots, tugging on the Wolf King's shoulders—but the Wolf King didn't move. He lay curled on the ground, covering his ears. Tears leaked from his eyes; his sweaty dark hair lay plastered to his pale skin.

"If you want to come with us, you'd better get up," Quicksilver said harshly, yanking him by the arm.

"I can't," he cried, his voice breaking—Ari's voice, singular and human and afraid. "They won't let me!"

A furious roar—five furious roars—exploded from the fight. The First Ones surged out of the chaos, five smoky streaks that sped across the cave, aiming right for Quicksilver.

The Wolf King shoved her away. "Go!"

Sly Boots tugged Quicksilver to the ground and threw himself over her, just as the First Ones surrounded them in darkness.

Hands grabbed Quicksilver. Teeth tore at her clothes. Cold

slipped across her skin, burning her like frostbite. Skulls butted against her own. In one moment, the First Ones felt solid; the next, they were merely shadows—dark and raging, choking her like smoke.

"Don't move, Quicksilver!" cried Sly Boots, his body shielding hers. "I've got you—"

He broke off with a pained cry.

"Give us the bones," moaned the First Ones. "Give them to us now!"

They clawed through her clothes, grabbed Fox's pack. He yelped, pawed the ground.

"Get off him!" Quicksilver pounded on the dark arms holding Fox. Her fists met cold, clammy flesh—then a cold mist that stung like needles.

Fox's pack ripped open. The starling and ermine skeletons spilled out onto the ground. Quicksilver and Fox scrambled for the nearest one, the ermine, and dropped it safely in one of Quicksilver's cloak pockets.

But the First Ones—they hooted and howled in triumph. Five pairs of hands held the glowing red starling skeleton high in the air. Five smoky bodies danced around it, swirling faster and faster.

The Wolf King, lying on the ground at the edge of the

fighting witches and wolves, let out a low groan. His mouth opened wide. A thin ribbon of pale smoke unfurled from his gaping jaws. The smoke slithered across the ground, growing larger and darker, shifting into a torso and arms and legs, and joined its five siblings.

Then, as one, the First Ones turned and rushed low over the ground toward Quicksilver, Sly Boots, and Fox.

"Quicksilver," they hissed, circling faster and faster, nearer and nearer. *"You've lost. GIVE US THE ERMINE."*

Sly Boots hugged Quicksilver close, and Quicksilver curled around Fox protectively, gritting her teeth as the First Ones clawed at them all.

Six First Ones. Quicksilver squeezed her eyes shut, buried her face in Fox's ice-crusted fur. Her nose and mouth and ears were filling with stinging, cold darkness. *Only one left. If they get the ermine skeleton, then they'll all be back. We're doomed, Fox.*

The faint sounds of the wolves battling Olli's coven brought her courage, but she could hardly lift her head against the force of the swarming First Ones, much less rise to her feet and run. Someone screamed in agony—Lukaas?

"Quicksilver?" Sly Boots whispered, his hand squeezing hers so tight it hurt.

"It's all right," she told him shakily. "We'll be all right." *Fox, can you get us out of here?*

Yes, I can, came his calm response—too calm, Quicksilver thought. Wasn't he frightened too? Shouldn't he be feeling her own fear on top of that? *But you won't like it.*

What? Why not?

A pause. *Do you trust me?*

Of course I do! Whatever it is, do it now! I want to help, but I'm not sure I can—Fox, they're strangling me—I can't breathe!

You can't help. Not this time. Hold the ermine skeleton close. Don't drop it, no matter what happens. And tell Sly Boots to hold on to you and don't let go.

Quicksilver did as he asked. Then Fox licked her cheek, nuzzling her. *I'm sorry, Quicksilver. I love you. I always have.*

All of a sudden Quicksilver felt a sick rush of fear. She tried to look for Fox but couldn't find him. The ermine skeleton rattled in her pocket. She clamped her hand over it, pressing it close to her chest.

Fox? What are you talking about? Where did you go?

A bright yellow light cut through the darkness, circling her and Sly Boots in a tight ring. The light was blazingly, brilliantly hot. She had to shut her eyes against it. Pain tugged at her heart, making her gasp and choke. She sensed that the magic binding her to Fox was about to break.

But that was impossible.

A monster could not live without his witch.

Fox! Whatever you're doing, stop right now!

He did not answer. Quicksilver struggled in vain to raise her head. The light was too bright, too close, too hot. It pressed closer and closer, burning and scorching—

The First Ones and their furious cries disappeared. The only thing Quicksilver could hear was her own roaring blood. The pain in her chest was becoming too immense; she was a girl no longer. She was only this searing ache that threatened to crack her chest in two, and the feel of Sly Boots's sweaty hand, gripping hers.

She searched the chaos for Fox, with her mind and her heart, and right as the light became its brightest yet, understanding came to her in a terrible flash. It smelled and felt like Fox—a burst of understanding, an ache of apology, a warm bloom of love.

You never could control me fully, master, came his faint, smug voice.

Quicksilver remembered, then, leaving the Shadow Fields.

How Fox had that sad, confused look about him, how he wouldn't look at her. How Anastazia had held him back to tell him something, privately.

Maybe, perhaps, to give him instructions?

Fear dropped into Quicksilver's belly like a boulder, sending a thick, queasy feeling flying up into her throat.

No. No. This could not be allowed.

He was *her* monster!

She was the witch, and *she* gave the orders!

No! Quicksilver thought to him, fighting with everything she had to call him back to her arms.

No, Fox! Stop it right now! You can't do this! I forbid it! Fox, listen to me. She was wrong, she didn't mean it. You don't have to do this. I'll never forgive you for it! Fox? Fox!

And then Quicksilver was falling, her only anchor Sly Boots's hand. Something deep inside her snapped, slid away from her like a broken rope, and was gone.

.45.

A Witch in Blood

The world was bright, swirling. Then, darkness. A sharp pain. A faint buzzing sound. They landed on a hard surface.

Quicksilver stumbled to her feet, swaying.

"Fox?" she screamed. "Fox! Where are you?"

"Quicksilver?" Sly Boots's voice was dazed. "Who is that screaming?" A pause, a gasp. Sly Boots shot upright, holding his head. "This is my attic. How did we get back here?"

Quicksilver ignored him and kept calling for Fox. She crashed through the attic, overturning chairs and digging through musty chests of folded linens. She stumbled, her vision blurred. She wiped her face and fell, scraping her knees. She got back up, drew aside the heavy, patched drapes that covered a small window. Nothing but glass and stars.

"Where are you, Fox? What did you do? Come here, right now!"

Sly Boots reached for her. "Quicksilver, I think—"

She slapped him away. "You don't know! You don't know anything about us! Fox, this isn't funny anymore! Stop playing! I'm your witch, and I command you, I *command* you . . ."

She sat on the floor, holding herself, heaving as she tried to fight off her tears and breathe away everything about this moment. There was a terrible, hollow pain in her chest, and she thumped against it with her fist, again and again, until her skin smarted. She put her face to her knees, wound her fingers in her hair, and pulled, drawing all the pieces of herself into a tight knot. She thought his dear name and pushed it through her mind like a reaching hand—*Fox? Fox, where are you? Come back, come back!* But the invisible magical cord that had helped her speak to Fox, and direct him and work with him, the cord that had hooked their two hearts together, was no longer there.

Her blood felt slow, her bones heavy. She lifted a strand of hair. It had lost its luster and was now a dull, faded red. The world around her didn't shine and shimmer; it was gloom gray and dust brown.

They were no longer in the Star Lands of long ago. They were in the Star Lands of *now*. *Their* now. The *now* from which Anastazia had taken them—was it weeks ago?

"Fox?" she whispered, but when she said his name aloud, she felt no answering tug in return.

Sly Boots crouched silently nearby. His hand was gentle on her shoulder, and that was the worst thing of all. Because it meant he understood, and this wasn't some horrible trick of Quicksilver's mind.

"He isn't," she whispered. "I promise you he isn't. Just wait. He'll show up. We'll wait for him."

"All right," said Sly Boots, sitting beside her on the floor.

But this was only an attic, dark and cluttered. There was no light. No sound of paws against the floor. No warm, musky fur to hide her face in.

In the back of her mind, a calm voice—which sounded rather like Anastazia when she was in the midst of a lecture—told Quicksilver that this meant she could no longer work magic. She was a witch in blood and always would be, but without a monster, she would never again be a witch in practice.

She found, however, that she didn't much care. For what was being a witch, without a Fox beside you?

.46.

WAITING FOR A LEGEND

For a long time, Quicksilver sat on the floor in the dim attic. She gazed blearily at the mess she had made—the overturned chairs, the spilled piles of clothes. Dust clouds drifted throughout the room, disturbed by her screaming and her crashing and her pointless searching. She watched the dust float, and she tried to find her way back into the gray cocoon of the Shadow Fields, where everything felt quiet and safe.

But no matter how hard she tried, she couldn't find that feeling again, couldn't slip back into the Shadow Fields. She was stuck here, in this attic, where the shadows were normal shadows, where she felt every horrible feeling it was possible to feel.

"He isn't," she whispered, whenever she found the breath to speak. "He isn't."

But he was, and she knew it. Fox was gone. He had saved her, and he had used his own life to do it. Anastazia had said, right from the beginning, that time-traveling magic was dangerous, that it required tremendous sacrifice—of both the witch, and her monster.

Which is why—Anastazia's words came floating back to her—*as far as I know, I'm only one of two witches to ever have done it.*

Now Quicksilver understood why.

"I'm sorry, Quicksilver," said Sly Boots, after a long time had passed. "What can I do?"

Part of her wanted to grab on to him, hide her face in his jacket, and never let go, simply because, at that moment, he was the only other person in her world.

But she would not let herself do that. Sly Boots had betrayed them; he had sent them down this path toward Anastazia's death, toward Fox's death. Maybe it hadn't been his fault, if the Wolf King and the First Ones really had tricked him into doing their bidding. Even so, she was not ready to forgive him. Not yet, not in this awful, empty moment in this awful, empty attic.

She glared at him, her vision still blurry with tears. "You can make yourself useful and help me do whatever needs doing. Fox died to save you. You'd better be worth it."

Instead of flinching or looking away, Sly Boots met her gaze. "I will. I promise."

"Your promises don't mean much to me." She got up, shaky, and shoved Sly Boots away when he helped steady her. Once downstairs, Sly Boots hurried ahead to his parents' bedroom, crying out with joy when he saw them there, just as he had left them.

Quicksilver followed slowly. Movement felt unfamiliar and difficult. Some stupid, oblivious part of her kept hoping that if she turned around and hurried back to the attic, she might catch Fox there. He had only been playing a game, and he would tease her, without mercy, for taking so long to find him.

But it was a lie, and so Quicksilver kept putting one foot in front of the other, because she did not know what else to do. Her feet took over, doing the thinking for her: left, right. Left, right.

Fox, she thought, she would forever think. *What am I to do now?* She remembered those nights at the convent when she had sat blubbering in the chapel, one arm around Fox, feeling lonely and sorry for herself. What had that girl known about loneliness?

"Someone's been here." Sly Boots inspected his parents' bedroom, frowning. "Things are different. I didn't leave that here, nor that there. And don't they look better to you? They seem better."

Quicksilver looked. "I suppose," said her tongue and her lips. How extraordinary, that they could function without her really caring whether they did or not.

Sly Boots paused, holding an empty bowl—the one he had thrown against the wall and shattered was gone. This was a different one, clean and whole. "I wish I knew how to help you."

Quicksilver turned away, her eyes stinging—and then a noise came from downstairs. A door opening. Someone was entering the house.

She whirled and ran, her heart in her throat and Sly Boots at her heels. It couldn't be Fox. *He is dead, remember? Dead, dead, dead. Say it enough, and you'll feel better. Say it enough, and your heart will go numb, and you'll never feel anything again.*

By the time Quicksilver got downstairs, they were already inside—a group of people wearing hooded cloaks. Quicksilver skidded to a halt, Sly Boots slamming into her back.

"Who are you?" she demanded. Automatically, she tried to fling Fox at them and failed, and nearly fell to her knees at the anguish of her own foolishness.

One of them lowered his hood, revealing a mop of strawberry-blond curls and a beaming, familiar smile.

Sly Boots gasped. Quicksilver stepped back, squinting. "Olli?" she asked.

"No," said the young man. He looked only a small handful of years older than them. "I'm Lars. I'm his great-great . . ." He paused to count, then shrugged jovially. "His grandson, many times over."

Quicksilver's mind felt like mud. She stared at Lars, noticing the similarities—and the differences. He had Olli's wide smile, but his hair was a light orange-gold, instead of a blinding, magic-bright white. His skin was a lighter brown than Olli's had been, and he had freckles, like Freja.

"Prove it." Sly Boots stepped in front of Quicksilver. "Either way, you're trespassing."

"I know, and I'm sorry about that." Lars nodded to the others, and they lowered their own hoods. "Olli made sure to pass on your story as well, Sly Boots. We've been tending to your parents in your absence. I think we've done a good job of it, too.

I know how to heal them, by the way, but it would require quite a bit of magic to do so, and we can't risk alerting the Wolf King to our presence. Besides, I need to save all the strength I can, while we're at war."

Sly Boots waited, his face hard.

"Olli and Freja survived, long ago in Valteya," Lars explained. "The great witches Lukaas, Aleksi, Bernt, and Lumi fought the wolves in that ice cave and gave them time to escape."

Quicksilver nearly sat down right there on the floor; the sadness felt too heavy for her to stand up any longer. Lukaas, Aleksi, Bernt, and Lumi—brave witches who had climbed a mountain and fought and been tortured, all because of her.

She fought through the heavy, sticky numbness trapping her whole body and croaked, "I'm sorry they died like that. I didn't mean for them to."

Lars smiled gently. "They are heroes in our history. Olli and Freja told their stories. They were on the road for a long time, hiding and grieving the loss of their friends. But they knew what they had seen, and what it meant—your Fox, Quicksilver, sending you and Sly Boots back to the future, along with the last skeleton. Someone had to survive, to tell others what had happened so someone would be here, waiting for you, when you came home."

When Lars said Fox's name, it woke something inside Quicksilver. She reached into her cloak and touched the pocket that held the ermine skeleton. Though it shifted at her touch, it did not bite or hiss. Perhaps now, as a magicless human, she was less interesting to it.

Lars's face sagged with relief. "You have it, then? It's safe?"

Wary, Quicksilver did not answer. "Tell me more."

"Olli and Freja traveled the Star Lands and told the story to any witch who would listen," Lars continued. "How you led Olli's coven into the mountains using collective magic. How Fox found the skeleton, and how you resisted the Wolf King's torture." Lars's face softened. "How Fox sacrificed himself to save the last skeleton from the Wolf King and send you home."

As she relived these moments—which for her had only just happened, and which for Lars were the stuff of long-ago story—a swift, sharp ache pierced Quicksilver's heart. *Fox's sacrifice.* Her eyes grew hot. She found Sly Boots's hand and grabbed on. His fingers pressed hers, gently.

"Ever since then," Lars went on, "we witches have lived in hiding, all throughout the Star Lands, waiting for your return. My family in particular has been charged with this task, ever since Olli told us where, and when, Fox would have been most likely to send you—somewhere safe. Back home, to Willow-on-the-River. My ancestors have lived in this town, in secret, for hundreds of years, waiting for Anastazia to come and take both of you back in time, as she had before. We had to make sure nothing kept that from happening." Lars gestured at the witches around him. "My coven and I saw you leave, weeks ago, when the Wolf King attacked. Then we waited for your return, watching Sly Boots's house and tending to his parents. When you came back tonight, we felt it. A sacrifice like Fox's sends out waves of magic." Lars paused, grim. "The Wolf King will have felt it too. We'll have to leave, very soon, before he tracks you here."

A cold, clean anger swelled within Quicksilver. "He still lives, then."

"Oh, yes, and he left much of Willow-on-the-River in ruins on the night you traveled to the past. We managed to protect your home and parents, Sly Boots. Now the town is rebuilding, but I'm sure it will be some time before it recovers." Lars looked sadly at Quicksilver. "The Wolf King is especially hateful of girls. I think they remind him of you. He takes them to the Black Castle, in the Far North, and . . . who knows what happens there?"

Quicksilver thought of her fellow orphans at the convent, and dug her fingernails into her palms. Not even Adele deserved a fate like that.

"It's not him, though!" said Sly Boots. "The Wolf King. He's being controlled by the First Ones. He wouldn't do these things if he were his own true self, I swear to you."

Sly Boots quickly recounted to Lars and his companions what he knew—how the Wolf King was enslaved to the First Ones' will, and how he longed to be free of them.

"If that's true," said Lars, "then the boy has my pity. But not my mercy."

His companions nodded in agreement. A squirrel monster, his fur a faintly lustrous orange-gold, poked his head out of Lars's cloak to gaze inquisitively at Quicksilver.

"Not now!" Lars said, and the squirrel retreated.

Quicksilver stared at where the monster had been, her head pounding. She could almost hear Fox's voice; if she closed her eyes, she would feel his fur beneath her fingers.

"I'm sorry," said Lars quietly. "They're just so excited to see you. All these years our people have been waiting for a legend, and here you are, at last." He paused, smiled. "They call you Foxheart, the monsters. Quicksilver Foxheart, in honor of him."

And Quicksilver understood then that these witches had instructed their monsters to remain hidden—because they had known Quicksilver would have no monster of her own, and that the misery of that would be fresh and raw.

We determine the fate of our world, Fox, she had told him, and Anastazia had told her—and she believed that. But how could she do such a thing, with this fist of grief squeezing her heart?

She did not know. But she knew she must begin to learn.

So she asked, "What do we do now? We have one skeleton, and he has six."

Lars knelt before Quicksilver, and his companions did the same, their faces kind and eager. "Now, at last, we go to the Black Castle to fight the Wolf King," Lars said, "and we would be honored, Quicksilver Foxheart, if you would join us."

.47.

THE MOST STUPID OF
ALL THE BOYS, EVER

Quicksilver sat on a chair in the corner, watching Sly Boots cool his parents' faces with a damp cloth and spoon broth into their mouths.

Feeding them was a painstaking process, and it made Quicksilver irritated just to watch. Sly Boots had to hold up their heads and slowly pour in tiny spoonful after tiny spoonful so they wouldn't choke. He ended up covered in more broth than he successfully fed to them, but not once did he lose his calm manner. Quicksilver couldn't conceive of such patience—but then she thought of Fox, and Anastazia. Would she be able to sit in patient silence and help them eat, if they were as sick as Sly Boots's mother and father?

The answer came to her at once: Of course she would, and gladly, for as long as they needed her.

Her bandaged leg throbbed with a dull, burning ache—but her chest ached even more. Would it ever stop aching? If only she had had the chance to care for Fox as he had cared for her. If only she had had the chance to say good-bye.

"I would have gotten you home to them eventually, you know," she said.

Sly Boots jumped, dropping the spoon. "You scared me half out of my mind!"

Despite everything, Quicksilver smiled—the barest twitch of her lips. So she had managed to sneak into the room without Sly Boots noticing her. At least some things hadn't changed.

"I'm not sorry," she said.

Sly Boots sighed and resumed feeding his mother. "I know you would have. Gotten me home, I mean."

"Then why did you betray us?"

"I told you everything got strange after you used mind magic on the Wolf King? He was controlling me. His thoughts were whispering to mine." He kept his gaze lowered, not looking at her. "I know that's no excuse, though," he added miserably. "I bet he wouldn't have been able to control *you*."

"Maybe he wouldn't have been able to control you so easily, if you hadn't been so angry at me in the first place." Quicksilver paused, her hands folded tightly in her lap. "You were awful to me, Sly Boots. You said horrible things."

"I know."

"How could you think I wouldn't do as I promised?"

Sly Boots put down the bowl and spoon, withdrew the Lady's heart jewel from beneath his shirt, and toyed with the necklace's sharp clasp as he gazed out the window, his brow furrowed.

"I don't have a good reason," he said. "I know now that you would have kept your promise. All I can say is this: even though I suppose it's good that I went with you, because if I'd stayed behind, the Wolf King would have killed me, and Lars wouldn't have known to protect my parents, so they probably would have died as well—even so, even knowing all those things . . . if it had been you instead of me, if you'd been far away while Fox stayed back at home, hurt and alone, and you couldn't get back to him, and you were trying to pretend like you were all right but really you were going slowly mad inside, worrying about him . . . wouldn't you have been the same way? Made the same mistakes?"

Quicksilver almost spat at him that no, of course she wouldn't have. She was better than that, and stronger.

But then she paused, and really thought about it, and knew he was right. If she had been separated from the ones she loved—from her dear Fox—she would have torn everyone and everything apart to get back to him.

"Maybe," she said quietly.

Sly Boots turned to her. "I really am sorry for what I did. Maybe there's nothing I can say right now that will make it better. But I never wanted to hurt you, or Fox, or even Anastazia—the great old bat."

Quicksilver smiled. "You liked her enough."

"I liked her whenever I remembered she was you."

Sly Boots's gaze dropped to the floor. Quicksilver watched him, a strange, warm feeling coiling deep inside her.

"Anyway, what I said to you the night of Princess Tatjana's birthday party . . . I shouldn't have said that, and I didn't really believe it. I was angry, and stupid."

Remembering those words made Quicksilver stiffen. "You *were* stupid."

"The *most* stupid," Sly Boots agreed.

"Of all the boys, ever," Quicksilver declared.

Sly Boots glanced up at her with a small smile. "Throughout all of time."

Quicksilver worked very hard to keep from smiling back at him.

"Can you forgive me, Quicksilver?" asked Sly Boots.

She considered him—his long, skinny arms, his soft, pale hair, the freckles across his cheeks. He wore such a gentle expression just then. If she had to put a word to the look in his eyes, she would have chosen . . . hopeful.

"Not yet," she said at last. "You really hurt me, Boots."

He did not look away. "I know."

"I don't know when I'll forgive you, in fact, or if I ever will."

"That's fair. In the meantime, I'll wait, and do whatever I can to help you. I'll spend the rest of my life helping you, if I must."

Quicksilver unfolded her hands, folded them again, unfolded them once more, and then realized she had no idea what to do with them. She fiddled with her boots so he would not see her flaming cheeks. "Yes, well. There's no need to be so weird and dramatic about it."

A soft knock on the door alerted them to Lars's presence. He poked his head in, smiling Olli's familiar smile. "Hello, you two. Quicksilver, you should get some sleep. We'll leave at nightfall, and the far northern road is a long and harsh one."

Sly Boots shot to his feet, his back straight as a board. "I'm coming with you."

"This is our fight, Sly Boots, not yours. You're not a witch."

"No, but I'm Quicksilver's friend," Sly Boots replied, "and I won't let her do this alone."

Lars raised an eyebrow, his mouth twitching. "Quite an admirer you've got, Quicksilver."

"He's hardly that," Quicksilver said, her cheeks growing even hotter. "He's just feeling guilty, is all."

Sly Boots stuck out his chin. "All right, so I feel guilty. But what does that matter? I can still help you. I know things about the Wolf King no one else knows. Let me prove to you how sorry I am, Quicksilver. Please?"

Lars shrugged, still far too amused for Quicksilver's liking. "It's your choice."

Quicksilver headed to the attic without once looking back at Sly Boots. "I suppose he can come, if he must," she said airily—but with a secret joy fluttering inside her. For she realized that, out of everyone alive, Sly Boots was the only person who had known her and Fox as witch and monster. And there was something special, even precious, about that.

She supposed, then, that she might be moved to someday forgive Sly Boots, if only so they could share stories about Fox, and remember him through the words.

.48.

The Far Northern Road

At first the journey north wasn't so terrible. They were six altogether, including Quicksilver, Sly Boots, and Lars. One of Lars's coven, an older witch with a bad knee, named Matias, volunteered to stay behind and care for Sly Boots's parents. They hoped, as frightening as it was, that the Wolf King would leave Willow-on-the-River alone and focus his attention on tracking the last monster skeleton—the ermine—stowed safely in Quicksilver's pack.

As they traveled north through Lalunet and then through Valteya, they joined with other covens who had been in hiding and waiting for Lars's arrival. These witches lived deep in forested mountain canyons, and in underground compounds, safe from the Wolf King's pack.

"But now that you've gone back in time and changed this future," Lars explained one cold night as they wound through a Valteyan forest of tall, whispering pine trees, "we witches are not so frightened as we once were." He stopped and looked at Quicksilver, his eyes shining but serious, just like Olli's had been. "We've been waiting—for you, Quicksilver. We've been waiting to fight. And we're not afraid."

Quicksilver didn't know what to say to that. The idea that generations of witches had been telling her story for so many long years, waiting for her to return so she could lead them into battle, made her feel, even after everything she'd been through, rather nervously floaty.

What if I mess things up for everyone after all this time, Fox?

No answer, of course—just the hissing pines overhead, the whispers and rustles of the coven, Sly Boots humming quietly to himself beside her.

Three days into the journey north, they stopped at a tiny mountain settlement of witches who lived in deep, narrow caves facing the northern horizon. The snow-covered mountains of the Far North loomed there—and somewhere within them was the Wolf King's Black Castle.

Witches crowded out of the caves, quiet and wide-eyed, some with shy smiles, some with beaming ones.

"We're glad to have you back, Quicksilver," said a man with faded rose-colored hair. "And glad to fight with you at last. Otto, at your service." He took off his cap and bowed. His monster, a pink and downy vole, stared at Quicksilver long after Otto had moved away to give others a turn.

A boy around Quicksilver's age, with a shaved head and a scarred scalp, attacked Quicksilver with a fierce hug.

"I'm Tommi," he said. "My father told me stories about you every night before bed, when I was little." He looked up, grinning. His red cat monster wound around his ankles. "He would have loved meeting you, my dad. He was never afraid to stand up to the Wolf King."

Quicksilver tried not to recoil at Tommi's words, nor at the scars running down his face. It wasn't that they were ugly to her; it was that they looked, horribly, like claw marks, and she wondered how many people would have been spared the Wolf King's wrath, had she not so thoroughly angered him, long ago.

And what if, after all that, they could not defeat him, even now? He had six skeletons, and she had one. The ermine skeleton in her pocket felt like a measly thing in the face of the Wolf King's power—and in the face of the losses these witches had suffered.

Two girls, a few years older than Quicksilver, one with faded grass-green hair, the other with pale sea-blue hair—but identical in every other respect—knelt at Quicksilver's feet.

"I am Irma," said the green-haired girl.

"And I am Veera," said the blue-haired girl.

"We are honored to fight for you, Quicksilver Foxheart," said Irma.

"And have been training since childhood to do so," said Veera.

"We will not fail you," they said together, with solemn nods.

Their monsters—two raccoons, one green and blue, one blue and green—stared at Quicksilver from their perches on Irma's and Veera's shoulders, whispering excitedly to each other.

An older woman with a white streak in her dark hair came forward, holding a steaming bowl of stew. "Thank you for saving us," she murmured. She clasped Quicksilver's hand and kissed it. "We won't fail you, Quicksilver Foxheart. My name is Karin, and I am ready to fight for you, as are all of us here." Karin's mottled black-and-white bat monster hung off her shoulder and peeked out at Quicksilver from behind its leathery wings.

"Foxheart," it whispered after her.

When Quicksilver bedded down to sleep that morning on the floor of one of the caves, she felt heartsick and tired. It had been a long night on the road, and then a long couple of hours talking to every witch in the settlement, accepting their thanks, accepting their careful hugs. Lars had finally steered Quicksilver away to a quiet corner of the cave, and given her a bedroll and a thick fur blanket, and instructed her to sleep.

But even though she was exhausted, Quicksilver found it difficult to shut her eyes. Her chest ached, her head ached; she felt hollow and brittle, like the slightest thing could break her in half.

After a few quiet minutes, the black-and-white bat fluttered over and curled up in the crook of her arm, its tiny claws hooked in her sleeve.

"What was he like?" asked the bat.

Quicksilver startled at the small voice, so near. "What?"

"Fox." The bat gently placed one of its wings on Quicksilver's chest. *Foxheart.* "What was he like? Will you tell us?"

"Us?" Then Quicksilver looked around, and realized that all the monsters of their new, growing coven hovered or crouched or coiled nearby—Karin's bat, and Lars's soft orange-gold squirrel. Otto's pink vole and Tommi's thin red cat. Irma's and Veera's green-and-blue raccoons. All of them watched her, bright eyed and eager.

Quicksilver swallowed hard. How to put into words what Fox was like? How to explain to these monsters what it had been like to know with certainty that she, Quicksilver, would never feel love—and then to receive it from Fox every day, every hour, even when she hadn't realized it?

How blind a girl she had once been.

She spotted Sly Boots, sitting with Lars at the mouth of the cave, on first watch. His eyes met hers, and he waved, his smile lopsided.

Quicksilver waved back and then took a deep breath. "Well," she began, "first of all, Fox was a dog, and so he of course loved sticks best of all. After me, of course."

The monsters nestled closer to hear, and as the morning sun crept through the cave, turning everything soft and drowsy, Quicksilver talked about Fox until Lars told her sternly to get some real rest. Night would come sooner than she'd like, and then they'd be on the road again.

So she lowered her voice, whispering so Lars couldn't hear, and when her eyes fell shut at last, the monsters curled protectively around her, she slipped into a warm and gentle sleep.

Foxheart, the monsters called her, and it was true. For there he was, inside her, and he always would be.

.49.

A WORLD FULL OF MONSTERS

By the time the coven—twelve witches and monsters, altogether—reached the Wolf King's castle, which was past the border of Valteya in the Far North, they had crafted a plan that, in the broad light of day, had seemed to Quicksilver both sound and promising.

But now, looking up at the Black Castle towering over them, she felt . . . differently.

The two moons, white and violet, cast soft colored shadows over the high, snowy mountains of the Far North—but the Black Castle did not shine. Its black stone swallowed up even the near moon's violet glow, leaving the castle looking like a dark castle-shaped hole cut out of the sky.

It was narrow and tall, its lines clean and sharp. It stood on a rocky plateau and seemed to loom over everything, even the cloud-piercing mountains that surrounded it. Hugged by snowy rock, crowned with pointy towers, it reminded Quicksilver of a beast scanning the mountains, poised and ready to hunt.

Beside her, Lars let out a long, slow breath. His squirrel monster, Naika, glared at the castle and snarled softly.

"That's quite a sight," muttered pink-haired Otto, his vole monster perched on his shoulder.

Sly Boots, on Quicksilver's other side, whispered, "Don't be afraid."

Quicksilver poked him. "I'm not!"

"I wasn't talking to you. I was talking to myself."

"Let's move in," Lars whispered, signaling to the others. Naika scurried ahead to scout.

They followed the icy road across the plateau and up a series of foothills, cloaked only by the shadows. If they used magic this close to the Wolf King, they would lose the element of surprise—which was their one real advantage.

Quicksilver tried not to think about when the First Ones

would sense the ermine skeleton and attack. Instead she focused on moving as quietly through the trees as she could. Maybe if she focused hard enough, she would stop thinking about Anastazia and Fox, and wishing desperately that they were there beside her.

Sly Boots seemed to know what she was thinking. "Feels strange to be going on adventures without them, doesn't it?" he whispered.

She glanced at his snow-dusted self and clamped down on a surprising feeling of fondness. "Just keep singing," she snapped. "And stay close so the bones can hear you."

Nodding agreeably, Sly Boots resumed singing "The Thief Dagvendr" under his breath. He had chosen that particular song at Quicksilver's request—a request she now deeply regretted. But this close to the Black Castle, the ermine skeleton in her pocket no longer seemed to care that Quicksilver was magicless, and had begun to fuss and scrape and snarl. She feared it might soon claw through Anastazia's thick cloak to freedom.

At last they reached the castle's front entrance, and Sly Boots fell silent. Stubby evergreen trees shivered around them; the ground was a choppy sea of rock and snow. The ermine skeleton thrummed and chattered, pricking Quicksilver's side with a stinging pain each time it thumped against her. She couldn't imagine how it would feel to have all seven of them in her possession at once—but she would soon find out.

She hoped.

Beside her, Lars's monster, Naika, transformed into a small orange-gold rat and disappeared with a soft puff of light.

Silent and tense, they waited, flat against the castle walls. The stone felt unnervingly strange—warm and damp and prickly. Quicksilver imagined she could feel the castle breathing against her back, and hoped fear was simply getting the best of her. Who knew what sort of spells the Wolf King might have crafted since she had last seen him?

One of the tall black castle doors creaked open. Naika, a squirrel once more, hurried back to Lars and curled around his boot. "The way is clear," she whispered to him, and Quicksilver forced herself to look at them, though their obvious connection made her miss Fox all the more.

She was Quicksilver Foxheart, and she would have to learn how to be alone in a world full of monsters.

If there was still a world left, after what they were about to do.

Lars placed his hands on her shoulders. "You'll be all right, Quix?" he asked one last time.

She nodded, bracing herself—and then someone screamed.
They whirled.

The Wolf King's black wolf was dragging Karin across the snow, his jaws tight around her leg. Karin's black-and-white bat monster shifted into a mountain cat and sprang onto the wolf's back with an ear-piercing yowl.

More wolves darted out from the shadows. The brown wolf lunged for Tommi, jaws open wide. Tommi ducked and swerved. His cat monster shifted into a great red stag and crashed into the brown wolf, antlers first. Another witch screamed, and another—the blue wolf, the gray wolf. Irma and Veera shifted their monsters into green-and-blue stallions and sent them galloping toward the blue and gray wolves. The blue wolf saw them first, let out a fierce howl, and leaped for the nearest horse, sinking its teeth into the horse's neck.

Otto bellowed a war cry. His pale pink monster, now a coiling, fat serpent, struck at the red wolf with glistening black fangs.

The First Ones—six long shadows with grinning faces and reaching arms—swooped down from the castle walls and rushed at them, a black tidal wave.

Quicksilver staggered back when they raced past her, choking on the sudden, shivering, furious cold. She couldn't breathe, she couldn't see. The howling shadows of the First Ones clogged the fight with thick, smoky darkness.

Lars threw himself in front of Quicksilver and Sly Boots.

"Ready?" he cried.

Quicksilver squinted through the darkness, found the tall, narrow castle entrance. One door still stood open.

She grabbed Sly Boots's hand, her heart a frantic drum. "Ready!"

Suddenly the gray wolf jumped out of the blackness, running straight for them.

Lars shifted Naika into a snarling wolverine and sent her flying toward the wolf.

"Go, Quix!" shouted Lars—but Quicksilver was already running, tugging Sly Boots after her.

They slipped through the open castle door and into a massive entrance hall. Seven staircases branched off in seven different directions. Behind each staircase was an immense painted-glass window. Each one depicted a First One, robed and imperious, with a monster: a starling, and a snowy hare. A hawk, a cat, a mouse. An owl. An ermine.

The ermine skeleton in Quicksilver's pocket rattled and

shrieked. Claws raked her skin through her cloak and winter clothes.

"Where do we go?" Sly Boots squeezed Quicksilver's hand, looking wildly about the massive room. "Which way?"

Quicksilver withdrew the ermine skull from her pocket and held it out in front of her. She had no Fox, and no access to her magic, so this time she could not use the Wolf King's stolen memories to help her. But the skull's excitement was obvious. It vibrated so hard she thought it would shatter. It jerked her body right, then left, then right again. Had she let go of it, it would have flown toward the second staircase from the right.

The staircase was crowned by the glass portrait of an ermine and its First One, painted in moon white and blood red, autumn-sky blue and shimmering moss green.

Quicksilver hoped the ermine skeleton wasn't trying to trick her.

"This way!" she cried.

The screaming sounds of the battle outside faded as she and Sly Boots raced up the stairs and down a series of shadowy corridors with high, arched ceilings. Quicksilver held tight to the ermine skull as it hissed and shook, letting it pull them where it wanted to go. Animal skeletons were everywhere—crowning each doorway, lining window panes, embedded in the very stone beneath Quicksilver's feet.

"Disgusting," Sly Boots muttered as they ran.

No, it's clever of the Wolf King, Quicksilver thought to Fox. *Who would ever think a few monster bones were special, when there are so many normal ones lying around?*

When Fox did not answer, Quicksilver gripped the ermine skull harder. She needed to *think*, not cry. Lars and his coven couldn't hold off the wolves forever.

The skull led them deeper into the castle and down a set of narrow stone steps. Quicksilver had to hold on to the skull with both hands to keep it from throwing itself down the corridor ahead of her. She was concentrating so hard on keeping it under control, in fact, that she almost stepped into a pit of stone.

Sly Boots grabbed her cloak and tugged her back to safety. Together they lay flat on their bellies and peeked over the edge into the pit. They had entered a throne room, with the pit at its center. Torches flickered between seven jeweled thrones carved into the pit's sloping stone walls. The walls themselves were crowded with narrow shelves, also carved into the stone, on which were displayed countless bones—for decoration? Perhaps trophies, relics of all those the Wolf King had killed. Ominous splatters of dried blood marked the walls and many of the bones. A set of wide, shallow steps curved around the pit, leading down to the floor.

There, a seven-pointed star surrounded by a circling pack of toothy wolves had been carved into the stone. In the star's center lay the Wolf King. He was pale and thin, his breath fast, ragged, and shallow, his dark hair drenched with sweat. He looked not a day older than when Quicksilver had last seen him—and just as sick. If Sly Boots was right about Ari . . . he had now been fighting the First Ones for hundreds of years. His body jerked violently—an echo of the battle outside?

For the sake of Lars and the coven, she hoped that, after so many years, the First Ones had grown as tired and ill as the Wolf King himself. It had to be exhausting, hunting and killing and living through another person's body.

"Ari!" Sly Boots whispered, scrambling to his feet. Pieces of stone crumbled off the ledge and fell to the pit floor below.

Quicksilver tugged him back down—but it was too late. The white wolf slunk out of the pit's shadows, sniffing, its eyes narrowed. Quicksilver froze, her hands tight around the shuddering ermine skull. The other skeletons *must* be near, but finding them with the white wolf on the prowl seemed impossible. She and Sly Boots lay still, hardly breathing.

The wolf grabbed the Wolf King by his collar, lifted him up into the air, and shook him with a growl.

The Wolf King's eyes fluttered open, his body hanging from the wolf's jaws like a rag doll. "Be quiet, you filth," he said.

"Who is he talking to?" Sly Boots whispered.

Quicksilver squinted through the gloom and nearly gasped. There, past the far side of the pit on the other side of the room, staring blearily through the bars of iron cages, were girls. Dozens of them—shivering and filthy, clothed in rags.

Her blood ran cold. "The Wolf King is especially hateful of girls," Lars had said. The dried blood on the walls took on a new, hideous meaning.

He feeds them to the wolves.

Sly Boots, following her gaze, gripped her arm hard. "What do we do?" he breathed.

Quicksilver's mind raced, searching for a plan. If there were cages, then there must be locks and keys, and if she could unlock the cages, free the girls, create a distraction . . .

She looked around wildly for inspiration. Then she saw the torchlight gleaming off the Lady's heart jewel, still hanging from Sly Boots's neck.

"Can you pick locks?" she asked.

"Yes." Sly Boots paused. "Well, mostly." He paused again. "My parents taught me. I get the general idea of it, but I'm not very fast."

It would have to be enough. "The clasp of that necklace might work." Quicksilver gestured at the heart jewel. "I'll distract the wolf while you pick the locks, free the girls, and run. Then *you'll* be distracting him, and I'll find the bones."

Sly Boots frowned, palming the jewel. "That seems risky. What if—"

"Just do it! And don't let him see you."

Quicksilver rose to her feet and made her way down into the pit, her hands—and the ermine skull—hidden beneath her cloak.

"Hello there!" she shouted.

The white wolf whirled, the Wolf King still dangling from its jaws.

"How did you—?" The Wolf King stopped. His eyes grew wide. *"You."*

"Yes, it's me!" Quicksilver reached the bottom of the steps and smiled sweetly. "Have you missed me, all these years?"

.50.

THE BEST THIEF IN ALL THE STAR LANDS

The white wolf dropped the Wolf King and howled such a furious, booming howl that the whole castle quaked and shifted. The wolf pawed at the floor, its claws scraping the stone and sending up sparks. Every hair on its body stood tall and angry like a forest of blinding white needles.

Quicksilver didn't even flinch, though her heart screamed, *Run, run, run!*

Stay quiet, please, she prayed to the ermine skull in her hands and the ermine bones in her pocket. *Please, just for a few more minutes. Tell me where to go—quietly, carefully—and then you'll be back with your brothers and sisters at last.*

The skull and the bones stayed quiet—humming, waiting. Had they heard her, somehow, even without her magic and her Fox? Or was she just lucky for the moment?

She hoped she stayed lucky.

"It's a lovely place you've got here." Quicksilver strolled around the bottom of the pit, circling past the seven thrones. The trembling ermine skull pulled in a particular direction, and Quicksilver wandered in the direction of that pull, letting the skull guide her toward the other skeletons.

At least, she hoped they were here, somewhere, hidden among all the others.

"Tell me," she asked, casually inspecting the curving shelves full of bones, "how long did it take to decorate?"

The wolf narrowed its glowing white eyes. Without further warning, it pounced, landing just shy of her. Its hot breath puffed against her cheeks. Its lips curled; a low growl rattled in its throat.

"Give me the ermine, witch," gasped the Wolf King, his sallow skin gleaming with sweat.

Over the Wolf King's shoulder and up above the pit, a shadowed figure darted to the cages. *Sly Boots.* But Quicksilver didn't dare look at him. She stared at the white wolf, nose to nose, willed Sly Boots to hurry, willed the imprisoned girls to stay quiet.

She stepped back, and back. The white wolf followed, heavy white paws silent against the stone. She leaned against one of the jeweled thrones. The wolf stayed close. Too close. Breath hot and teeth gleaming and shoulders hunched, ready to attack.

The ermine skull jumped and whined in Quicksilver's hands. She yawned to cover the sound. The white wolf's ears pricked. Its nose twitched, sniffing. Its eyes darted to her cloak.

Quicksilver's skin shivered hot and cold.

"What'll you give me for it?" she asked, sounding bored.

The Wolf King let out a weak puff of laughter. "Too late for that, witch. I've waited—"

He gasped, clutched his head. The white wolf whipped around to stare and growl.

"Leave me alone!" the Wolf King gasped.

Quicksilver's world narrowed down to him—this one pivotal point.

He was fighting them. After all these years, Ari was still fighting the First Ones' control.

"Ari?" Quicksilver took a few cautious steps forward. She

felt the wolf follow her, heard it sniffing. "Ari Tarkalia?"

The Wolf King's gaze flicked toward her. "Please . . ." he gasped. Him, Ari—and him alone. A lone boy's voice, tired and frightened.

The white wolf howled and lunged at Quicksilver. She ducked, spun, dodged him—*like running from Mother Petra, like slipping away to climb the roofs*—and hurried across the pit.

The wolf followed, slow and easy now, shaking its head. It could kill her in a moment. It was toying with her. It—and all the wolves, and the First Ones—had been waiting hundreds of years to kill her.

They planned to enjoy killing her.

Her mind screamed now, and her heart, and every muscle in her body: *Run, fool girl! Run and hide!*

But she wouldn't. This fight ended here.

Quicksilver wagged her finger at the wolf. "Ah-ah-ah! I wouldn't kill me just yet."

The wolf stopped. The fur on its back stood up, and its tail lashed from side to side.

"And . . . why . . . is that?" gasped the Wolf King, huddled in the center of the pit. His voice darkened once more as the First Ones spoke through him.

"Because, *Ari*," said Quicksilver, "I'm sorry to tell you that I forgot some of the skeleton back home. I used one of the thighbones to flavor a stew, and it's sitting in a pot on my stove right now. And—oh, yes! Dear me." She smacked her forehead. "I've just remembered. I left a whole pile of bones on the roof for the pigeons to peck at." She clucked her tongue. "And don't you need all of it, every last bone, in order to bring your little friends back to life? How thoughtless of me."

She slowly backed away, following the ermine skull as it tugged at her hands—to the left, to the right, and straight behind her. Left, right, straight behind. Left, right, straight behind. Over and over, it pulled in these three directions.

Three directions. Three skeletons? To her left, to her right, and behind her?

If only she could turn and grab them!

"You lie, witch," spat the Wolf King. "A bone cannot be separated from its skeleton. All the pieces *want* to be together." He grinned, horribly. So did the wolf. "You know this. I'm sure the old woman told you."

Quicksilver's heart pounded so hard she knew the wolf must be able to hear it.

"So far as *you* know," she said, flashing him a tiny coy smile.

"You wouldn't believe some of the tricks I've managed to learn over so many lifetimes of hunting you. Shall I tell you about some of them?"

The Wolf King roared in rage. He lurched up from the floor, his body twisting. Darkness shifted underneath his skin.

"I will bathe my wolves in your blood!" he bellowed.

"If you say so." She shrugged, continuing her slow circle around the pit, making sure the Wolf King kept looking at her—and not at the cages above and behind him.

The wolf slunk after her, its bright eyes trained on her cloak.

"*I'd* think twice before killing me," she said. "Without me, you'd have no idea where to find the bones. But if you feel it's worth the risk—"

The white wolf pawed at the ground.

Quicksilver glimpsed small, swift shadows moving up above. Sly Boots? The girls? Had he freed them?

Don't look, don't look. Hurry, Sly Boots, hurry.

"I could make you a deal," Quicksilver offered. A jolt of heat in her hands: the ermine skull jerked and leaned—another skeleton, behind her to the right. Another, to her left on the highest shelf.

She had found five, then. One more remained.

"What kind of deal?" asked the Wolf King. The white wolf growled, pacing back and forth between him and Quicksilver.

"I'll give you the bones I have with me," she said slowly, "and tell you where I've hidden the rest, *if* . . ."

She paused, considering. Behind the Wolf King, above the pit, a gold glimmer of light flashed. The lady's heart jewel?

The air was heavy with silence. She hoped Sly Boots and the girls were ready.

Quicksilver squeezed the ermine skull hidden under her cloak. The skull jolted, pushing her hand toward shelves that stretched high above one of the jeweled thrones.

There. The sixth skeleton.

"If?" the Wolf King cried. Ari's voice was faint within the seven roars of the First Ones. "Speak, witch!"

"If," said Quicksilver, "you free your slaves."

The Wolf King and the white wolf whirled around to see the rows of empty cages above the pit—and Sly Boots and the girls, running for the throne-room doors.

"What have you done?" wailed the Wolf King—although a ghost of a smile toyed at his mouth, and Quicksilver thought that, however deeply he was trapped inside himself, the boy Ari Tarkalia was glad.

The white wolf bounded across the pit, sprang up over the wall, crash-landed in the middle of the running pack of girls. The girls scattered, screaming, but they did not flee.

Sly Boots had a small one in his arms. "Now!" he cried.

The girls flung stones at the white wolf, found bones along the walls and floor and sent them flying. The wolf whined and howled, bones and rocks raining down on him. He smacked the bones from the air.

Quicksilver raced around the pit. She climbed the shelves, digging frantically through piles of bones while holding tight to the ermine skull. The useless bones didn't bother her; the bones of monsters bit and snarled and clawed at her. Above the pit, Sly Boots and the girls fought the white wolf. Quicksilver heard their screams, heard Sly Boots shouting, "You have him! Watch out!"

Tears stung Quicksilver's eyes, tears of pain and panic. The ermine's ghostly teeth bit her palm, drawing blood. She let the skull pull her arm ahead of her, dragging her on, through the shelves and around the bone-strewn pit.

One by one, she collected each skeleton and tucked them into the pockets of her cloak—the starling, and the snowy hare. The cat and the mouse. The hawk and the owl, which she hadn't seen before.

But the four she had once carried . . . As she ran through the pit, touching each skeleton brought memories rushing back—Fox helping her search the treasure in the Rompus's lair. Fighting the undead army in King Kallin's catacombs. Running from the unicorns in the world beneath the Lady's tree. Climbing up the mountain with Olli's coven.

Fox, Quicksilver thought to the world, to the stars, to the Shadow Fields, *I wish you were here to see this. It doesn't feel right without you.*

The last skeleton, the starling, was on the highest shelf, above one of the thrones. She climbed up, strained to reach, grabbed the bones and shoved them in her pocket, tried to pull herself up the rest of the way and out of the pit—but something grabbed her foot and yanked her down.

She smacked her chin against the stone shelves, hit her head against the stone floor. The world wobbled, drifting to blackness and back.

A piercing pain shot through her. She screamed, twisting on the floor, only to see the white wolf biting down on her bandaged leg. He had bit her there before, hundreds of years ago, in that icy mountain cave.

The white wolf snarled, dragged her across the floor. Her leg was on fire; she could not breathe. She patted her cloak, felt the full pockets.

Stay put, she told them, not knowing if they could hear or would obey, if they could.

"Give . . . me . . . the bones." The Wolf King crawled toward Quicksilver.

Her vision spotting, she looked up, searching the throne room above the pit. The girls and Sly Boots were nowhere to be seen. She fell slack against the floor. She hoped they'd escaped, at least—even if she wouldn't.

The white wolf pinned her to the floor, his claws digging into her cloak. He opened his mouth—and then he was gone, ripped away from her.

She sat up, cloudy with pain, and saw the Wolf King struggling with the white wolf, his arms wrapped around him. The wolf gnashed his teeth and howled.

"Go!" the Wolf King yelled, his voice completely his own— completely Ari's. "I've got him! Run!"

Quicksilver tried not to think about how normal he had looked just then—a frightened but resolute boy. She fled up the steps, out of the throne room, and back through the castle hallways. When she burst out into the entrance hall, she saw the girls hovering on the landing, peering down. Sly Boots stood with them. A couple of the smaller girls clung to him, hiding their faces in his jacket.

Down below, on the main floor, Lars, Otto, Tommi, Karin, Irma, and Veera fought the wolves and the First Ones. The huge windows had been shattered; shards of colored glass littered the floor. The room smelled of blood, and the smoky burn of monsters at war.

Monsters flashed, wolves pounced, witches screamed in pain and yelled in triumph. The First Ones fogged the room with darkness. One swooped down, coiled around Tommi like a great snake. His cat monster shifted into a wildcat and enveloped Tommi in bright red light. The First One hissed and shrank away. Another dove between Irma and Veera, winding around their ankles and slamming them into the ground. Their monsters shifted into blinding fire and charged.

Quicksilver ran down the steps into the fight. Otto's monster blazed past her, an arrow of pink light, and pierced the blue wolf's side.

A slam, a scream—Quicksilver dodged Karin's body as it skidded across the ground toward her. She wanted to stop and help her, but she ran on, ducking behind a stone pillar right before the gold wolf crashed into it. The pillar swayed; dust rained down from the ceiling.

Quicksilver peered around the pillar. The gold wolf shook himself, then tore back into the fight. Quicksilver ran after him. A streak of monstrous light zinged past her, burning her skin. The black wolf spotted her, leaped for her; she ducked low, and he flew right over her.

Darkness fell. She looked up—the six long shadows of the First Ones plunged toward her, their mouths open and roaring:

"GIVE US THE BONES!"

"Quix!" called Lars, sending Naika flying at the First Ones in a fiery streak of stars. "Over here!"

Quicksilver ran to him—Naika arching brilliantly over her head—and flung off her cloak at Lars's feet. Inside it, the skeletons shrieked and hissed and howled.

The wolves froze, snapped their heads around to stare.

The First Ones punched past Naika's light and reached, reached with seeking black claws, reached with centuries of rage and hatred.

Quicksilver faced them and smiled.

For Anastazia. For Fox.

For all the witches—including me.

"Many will be mighty!" Quicksilver yelled. The witches

turned at the cue—Karin, her arm bloody but her eyes fierce. Otto, standing tall. Tommi, his scarred face bright and ready. Irma and Veera, hand in hand.

Being a witch without a monster, Quicksilver could not feel it when the other witches joined their magic—but she could see it. Their six monsters rushed at one another and collided, coalescing into a spinning ball of colored light that reminded Quicksilver of the stars. Each witch raised an arm to direct the light brighter, larger, faster.

The First Ones flew at them, their screams deafening.

But Quicksilver stood tall, dizzy with pain, and made herself listen. Shivering without Anastazia's cloak to shield her, she watched as the spinning light expanded. Six strands of colorful light wove a thick, shimmering web around the coven. The wolves cowered before the brilliant light, huddling together. The First Ones raged, tried to slink through the web. But the coven's magic was too powerful. Blinding white fire clung to their shadowy bodies. They shrank back, moaning and yowling, trying to shake free of the sticky flames.

One witch was not enough to destroy the bones. Even Anastazia had never been able to do that, with all her lives. But many witches, working together . . .

"Many will be mighty," Quicksilver whispered over and over, watching the coven move as one. They pulled six spools of light from their monsters' protective web and sent the spools toward Quicksilver's abandoned cloak. The First Ones were a howling storm, the wolves a slathering frenzy, and yet the light burned on, the spools spinning into a blinding cyclone. It engulfed the cloak, and the bones within, and became a crackling white fire that snapped between Lars and his coven like lightning. When the bones caught fire, the skeletons screamed, high and shrill.

And the First Ones fell to the floor, crumbling into shapeless piles.

One of the piles crawled toward Quicksilver and reached for her with a charred hand.

Quicksilver glared down at it. "This war is finally over," she said coldly, "and I've won."

Then she stomped hard, and the hand collapsed into a pile of ashes.

The hunt, at last, was finished.

There was one final pulse of light, and then the web of magic surrounding the coven twisted and dimmed, shifting back into their monsters. The red cat jumped into Tommi's arms, butting his chin with her head. The black-and-white bat flapped to Karin and hugged her neck with its wings.

The wolves scattered, slinking off into the shadows.

"Quicksilver!" called Sly Boots, racing down the stairs toward her, the freed girls at his heels. "You did it! *You did it!*"

"I did," she whispered faintly, just before Sly Boots crashed into her with a ferocious hug.

"The best thief in all the Star Lands!" he shouted, and Lars and his coven took up the call. "The best thief in all the Star Lands! Quicksilver Foxheart! Foxheart! Foxheart!"

Dear Fox, thought Quicksilver, smiling as Sly Boots and the girls and the coven and their monsters surrounded her, clapping her on the back and whistling and cheering her name. *We did it. You and me. Me and you. Forever.*

.51.

QUICKSILVER FOXHEART

W hen Quicksilver awoke, she was lying in something soft and warm. When she tried to move, a dull pain drifted up her right leg.

"Don't move too much just yet," said Sly Boots, hurrying over.

"Where are we?"

"My house in Willow-on-the-River."

She shot upright. "Did we—?"

"Everything's all right. The First Ones are gone. Their monsters' skeletons, too. They won't be coming back ever again."

"And the wolves?"

"Run off into the wild. They're just wolves now, Lars said, since no one's forcing them to be monsters anymore."

"Does that mean . . . what about the Wolf King?"

"Ari's resting. The white wolf nearly tore him apart, in that throne room." Sly Boots paused, looking grim. "He almost didn't make it."

Quicksilver settled back into what she now realized was a small but cozy bed. "*I* wouldn't have made it, if he hadn't held that wolf back for me."

Sly Boots nodded. "I know. I told you he wasn't as bad as all that." Then he tossed a clean white cloth over his shoulder and lifted up the blanket covering Quicksilver's legs.

She yanked the blanket from him, all thoughts of the Wolf King shooting straight out of her head. "What do you think you're doing?"

Sly Boots flushed bright red. "I'm only checking your bandages."

"Can't someone else do that?" Quicksilver scrambled to cover herself. Even though she seemed to be wearing a perfectly decent nightgown, the idea of Sly Boots doing anything near her legs made her insides scrunch up and twist around.

It was not an *entirely* unpleasant feeling.

"Someone else could," Sly Boots agreed, moving about the

room to gather additional fresh bandages, a bowl of broth, a cup of water, "but I'm the one in charge of tending to Quicksilver Foxheart, and that's an honor I don't want to lose." He paused, then looked stricken with a sudden, quiet panic. "You won't make me leave, will you?"

Quicksilver had to bite down hard on her lip to keep from grinning at him. "Fine," she said, gesturing imperiously at her bandaged leg. "You may proceed, boy."

Sly Boots stood tall, beaming, and then bowed with a flourish. "Thank you, Quix."

"Not so terrible a nickname, is it?"

"Nothing about you is terrible," Sly Boots mumbled with a quick, blushing glance.

Quicksilver opened her mouth and shut it again, not knowing how to respond. As Sly Boots changed her bandages, they said not a word, trapped in a thick, tight silence that became so unbearable Quicksilver was tempted to kick him in the face just to remind them both about the true status of their relationship.

But she could not bring herself to do it, and instead stared at the ceiling and contented herself with imagining it.

A man and a woman entered the room just as Sly Boots

finished working. It was so strange to see them up and about that at first Quicksilver didn't recognize them.

Sly Boots caught her staring. "Oh! Quicksilver, these are my parents—Henna and Jari."

"You're healed!" Quicksilver said.

Sly Boots's mother, Henna, grinned. "Indeed we are. Turns out your witchy friend Lars knows quite a lot about how to undo curses. And can we just say we are honored to meet the girl who we have heard is the . . . what did they say, Jari? The best thief in all the Star Lands?"

"Yes, I believe you're right." Sly Boots's father, Jari, leaned closer and raised an eyebrow. "I think we'll be the judge of that, however."

Remembering that Sly Boots's parents were thieves themselves, Quicksilver straightened and tried to look as formidable as it was possible to look while sitting propped up against many fluffy pillows.

"You just wait and see," she said. "Once I'm well again, I'll show you how it's done, this whole thieving thing. I'm sure you're out of practice by now, having been ill for so long."

"Or," Henna suggested, her eyes sparkling, "we could go on jobs together. All three of us."

"We've never worked with a witch thief before," said Jari, stroking his beard and looking a bit dreamy eyed at the possibility. "Soon enough we'll be swimming in riches."

Sly Boots, straightening Quicksilver's blankets, rolled his eyes. "Or you could, you know, get an honest job and *not* steal things."

Henna and Jari stared at him, aghast. "But where's the fun in that?" asked his mother.

"And anyway, I'm not a witch anymore," Quicksilver said, fiddling needlessly with her pillows. "So I wouldn't be any help to you in that way. If you want a witch thief, you'll have to find someone else."

There was a moment's pause, and then Sly Boots shooed his parents out of the room.

"Lovely to meet you!" Jari called back to Quicksilver.

"We'll talk more later!" Henna added. "We've got lots of ideas!"

Once they had gone, Sly Boots returned to the chair at Quicksilver's bedside and started folding a stack of clean bandages.

"You'd think a botched job like the one they went through would have scarred them for life and put them off thieving forever," he muttered. "But I swear to the stars, between them they haven't got a lick of sense."

Quicksilver twisted the edge of her blanket in her hands. "Boots?"

"Yes?"

When she did not immediately reply, Sly Boots looked up. "Are you all right?"

"Yes, it's just . . ." Quicksilver sighed irritably and looked away. "What am I supposed to do now? I'm a witch, because it's in my blood, somewhere, and I've *been* a witch . . . but I've no monster anymore, and so I'm not *truly* a witch like the rest of them. So what does that mean about me? What am I? Am I a witch? Am I just a girl?"

"You're Quicksilver Foxheart," Sly Boots said simply, taking her hand, "and you're the only one there is. That's all that matters."

Quicksilver glared at their hands. "*What* do you think you're doing?"

"Er." Sly Boots retracted his hand. "Comforting you?"

"You're a little too close to be comforting, Boots."

Agreeably, Sly Boots scooted his chair toward the door.

Quicksilver exhaled sharply. "Not *that* far away, Boots!"

He returned to her bedside, looking more than a little bewildered.

"Just . . . keep your hands to yourself," said Quicksilver, "unless I instruct otherwise."

Sly Boots's eyebrows shot up. "Well. Shall I sing to you instead?"

"Don't even think about it."

.52.

A Fuzzy Half Creature

Later that night, Quicksilver lay awake in her bed, unable to sleep. She listened to Sly Boots snoring in the chair beside her, and his house creaking and groaning.

She could not sleep because she kept thinking of too many things—the cages where the girls had been kept at the Black Castle. Whether or not she wanted to visit the convent. How long it would take for the witches who had survived the hunt to come out of hiding and rebuild. How the people of the Star Lands would learn to trust and live alongside witches again, and how long that would take, and if there would be violence in the meantime. They had been taught to hate magic and witches for so long. What would they think of it all now?

What would this world be, without a Wolf King?

Quicksilver turned over, away from Sly Boots, and stared out the window. The open shutters let in a soft, warm breeze.

For a time, when they had been in the Star Lands of long ago, Quicksilver had felt like she was becoming the person she was supposed to be, that all the unhappy years at the convent had simply been a hardship to endure so she could be rewarded with magic and witchiness. But with Fox's death, everything had been ripped away from her. She was now neither witch, nor girl, but something fuzzy between the two. How was she to live in this strange new world—a fuzzy half creature with a Fox-sized hole in her heart?

Sly Boots had said she was herself, Quicksilver Foxheart, and that was all that mattered. But she wasn't sure he was right.

She crept out of bed and retrieved the crutches Sly Boots had fashioned for her. Tottering down the stairs seemed ill-advised, but if she stayed in bed any longer, she would go mad from thinking too much.

Downstairs, snoring witches slept on the floor in the foyer, using rolled-up cloaks for pillows: Lars and Otto, Tommi and

Karin, Irma and Veera, and old Matias, who had tended Sly Boots's parents when the coven went north. Quicksilver tried not to look at their bandages and bruises, nor think about how awful it must have been for them to fight the wolves and the First Ones while so many of their friends died around them.

A door in the wall beneath the staircase creaked open, revealing a tiny room warm with candlelight.

A vaguely familiar voice whispered from inside. "Who's there?"

Curious, Quicksilver hobbled over and peeked in.

The Wolf King sat on a pallet of blankets, his arms, his chest, and half of his face bandaged. His smile was cautious; either he was in pain or he was frightened of her.

Quicksilver hoped for both.

"Oh," he said, "it's you. Hello."

"You survived," said Quicksilver flatly.

"Mostly. Lars told me I'll have a lot of scars."

"Good."

The Wolf King lowered his eyes. "I understand why you feel that way. I do too. It feels like I've been living in a nightmare for hundreds of years, and no matter how hard I tried, I couldn't wake up from it."

Quicksilver could not match up what she knew the Wolf King to be—and what he had done—with the boy now in front of her. Without his monsters, without the First Ones, he seemed small and unimpressive. She stood there, shifting her weight on the crutches, unsure how to deal with him.

"If you want to yell at me," said the Wolf King quietly, "I suggest you wait until morning. We shouldn't wake the others."

Quicksilver's eyes narrowed. "Interesting that you should care about them *now*."

The boy was quiet for a long time, while Quicksilver glared at him, trying to sear her grief and anger into his skin using only her eyes.

"I won't say I'm sorry," he said at last. "I mean, I am, but no one wants to hear me say that. It's not enough, after everything that's happened."

Quicksilver gripped her crutches hard. She knew she should pity him, and she did, but if he wanted to be soothed and fussed over, he was talking to the wrong girl.

He gave a soft laugh. "You know, it's funny. All the horrible things I've done, all the pain I've caused—and received," he added, wincing as he tried to stretch out his leg. "And all I can think about is how I miss them. The wolves, I mean. I suppose it's what I deserve, of course, and they did terrible things while they were bonded to me, but . . . they were still my monsters, even if the worst part of them belonged to the First Ones, too. And now, without them, I feel . . ." He paused, frowning. "I don't know why I'm talking to you, of all people, like this. I'm sorry."

"You feel like part of you is missing," Quicksilver said, moving closer. "Like part of you—the biggest part—has been cut out."

The Wolf King's face brightened. "Yes, that's exactly it!"

"Like you're not a witch anymore, but you're not a human either."

"Like you're somewhere in between."

Quicksilver felt him watching her and stared stubbornly at the floor. She wished she had not said anything, but she knew no one else who had once had a monster, and now did not. Despite herself, she itched to talk to him about it—him, the Wolf King!

She scowled, toeing the floor with her unbandaged foot. "So what will happen to you now? I hope it's something along the lines of throwing you into a dark and lonely prison as punishment for your crimes."

"I will be tried by the Council of Lords," the Wolf King

said quietly. "But Lars and his coven said they would vouch for me, explain what happened. I have family left, he said. Some Tarkalias, up in Valteya. One of them's Lady Lovisa. She's trying to change the name Council of Lords to Council of Thrones. You know, because there are women ruling now, too. She sounds nice, don't you think? Distantly related, of course." The Wolf King laughed, a soft, sad sound. "I thought I had killed all my family, long ago, but apparently I missed a few."

Quicksilver looked up at that, and immediately regretted it, for the Wolf King seemed so miserable and lost, sitting there covered in bandages, that she found herself pitying him. She remembered one of the memories she had stolen from him—the lonely witch boy, unlucky enough to be born without much magic in him, chasing after a deer and longing for a monster of his own.

"Perhaps," she said, "we should start again." She tried to extend her hand without falling over and realized it would be easier to simply extend the crutch. So she did, and said, "I'm Quicksilver. I'm a thief and a witch, but don't ask me to make any spells for you. I can't do that anymore."

The Wolf King's watery smile grew larger. "And I'm Ari Tarkalia," he said. "I used to be an evil king, but now I'm just a boy. And don't ask *me* to make spells for *you*, because I've got no magic in me, and . . . I'm all right with that."

They slapped hands, palm to crutch.

"Don't think this means I like you," Quicksilver warned him. "You've a long way to go there, Ari. I hope you know that."

He nodded, taking a deep breath. "I know. But I'm ready for it. Anything's better than where I've been."

And Quicksilver saw then, in the serious set of his face, the king who should have been: Ari Tarkalia, son of a powerful witch family. Not much magic of his own, the poor boy—but perhaps, Quicksilver thought, magic wasn't everything.

She sat beside him until the sun rose—not for the conversation, she told herself, nor for the comfort of being near another half creature like herself, but because someone had to keep an eye on him, and it might as well be her.

.53.

A STRANGE KIND OF FAMILY

As Quicksilver watched the Willow-on-the-River market from her perch on the church belfry, she munched on a stolen sugar cake and considered things.

Much had changed, and was still changing.

There were witches in the world, slowly coming out of hiding. Someday the Star Lands would be bright with magic once more, as they had been so long ago. Quicksilver reached into her dull and faded hair, found the one flaming lock of red—fire-bright and shimmering—and wrapped it absently around her finger. Every time she saw these shining strands, she felt her heart lift to remember how beautiful the world had once been—and how it would be so again.

Lars and his coven came and went, working with the newly renamed Council of Thrones to abolish the Scrolls and teach the people of the Star Lands what witches were *really* like. They often showed up at Sly Boots's house in the middle of the night with no warning, hungry and boisterous, and though Sly Boots's parents reminded them often that their home was not, in fact, a travelers' inn, they could never find it in their hearts to turn them away.

The Council of Thrones had decided to pardon Ari Tarkalia, and he was now on his way to Valteya with Lady Lovisa Tarkalia, who, at their first meeting, had taken one look at him and wrapped him into a ferocious embrace, proclaiming for all to hear that he was family, and if anyone didn't like that, she would, as the ruler of Valteya, be happy to explain it more fully with the help of her royal guard.

Sly Boots, after a long conversation in which he explained to his parents—using numerous real-life examples—that he would never be a good thief, had, at last, convinced them that this was true. Then, with his parents' help, he had opened a small apothecary and healer's shop on the ground floor of their house. On occasion, Quicksilver stole from his stores, just to make sure he was paying attention to his surroundings as he ought to. She always returned the stolen goods—if Sly Boots asked nicely.

The girls and sisters at the convent were not entirely the girls and sisters Quicksilver had once known—Adele wasn't there, for one, and neither was Mother Petra. When Quicksilver visited, she saw some familiar faces, and some unfamiliar ones, and felt so entirely disturbed when she stopped to think about all that might have changed in this time, thanks to her actions in the past, that she never visited the convent again.

And yet, Quicksilver thought, finishing off her sugar cake, as much as some things had changed, much was still the same. She was, as ever, an orphan and a thief, and she still enjoyed sleeping on rooftops more than in beds, even the perfectly comfortable one Sly Boots had made up for her in the now clean and tidy attic.

Sometimes she still looked north and wondered about her parents. But not knowing who they were or where they had gone or why they had left her no longer cut her heart as deeply. She had found a family of her own—a strange kind of family, made up of witches and boys, thieves and monsters, lords and ladies— but it was hers, nonetheless, and it was all she needed.

Quicksilver licked her fingers clean, grinning as she watched the baker count over his cakes down below. When he realized he was one short, he scowled and muttered what she was sure was her name, followed by a few choice curses. He pushed back his cap and scanned the rooftops for her, but she was well hidden, and besides, she couldn't worry too much about him at the moment.

She had just seen something far more interesting.

On the other side of the church, on a quiet corner, a farmer had set up a small pen full of puppies. Quicksilver crept down the church roof to see better.

"I already have three dogs for my sheep," the farmer was explaining to a man and his small daughter. "Can't take care of eight more!"

Quicksilver crept even closer, clinging to the gutter with a pounding heart. It was stupid to hope, stupid even to *think* it. . . .

"Five silvers for this one." The farmer held up a wriggling pup with a speckled gray coat. "I think he likes you."

"Can I, Papa?" asked the girl, tugging on her father's sleeve.

"I won't be cleaning up after it," said her father sternly.

The girl's face took on an utterly serious expression. "I'll clean up *everything*, Papa. You won't ever have to!"

"Right." The man rolled his eyes, but he couldn't hide his smile. "Five silvers, then?"

Quicksilver watched, hidden behind a wolf-shaped gargoyle, while the day stretched on and the litter of puppies dwindled. None of them looked remotely like Fox, but there was one—the floppy-eared shaggy-haired runt of the litter—who caught her eye. He was black all over except for two white socks and a white chest and belly. He wagged his tail hopefully every time someone walked by.

"He's quite small," said a woman, stopping to look when the runt was the only one left. "And his face is a bit smashed, isn't it?"

"Sometimes that happens with runts," said the farmer. "But he's the gentlest of the bunch, I'll tell you that."

The woman smiled politely and shook her head, moving on.

The farmer sighed and put his hands on his hips, looking up and down the street. The sun was setting, and the market would close soon.

"What am I going to do with you, little one?" he asked the empty road.

Quicksilver moved like lightning, climbing down the church wall, sprinting across the road, scooping the pup into her arms, and hurrying back to the church roof before the farmer had even turned around. She made sure to leave five silvers in the pen, for the farmer seemed a nice sort.

It was difficult, climbing up to the belfry with a puppy tucked into her coat. She would have to fashion him a bag, just as she had for Fox.

"Hello," Quicksilver whispered to him once she had settled back in her spot. She touched noses with him and scratched his belly, which made him wriggle with delight in her lap. "My name is Quicksilver," she told him, "and I think I shall call you Bear, for I can already tell you'll grow up to be fearsome and strong, no matter what anyone else thinks."

Bear blinked up at her and yawned.

"Yes, it's quite tiring, being a thief, but you'll get used to it." Quicksilver tucked her coat about him and settled back against the wall. For a moment—a tiny moment—she felt a twist in her heart at the thought that this pup would never be her Fox, that she would never again work magic. A monster, for a witch, only happens once, and she had had so little time with hers.

But as she turned over these thoughts in her mind, she realized they did not bother her as much as they once had. After all, she had lived many lifetimes of magic as Anastazia, as a witch with her Fox. And as Quicksilver—as only herself—she had saved her kind and stopped a great evil from returning to the world. That was enough for her.